continued . . .

5

"I was mesmerized, awed, and totally entertained. Only rarely do I read a book that I literally can't put down, that draws me so deeply into the world created by the authors that I feel a part of it and don't want to let it go. It happened with [*Local Custom*]. I loved the action, the conflict of cultures, the characters, and the romance. But best of all, and what makes each story enduringly special to me, is the strong sense of honor that impels the actions of the main characters and is often the basis of the conflicts among them. The Liaden world is an admirable world." —Mary Balogh, author of *No Man's Mistress*

"The plot threads are intricately interwoven. . . . The plotting is careful and well-balanced . . . the great excellence lies in the relationships." —*Analog*

"One of the never-failing joys of [*Local Custom*] is the crisp language, the well-turned phrases, the very exciting action, not to mention the confrontation of two vastly different cultures." —Anne McCaffrey

"Space opera isn't just ripsnortin' adventure, though Lee and Miller give us plenty of that. The thing about space opera is it's more than nifty science, the clash of customs, the evolution of ideas, interesting planets, cool tech, and new pioneers, it's also and above all about character . . . and one cares about the characters, about their further adventures, and their families' adventures, and even about the villains. The Liaden Universe stories are very good space opera." —Sherwood Smith, author of *Journey to Otherwise*

"Lee and Miller have taken standard space adventure fare, added a touch of romance, and turned the whole into powerful stories." —Melisa Michaels, author of *Cold Iron*

"Ambitiously creating a complex emotional environment, Mr. Miller and Ms. Lee pique our curiosity with an equally complicated plot development." —*Romantic Times*

"No other authors can compare to their skill at bringing characters to full and robust life, half convincing me that there is a time portal to the future, hidden up in Maine through which Sharon and Steve have been watching and recording the lives of the Liadens for years." —Jennifer Dunne, author of *Raven's Heart*

carpe diem

sharon lee and steve miller

ACE BOOKS, NEW YORK

CARPE DIEM

An Ace Book / published by arrangement with
Meisha Merlin Publishing, Inc.

PRINTING HISTORY
DelRey mass-market edition / October 1989
In Meisha Merlin Publishing, Inc. hardcover and trade paperback
editions of *Partners in Necessity* / February 2000
Ace mass-market edition / February 2003

Copyright © 1989 by Steve Miller and Sharon Lee.
Liaden Universe registered ® 2000 by Sharon Lee and Steve Miller.
Cover art by Michael Herring.
Cover design by Rita Frangie.
Text design by Julie Rogers.

Visit our website at
www.penguinputnam.com
Check out the ACE Science Fiction & Fantasy newsletter!

ISBN: 0-441-01022-9

ACE®
Ace Books are published by The Berkley Publishing Group,
a division of Penguin Putnam Inc.,
375 Hudson Street, New York, New York 10014.
ACE and the "A" design
are trademarks belonging to Penguin Putnam Inc.

PRINTED IN THE UNITED STATES OF AMERICA

10 9 8 7 6 5 4 3 2 1

SECOND QUADRANT

RAMAL SECTOR

The pilot stared at the readout in disbelief, upped the magnification, and checked the readings once more, cold dread in his heart.

"Commander. Pilot requests permission to speak."

"Permission granted," Khaliiz said.

"The vessel which we captured on our last pass through this system is moving under power, Commander. The scans read the life forces of two creatures."

"Pilot's report heard and acknowledged. Stand by for orders. Second!"

"Commander."

"It was reported to me that none were left alive aboard yon vessel, Second. Discover the man who lied and bring him to me at once."

His Second saluted. "At once, Commander." He turned and marched from the bridge.

Khaliiz eyed the screen, perceived the ship-bounty slipping through his fingers, and was displeased.

"Pursue."

Val Con cursed very softly, then snapped back to the board, slapped the page into its slot, and demanded data: coords, position, speed, and amount of power in the coils.

"Could we leave now?" asked a small voice to his left.

He turned his head. Miri was sitting rigidly in the copilot's chair, her eyes frozen on the screen and the growing shape of the Yxtrang vessel. Her freckles stood out vividly in a face the color of milk.

"We must wait until the power has reached sufficient level and the coordinates are locked into the board," he said, keeping his voice even. "We will leave in a few minutes."

"They'll *be* here in a few minutes." She bit her lip, hard, and managed to drag her eyes from the screen to his face. "Val Con, I'm *afraid* of Yxtrang."

Aware of the tightness of the muscles in his own face, he did not try to give her a smile. "I am also afraid of Yxtrang," he said gently. His eyes flicked to the board, then to the screen. "Strap in."

"What're you gonna do?" Miri was watching him closely, some of the color back in her face, but still stiff in every muscle.

"There is a game Terrans sometimes play," he murmured, dividing his attention between board and screen, fingers busy with his own straps, "called 'chicken' . . . Strap in, cha'trez."

He flipped a toggle. "I see you, Chrakec Yxtrang. Pass us by. We are unworthy to be your prey."

There was a transmission pause—or did it last a bit longer?—then a voice, harsh as broken glass, replied in Trade. "Unworthy? Thieves are always worthy game! That ship is ours, Liaden. We have won it once."

"Forgive us, Ckrakec Yxtrang, we are here by no fault of our own. We are not worthy of you. Pass by."

"Release my prize, Liaden, or I shall wrest it from you, and you will die."

Miri licked her lips, steadfastly refusing to look at the screen.

Val Con's face was smooth and calm, his voice nearly gentle. "If I release your prize, I shall die in any case. Pass by, Hunter. There is only I, who am recently wounded."

"My scans show two, Liaden."

Miri closed her eyes. Val Con, measuring board against screen, eased the speed of the ship higher, toward the halfway point.

"Only a woman, Ckrakec Yxtrang. What proof is that of your skill?"

There was a pause, during which Val Con slipped the speed up another notch and pressed the sequence that locked in the coords.

"Will it please you, when you are captured, Liaden, to watch me while I take my pleasure from your woman? Afterward, I shall blind you and give you as a toy to my crew."

"Alas, Ckrakec Yxtrang, these things would but cause me pain." Coils up! And the Yxtrang were finally near enough, beginning the boarding maneuver, matching velocity, and direction . . .

"It would give you pain!" the Yxtrang cried. "All things give Liadens pain! They are a soft race, born to be the prey of the strong. In time, there will be no more Liadens. The cities of Liad will house the children of Yxtrang."

"What then will you hunt, O Hunter?" He flipped a series of toggles, leaned back in the pilot's chair, and held a hand out to Miri.

Slowly the ship began to spin.

There was a roar of laughter from the Yxtrang, horrible to hear. "Very good, Liaden. Never shall it be said, after you are dead, that you were an unworthy rabbit. A good maneuver. But not good enough."

In the screen, the Yxtrang ship began to spin as well, matching velocity uncertainly.

Miri's hand was cold in his. He squeezed it, gave her a quick smile, and released her, returning to the board.

More spin; a touch more acceleration. The Yxtrang moved to match both. Val Con added again to the spin but left the speed steady.

"Enough, Liaden! What do you hope to win? The ship is ours, and we will act to keep it. Do you imagine I will grow tired of the game and leave? Do you not know that even now I might fire upon you and lay you open to the cold of space?"

"There is no bounty on ruined ships, Ckrakec Yxtrang, nor any glory in reporting that a Liaden outwitted you. But," he said, sighing deeply, "perhaps you are young and this your first hunt—"

There was a scream of rage over the comm, and the Yxtrang ship edged closer. Val Con added more spin. Ship's gravity was increasing—lifting his arm above the board the few inches required to manipulate the keys was an effort. His lungs were laboring a little for air. He glanced over at Miri. She grinned raggedly at him.

"How much faster will you spin, Liaden? Until the gravity crushes you?"

"If necessary. I am determined that you will collect no bounty on this ship, Chrakec Yxtrang. It has become a matter of honor." More spin. He paused with his hand on the throttle.

"Speak not to me of honor, animal! We have toyed long enough. We shall—"

Val Con shoved the velocity to the top, slammed on more spin, hesitated, counting, eyes on the board—

Jump!

LUFKIT

NEEFRA'S TAVERN

The Terran creature's name was Jefferson, and it was sweating; it talked jerkily, swigging warm beer down its gullet, moving its big, rough hands aimlessly about, occasionally plucking at its companion's sleeve—and talking, always talking.

Much of what it said was of no value to the Liaden who stood beside it, delicately sipping at a glass of atrocious local wine; but Tyl Von sig'Alda was patient, by training if not by inclination, and the bits of useful information mixed in among the trash were jewels of very great price.

"Yxtrang," the creature was saying, fingering its empty mug in agitation. "Well, it had to be Yxtrang, didn't it? Stands to reason—the way the ship was cleaned out but not ruined. Coming back for it, Tanser said. Sure to come back for it. Yxtrang get a bounty for captured ships . . ." It faltered there, and its companion waved at the barkeeper for another beer. The creature took it absently, drank, and wiped its mouth with the back of a hand. It glanced furtively around the noisy bar and bent close enough for its listener to smell the beer on its breath, the stink of its sweat, and the reek of its fear. It was all sig'Alda could do not to recoil in disgust.

"Tanser knew it was Yxtrang," Jefferson whispered, voice rasping. "*Knew* it. And he left 'em there. Alive. Could've put a pellet into 'em—something quick and clean. But the turtle'd said let 'em go and the boss said okay . . ."

Horror seemingly choked it, and it pulled back, eyes glistening, showing a plentitude of white all around the irises. The one beside him sipped wine and murmured soothingly that of course the ways of the Clutch were mysterious, but that he had understood them not to involve themselves so much with the affairs of—men.

"This one did," Jefferson said fervently. "Claimed some kind of kinship with 'em both—brother and sister." It swigged beer.

"Crazy alien."

Most assuredly the victims were Val Con yos'Phelium and the female companion; though why an agent might be traveling with such a one was more than could be fathomed. Tyl Von sig'Alda assayed another sip of syrupy wine. The female . . . Headquarters had assumed a mischance during the journey home, assumed that the female had, perhaps, served for a time as camouflage. A sound enough theory.

Unless, sig'Alda thought, training was somehow broken? At once the Loop flickered to life, showing .999 against that possibility. He was aware of some dim, faraway feeling of relief. The Loop was the secret weapon of the Department of the Interior, an impartial mental computer implanted only in the best of its agents. Its guidance was essential to the Department's ascendancy over the enemies of Liad. It was an essential part of training. Training could not be broken.

Jefferson leaned close, breathing its beery breath into sig'Alda's face. "I have a son," it said hoarsely.

"Do you?" he murmured. And then, because the creature seemed to await a fuller response, he said, "I myself have a daughter."

It nodded its head in barbaric Terran agreement and withdrew slightly. "Then you know."

"Know?"

"Know what it's like," the creature explained, a trifle

loudly, though not loud enough to signify within the overall clamor of the tavern. "Know what it's like to worry about 'em. My boy . . . And that turtle telling—bragging on himself, maybe. Maybe not even telling the truth. Who can tell what's truth to a turtle?"

Was that relevant, or more of the creature's ramblings? sig'Alda gave a mental shrug. Who could tell?

"But what did he say?" he inquired of Jefferson. "The turtle."

"Talking about how his clan or family or egg or whatever it is will hunt down the first and the last of a family, if you don't do what he says to do." Jefferson gulped the last of the beer and set the mug aside with a thump, black despair filling its half-crazed eyes. "And Tanser put 'em right in Yxtrang's path, after the turtle'd said let 'em go free. Gods."

There was a long moment's silence, while the Loop presented the chances of survival for Val Con yos'Phelium and his female, whomever and whatever she was, stranded in a ship marked for Yxtrang reclamation and deprived of coords and coils.

.001

So, then. He smiled at Jefferson. "Another beer, perhaps?"

"Naw . . ." The Terran was twitching, suddenly eager to be off, perhaps conscious all at once that it had been spilling secrets wholesale into the ear of a stranger.

sig'Alda laid a gentle hand on its sleeve. "Tell me, did anyone check to see if the ship was still there? Even the Yxtrang might make an error from time to time."

The despairing eyes gazed back up at his face. "It was gone when we dropped back to look." It swallowed harshly. "Tanser laughed." Another painful working of the throat. "Tanser ain't got any kids."

It stood away from the bar abruptly and held out a horny hand. "Got to be going. Thanks for the beers."

sig'Alda placed his hand into the large one, forcing himself to bear the pressure and the up-and-down motion. "Perhaps we will meet again."

"Yeah," Jefferson said, not very convincingly. "Maybe." Its lips bent upward in a rictus that might have been meant as a smile. "G'night, now." And it turned and strode away, leaving Tyl Von sig'Alda staring into the depths of his sticky glass.

Jefferson went rapidly through side streets and back alleys, cursing his tongue and his need and the horrible, ever-present fear in his belly.

The man had been Liaden—and maybe the woman, too. Yxtrang and Liaden had been enemies, blood and bone, for longer than Terrans had been on the scene. Jefferson swallowed against the fear's abrupt nausea. Yxtrang would have special ways to treat a couple of representatives of their old, most-hated enemy . . .

Jefferson leaned against a convenient light post to get his breath and wait for the shaking to ease—but he only shook harder, gripping the post in misery and closing his eyes.

He never saw the slender shadow take aim in the empty street, never heard the gun's discreet, genteel cough or felt the pellet enter his ear and rend his brain.

The Terran crumpled slowly, as if falling into a swoon, and lay still in the puddle of light. Tyl Von sig'Alda slid his weapon away, glanced up and down the street, then walked carefully over to the carcass. He made short work of stripping the pouch and pockets of anything remotely valuable— it was to appear a mere murder for gain, as might happen to anyone walking alone in the dark back streets of Lufkit.

Jefferson had given much information freely; its continued existence had been a threat to sig'Alda himself. More, its elimination was a minor balance for the act of putting a Liaden—any Liaden—in the way of the Yxtrang. That the Liaden had been a member of his own Department and one of its best was a sad fact. Tanser's name had been duly noted; sig'Alda's report would mention it, and another bit of balance would no doubt follow.

sig'Alda stepped back, noting that the Loop gave him excellent chances of attaining the shuttle to Prime Station and the deck of *Raslain*, his passage away. Yet he hesitated, nagged by a consideration that was by rights none of his, he who was assigned to determine what had become of Val Con yos'Phelium, lost en route to his debriefing. And still there was the damned female . . . No. He would leave tonight, information pertinent to the mission having been gathered on Lufkit. His report to the commander would reflect Jefferson's certainty that yos'Phelium and the female had fallen to the Yxtrang bounty-crew, as well as the corroboration of the Loop. It was futile to spend time backtracking the female. He was not assigned to provide her a eulogy.

So thinking, he turned and faded into the shadows, leaving the street to the puddle of light and that which lay within it.

LIAD

TREALLA FANTROL

"No! Absolutely not!"

"Shan . . ." Nova yos'Galan flung forward and caught her brother's sleeve in one slim hand. Head tipped back, she stared up into his face, seeing the ice forming in the silver eyes and the lines of Korval stubbornness tightening around the big mouth. "Shan, by the gods!"

He made the effort—he took a deeper breath, then another. "You tell me that the First Speaker wishes me to contract-wed. Why now? Why not last week or next week? Have you some sweet offer for the stupidest of the Clan? This is arbitrary beyond sense, sister!"

She recoiled from the anger in both his words and his face. "It is Val Con! I—I must consider what is proper. He has been missing all this while . . ."

"Is he truly missing? I know I haven't seen him for some time, but missing?"

Nova held up her hand, moved to the console, and touched several buttons, bringing the computer screen to life.

He moved closer as she scrolled the information there, finally settling on a spot.

". . . the First Speaker's point is, however, valid insofar as it concerns the necessity of the Nadelm's education," she read. "I shall undertake to make myself available as soon as practicable following my thirtieth anniversary Name Day for instruction on the proper administration of a Clan from both the First Speaker and Korval's man of business. It is made extremely clear by the First Speaker, my sister, that I am expected to graduate to Delm very quickly."

Shan sensed the underlying impatience in those few words as clearly as he felt the tension singing in Nova.

"His *word*, from the last letter I had of him, nearly three Standards gone. His Name Day is more than a relumma past, and I have heard nothing! I must prepare, for the benefit of Korval. *yos'Galan must prepare, as well!*"

"Is he dead, then?"

His query was quite calm. Had she been less wrought up herself, she might have mistrusted such calmness. As it was, she gasped and stared up at him, dimly aware that somehow during the course of the interview the lines of melant'i had shifted so that it was no longer Korval's First Speaker, eldema-pernard'i, in conference with the Head of Line yos'-Galan, but a younger sibling pleading with an elder.

"Dead?" she repeated, golden fingers snaking about each other in agitation. "How can I know? They answer no questions! The Scouts say he was placed on detached duty to the Department of the Interior these three years gone by. The Department of the Interior says he has been offered leave and refused it; that it is not their part to force a man to go where he would rather not. They refuse to relay the message that he come to his Clan, when next he is able . . ."

And that, Shan thought, was not as it should be. Even the Scouts, who had little patience with many things Liaden— even the Scouts, appealed to in need, had sent broadbeam across the stars that Scout Captain Val Con yos'Phelium was required immediately at home, on business of his Clan. So had Val Con come, too, in remarkably short time, shaky with too many Jumps made one after another, to stand and weep with the rest of them at his foster mother's bier.

"If he will not come to us—" Nova was saying distractedly, "If he is so angry with me, even now . . ."

And there was the nub of it, Shan knew. When last he had been home on leave, Val Con had quarreled with his sister, the First Speaker, over her insistence that he take himself a contract-bride and provide the Clan with his heir. That quarrel had been running for several years, with subtle variations as each jockeyed for position. There was very little real pressure that Nova as Korval-in-Trust could bring upon Korval Himself, whether he chose at the moment to take up the Ring and his Delmhood, or remain mere Second Speaker. However, the Second Speaker was bound to obey the First, as was any Clanmember, and the Clan demanded of each member a child, by universal Clan Law. A pretty problem of melant'i and ethics, to be sure, and one Shan was glad to contemplate from a distance. Obviously even Val Con had bowed to at least part of melant'i's necessity, as evidenced by that snappish letter. But still . . .

"That's hardly like him, denubia. Val Con's never held a grudge that long in all his life."

His attempted comfort backfired. Nova's violet eyes filled with tears, and her hands knotted convulsively.

"Then he is dead!"

"No." He bent to cup her face in his big brown hands. "Sister, listen to me: Has Anthora said he is dead?"

She blinked, gulped, and shook her head so the blond hair snared his wrists.

"Have you asked her?"

Another headshake, fine hairs clinging to his skin like grade-A silk, and he read the two terrors within her.

"Anthora is dramliza," he said patiently, beginning to pay out a Healer's line of comfort as pity overtook him. "She holds each of us in her mind like a flame, she told me once. Best to ask and know for certain."

Nova touched the tip of her tongue to her lips, hesitating.

"Ask," he urged, seeing with satisfaction that her agitation quieted under his weaving of comfort and gentle hope. "If this Department of the Interior flouts Clan tradition, then we will search ourselves. Korval has some resources, after all."

"Yes, of course," she murmured, moving her cheek against

his palm in a most un-Novalike demonstration of affection. Shan cautiously lowered his level of input and pulled his hands away. She would do, he judged. Korval's First Speaker had a cool, level head. Even without his aid, she would have taken up her charge again very shortly and done all she perceived as necessary to keep the Clan in Trust for Korval's Own Self.

Shan shook his head slightly. He had briefly held the post Nova now filled and did not envy her the necessity of running a Clan composed of such diverse and strong-willed persons. *Dutiful Passage* was more to his taste, more in keeping with his abilities; yet the trading life had bored Nova to distraction.

He smiled down at her—the only one of the three yos'-Galans who had inherited all their Terran mother's height. "Ask Anthora," he advised again. "And tell me what I can do to help us find our brother."

She returned his smile faintly, a bare upward curve of pale lips. "I will think upon it. In the meanwhile, do think upon what we discussed earlier . . ."

Anger flared, but he held it in check, unwilling to give her cause to fear the loss of another brother. "I will not contract-wed. I have done my duty, and the Clan has my daughter in its keeping. I have done more than my duty—I hear that the child Lazmeln got from me aspires to be a pilot. Leave it."

"If Val Con is dead—if he is eklykt'i—then yos'Galan must be ready to assume its position as Korval's First Line. You are Thodelm yos'Galan—head of our Line! *You* are A'nadelm, next to be Delm, if Val Con—"

"*If* Val Con!" The anger clawed loose for an instant before he enclosed it. "If Anthora claims our brother dead, I still demand to see the body: my right as kin, my right as cha'leket, my right as A'nadelm! You do not make me Korval so easily, sister. Nor do I contract-wed again, and so I do swear!"

Her face was stricken; he felt the grief roiling off her like bitter smoke and made his bow, utterly formal.

"With the First Speaker's permission," he said precisely, and left her before it was given.

LIAD

SOLCINTRA

Shan reached Priscilla's house at first dark, when the fairy lights within the transparent walkway glowed under his boots like snowflakes. Taking the four steps to the town house's narrow vestibule in two strides, he laid his palm against the door. It slid open to admit him, and his heart clutched in wonder of it, even after so many years.

In the study, Priscilla lounged on pillows before a newly laid fire, papers in drifts around her, while Dablin, the resident cat, lay stretched in striped orange glory upon the scrubbed wood floor. His ears twitched at the sound of Shan's footsteps, but he did not deign to turn his head; the woman looked up, black eyes smiling, emotive grid a scintillation of joy/affection/caring/desire.

"Hello, love."

"You really should see to that door, Priscilla. Anyone might walk in."

She laughed softly as he crossed the room, open to and treasuring her joy, knowing that she read his emotions as clearly as he read hers—or did she read more clearly? Priscilla was not a mere Healer, after all; she was of the dramliz—a full-scale wizard, though on Sintia, the planet of her birth, the proper term was "witch."

"Have you eaten?" she asked, putting aside a sheaf of papers and extending a hand. "I can have Teyas bring you something."

He took her cool hand in his and, obedient to the gentle downward tug, settled to the pillows, chin propped on fist. She curled around to face him, cheek resting on a white arm. She was naked to the waist, as was her custom at home, and the platinum hoops in her ears gleamed in contrast to her short mop of thundercloud curls.

"I'm not hungry," he said, laying a hand over one breast; the nipple hardened against his palm, and he caught a flash of sheer lust from her. He looked up and smiled. "Hello Priscilla."

"Hello, Shan." One long finger traced the stark line of his cheek and lifted to follow the slant of a frost-colored eyebrow. "Nova made you angry."

"She has a very talent for it. Too like our father, poor child. Afraid she's driven Val Con away for once and all, or that he's gone and she must now command the Clan."

His father had been two years dead before Priscilla Mendoza had taken berth on the *Dutiful Passage*. However, she knew Nova and Val Con—Dablin, beginning the opening moves of his bathing ritual there before the fire, had been Val Con's gift to her.

Priscilla frowned. "Surely that's not like him? Has she contacted the Scouts? Left word for him to come home?"

Shan sighed and leaned back across the pillows, light eyes on the ceiling tiles. "She tried; but here's an oddity for you, Priscilla. The Scouts say Commander Val Con yos'Phelium hasn't been with them for more than three years, that he's on detached duty to something called the Department of the Interior. Ring any bells with you?"

She shook her head.

"Well, with me either, if it comes to that. Something to check on . . . At any rate, Nova calls this Department of the Interior, requests that a message be delivered to Commander yos'Phelium—kin-right, she tells them; his First Speaker requires him at Trealla Fantrol, on business of the Clan."

"The Department of the Interior is delighted to comply," Priscilla suggested when the silence had stretched a time.

Shan snorted. "The Department of the Interior informs Korval's First Speaker that Commander yos'Phelium is not at the moment available and adds that it is not Korval's lackey, to be delivering messages here and there around the galaxy. Nova points out that they are in violation of Clan Rule in that the commander has not returned home on leave in all the three years he has been with the Department. The

Department replied that he has been offered leave several times and refused it; nor are they in the business of forcing a man to go where he would rather not."

"Nova hangs up in a fury," Priscilla murmured.

He laughed sharply. "Too true!"

"But what did she want you to do? Certainly the voice of Korval eldema-pernard'i carries more weight than that of Thodelm yos'Galan?"

"The First Speaker, in her wisdom, desires Thodelm yos'-Galan to contract-wed."

Shock lanced through her, edged with astonishment, confusion, and the beginning of grief.

"Priscilla . . ." He reached for her, with both mind and hands, pulling her back down to lie beside him, her hand fisted on his chest despite the tide of comfort and love he poured out for her reading. "Priscilla, it will not happen! I will not allow it, and so I told her! My duty is done and—"

"If the First Speaker commands it, you'll have to. But why?" Anguish was added to the blare of other pains, and betrayal; she counted Nova among her friends. "Val Con's dead, is that it? The Department of the Interior—they lied to her. No, they said unavailable—truth. Of a kind. If Val Con's dead . . ." She raised herself up on her elbow and looked down on him with wide black eyes.

"You're Delm, aren't you? Korval Himself."

"I am *not* Delm, Priscilla. Strive for some sense! Scan me! Do I grieve for him—for my heart's own brother? Do I?"

"No."

He took a breath, feeling the warmth of her affection seeping into his bones like a draught of strong brandy. "Nova's duty as First Speaker is first to hold the Clan in trust for Val Con, who *is* Korval Himself. But the Clan exists even if Val Con doesn't, and a prudent Speaker must consider all contingencies, make plans for each—like captain and first mate, eh?" That drew a slight smile, though her eyes were tight on his face.

"Nova must consider the possibility of Val Con's death, as well as the chance that he's left the Clan," he went on. "But her guilt makes her favor the worst of all worlds above any other. With some reason—yos'Pheliums lately seem prone to leaving the Clan.

"There's Uncle Daav, for instance—Val Con's father—gone these twenty-five Standards and more. Nova forgets that he went for Balance, not anger. Not that it makes much difference, gone being gone. But you understand that the First Speaker must plan for yos'Galan to take its place as Korval's Prime Line, should Val Con's thirty-fifth birthday pass and he not, in fact, take up the Ring. She's simply beginning her strategy too early, and with too little information in hand. Korval must find its Nadelm, and the First Speaker must put the question to him plainly. That's all."

"How old is Val Con? Thirty?"

"Just turned," he agreed. "We've got five whole years to find him."

She did not say that a Scout might easily stay hidden for twelve times that long, or that the universe was wide. Instead she bent close, eyes locked on his, lips above his mouth by the breadth of one of Dablin's whiskers.

"You are my man," she said. It was not a command; it was a statement of her belief, open to his contradiction.

He lifted his hands and ran brown fingers roughly into her curls. "With all my heart."

The small gap closed, and she kissed him leisurely, then, yielding to his urgency, harder, hands at his shirt, at his belt; and they made love with body, heart, and mind, scattering pillows and papers every which way and boring Dablin to yawns.

Much later, when they both had had a glass or two and a bit to eat, and had gone upstairs to the bedroom and curled beneath the coverlet, she spoke into his ear. "*Do* you think Val Con's okay? Even if he's not dead, he could be—in trouble."

Shan laughed sleepily and pushed his face into the hollow of her neck. "Trust me, Priscilla. Wherever Val Con is at this moment, he has the best of everything possible."

ORBIT

INTERDICTED WORLD I-2796-893-44

Miri rapped sharply on the wall at about the height of her shoulder and was rewarded with a solid metallic *thunk*. She sighed in equal parts of relief and frustration. The hallway had no hidden compartments, which meant that she would not have to deal with another bushel of amateur telescopes, or dolls, or jewels—but it also meant that there was nothing resembling a vegetable or vitamin anywhere on this tub, and she had, after all, a half-convalescent soldier on her hands.

One of the other hideys had yielded up a solitary platinum necklace, set with twelve matched emeralds. Val Con had handed it to her with a flourish and a smile. "For you—a hand-cut set."

"You keep it," Miri had told him. "Matches your eyes."

He had insisted, though, and now the thing was in her belt pouch, sharing space with a flawed sapphire, a matching ring and necklace, an enameled disk, a harmonica, and a couple of ration sticks. She would have traded the whole bunch for a handful of high-potency supplements.

"Damn it," she muttered, and settled her back against the cool wall, glaring at the pilfered elegance around her. Val Con had had a lot to say—for him, anyway—about the fineness of the yacht, pointing out the up-to-the-second water purification system, the lighted ceilings and side walls, and even the style and power of the coils they had blown to bits in that desperate Jump away from the Yxtrang.

The boarding crew had pretty well cleaned things out in the initial raid. The galley was bare—even the menuboard had been dismantled and removed. It was just plain, dumb luck that the Yxtrang had not been looking for secret compartments, or else she and Val Con would not even have had salmon and pretzels to eat.

What the hell are you doing here, anyway? she asked herself suddenly. Everything had happened so fast. Married. How in the name of anything holy had she wound up married?

"Damn Liaden tricked me," she told the empty hall. She laughed a little. Tricked three ways from yesterday—married and partnered to a Liaden; sister to an eight-foot, bottle-green Clutch-turtle with a name longer than she was; stranded on a coil-blown pleasure yacht around a world her new husband assured her was most likely Interdicted.

"Bored, were you, Robertson? Life not exciting enough with just the Juntavas after you?" She laughed again and shook her head, pushing away from the wall and starting back toward the bridge. Life . . .

The bridge was a racket of radio chatter and computer chimes in the midst of which a slender, dark-haired man sat quietly. Miri froze in the doorway, heart stuttering, eyes sharp on the stillness of him, remembering another time, not so many days before, when he had been that still and a deadly danger to them both.

Quietly she approached the pilot's board, noting with relief that his shoulders carried only the normal tensions of weariness and concentration—nothing of shock or the abnormal effort of attaining freedom.

Nonetheless, standing unheeded beside him and watching the absorption on his face as he extended a long-fingered hand to minutely adjust a dial, she felt dread stir and chill her, and impulsively put her hand on his wrist, interrupting the adjustment.

"Stop!" he snapped, glancing up quickly.

"Still here, huh, boss?" She pulled her hand away. "Time for a break."

"Later." He turned back toward the board and the senseless chatter coming up from the planet surface.

"I said *now,* spacer!" Her voice carried all the authority of a mercenary sergeant, and she braced herself for retaliation.

His eyes, brilliantly green, flicked to hers, his mouth straight in that look that meant he was going to have his way, come hell or high water—and suddenly he smiled, pushing the hair out of his eyes. "Cha'trez, forgive me. I was lost in the work, and only meant to say that I am attempting—"

"To put yourself in a bad spot," Miri interrupted. "I don't think you been outta that seat for ten hours. You gotta eat, you gotta walk around, you gotta rest—wasn't all that long ago the only things between you and the Last Walk were an autodoc and a scared merc."

There was a long pause during which green eyes measured gray. He was the first to sigh and drop his gaze.

"All right, Miri."

She looked at him suspiciously. "What's that mean?"

"It means that I will take a break now—walk a bit and join you for a meal." He grinned weakly and reached up to brush her cheek with light fingers. "I do tend toward singlemindedness occasionally, despite my family's best efforts." The grin broadened. "I would not have you think that I was brought up as poorly as that."

"Sure," she said uncertainly, sensing a joke of some kind. She pointed at the board. "You still doing the hunt-and-compare bit? 'Cause I can give a listen while you're off-duty."

"It would be of assistance," he said, standing and stretching to his full height. Miri grinned up at him, liking the slim, graceful body and the beardless golden face. She extended a hand to touch his right cheek, and he shifted to drop a kiss on her fingertips. "Soon," he said, and slipped silently away.

Shaking her head at the hammering of her heart, Miri dropped into the pilot's chair and picked up the earphones.

Dinner was prime-grade Milovian salmon, Boolean pretzel-bread, and water, consumed while seated cross-legged on the carpet amid the desolation that probably had been the private quarters of the yacht's owner.

Val Con ate his ration with neat efficiency, as if he were stoking his furnace with protein, Miri thought; as if taste and variety had nothing to do with the act of eating.

She ate more slowly, weary of the taste but forcing herself to finish every bit of the stuff, and finally she looked up to find Val Con watching her closely.

"This whole ship's a loony bin," she groused. "Triple-A prime salmon, telescopes, dolls, jewelry, secret compartments, and a coordinate page filled with Interdicted Worlds. How come?"

"The luxuries are bribes," Val Con said softly. "And the extra compartments are to hide them. Simple."

"Yeah?" She blinked. "Somebody's trading with Quarantined Worlds? But that's—"

"Illegal?" He shrugged. "It's only illegal when someone catches you."

"Hell of an attitude for a Scout."

He laughed. "Did I ever tell you about my grandmother?"

"Don't know when you would've had a chance. What about her?"

He smiled. "She was a smuggler."

"That a fact?" Miri said calmly. "What's the old lady doing now?"

"Forgive me," he murmured. "I should have said my many-times great-grandmother, Cantra yos'Phelium, co-founder of Clan Korval."

She grinned. "Not likely to go around embarrassing all the relatives then, is she?" Then she did a double-take. "Cantra, like the money?"

"Indeed," Val Con said around a sudden yawn. "Exactly Cantra, like the money."

"Better get some sleep, boss," she advised, hoping against all reason that he would forget about the blithering radio and the strings of signals to be overlaid and recorded.

"Not too bad an idea." He yawned again and without ado stretched out, putting his head on her lap.

"What the hell's wrong with you?"

"I'm tired, Miri."

She glared down at his shuttered face. "And you gotta put your head right there?"

One green eye opened. "Shall I put it on the floor?"

"Should you—I'll tell you what's wrong with you. You're spoiled."

The eye closed. "Undoubtedly."

"Rich kid from the good part of town; never had no trouble; never had to rough it; always a soft place to put your head . . ."

"Inarguably. Absolutely. Cantras and coaches. Satins and silks. Malchek and feeldophin."

She eyed him warily, noting without meaning to the long dark lashes and the firm, sweet mouth. "What's malchek and feeldophin?"

Both eyes opened wide, staring upside down into hers. "I don't know, Miri. But I'm certain they must be something."

"Think I'd learn." She sighed heavily and moved a hand to brush the hair away from his eyes. "I ain't good at sleeping sitting up, though."

"Ah. A compelling reason for me to put my head on the floor, I agree." He did so and opened his arms. "Come to bed, Miri."

Laughing, she stretched out beside him and put her head on his shoulder.

LIAD

SOLCINTRA

The priority gong clanged, and Shan was up in an eruption of bedclothes, slapping the stud before he was fully awake.

"yos'Galan," he snapped into the speaker, only then aware of Priscilla at his side.

"Tower here, Cap'n. Sorry to disturb you."

"That's quite all right, Rusty; I enjoy having my rest broken for crew maneuvers. I assume that you *are* doing a dry run and that there really *isn't* a priority message for me lying somewhere around the Tower?"

"Nosir—I mean, *yessir,* there's a message, all right, pin-beamed to you by name, priority wrap, balance in code. Hit about three minutes ago. But here's what's funny, Cap'n . . ."

"I knew there was a punch line! Don't disappoint me, Rusty."

"Yessir. We tagged the source of transmission as local— just north of Solcintra. Thought you'd want to know."

"We're in northern Solcintra . . ." Shan frowned. "You didn't by any chance send a priority message to me via the *Passage,* did you, Priscilla? There are more seemly ways to get my attention."

"The thought had occurred to me," she admitted, grinning.

"But action did not follow. Well, I doubt it's someone wanting to sell me a cloak." He touched a quick series of keys. "Transmit at will, Rusty—and thank you for your patience. It occurs to me that I'm becoming ill-tempered in my dotage."

Laughter burst from the comm as the receiver lit and beeped. "How long've we known each other?"

"Gods alone know. I recall the day they carried you onship, a babe in arms—"

"And you a gleam in Cap'n Er Thom's eye! Tower out."

"Good-bye, Tower." He shook his head and tapped keys— and the screen lit, displaying a bare line of gibberish, the word PRIORITY shrieking across the top margin. Shan sighed. "What day is it, Priscilla?"

"Banim Seconday."

"Ah, yes, and we're in the second relumma, year Trebloma . . ." He keyed in the information, added his ship-code, and stepped back, slipping an arm around her waist. Before them, the screen shimmered, null-words breaking, re-forming, then becoming intelligible.

INFORMATION RECEIVED RE PROBLEM VIA GREENTREES.
COME HOME.

"My sister studies espionage. How refreshing." He sighed again and gave Priscilla a slight squeeze before he withdrew his arm. "Adventures, Priscilla! Were you growing bored?"

"Not especially." She hesitated. "Shall I come with you, Captain?"

He reached to touch her cheek. "This is a Clan matter,

beloved, not a ship matter; the first mate has no need to be with me. However, I was to have seen Sennel this morning—if you would do the kindness?"

He read her disappointment, a reawakening of the previous night's uncertainties. "Fear not!" he cried with a gaiety his pattern did not reflect. "I very much doubt that this is a clever plot to whisk me away and marry me against my will to some lady from an outworld Clan—"

She laughed in spite of herself as he went across to the dressing room. He was out again in a handful of minutes, sealing the cuffs of a wide-sleeved blue shirt.

"Only see how obedient I am! My father would have expired of astonishment. First mate and captain are to meet with Delm Intassi this afternoon to discuss a possible cargo. If for some reason I cannot go, take Ken Rik with you and present my assurances to Intassi that nothing less than my First Speaker's word would have kept me from such an important appointment."

"Yes." She had flung the balcony door wide and was staring down into the inner garden, her pattern overlaid with the hum that signaled concentrated thought.

Shan stepped to her side and touched her shoulder. "Priscilla?"

She started just slightly, ebon eyes flashing to his face.

"Will you dine with me this evening? It seems we'd best talk again about the maggot in Nova's head." He took her pale hand and kept his eyes steady on hers. "I will marry no other lady, Priscilla. I swear it to you."

Her eyes filled, even as his did. "Shan . . ."

"Yes?"

She took a hard breath, and then the words came in a rush. "Can't we declare ourselves lifemates? If we—act according to Liaden law . . . Nova can't insist you contract-wed if you're lifemated, can she?"

"No, of course not. But Thodelm yos'Galan owes allegiance to Korval. Since we have no Delm, I must ask the First Speaker's permission to a lifemating and—"

"The timing's bad."

"Dreadful might be more accurate." He glanced down at their linked hands, saw the Master Trader's amethyst gleaming against his brown skin, bracketed by her slim white fingers, and looked back to her face. "The last time we were in port I went to the First Speaker to ask her permission . . ."

Priscilla stiffened. "She refused?"

"I never asked. Already the time was bad. I'm a Trader, Priscilla! It's lunacy to deal at a known disadvantage!" The bedside clock chimed their usual hour of rising, and he shifted. "I should go."

"Yes." She loosed his hand and stepped back. "Give my love to your sisters."

"Always." He hesitated on the edge of a kiss, read in her a desire for reserve, and so merely bowed the bow of affection and esteem. "I'll see you soon, Priscilla."

"Walk the day in joy, my love."

LIAD

TREALLA FANTROL

Shan sent the fast little groundcar through the curve at the top of the hill, slipped the stick, and spun into the drive with a purring uptake of speed. At the base of the first hill, he downshifted in deference to the possibilities of children, cats, and dogs and proceeded at a pace only another pilot might have called sedate.

Damn it, he thought, guiding the car through twists and turns he knew like the rhythm of his own heartbeat. It wasn't like Nova to indulge in espionage! That Department of the Interior had got her worried beyond sense.

Or worried in very good sense. The car slid beneath a flowered archway and continued down a straight road lined with fragrant colmeno bushes. Shan felt a finger of cold down his spine and shivered in the warm Liaden sunshine.

The car negotiated the final right turn, left turn, sharp right, and pulled into a space near the garage doors. Shan got out and slammed the door.

The south wing was quiet. Despite the lesson of past experience, it seemed as if Padi and Syl Vor might actually be with their tutors this morning—or engaged in quiet mayhem in another part of the house. Anthora's brand-new twins would be sleeping or gurgling in the nursery, charming those who had them in their care into the belief that *this* set of yos'Galans, at least, were as even-natured as they were sweet-tempered.

Nurses were so easy to fool. Shan shook his head and moved with lazy haste toward the main corridor, ears tracking the growing rumble of wheels across strellawood flooring. In contrast to nurses and tutors, Trealla Fantrol's butler was damn near impossible to fool.

They met at the intersection of corridors. The butler rotated the orange glass ball that served as his head and waved two of three arms in salute.

"Master Shan. Good day, sir. The First Speaker awaits you in the study." The voice, male and middle-aged, spoke Terran with the affected drawl of the upper classes and originated somewhere near the plate steel midsection.

"Jeeves," Shan said calmly. "Good day to you. Have you seen the children lately?"

"Miss Padi is in the garden with Mr. pel'Jonna, partaking of a botany lesson. Master Syl Vor and Ms. Gamkoda are engaged in geography, and Miss Shindi and Master Mik are having an early-morning nap."

"Dear me, what exemplary behavior! I believe they may be ill."

"On the contrary, sir, they enjoy their customary robust health. I believe, if I may say so, that this morning's quietude may be attributed to Miss Nova's promise that they would be allowed to visit you only if they behaved as became those of Korval."

"Ever more terrifying! But perhaps they don't yet have a firm grasp of family history."

"As you say, sir."

Shan grinned and turned right. "To my sister in the study, then! Be well, Jeeves."

"Be well, sir."

He went perhaps half a dozen paces before turning back. "Jeeves!"

"Sir?" The midsection rotated, and the orange ball lit in inquiry.

"Is Miss Anthora in the house? And Gordy?"

"Miss Anthora is with the First Speaker in the study. Your foster son has contracted an alliance of pleasure with Karae yo'Lanna and spent last evening in her company. Shall I contact Glavda Empri and inquire for him?"

"Ken Rik's granddaughter, is it? No, don't disturb the child; just ask him to call me at his earliest opportunity. The *Passage* will know where I am, if he doesn't find me here or at Pelthraza Street."

"Very good, sir." Jeeves rotated once more and wheeled off in pursuit of other imperatives. Shan grinned and headed for the study.

The door slid away and two heads turned toward him—one blond and one dark, violet eyes and silver. Anthora stood and came forward, small hands outstretched, welcome riding a warm wave between them.

"Shan-brother."

He ignored the hands and bent to hug her. "Hello, denubia. How's the contract-husband?"

She laughed, nose wrinkling. "Many days gone, thank the gods! But the twins are very good, don't you think?"

"Very good, indeed. I could have done no better."

That earned another laugh as a tug on his sleeve pulled him across the carpet to where Nova waited in cool uncertainty.

"Sister." He smiled and extended a hand, marking with what relief she took it. Not for the first time, he regretted that Nova's talent was one that gave her access only to the memories of those already dead, rather than to the living emotion all about her.

"Brother. Thank you for coming so promptly."

"The least I could do, when you'd gone to so much trou-

ble and expense! Only why a pin-beam to the *Passage,*
denubia, when a local call might have gotten you the same
result?"

She looked coldly into his face, every inch the First
Speaker of Liad's First Clan, her hand gripping his until he
feared for the bones.

"Local calls can be too easily traced," she said. "Come see
what we have." She waved to the comm on its corner of the
wide desk.

"I've seen it," Anthora said to his hesitation, her emotive
grid suddenly and suspiciously bland. "Would you care for
some morning wine to help you read, brother?"

"Wine by all means—but not morning wine. A glass of the
red, if you please." He glanced at Nova's face, but saw only
waiting there while her pattern glimmered, chameleonlike,
too changeable to read.

He slid into the desk chair and tipped the screen to
the proper height. Amber letters spelled out words in High
Liaden:

COMMUNICATION BEGINS

GREETINGS.

    TO NOVA YOS'GALAN FIRST SPEAKER-IN-TRUST CLAN
KORVAL, SHE WHO REMEMBERS, FIRST SISTER TO OUR
SHARED BROTHER, VAL CON YOS'PHELIUM SCOUT, ARTIST
OF THE EPHEMERAL, SLAYER OF THE ELDEST DRAGON,
KNIFE CLAN OF MIDDLE RIVER'S SPRING SPAWN OF
FARMER GREENTREES OF THE SPEARMAKER'S DEN, TOUGH
GUY.

Shan blinked and leaned back in the chair, absently accepting the glass from Anthora's hand, wondering at the sig-
nificance of the final two words being rendered in Terran.

    KNOW THAT ON THE TWO HUNDREDTH AND FORTY-SEC-
OND DAY OF THIS STANDARD YEAR NUMBERED 1392 OUR
BROTHER AND HIS LIFEMATE, MIRI ROBERTSON MERCE-
NARY SOLDIER, RETIRED, PERSONAL BODYGUARD, RE-
TIRED, HAVE WEAPON WILL TRAVEL, DEPARTED FROM
LUFKIT PRIME STATION BY TESTIMONY OF HE WHO

WATCHES ON A SHIP OF THE CLAN, FLEEING NAMELESS
ENEMIES.

KNOW FURTHER THAT ON THE TWO HUNDREDTH AND
FORTY-SIXTH DAY OF THIS STANDARD YEAR OUR BROTHER
AND MY SISTER HIS LIFEMATE FELL INTO THE HANDS OF
CLAN JUNTAVAS OF THE LINE WHICH LOOKS TO ELDER
JUSTIN HOSTRO IN WHICH MISFORTUNE OUR BROTHER
TOOK INJURY FROM THE KIN OF ELDER HOSTRO

Dear gods, Shan thought. He damped his output, so that
Anthora would not be pummeled with his dread. He sipped
wine and touched the advance key.

NEGOTIATION WITH ELDER HOSTRO PROVED SATISFAC-
TORY TO THE POINT THAT OUR BROTHER'S INJURY WAS
HEALED. IT WAS FURTHER NEGOTIATED THAT OUR KIN BE
RETURNED THEIR KNIVES AND GIVEN A SHIP ON WHICH TO
CONTINUE THEIR JOURNEY, THE SHIP OF THE CLAN HAVING
RESUMED ITS LABOR DURING THE TIME THEY WERE HELD
BY CLAN JUNTAVAS. EVIDENCE INDICATING THAT THESE
THINGS WERE DONE PROVIDED BY JUSTIN HOSTRO AND
FORTHCOMING TO YOURSELF VIA HASTIEST COURIER
AVAILABLE.

IT HAS COME TO MY ATTENTION THAT JUSTIN HOSTRO IS
THE MOST MINOR OF ELDERS WITHIN CLAN JUNTAVAS AND
CANNOT GUARANTEE THE ACTIONS OF THE REMAINDER OF
HIS CLAN. IN THIS CIRCUMSTANCE, I GO TO NEGOTIATE
WITH THE ELDEST ELDER OF THE JUNTAVAS ON THIS, THE
TWO HUNDREDTH AND FIFTY-FIFTH DAY OF STANDARD
YEAR 1392. I UNDERTAKE THIS NEGOTIATION AS MIRI
ROBERTSON'S BROTHER AND T'CARAIS AND AS THE
BROTHER OF OUR SHARED BROTHER WHO TRAVELS AT HER
SIDE.

KNOW AT LAST THAT OUR BROTHER'S STATED DESTINA-
TION WAS VOLMER DESIGNATION V-8735-927-3 AND THAT
HE HAS NOT YET ARRIVED AT THAT PORT THOUGH A SHIP
OF THE CLANS OF MEN MUST HAVE TAKEN HIM THERE BY
THIS DAY. NOR HAS HE CONTACTED ME AS I FEEL HE
WOULD HAVE DONE WERE ALL WELL.

THAT JUSTIN HOSTRO MAY NOT HAVE BARGAINED IN
GOOD FAITH IS A MATTER I SHALL DISCUSS WITH THE MOST
ELDER OF THE JUNTAVAS. THAT OUR BROTHER AND SISTER
HAVE ATTAINED THAT STATE KNOWN TO MEN AS "MISSING"
IS INFORMATION I FELT THEIR REMAINING KIN MUST HAVE
WITH UTMOST ALACRITY SO THAT A SEARCH MAY BE UN-
DERTAKEN WITH ALL HUMAN SPEEDINESS.

IN SHARED KINSHIP AND DUTY I SALUTE YOU. MAY SUC-
CESS MEET OUR MOST STRINGENT EFFORTS.

BEAMED THIS DAY 255 STANDARD YEAR 1392 BY:

TWELFTH SHELL FIFTH HATCHED KNIFE CLAN OF MID-
DLE RIVER'S SPRING SPAWN OF FARMER GREENTREES OF
THE SPEARMAKER'S DEN, THE EDGER.

COMMUNICATION ENDS

Shan leaned back and closed his eyes, thoughts tumbling.
The first was that the message came from the old boy himself, Val Con's very brother Edger, in whom Shan had never
quite believed, no matter how well told the tale. The second
was that, of course, it would have to be checked, fraud being
however dimly possible.

The third thought bestirred him to open his eyes and lean
to the comm, touching keys, banishing Edger's message to
memory as he opened a line to the *Passage*.

"Shan—" Nova began, her worry apparent.

He finished his query, hit SEND, and picked up his glass.
"Annie, my own."

"Shan-brother?"

"Is Val Con alive, denubia? Progress report, please, as of
this very moment, if possible."

"Alive?" She blinked at him. "Of course."

"Good. Wonderful, in fact." He stared at her over the rim
of his glass. "Where?"

He sensed confusion; frustration quickly sublimated into
thought. Anthora closed her eyes, casting this way and that,
for all the worlds like a dog hunting a scent. Nova stirred and
began to speak, but Shan held up a hand, his eyes on the
youngest of them all.

"There!" she cried suddenly, finger pointing roofward and
beyond, to what might be the Second Quadrant. She opened

her eyes. "But a long way away, Shannie. I don't—when *you're* on Volmer you don't feel nearly so far away . . ."

"How far beyond Volmer?" He caught the edge of her frustration again and leaned forward. "Have I ever felt that distant? If you remember an approximate time, we can check the log on the *Passage*—"

But Anthora was shaking her head. "None of us has ever been that far—no. When Father—when Father was dying, at the very end—the day before he—he was that distant then . . . Oh, no!" Nova's pain broke over them, and Anthora flew forward to hug her and shake her. "He's *alive,* sister! *Physical* distance, not spiritual! I can't tell you how I know the difference—but there is one! And another difference—" She paused, looking to Shan, who nodded.

"There's a—an—echo—around Val Con. It's like—it's like how I sense Priscilla—not directly, you see—but through Shan . . ."

"His lifemate," Nova murmured, and suddenly spun. "Lifemate! Did you know of a lifemate? Who is she?"

Shan sipped wine. "I'd say she's a person with a sense of humor: 'Miri Robertson Mercenary Soldier, Retired, Personal Bodyguard, Retired, Have Weapon Will Travel'? Also a person to treat with a bit of respect. As for who else she is, as soon as the *Passage* gets through to Terran Census—aha! Right on cue!"

He touched the glowing purple stud and the screen filled with amber letters once more, this time forming Terran words.

"Well, let's see: Planet of origin: Surebleak . . . Date of Birth: Day 28, Standard Year 1365; Tag: mutated within acceptable limits. Parents: Katalina Tayzin; Chock Robertson. Job Fee paid: Half-bit; Day 116, Standard 1375, poor child . . . Outmigrated Day 4, Standard 1379 . . . Reason for Migration: Job opportunity. And the job? Ah, here we are . . ." He hit ADVANCE and shook his head. "Apprentice soldier, Lizardi's Lunatics, Fendor. Angela Lizardi, Senior Commander. Poor, poor child."

"Mutated . . ." Nova was hanging over his shoulder, frowning at the screen.

"Within acceptable limits," Shan completed. "Now, on a

backward, low-tech world like, shall we say, Surebleak, the phrase 'mutated within acceptable limits' can mean several things. But mostly it means 'half or full Liaden.'" He tapped the screen. "My guess is that Katalina Tayzin has gotten her name mangled into something more or less Terran-sounding. Chock Robertson seems rather definite."

"But who *is* she?" Nova demanded, running the advance down to blank screen.

"She's a soldier, sister!" Shan snapped. "Where have your wits gone begging? We'll run an employment check on her through the *Passage* if you like, to find where she went after being apprenticed to Lizardi's Lunatics—but you already know the most important thing about her."

Nova drew herself up and glared down at him. "Which is?"

"She's Korval's Own Lifemate," Shan said, and drank his wine.

ORBIT

INTERDICTED WORLD 1-2796-893-44

Flesh against flesh was warm, promoting drowsy comfort, though her exposed right flank was getting damn cold.

Unwilling yet to let go of the drowse, Miri nestled closer to Val Con's warmth, too comfortable even to care that a long lock of her hair was trapped under their combined weight and pulled at her temple. She smiled a little to herself.

Things had gotten pretty intense there, for a bit. It had started with her reaching to touch his right cheek—the one the Juntavas had cut—by way of saying "good night."

His eyes had opened wide; his fingers had lifted and traced the line of the scar. "It does not repel you?"

"Huh?" She blinked, then shook her head against his

shoulder. "People get hurt in fights sometimes. Better a scar or two than something more fatal."

"Ah." Once more his fingers passed lightly across his own cheek; then they were at the lacings of her shirt, baring her breast and touching the faint white pucker where she had caught a near-spent pellet, way back on Contrast. Rolling with her so that he was half on top, he bent his head to kiss the scar.

Miri had had her share of scrapes—maybe more than her share of scars, what with her father . . . But Val Con, unlike one loobelli of a civilian she had slept with, did not ask where they were from, but just patiently and thoroughly sought each one out to kiss and caress until she had gotten a little intense, herself.

Now she snuggled even closer to his side, the steady beat of his heart filling her ears. He had even found the scars on her feet, from when she had kicked the grille out of the door and tried to walk away from the rehab center, her light house slippers hanging in bloody rags. She would have made it, too, except Liz had found her and made her swear to finish the therapy.

No sense, of course, she thought. Went to all that trouble to make sure Klamath didn't get me and almost let Cloud have me for nothing.

She stirred sharply, completely awake and almost breathless, as if she had suddenly found herself standing at the very edge of a sheer drop. Cloud. She had jammed so much of the stuff into her system by the time Liz had dragged her to rehab, she had barely remembered her own name.

And what if he asks you where you got them scars? she demanded of herself. You gonna tell him the truth, Robertson? Huh? Rich kid from Liad, hobnobs with the best people? Think he's gonna stand by words he said to some snip from Surebleak who was so addicted to Cloud it's a wonder she ever came away whole? Think it's gonna matter to him how long you been clean?

"Cha'trez?" His arms tightened, and he craned to see her, green eyes hazy and half asleep. "Is something wrong?"

She started, then reached up, touched his lips, and brushed her fingertips over the scar, aching at the beauty of him.

"You're on my hair," she said.

• • •

MIRI woke alone, her head pillowed on Val Con's folded
vest. She sighed, stretched deliberately, and was wide awake
by the time the stretch was done. From the bridge she heard
the radio's unceasing blather; she sighed again, rolled to her
feet, and hurriedly pulled on her clothes before heading that
way, his vest swinging in her hand.

Val Con stood, deep in thought. The bottle-shaped continent from the planet below had taken on three dimensions,
overrunning the bridge: the neck of the bottle started in the
companionway, and its bottom ran into the pilot's chair.

Miri shook her head in wonderment and leaned against the
doorjamb to watch.

Duct tape from the repair box was rumpled into mountain
ranges running north and south, gaps precisely cut out to
allow river systems their courses. Spare instrument lamps
dotted the map, some singly, others clustered. There were
several pipe pieces in the map, each with a number written on
the floor next to it.

Marking pens had also been used with art. The rivers had
boundaries of blue, while some areas were enclosed by curly
green lines and others simply outlined in brown. Three paper
spaceships sat next to the three largest lamp-clusters; Val Con
held another in his left hand. In his right was a ragged block
of metal the Yxtrang had torn from somewhere.

Miri gazed at the arrangement thoughtfully. "If you bring
your transport down 'round the oceanside of the blue lamps,
you can take out the red ones before they know what hit 'em,
then use their supplies to take the ship. Blue's gonna have to
get involved to protect themselves, so you sit tight and let
'em bang their heads against your position for a bit, then mop
up and go on a tiger hunt for green . . ."

He looked up, grinning and bright-eyed. "Are we invading, then, Sergeant?"

"Sure looks like a situation map to me, Commander."

Val Con stepped out of his construction, gently placing the
fourth paper spaceship near one edge of the continent before
moving to her. He kept the chink of metal in his hand.

"I don't doubt your invasion would work," he said, "but I
am not a general, alas, and would hesitate to direct it."

"Don't blame you. Invasions are messy. Course, garrison duty's boring."

"And limited by supplies."

"Like us." She nodded at the map. "What's with the world view?"

He turned carefully to avoid stepping on a mountain range and pointed. "The lamps are towns, as lit when we pass over them at night. More lamps become a city—like here—and fewer are villages or less. So the blue is a large town or a small city, one with four transmissions from it."

"The pipes are transmission towers?"

He nodded. "The green is the largest city, and I suspect it has an airport of some consequence."

"And that?" She pointed at the metal block in his hand. "Where does that go?"

He hefted it, walked two graceful steps into the map, and very precisely placed it between the coastal mountains and a single red lamp, not far from where he had placed the paper spaceship. "There."

"Fine," Miri approved. "What is it?"

"Us."

She frowned at the map, letting the picture build in her mind. "The idea is to leave the ship in the mountains, then walk down that pass there—if it is a pass—and hope there's some way we can work things out to meet people *before* we go to town?"

He nodded. "It is the best course of action I can envision, given the limited data we have been able to gather." He sighed. "This is not a Scout ship." He seemed genuinely annoyed with the yacht for that shortcoming, and Miri grinned briefly before walking the perimeter and stepping in beside him.

"When do we land?"

"When the time is propitious," he murmured, idly adjusting the metal block with his foot.

"You figure the propitious time will he soon?" she persisted. "Reason I ask is we only got another two days of fish and maybe three of crackers, and then what we got is water."

"Ah," he said, shifting slightly to take another look at his creation before turning and smiling down into her eyes. "In that case, I would say that the most propitious time is immediately after lunch."

LIAD

TREALLA FANTROL

Korval's man of business was closeted with the First Speaker, but before being whisked away he had managed one minor bit of magic and produced a credit history on Miri Robertson, Terran citizen. Shan slid the disk from the old gentleman's fingers with a smile. "Exactly what I was needing, sir. My thanks," he said, and carried it off.

Alone in his rooms, he fed the information to the computer and took a sip from his glass.

Apparently financial institutions did not consider mercenary soldiers good credit risks. There was a string of six "Applied. Credit Denied" before a surprising "Loan granted, Bank of Fendor, one-half cantra to Miri Robertson payable over a period of not more than four Standard Years at interest of 10.5%. Co-signator, Angela Lizardi. Collateral in form of Pension Fund 98-1077-45581 carried by Ilquith Securities. Transaction completed Day 353 Standard 1385."

Angela Lizardi again—apparently a commander who took active interest in her soldiers. And Miri Robertson pledges her pension for half a cantra cash, he thought. I wonder why.

The screen supplied no answer, but it did reflect an exemplary payment record, and then the notation "Balance paid in full, Day 4, Standard 1388."

She earned a bonus and killed the thing, Shan surmised, sipping wine. It was the best she could have done at ten point five. He touched a key and the credit file faded, to be replaced a heartbeat later by an employment history.

1379: APPRENTICE SOLDIER, LIZARDI'S LUNATICS.

The Lunatics had taken and fulfilled a series of contracts on a number of worlds: Eskelli, Porum, Contrast, Skittle, Klamath.

Shan froze. *Klamath?*

He had just extended a hand to request more information when the annunciator chimed.

"Come!"

The door whispered open behind him as he impatiently tapped keys.

"Klamath?" Anthora asked, leaning on his shoulder. "What's Klamath?"

"That is what we're trying to find out. We are, in fact, hoping my memory has finally deteriorated to the point that someone must be assigned to lead me about. Exercise your influence, sister, and see that it's Priscilla?"

She laughed. "As if I had any! And what use would you be to Priscilla without a memory?"

"The same use I'll be to her with impaired hearing. Do stop bellowing in my ear."

She stuck her tongue in it.

"That will do," he said. "Bring a chair over and sit nicely or leave."

"Yes, Shan-brother."

He glanced up as she moved away. "Tell me, denubia, did the contract-husband leave with all faculties intact? If yos'Galan owes for mental disability it would be best for me to settle it before the *Passage* leaves."

"I was very nice to him, Shannie. Truly I was." She dragged the chair into place and sat primly, hands folded in her lap. "Like this?"

"Precisely like that. Pretend you've had upbringing. Now if only the damned computer—Aha! Progress!"

The screen filled with amber letters, scrolling. Shan let it run, then slapped PAUSE and was silent for longer than it should have taken him to read the information there.

Anthora leaned back from her own perusal, frowning at his face and at his pattern, which had suddenly gone flat with pity.

"The world shook apart?" she asked tentatively. "It is

horrible, Shannie, but why are we looking at it? I thought you were trying to find out about Val Con's lady."

"I am," he said expressionlessly, allowing the screen to continue a slow scroll. "She was there. Lizardi's Lunatics was one of the mercenary units hired to fight in the local civil war. A handful of people got off-planet before things went so unstable that rescue were hopeless. Countless people died, civilians and soldiers . . ." He touched PAUSE once more. "Survivors, Lizardi's Lunatics: Angela Lizardi, Senior Commander, Roth MacNealy, Brevet Lieutenant; Miri Robertson, Sergeant; Scandal Arbuckle, Private; Lassiter K. Winfield, Private. *Five*. Gods, a full-staffed unit is nearly three hundred!"

"She has the luck," Anthora said gravely, and Shan felt the hairs rise on his neck.

"Does she?"

But his sister was frowning. "Isn't it odd? I always thought Val Con would chose a lady who was a musician, like he is."

"We don't know that she's not," Shan pointed out. "Though gods alone know what she might have to sing about."

Anthora turned wondering silver eyes on him. "She's alive."

"So she is." He tapped another series, recalling the employment history. "Let's see what else she's done with her life, then, shall we?"

Lizardi's Lunatics had been deactivated in 1384, and there was a two-year blank in Miri Robertson's record until she showed up again as sergeant with the Gyrfalks, under Senior Commander Suzuki Rialto and Junior Commander Jason Randolph Carmody. There followed another list of contracts accepted and fulfilled, interspersed with notations of the excellence of Sergeant Robertson's performance. In 1388 her rank was increased to sergeant master. In 1391 she resigned. Commanders Rialto and Carmody let the record show their sorrow at that decision and their willingness to take the sergeant back into the Gyrfalks at any time.

Some months later Miri Robertson was certified as bodyguard to a Sire Baldwin of Naome, and there the record ended, except for a muted chime indicating that auxiliary information was available.

Shan glanced at Anthora. "Well, sister? Do we press on?"

"By all means!" she cried, and wriggled a little to show the intensity of her interest.

Grinning, Shan touched the proper key. The auxiliary file clicked in and his grin faded.

In 1392, five Standard months after Miri Robertson had become Sire Baldwin's bodyguard, a party of Juntavas attacked the estate, killing many of the household staff. Of those listed missing and presumed escaped: Baldwin himself . . . and Miri Robertson.

The aux file faded, and Shan leaned back in his chair. "Well, sister? Does she still have the luck?"

"It seems so," Anthora said softly. "After all, she got from Naome to Lufkit, and then from Lufkit to Lufkit Prime Station and as far as wherever she and Val Con are now, and they're both alive." She tipped her head. "Doesn't that sound like the luck to you, Shannie?"

"Unfortunately," he said after a small pause. "it does." He sighed and rubbed the tip of his nose. "Does it occur to you that Clutch-turtles might well mistake relationships between humans? By Space, we don't even know that that damned message is from Edger!"

"Mr. dea'Gauss had a tracer put on the pin-beam," Anthora said. "Verification hasn't been made yet, but he feels there's small doubt that the message is genuine. And I *told* you, brother—I can see Val Con's lady through him, just like I see Priscilla through you!"

He turned to stare at her. "So you did." He touched keys, shut down the screen, reclaimed the disks, and slipped them safely away. "Which reminds me that I'm to dine with Priscilla this evening. Talk about a coil! If Val Con had his heart set on the woman, why couldn't he bring her home? And when did he have time to court and lifemate anyone? Unless . . ." He pushed away from the desk, stretching to his full six feet, reducing Anthora to a plump, precocious child.

"Unless?" she asked.

He bent to kiss her forehead. "A question for Jeeves on my way out, that's all. Please assure Nova that I'm at her command. We'll be dining at Ongit's before going back to Pelthraza Street. And tell Gordy I'll expect to see him here early tomorrow morning. He's loafed long enough."

"Oh, no," Anthora said earnestly. "He's been working very hard! Karea seems particularly pleased."

"I'm delighted for them both." He gave her a gentle shove toward the door. "I'm off to visit Syl Vor and Padi—then a quick word with Jeeves and away! Be a good child, now, and help your sister."

"All right, Shannie," said the most powerful wizard on Liad, and went docilely down the hall.

With some difficulty Jeeves was discovered crouched in a corner of the hearthroom, swaddled in cats, head-ball dim in what Val Con had used to call "sleep." Shan cleared his throat.

"Sir?" The ball glowed to gentle orange life.

"Please don't get up! I only need to ask you a question— you *are* available for questions, aren't you, Jeeves? It wouldn't concern me quite so much except that you're the brains to Trealla Fantrol, and if we were to have an intruder while you're napping with the cats I don't know what would happen."

"The intruders would be repelled, sir. I was not asleep, but merely offering comfort."

Shan rubbed the tip of his nose. "Comfort? I am to understand that the cats are distressed?"

"They miss Master Val Con, sir."

"They do." Shan considered the various and varicolored felines draped around Jeeves's metallic person. "I hesitate to mention this—but Pil Tor and Yodel have never *met* Master Val Con."

"Quite right, sir. But Merlin has told them all about him, so they feel his absence as keenly as the rest."

A grizzled gray tabby curled near the head-ball opened one yellow eye, as if daring a challenge to that explanation.

Shan swept a bow. "Never would I doubt you, sir."

The cat closed his eye, and the man swallowed a laugh. "Jeeves, if I might ask you to cast your mind back seven or eight Standards—possibly more: Has my brother ever mentioned the person Miri Robertson in your presence?"

There was silence. Shan bore it for nearly a minute.

"Jeeves?"

"Working, sir. I anticipate completion of the match in approximately—done. Master Val Con has never spoken of or to Miri Robertson in my presence." After a slight and unrobotic hesitation, Jeeves said, "Forgive me."

"There's nothing to forgive, old friend. I had a notion Val Con had been lifemated for a few years and had simply forgotten to let us know. Exactly the sort of thing that might slip one's mind, after all. It was dimly possible that he'd said something to you, however, the dangers of Scouts and soldiers being what they are."

"You speak in the context of a will."

"Exactly in the context of a will."

The orange ball flickered, and Merlin flicked a reproachful ear. "The will I have on file for Master Val Con has not been altered since Standard 1382. It does not mention Miri Robertson."

"And that," Shan said, "would seem to be that. Thank you, Jeeves, you've been very helpful. Do continue comforting the cats."

"The comfort is two-way, sir."

Shan sighed. "Are you distressed, Jeeves?"

"It is merely that I, too, miss Master Val Con."

"I see. Forgive me if this offends, but Val Con and I built you, which means—"

"I was Master Val Con's idea."

Shan blinked. "I beg your pardon?"

"I was Master Val Con's idea," Jeeves repeated, moving an arm to rub a restive tigerstripe. "You said so yourself, sir, several times during my construction."

"So I did." And a more cork-brained scheme, he added silently, may I never again be party to! "My thanks for calling that to my attention. Carry on."

"Thank you, sir. Good evening, sir."

Shan's footsteps faded down the hallway, and in a moment Jeeves noted the opening and closing of the door to the south patio. One of the younger cats, Yodel, mewed faintly and twitched in her sleep. Jeeves moved a hand to stroke her.

"There, there," he said. "There, there."

ORBIT

INTERDICTED WORLD I-2796-893-44

The sound of the ship around them went from solid hum to pulsing throb as Miri slid into the copilot's seat. Val Con sat in the pilot's chair, hands moving with precision over the switches and keys and toggles as if he were playing the omnichora. All screens were up, showing different and changing views of the world below while the radio mumbled to itself. A number of the lights on the central board glowed red, a fact that Miri decided to ignore.

"No power left to shunt from the coils," Val Con murmured. "Altitude control jets low on fuel. Rocket thrust? Ah, well, rockets are only a luxury, after all . . ."

Miri considered the side of his face. "Is this dangerous?"

"Hmm? Strap in, please, cha'trez. We are approaching a mark." A slim finger touched a readout that was counting large blue numbers down from ten. Miri engaged the webbing as the numbers ran down. There was a sharp push and a heavy vibration as zero flashed. Val Con flipped a quick series of toggles, and the worst of the vibration faded.

"Is—this—dangerous?" Miri asked again, spacing the words and increasing the volume a tad, on the slim chance he hadn't heard her the first time.

His smile flickered, and he reached to take her hand. "Dangerous? We are descending with neither reserve rockets nor jet power to a planet without landing beacons, without an actual touchdown point chosen, and without being invited." The smile broadened. "A textbook exercise."

"Sure," Miri muttered. "And how many people get hurt when a textbook crashes?"

Val Con raised an eyebrow. "You doubt my skill?"

"Huh?" She was startled. "No, hey, look, boss, I ain't a pilot! I just gotta know if we're gonna get down—" She stopped because he was laughing, his hand warm around hers.

"Miri, I will contrive to bring us down as safely as possible, considering circumstances." He squeezed her fingers and let them go, turning back to his board. "As for whether we *will* get down, the answer is yes. We are no longer moving rapidly enough to maintain orbit."

She watched him go through another series of adjustments, then shook her head as he leaned back in the chair. "Tough Guy," she murmured.

He glanced over. "Yes."

"Tell the troops just enough to keep 'em honest, doncha?" she said, not sure if she felt admiration or frustration. "Got some guts—this stuff here." She waved a hand at the red-lit board. "Playing chicken with the Yxtrang . . . What were the chances of us getting out alive, when you pulled that hysteresis thing and we Jumped outta there?"

"Ah." He faced her seriously. "The pilot did not expect to reenter normal space."

"Thought we'd come apart in hyper," she translated and nodded to herself, thinking.

At the conclusion of thought, she reached over and patted his arm. "Good. Best choice there was. Yxtrang boarding party, against us two, even if we are hell on wheels . . ." She shook her head. "And I wouldn't want to have to shoot you. Heard that was the best thing to do for your partner, Yxtrang ever gets you cornered."

"There are sometimes," Val Con murmured, "other options."

"Yeah? How many Yxtrang you ever talk to in person?"

"One," he said promptly. "Though it is true that I took him unaware."

Miri blinked at him, then glanced at the ruddy board and at each of the screens in turn. "Remember to tell me about it," she managed at last. "Later."

"Yes, Miri," he said, sternly controlling his twitching lips, and turned back to the board.

The planet spun beneath them five times on the inbound spiral.

Miri watched the screens in fascination—she had never been on the flight deck of *anything* on a trip downworld before—and meticulously copied information Val Con read off to her: coordinates of major features, drainage patterns of important river basins, the direction and strength of atmospheric jet streams.

Her duties also included monitoring the radio, which still gave out its gabble of nonsense words and earsplitting music. But on the third pass over the continent south of their target something different came over the speaker.

Bringing the volume up, Miri heard the excited voices and the boom and thunder of heavy guns.

"Boss?" she asked quietly.

He glanced away from his board, frowning at the radio noise.

"Somebody's having a war," Miri said, and he sighed, hands and eyes already back to the business of piloting.

Miri kept with it, hearing the despair in the man's voice on the radio and counting the rhythms of the bursts and explosions until they were out of range. She found the station again on the next pass, but it was only playing music. And on the next pass they were inside the ion shield and could not hear anything at all.

The meager stars had given way to local dawn when Val Con finally brought the ship down. Miri found the switch from a ballistic trajectory to magnetic control unexpectedly harrowing: the deceleration reminded her all too vividly of their close call with the Yxtrang. The final lurch brought forth an involuntary burst of swearing, which she squelched in embarrassment, for by that time the ship was flying smoothly.

• • •

Val Con sealed the hatch behind them and slid the key into his pouch, shivering in the crystal air.

Miri tipped her head. "You cold?"

"Only a little," he murmured, lifting a brow. "Aren't you?"

She grinned, stretching tall on her toes. "Where I come from, Tough Guy, this is high summer." Then she, too, shivered as a random breeze ran through the ravine. "Course, when you get as old as me, your blood starts to thin out."

"So? I had no idea you were as old as that."

"You didn't ask; I didn't say." She frowned at the crouched ship, a pitted metal boulder among a tumble of rock. "Should we hide it better?"

"This should suffice. The country does not look well traveled, and from the air it will seem just another rock. We are only in difficulty if local technology proves to include long-range metal detection." He sighed. "We could send it into orbit, but there might be a way to repair . . ." His voice drifted off.

"So, for better or worse." She came closer and slid a small hand into his. "*Carpe diem,* and all like that." She grinned, and he smiled faintly, squeezing her hand as she looked around. "Well, where's this town of yours? I could sure use a cup of coffee."

"West," he said, and smiled at her confusion. "*That* way," he elaborated, pointing.

"Whyn't you say so? Though how you can tell up from down this soon after 'fall beats hell out of me." She shivered again in another eddy of breeze and wrinkled her nose. "Guess we better start walking."

"It would seem best," he agreed. He slipped away, moving like a shadow over the broken shale, Miri silent at his back.

An hour later they rested by a stream. Val Con knelt, cupped a hand into the rapid current—and turned his head as if he had heard the cry of protest she had stilled.

"Cha'trez, the water is good," he assured her. "Nor do I think the vegetables or grains will do us harm. The meat should also be edible. Whether all the nutritional needs of our

bodies are met we must wait and see." He cupped his hand
again and drank, then rose, sighing. "Had we been abandoned in a Scout ship instead of a smuggler's yacht we would
have known these things with certainty before landing. As it
is, we ride the luck."

Miri closed her eyes as he came to sit beside her. *"Carpe
diem,"* she muttered, willing herself to relax.

"What is that?"

She opened her eyes to find him watching her. "What's
what?"

"Carpe—diem? It does not sound Terran—and you have
said it several times."

"Oh." She frowned. "Actually, it is Terran—at least, it's
from Terra. Latin, I think the language was. Real old. I remember reading that two or three of the languages Terran de-
rives from came from Latin, first." She paused, but he was
watching her face with apparent interest.

"Time I was—sick—right after Klamath," she continued,
"I got to read lots. Book I liked best was called *Dictionary of
Phrase and Fable*. It was sort of a list of things that people
had said or believed—and sometimes *still* said—and next to
each one was an explanation of what it was really supposed
to mean.

"*Carpe diem,* now—that's supposed to mean, 'seize the
day,' enjoy yourself while you can. Seemed like good advice." She shook her head and smiled. "Great book. Sorry I
had to give it back."

"How long were you able to spend with the book?" he
asked gently. "After Klamath?"

"Hmm? Ah, not too long. Got busted up toward the end of
things—my own damn fault. Got cocky." She shifted, breaking his gaze. "You want a sandwich before we get on?"

Both brows rose. "Salmon?"

"Got four," she told him earnestly.

"I think that I am not hungry, thank you." He came to his
feet in one fluid motion and reached down to help her up,
though he knew she could rise as easily as he, unaided.

"Besides," he said, pressing her hand warmly before letting her go. "I thought you wanted that cup of coffee."

•   •   •

The town sat in a three-sided bowl made of mountains, clustered in the center of a valley that was merely a widening of the pass they walked through. It was not a large town, which was good, and no one was yet abroad, though the sun had been up for several hours. In the near distance Val Con made out a field of some type of grain, while closer in—

Miri was not at his back.

He turned slowly and found her seated astride a fallen log, staring down into the protected little town, tension sharp in the lines of her face, in the set of her shoulders, and in the slender hands folded too still upon her knee.

He moved, deliberately scraping boot heel against stone. She started and looked at him.

"Mind if I rest a minute?" she asked, tension singing beneath the words.

"As long as you like." Silent again, he went to the log and sat behind her, putting his arms loosely around her waist, feeling her taut in every muscle. Laying his cheek against her hair, he exhaled gently. "What is it, cha'trez?"

"*I* was gonna ask *you.*" She flung her hands out with suppressed violence, directing his attention to the valley below. "What is it?"

He considered. Then, he said softly, "A town. Civilians. Not, it is true, a very large town—but sufficient for our present needs. A pattern such as this many times includes outlying farms or homes. If this place is true to that pattern, then that is very good for us. It may be possible for us to go to a single home and offer to trade labor for—language lessons."

She drew a deep breath. "*That's* a town?"

"Certainly it's a town," he said, keeping his voice matter-of-fact. "What else would it be?"

"The gods alone know. It's so small . . ." Her voice faded, significant of growing tension.

"So? Then perhaps we should take a few moments to study what we see." He raised an arm, pointing. "That large affair, there, with the many windows? That's probably a government building of some kind. It seems to have the proper hauteur about it."

She chuckled—a good sign—and it seemed that she

relaxed, ever so slightly. "And that squatty one, with the railing around the front?"

"A trading post," he guessed. "Or a small store." He pointed again. "What do you make of the little blue one?"

"A barbershop? Or a bar?" She laughed a little, and the tension was definitely easing. "Both?"

"Perhaps—though I think it would be a bit crowded for either. And the metal objects—they do seem to be metal, do you think?—along the sides of the thoroughfare?"

"Cabs!" Miri announced with certainty, relaxing back into him. He moved his cheek away from her hair and slanted a glance at the side of her face. She was smiling slightly. Good.

"So? Then tell me about that one—you see? Over behind the little blue one—with the tower and the knob on the top?"

She was silent for a moment, then blinked and grinned. "A bordello."

"Do you really think so?" he murmured. "Perhaps we should go there first."

She laughed—a true laugh—her head against his shoulder, then abruptly sobered. "Val Con?"

"Yes?"

"You're a sneak."

He lifted a brow. "It is a common failing, I am told, among Liadens."

"That's what Terrans say." She frowned. "What do Liadens say?"

"Ah, well. Liadens . . ." He tightened his arms around her in a quick hug. "Liadens are very formal, you know. So it is likely that they would not say anything at all."

"Oh." She took a breath. "What do we do now?"

"I think we should take off our guns and put them in our pouches. In some places the possession of a weapon makes a person suspect, even, perhaps, a criminal. And I think we should each have another sandwich—so that we do not grow proud—" He echoed her laugh softly. "After we eat, we should go down into the valley and look for one of those outlying farms I spoke of, to see if we might not trade the labor of our strong young bodies for a roof and food and lessons in language."

"All that on a sandwich? Well, you're the boss."

"And when," he inquired, "will you be boss?"

"Next week." She stood, pulled a plastic-wrapped package out of her pouch, and handed it to him to unwrap while she stripped off the gun and holster and stowed them away.

VANDAR

SPRINGBREEZE FARM

"Borril! *Here*, Borril! Wind take the animal, where—ah *ha!* So there you are, sir! No skevitts this morning? Or did they all sit in the treetops and laugh at you? Ah, now, old thing . . ." She finished in a much sweeter tone, as the dog flung himself at her feet with a *whuff* and lay gazing up at her, worship in his beady yellow eyes.

She bent carefully, rubbed her knuckles briskly across his head ridges, and yanked on his pointy ears. Straightening, she sighed and eased her back, her eyes dwelling on the marker before her: "Jerrel Trelu, 1412-1475. Beloved zamir . . ."

Beloved zamir—what bosh! As if it had not just been Jerry and Estra, working the farm and raising the boy and doing what needed to be done, one thing at a time, side by side, him leaning on her, her leaning on him. Beloved husband, indeed!

A wind blew across the yard, straight down from Fornem's Gap, ice-toothed with winter, though it was barely fall. Zhena Trelu shivered and pulled her jacket close around her. "Wind gets colder every year," she muttered, and pulled herself up sharp. "Listen at you! Just the kind of poor-me you hate in Athna Brigsbee! Mooning the morning away like there wasn't any work to do!"

She snorted. There was always work to do. She bent creakily and gathered up the sweelims she had picked for the parlor—she liked a bit of color to rest her eyes on in the evening when she listened to the radio or read. "Let's go, Borril. Home!"

The wind sliced out of the gap again, but she refused to give it the satisfaction of a shiver. The signs all pointed to a bad winter. She sighed, her thoughts on the house she and Jerry had lived a lifetime in. The shutters needed mending; the chimney had to be cleaned and the tin inspected for corrosion—though what she could do about it if the whole roof was on the verge of falling in was more than she knew. It was a big, drafty old place, much too big for one old woman and her old dog. It had always been too big, really, even when there had been Jerrel and the boy and, later, the boy's zhena—and the dogs, of course. Always four or five dogs. Now there was only Borril, last of a tradition.

As if her thought had reached out and touched some chord within him, the dog suddenly bounded forward, giving tongue in mock ferocity, charging around the side of the house and out of sight.

"Borril!" she yelled, but any fool would know that that was useless. She picked up her pace and arrived at the corner of the house in time to hear Borril, in full stranger-at-the-gate alarm.

Across the barking cut a man's voice, speaking words Zhena Trelu understood to be foreign.

She rounded the corner and stopped in surprise.

Borril was between her and two strangers—barking and wagging his ridiculous puff of a tail. The taller of the two spoke again, sharply, and the barking subsided.

"Be quiet, dog!" Val Con snapped. "How dare you speak to us like that? Sit!"

Borril was confused. The tone was right, but the sounds were different than the sounds She used. He hesitated, then heard Her behind him and ran to Her side, relieved to be out of the situation.

"Borril, you bad dog! Sit!"

That was better. Borril sat, tail thumping on the ground.

"I *am* sorry," Zhena Trelu continued, trying not to stare. "Borril really is quite friendly. I hope he didn't frighten you."

Again, it was the taller who spoke, opening his hands and showing her empty palms. Zhena Trelu frowned. It did not take a genius to figure out that he did not understand what she was saying.

Sighing, she stepped forward. "*Stay,* Borril." As she moved, the two men came forward also, stopping when shock stopped her.

The shorter man was not a man at all. Not, that is, unless foreigners of whatever variety these were allowed a man the option of growing his hair long, braiding it, and wrapping it around his head like a vulgar copper crown. A woman, then, Zhena Trelu allowed. Or, more precisely, a girl. But dressed in such clothes!

Zhena Trelu was not a prude; she knew quite well what useful garments trousers were—especially working around the farm. But these . . .

First, they seemed to be made of leather—sleek, black leather. Second, they were skintight, hugging the girl's boy-flat belly and her—limbs—and neatly tucked into high black boots. The upper garment—a white shirt of some soft-looking fabric—was acceptable, though Zhena Trelu thought it might have been laced a little closer around that slender throat; and the loose leather vest was unexceptional. But what in the name of ice did a woman want to wear such a wide belt for? Unless it was to accentuate the impossible tininess of her waist?

"Am I *that* funny-looking?" Miri asked, and Zhena Trelu started, eyes going to her face.

No beauty, this one, with her face all sharp angles and freckles across the snubbed nose. The chin was square and willful, the full mouth incongruous. Her only claim to pretti-ness lay in a pair of very speaking gray eyes, at present rest-ing with resigned irony on the other woman's face.

Zhena Trelu felt herself coloring. "I beg your pardon," she muttered. She moved her eyes from the girl to her compan-ion—and found herself staring again.

Where the angles of the girl's face seemed all at odds with each other, the lines in her companion's face worked toward a cohesive whole. High cheeks curved smoothly to pointed chin; the nose was straight and not overlong; the mouth was generous and smiling, just a little. His hair was dark brown, chopped off blunt at the bottom of his ears, and one lock of it straggled across his forehead, over level dark brows and quite nearly into the startling green eyes. His skin was an odd golden color, except for the raw slash of a recent scar across his right cheek.

He was dressed in the same sort of clothes as the girl, the clinging leather and the wide belt keeping no secrets regarding his own thinness.

Zhena Trelu frowned. The girl's skin was pale, doubly so when compared to the man's rich complexion. And they both looked tired. Skinny, too—never mind the outlandish clothes—and foreigners to top it all, without even a word of the language.

The wind sliced across the open lawn; the girl shivered—and that decided it. If the child was sickening for something she needed to be out of the wind. What was her zamir thinking of, to have her out in the chilly autumn weather with no jacket on and that shirt laced up so loose? Zhena Trelu glared at him, and one of his eyebrows rose slightly as he tipped his head, rather like Borril trying to puzzle out one of the rambling monologues she addressed to him.

"Well," she told the young zhena sharply, "you might as well come on in. There's soup for dinner to warm you up, and you can have a rest before you get on." She turned and marched up to the house, treading carefully on the creaky porch steps.

Realizing that he was in danger of being left behind, Borril jumped up and galloped across the lawn, taking the three wooden steps in a bumbling leap. Zhena Trelu, fidgeting with the chancy catch on the wind door, grumbled at him.

"Borril, sit *down,* you lame-witted creature. *Borril!*" she raised her voice as he jumped, almost knocking her down.

"Borril." From her back, a steady voice spoke, firm with command. Woman and dog turned to look.

The slender zamir stood on the second step, bent slightly forward, one golden hand extended. "Borril!" he repeated firmly. "Sit."

Zhena Trelu watched in fascination as the dog waggled forward and thrust his blunt nose into the outstretched hand. "Sit," stated the owner of the hand again.

Borril sat.

The man reached out and tugged lightly on a pointy ear, turning his head as the girl came to his side.

"Borril?" she asked, extending a wary hand. The silly creature *whuffed* and pushed his head forward. In careful imitation of her companion, she tugged on an ear. Borril flung himself onto his side in ecstasy, rolling his eyes and sighing soulfully. The girl threw back her head and laughed.

Zhena Trelu turned back to the catch and pulled the door wide.

"Well, come on," she snapped when they just stood there, staring at her from the second step. "And don't pretend you're not hungry. Doesn't look like you've had a full meal between you since last harvest-time." Irritably, she transferred the sweelims to the hand holding open the door and waved at her hesitant guests with the other.

After a moment, the man moved, coming silently up the last step and crossing the porch into the hall; the girl trailed him by half a step, and Zhena Trelu bit back a sharp lesson on manners. Did the girl think the house was a den of iniquity, that she sent her man in ahead?

They're foreigners, Estra, she reminded herself as she led them down the hall. You're going to have to make allowances.

She dumped the flowers into the sink, turned the flame up under the soup pot, and looked back to find them standing side by side just inside the door, looking around as if neither one had ever seen a kitchen before.

"Soup'll be ready in a couple minutes," she said, and sighed at the girl's blink and the man's uncomprehending head-tip.

Feeling an utter fool, she tapped herself on the chest. "Zhena Trelu," she announced, trying to say each word clearly and pitching her voice a little louder than normal.

The man's face altered, losing years as he grinned. "Zhena Trelu," he said, matching her cadence.

So, it works, she congratulated herself. She pointed at him, tipping her head in imitation of Borril.

He moved his shoulders, lips parting for an answer.

"Tell the truth, Liaden," Miri muttered at his side.

His eyes snapped to her face, both brows up. Smiling in

rueful resignation of what he found there, he turned back to the old woman and bowed very slightly, fingers over heart. "Val Con yos'Phelium, Clan Korval."

Zhena Trelu stared, trying to sort the sounds. Valconyos Fellum Can Corevahl? What kind of name—no, wait. Corevahl? He was a foreigner, after all, with wind only knew *what* kind of barbaric accent. She pointed. "Corvill?"

The level brows twitched together, and he frowned, green eyes intent. "Korval," he agreed warily, though still thumping harder on the last syllable than the first.

"Corvill." Zhena Trelu decided, and pointed at the girl, who grinned and shrugged.

"Miri."

"Meri?" Zhena Trelu asked, frowning.

"Miri," she corrected, refusing to look straight at Val Con, though a glance out of the corner of her eye showed him grinning widely.

"Meri," Zhena Trelu repeated, and brought her finger back to Val Con. "Corvill."

He inclined his head, murmured, "Zhena Trelu," and jerked his chin at the dog, curled on his rug next to the stove. "Borril."

"Well, that's fine. Now we're all introduced, and dinner's almost ready." The old woman went across to the stove, lifted the pot lid, and stirred the soup with a long wooden spoon. Going over to the cupboard. she pulled out three bowls and three plates, shoved them into the girl's hands, and waved at the table. "Set the table, Meri."

The girl turned hesitantly toward the table. From the depths of the cupboard, Zhena Trelu produced three glasses and three mismatched napkins, which she handed to the man. He took them without apparent confusion and headed for the table. Zhena Trelu nodded to herself and went back to the sink to rescue the languishing sweelims.

"Hello, Meri," Val Con murmured, setting the glasses by the bowls and plates she had laid out.

"Hello yourself, Corvill, my friend. Sounds like you rhyme with Borril. Speaking of which, what *is* Borril?" She looked up at him. "Besides ugly, I mean."

"Hmm?" He was considering the napkins—one each of

white, green, and pink. "Borril is a dog, Miri—or, no," he corrected himself. "Borril is of the species that fills the watch-pet niche here." He smiled at her. "For all reasonable purposes, a dog."

"Oh." She looked at the napkins. "Who gets what color?"

"An excellent question. I was wondering the same." He placed them carefully in the center of the table. "We shall discover."

She grinned. "Clever. Something still missing though—oh." She turned and made her silent way across the kitchen to where the old woman was fussing with her flowers. "Zhena Trelu?"

Zhena Trelu started, nearly overturning the vase, and recovered with a breathless laugh. "Goodness, child, but you gave me a fright. What is it?"

Miri blinked at the unintelligible tirade, opened her mouth to ask for the missing items—and closed it again. The old lady wasn't going to understand any more than she was understood.

All right, Robertson, she directed herself. Use your brain—if you got one.

She looked about, then picked up the wooden spoon lying on the stove and showed it to Zhena Trelu. She turned and pointed at the table, beside which stood her partner, watching the proceedings with interest.

The old woman looked at the spoon, looked at the table, and then laughed. "Oh, is my memory going back on me! Silverware, is that it?" she asked the girl, who only smiled, uncomprehending.

Taking the spoon and putting it back where it belonged, Zhena Trelu went to the cupboard once more. "*Spoons,*" she said clearly. "*Knives. Forks.*"

"*Spoons,*" the girl repeated obediently as each set was placed in her hands. "*Knives. Forks.*"

"That's right," Zhena Trelu said encouragingly. She made a sweeping motion with her hands, trying to indicate *all* the items the girl held. "*Silverware.*"

Meri's brows pulled together in a frown. "*Silverware,*" she said, and the other woman smiled, and went back to arranging flowers.

"Spoons," Miri told Val Con, shoving them into his hand. *"Knives. Forks."* She frowned. "That all seems simple enough. You savvy *silverware,* boss?"

"Perhaps *knives, spoons,* and *forks* are separate names and *silverware* is the name for all together?"

"Not too bad, for a bald-headed guess."

He laughed softly. "But that is what being a Scout is—guessing, and then waiting to see if your guess was correct."

"Yeah?" She looked unconvinced. "Ain't the way I heard it."

"Ah, *you* heard we were heroes, risking our lives among savage peoples, magically able to speak any language we hear and never misunderstanding custom or intent." Mischief glinted in the bright green eyes.

"Naw. Way I heard it, only things Scouts're good for is drinking up fancy liquor and tellin' tall tales 'bout the dragons they killed."

"Alas, I am found out . . ."

"Meri! Corvill! Bring your bowls over here now. Soup's hot."

Miri grinned at him. "That's us—wonder what we're supposed to do now?"

He glanced over his shoulder in time to see the old woman pull a ladle from its hook over the stove. "Bowls, I think," he murmured, and picked up two, moving toward the stove with a deliberately heavy step.

Miri blinked at the unaccustomed noise, then shrugged, picked up the remaining bowl, and followed.

Zhena Trelu smiled and ladled soup into the two bowls Corvill held ready. Then she filled Meri's bowl and touched the girl's shoulder. "Wait."

She opened yet another drawer, produced a half-loaf of bread, and held it out. Miri took it in her free hand and carried it to the table.

Zhena Trelu hesitated, nodded to herself, and went to the icebox, pulling out butter. Her hand hovered over the cheese for a moment before descending. Skinny as they were? How could there be a question?

Butter and cheese balanced in one hand, she hefted the milk pitcher with the other and pushed the door shut with her knee. At the table she poured milk for all before looking around for her seat.

They had left her the chair at the head of the table, she realized then: Jerrel's place. The two of them sat next to each other, in what in later years had come to be the boy's chair, and his wife's.

Zhena Trelu smiled, pleased to see that they had not touched their soup. Manners, then, foreign or no. She picked up her spoon and had a taste, and they followed suit. Certain that they understood they were free to go on without her, she laid her spoon down, pulled the bread toward her, and laboriously sawed off three ragged slices. Then she took the cheese out of its paper and hewed off a largish chunk for each of them, laying it on the plates next to their bread.

Her own slice she slid into the toaster, reminding herself to pay attention to it. There was something wrong with the contraption; lately it burned bread to cinders without ever giving warning that it was done.

She picked up her spoon again and addressed the soup, watching her guests but trying not to stare.

The boy was left-handed and ate seriously, giving his whole attention, apparently, to the meal.

Meri was right-handed and appeared distracted, darting quick bird-glances around the room. She picked up her bread and broke it in half, using it to soak up some broth while she said something to the boy, who laughed and reached for his glass, and then jerked his head up, staring at the toaster.

"Oh, wind take the thing!" Zhena Trelu cried, smacking the release. The toaster *chingged!* and discharged a scorched rectangular object that smoldered gently and dripped charred bits onto the tablecloth.

"Damn you," she muttered, mindful of her company, and pulled the plug vindictively. She sawed off another piece of bread and buttered it, sighing.

She offered her guests more of everything, but they either did not understand or were too shy to avail themselves of her hospitality. Zhena Trelu finished her milk, wiped her mouth carefully, and folded her hands in front of her, wondering what to do. The most reasonable course was so send them on their way; and, truth told, they did look more rested, though Meri's face was still paler than Corvill's.

Miri tipped her head, catching Val Con's eye. "Now what?"

"Now we pay for the meal," he murmured. He pulled the toaster toward him, turned it around, pushed down on the lever, and peered inside the bread slot. Miri watched him for a minute, then slipped out of her chair and gathered the dishes together.

As she carried them to the sink, she heard Zhena Trelu address one of her incomprehensible comments to "Corvill," and glanced over her shoulder.

The old woman had risen and was beckoning to Val Con, indicating that he should follow her. Picking up the toaster, he obeyed, throwing Miri a quick smile as he left the room.

She swallowed hard, slamming the lid on an unexpected need to run after him. Deliberately she turned to the sink and worked out the gimmick for the water, then puzzled out the soap and stood holding it in her hand.

Month ago you didn't know the man existed, she told herself sharply. Now you can't let him outta your sight?

Adjusting the water temperature, she began to lather the soap, carefully thinking of nothing. By the time Zhena Trelu returned alone, the glasses were washed and draining, and the girl was scrubbing diligently at a bowl.

VANDAR

SPRINGBREEZE FARM

What with one thing and another, it was only rea-sonable that they spend the night. Corvill fixed the toaster like a charm; it took him the better part of the afternoon, but Zhena Trelu was not critical. She could not have fixed it at all.

Meri had been set to dusting after the dishes were done, and Zhena Trelu went out to milk the cow. By the time she came back, Corvill was waiting to show her the repaired toaster, and she exclaimed over that for a bit, even toasting a celebratory piece for everybody and doling out the last of the poquit jam.

A startled glance at the clock about then told her it was time to start making supper, for which she drafted Meri's help, first directing Corvill's attention to the carpet sweeper.

After supper, she went out to give the scuppins their evening grain while Meri and Corvill did the dishes. On the way back to the house she stopped, shivering in the wind, to look up at the rock-toothed gash that was Fornem's Gap. It was fixing to rain tonight, for sure . . .

And who but a two-headed, heartless monster would send the pair of them on their way with night coming on and a cold rain due out of the gap before morning?

On the porch she paused again, listening to the soft sound of their voices, talking their foreign talk as if the weird word-sounds actually meant something. Shaking her head, she tramped back into the kitchen.

Meri was in the middle of a yawn, which she belatedly covered with a slender hand.

"Tired?" Zhena Trelu asked, and sighed at the girl's blank smile.

She reached out and firmly grasped one small hand. "Come with me."

Turning down the right-hand hallway, she marched the two of them up the main flight and turned left, past the upstairs parlor and the attic stairs to the boy's old room. Pushing the door open, she yanked on the light cord and finally released Meri's hand to point at the double-wide bed where Granic and his zhena had slept—the same bed the young zhena had died in, struggling to birth a child too big for her.

"You sleep there," she told Meri.

The girl moved soundlessly over the rag rug and scrubbed floorboards to sit on the edge of the bed. She smiled and raised her hand to cover another yawn, while Corvill waited quietly by the door.

"That's fine," Zhena Trelu said. "Good night, Meri." She nodded to the man. "Good night, Corvill."

"Good night, Zhena Trelu," she heard him say softly as she pulled the door shut behind her.

Val Con turned down the bed and undressed, folding his clothes onto the bench against the wall. Slipping under the covers, he took a deep breath, consciously relaxing, and let his eyes rest on Miri.

She undressed, letting her clothes lie where they fell, and went to the mirror across the room, unwrapping the braid from around her head. It seemed that she swayed slightly where she stood, but he was tired enough to believe it only a trick of his eyes.

"Come to bed, cha'trez."

She turned her head and gave him a faint smile. "You convinced me."

It took her too long to walk across the room—she was, indeed, swaying—and she sat on the edge of the bed with a *bump*. "Why'm I so tired?"

"Altitude, perhaps. Also, we have had to think very hard today—everything is strange, the words must be heard and remembered . . ." He shifted, pulling back the covers. "Miri, come to bed; you're cold."

"Nag, nag." But she slipped under the covers, her face beginning to relax as she closed her eyes—and tensing again as she snapped them open. "Light. Aah, the hell with it." She closed her eyes with finality.

The hell with it, he agreed silently, and closed his own eyes, letting the tide of weariness take him.

Someone shouted his name; there were rough hands on his shoulders, and he was fighting, and the voice cried his name again, and it seemed familiar, and he opened his eyes with a jerk, staring uncomprehending at the face suspended above him.

"It's Miri," she told him, breathlessly.

"Yes." He was shaking, he realized, even more bewildered. The room beyond Miri's shoulder was brightly lit, composed, empty of threat. He looked back into her eyes. "What happened?"

She let out a shaky breath. "You were having a nightmare. A bad dream." She released his shoulders and slid to one side, her cheek resting on her hand.

A bad dream? He cast his mind after—and found it immediately; he recognized it for what it was and knew he was shaking harder. The bedclothes were stifling, in spite of his chill. He pushed them away and began to get up.

"Val Con?"

He looked at her, and she saw the lines etched around his mouth and the shadow of fear in the green eyes. He was trembling so hard she could *see* it. She put out a hand and covered his, feeling the cold and the shaking.

"There's this old Terran cure for nightmares," she said, trying to keep her voice steady. "Goes like this: You have a bad dream, you tell somebody. Then you never have it again." She offered a smile, wondering if he heard her. "Works."

He took a slow, deep breath, then lay back down like a thing made of wood and pulled the cover back over him.

Miri moved closer, not touching but offering warmth, hoping to ease the trembling. She reached out to brush the hair from his eyes.

"Not a dream," he said, and his voice was as rigid as his body. "A memory. When I was put on—detached duty—from the Scouts to the Department of the Interior I—received my orders and went to fulfill them—immediately, as instructed. I entered the proper building and walked down the proper hallway—and every step I took down that hall it seemed there was something—crying out?—screaming—in me—telling me to run, to go far away, to on no account continue forward . . ."

"And did you?" she asked softly.

He made a sound, which she did not think was laughter. "Of course I did. What else would I have done? Disobeyed orders? The dishonor—the disgrace . . . Gone eklykt'i? My Clan . . ." He was holding himself so stiffly that she thought he would break.

"I continued down the corridor, fighting myself every step

of the way—against every instinct I had otherwise. Against my hunch. The only time in my life I failed to heed a hunch . . ." He closed his eyes.

Miri shifted beside him, worriedly.

"I went down the hall," he said tonelessly, "through the proper door, handed my papers in, and commenced training as an Agent of Change. And they lied, gods, and made it seem truth and twisted what I saw and how I knew things and pushed and pulled inside my head until Val Con yos'Phelium was hardly more than a memory. And it hurt . . ." He took a breath that could not have filled his lungs—and suddenly the horrible control snapped and he was rolling toward her, his arms locking around her, his head burrowing into her shoulder.

"Ah, Miri," he cried, anguish twisting in his voice. "Miri, it *hurt* . . ."

And he burst into tears.

She held him until it subsided, stroking the dark hair, running her hands down his back, feeling the tension going, going—gone, finally, with the sudden last of the tears. She held him a little longer and sighed; his breathing told her he was asleep.

She shifted, trying to ease away, but his arms tightened, and he moved his head on her shoulder, muttering, so that she sighed, resigning herself to a cramped and sleepless night.

She woke to find him looking very seriously into her face.

"Morning," she said fuzzily. "*Is* it morning?"

"Early morning," he said softly. "I do not think Zhena Trelu is about yet."

"Good." She moved, meaning to give him a kiss—and stopped.

"What is wrong?" he asked.

She shrugged, glancing away from the brightness of his gaze. "I'm never sure whether you want me to kiss you or not."

"Ah, now that is very bad," he said. "A problem in communication. I suggest that the best course is for you to kiss me whenever you wish to do so. In this way you will eventually be able to ascertain when it is I most wish to be kissed."

"Yeah?" She grinned and swooped down, intending the veriest peck on the cheek, but he shifted his head and caught her lips with his. His fingers were as suddenly in her hair, loosing the braid, stroking lightly . . .

When the kiss was over, Miri lay trembling on his chest, looking at his face, all blurred with longing and lust and love. "Any more kisses like that," she said, hearing that her voice shook as well, "and I ain't guaranteeing the outcome."

He smiled gently, one eyebrow slipping up. "It's early."

She closed her eyes against the sight of him, against the sudden stab of—what?

Robertson, she pleaded with herself, don't go sappy on me. She felt his fingers, feather light and trembling, moving down her cheek, stroking the curve of her throat.

"Please, Miri," he said wistfully. "I would *like* another kiss."

Opening her eyes, she obliged him to the fullest extent possible.

LIAD

SOLCINTRA PORT

Yes, the middle-aged voice assured Cheever in up-town Terran, the First Speaker would be delighted to see Mr. McFarland as soon as he arrived. Should a car be dispatched from Trealla Fantrol, or did he have his own transportation?

"I got cab fare," Cheever growled, mistrusting the voice, the featureless grid from which it emanated, the packet in his inside vest pocket, and very nearly the turtle who had gotten him into this, except there was no sense to that. The turtle had dealt straight. Turtles always dealt straight.

"Very good, then, sir," the voice told him. "The First Speaker awaits your arrival." The connection stud went dark.

"Yeah, great," Cheever muttered as he stepped out of the booth into the noisy tide of Port traffic.

He was nearly to the city gate before he saw a cab and waved it frantically to a halt. The Liaden woman in the driver's slot slanted him a look he was not sure he liked as he settled in the passenger's seat.

"I want to go to Trealla Fantrol," he snapped in Trade.

"Ah."

Cheever glared at her. "You know how to get there, or doncha?"

"I know the way. The question becomes, 'Can you afford the fare?' "

He took a deep, frustrated breath. Damn Liaden was laughing at him. "You want your round-trip upfront, is that it? Name your choice: Unicredit, bits, or Liaden money, if you got change for a cantra."

She stared at him for a long moment, apparently oblivious to the confusion her motionless vehicle was causing among Port pedestrians. "*You* wish to go to Trealla Fantrol."

Cheever clamped his jaw and refused to look down at his worn leathers, though the shirtsleeve he saw from the corner of his eye was far from clean.

"Yeah, I do. This is a cab, ain't it? You can take me to Trealla Fantrol, right?"

"Indeed, this is a cab. As for taking you to Trealla Fantrol . . ." The shoulders rippled, conveying nothing. "It is a pleasant morning for a drive."

Abruptly the cab swerved into traffic, gained momentum, dashed down a side street, and, a moment later, sped through the main gates. Cheever sat back in the seat, swearing at shortened leg room, and stared out the window, thinking about his ship.

Solcintra went by in a blurring zigzag of tree-lined streets. The ground pilot knew her quadrant inside out, Cheever allowed grudgingly, then snapped upright in the short seat as they sailed through a second gate—this one old and stone and shrouded with purple blossoms—and were abruptly in open country.

"Hey!"

The cabbie turned her head, forward velocity unchecked.

"Where the hell we going?" Cheever yelled, staring in confusion at jade-green meadow on one side, trees on the other, and a twisty road running toward some kind of tower leaping up out of a stand of trees way on the far side of the valley.

"We are going to Trealla Fantrol. It is the destination you chose. I merely agreed to take you—as far as we are allowed to go."

There was an unmistakable note of malice in that last bit. Cheever silently cursed the Liaden race, this specimen in particular, and his own stupidity in mentioning that he had a cantra on him. She was going to take him to Trealla Fantrol, okay—the long way.

"Where I want to go's in Solcintra," he tried, keeping his voice reasonable.

"Then you do not wish to go to Trealla Fantrol."

"Oh." He frowned out the window, where the tower across the valley was taking on more details by the second. In fact, it did not look like a tower at all, but a tree, except who had ever heard of a tree that tall? He pointed at it. "That Trealla Fantrol?"

The cabbie laughed. "Indeed it is not. That is Jelaza Kazone. Perhaps you'd rather go there? Though I hear the Korval is not presently in residence."

"Trealla Fantrol," Cheever said firmly, "is where the First Speaker of Clan Korval lives. I *know* that."

"Do I dispute it? Look to your left hand and you will see the chimneys."

He found seven of them, crowning a tight cluster of trees, then lost sight of all as the cab plunged down a steep incline, dashed left into a sudden roadway, and proceeded at an abruptly conservative pace.

They had gone perhaps a quarter mile when she glanced at him once more. "It appears you are expected."

He looked back, laconic in the face of her surprise. "What makes you think so?"

"The last fare I had to Trealla Fantrol was stopped a cab's length inside the grounds." There was another ripple of thin shoulders. "One assumes that she was not expected."

They passed beneath an archway, and the perfume of the flowers was momentarily overpowering until driven away by a sharp, lemony scent from the bushes on both sides.

The bushes ended and the cab spun through a quick right turn, left turn, emerged into a sweeping elliptical drive, and stopped smoothly at the base of a stairway.

Cheever stared, hand curling into a fist on his thigh; the weight of the package in his pocket trebled, and he wished fervently that he had taken the time to buy a new shirt.

"Trealla Fantrol," the cabbie said. "I will take Unicredit."

He fumbled it out of his pouch and never even looked to see how much she charged him. The turtle had said it was urgent, that Cheever was to deliver the turtle's package to the First Speaker of Clan Korval at Trealla Fantrol, Solcintra, with all possible speed.

The cabbie shoved the card back into his slack fingers. "My thanks, Jump pilot. Fare you well."

He started, dropped the card back into his pouch, and took a deep breath as the cab door swung aside. "Thanks. Errr . . . maybe you better wait."

"A waste of my time. Trealla Fantrol expects you. It is unlikely you will be sent forth in a cab." The door slid closed, and the cab was moving, taking the rest of the ellipse in smooth acceleration before vanishing down the long drive.

Cheever squared his shoulders and went up the stairs.

He laid his palm against the center plate in the big wooden door and composed himself to wait. They were not going to like him, the people who lived here. He had a sinking feeling that they were going to like the turtle's message even less.

Beyond the door, there was a brief rumble. Then the door was pulled open from the inside, and the voice from the Port phone inquired, "Mr. McFarland?"

For an instant he wanted desperately to deny it, to run down the stairs and the long drive, back to the Port and the loaned ship. Wanted to ditch the package and forget he had ever said he would deliver it.

Wanted to back down on his guarantee to a Clutch-turtle?

"Yeah," he managed, if a little hoarsely.

"Do step inside, sir. I've been instructed to place you in the small salon. Please come with me."

He stepped into the velvet-dim hall, turned toward his host—and felt his jaw drop. The squat metal cylinder did not seem to notice; indeed, it may have been too busy closing the heavy door to pay any attention to Cheever's lapse of courtesy.

Door closed, the 'bot rotated on its axis and gestured with one of its three flexible arms. "Right this way, Mr. Mc-Farland."

"Okay . . . Uh, didn't I talk to you on the phone?"

The orange ball balanced on top of the monstrosity flickered, and all three arms waved gently. "Quite right. I am the butler, sir; Jeeves. At, I might add, your service."

"Sure you are," Cheever said. He shook his head slightly. "We're going to the—small salon?"

"Exactly so. If you would be good enough to come with me, sir? It's just a step down the hall."

Jeeves's step was most people's hike, Cheever decided some minutes later. It took more time to cross the slippery marble foyer than it did to go through a normal Terran house, and he added a second or two to the trip by stopping to stare at the sweep of strellawood stairs.

"The grand staircase," Jeeves murmured as they moved on. "Each riser hand-carved with an episode from the Great Migration and other illustrious points of history. I'm told it's quite impressive."

"Uh . . . yeah. Yeah, it's real nice," Cheever said, and followed the 'bot down a side hall only a little less wide than the foyer.

There were wooden doors with crystal knobs set dead center; there were impossibly delicate lights glimmering here and there on the wood-paneled walls; there was more wood underfoot, resilient beneath his boots, muting the rumble of the 'bot's wheels. Cheever shook his head to clear it and nearly fell into his guide.

"Here we are, sir. I trust you'll find the aspect pleasant, what with the ethaldom in bloom. Lord yos'Galan will be with you shortly."

Three steps into the room, Cheever spun. "*Lord* yos'-Galan!" But the 'bot was gone.

"I want to see *Lady* Nova yos'Galan," he told the empty room. "First Speaker of Clan Korval. The turtle *said* Lady Nova yos'Galan . . ." Hands tucked into belt, he prowled the perimeter of the room, wincing at the smudge his boot had left on the creamy carpet. Bookshelves filled to capacity—bound books mostly, which told how rich they were even if he had not had the evidence of the house, the grounds, and the grotesque, efficient robot. People who owned books at all owned book-tapes; Cheever's personal collection included several piloting manuals and the general concordance for the Traland Three Thousands, though of course he had done his own mods on *LucyBug* . . .

The door at his back clicked and creaked, and Cheever spun with pilot quickness, the weight of the package pulling his vest a little wide.

"Good morning!" an affable voice cried in Terran unsmirched by uptown twang or Liaden blurring. "Mr. McFarland, isn't it? I'm so very glad to meet you, sir!"

The man coming toward him was Terran-high, though an inch or two shorter than Cheever himself, and dressed in exquisitely clean trousers and a full-sleeved, claret-colored shirt that set off the white hair shockingly. Beneath the old man's hair was a young man's face: big nose, wide mouth curved in a grin, pale eyes warm under slanting, silver brows. He held out a large, square hand on which an amethyst ring gleamed.

"Shan yos'Galan at your service."

Cheever grinned and slapped his own hand around the one offered. "Cheever McFarland. Pleased to meet you."

"As I am to meet you—but I said that already, didn't I? Mustn't repeat myself. Has no one given you wine? My dear man . . . Our hospitality has been wanting, and you fresh from the Port. Very dusty sort of place, Solcintra Port. Don't you find it so?"

"Errr . . ." Cheever said as the big hand came to his shoulder and coaxed him toward a discreet onyx counter.

"Precisely," his host said. "Will you have some morning wine? Whiskey? Misravot? Brandy? We have an excellent jade and a passable white, but I confide in you, sir—the red excels them both."

Whiskey . . . Cheever could almost taste it. A whiskey would be real good. Regretfully, he shook his head. "You wouldn't maybe have some coffee?" He smiled a little sheepishly at the other man. "Been up for a while, see? 'Fraid the booze'd go straight to my head."

"We can't have that, can we? Jeeves," he said, apparently to the room at large. "Please bring Mr. McFarland some coffee."

Glass clinked against crystal as he poured himself a healthy swallow of red wine. "I can't help noticing the insignia on your vest. Bascomb Lines, isn't it?"

Cheever's hand went to his left breast, where the once-bright Sol System insignia had almost faded away. "Yeah . . ."

"Do you work for the line?" Shan asked, lifting his glass. "I've just recently concluded some business with Ms. Lillian Bascomb and Captain Barney Keller—do you know them?"

"Lillian—I know—knew Lillian real well. Barney an' me ran the board together on the big bruiser—he wasn't no captain then."

"A pilot of some skill! What's it like, piloting a big cruise ship? Exciting?"

Cheever shrugged. "It's okay. But I like a little ship—better handling, faster, put 'er in and out of someplace tight before anybody knows you been there. Can't do that kind of stuff with the big ones. Got to play it straight." He nodded. "Like running my own boat."

"Do you?" Shan murmured as the door swung open to reveal robot and tray. "Reprieved, sir! I hope you find the coffee to your liking. Jeeves, Mr. McFarland tells me he's been up for days and that only a cup of your finest will see him safely through the next hour. Cream, sir? Sweetening?"

"Just black, thanks." He took the steaming cup from the

'bot, stomach cramping as he remembered that the past days hadn't included too many meals, either.

"I'm amazed," Shan yos'Galan was saying, "to see you so quickly. We were warned to look for you only yesterday."

Cheever grimaced as he burned his tongue. "I left two days ago."

"Really? You must have been very far away."

"Farther than you think," Cheever told him with a glint of pride. "All the hell and gone in the Second Quad."

"Quite a trip," Shan murmured appreciatively. "And so quickly! No wonder you're tired. If you like, I can take your charge to my sister. I should have made her apologies to you sooner—my dreadful manners, sir, do bear with me! She was called to speak with our man of business. But I assure you that I am completely trustworthy to—"

Cheever set his cup on the bar with a *thckk*. "Turtle said to give the package to First Speaker Nova yos'Galan. Said I was to put it in her hands."

The light eyes quizzed him over the cup's fragile rim. "Commendable." He turned his head slightly. "Jeeves."

"Your lordship?"

"Please inform my sister that Mr. McFarland can deliver his package into no hands but her own. I trust her manners are equal to the task of excusing herself from Mr. dea'Gauss for half an hour."

"Certainly, sir." The 'bot wheeled out of the room, dragging the door shut behind it.

"She'll be by in a moment or two, and then we'll get you to bed, sir, never fear."

"Huh?" Cheever frankly stared. "Hey, look—I mean, that's really nice and all, Mr. yos'Galan, but you don't need to put me up. I'll snatch a couple hours at the Port while I'm waiting for clearance—it's a borrowed ship, see? Turtle's deal was he'd pay for repairs to *LucyBug* if I delivered this stuff for him. Came into the bar asking for the hottest pilot there. I said I was—not bragging; stupid to lie to a turtle— and the rest of 'em said yeah, that's right."

"I see. Very nice of the turtle. What was his name, by the way? My ghastly memory!"

"Edger, he said to call him. *Big* somebody. Voice like to

crack your eardrums." Cheever picked up the cup and gulped down the contents. "Real character, ain't he?"

"So I've been told. But I really must insist that you guest with us, sir. It's the least we can do for the trouble you've gone to on our account! Do let me convince you!"

"No, listen, that's—"

"Shan?" The voice was soft, accented and thoroughly lovely.

And the person who came with it was slim and small and golden and perfect. The violet eyes were huge in an adorable pointed face, framed by spun-gold hair. Cheever frankly stared.

The diminutive goddess stared back, infinitesimal frown shadowing the smooth expanse between flawless brows.

Into the growing silence swept Shan yos'Galan. "Ah, there you are, sister! Allow me to present Mr. Cheever McFarland, who has something he must deliver only to you."

She bent in a bow so graceful that Cheever felt tears start to his eyes. "Cheever McFarland, I am happy to meet you."

"And I'm ha—happy—to meet you . . ." Some nearly paralyzed grain of sense stirred. "I've got something to deliver to Nova yos'Galan, First Speaker of Clan Korval."

"I am that person," she said softly. "You may unburden yourself."

His hand started toward the inside pocket, then checked. "I'm sorry, but see—since I don't know you and all. Edger said I was to ask you to tell me your name."

"My name." The frown line became more pronounced, and it was all Cheever could do not to go down on his knees and beg her not to tease herself about it; he would *give* her the damn package, if only . . .

"My name," she began, quite seriously, "is Nova yos'-Galan First Speaker-in-Trust Clan Korval, She Who Remembers, First Sister to Val Con yos'Phelium Scout, Artist of the Ephemeral, Slayer of the Eldest Dragon, Knife Clan of Middle River's Spring Spawn of Farmer Greentrees of the Spearmaker's Den, Tough Guy."

It was music; it was angel-song. He could have listened to her voice for hours—days—years. It was inconceivable that he would ever tire of hearing . . .

"Uh—yeah," he stammered, reaching in at last and drawing the thing forth. "Here you go."

She took it gravely in small hands and bowed once more. "My thanks to you, Cheever McFarland, for the service you do Korval. Please allow Jeeves to show you to the guesting room."

"Yeah . . ." he said again, and managed a rough bow, mere parody of her smooth perfection. "I'll, umm, I'll see you later."

"We will speak again," she agreed.

He glanced back once as he followed the 'bot down the hall, and saw her hands already busy at the sealing tape.

LIAD

TREALLA FANTROL

"Cut that out!" Gordy brushed the screen, diverting Lady Pounce's attack from the cursor to his hand. "Cut that out, too! Dumb cat."

She blinked angelic and slightly crossed blue eyes at him and tucked her paws neatly beneath her snowy chest.

Gordy sighed gustily. "If you want to stay up there, you stay just like that. No more killing the cursor, hear me? I've got to finish this check."

Lady Pounce slitted her eyes in amiable acquiescence and even purred a few notes, though Gordy did not believe a word of it. He turned his attention back to the gridwork of equations that represented the contents and balancing of the *Dutiful Passage's* holds. The grid had already been checked by Cargo Master yo'Lanna, who had generated it; by First Mate Mendoza; and by Captain yos'Galan. Scant chance Gordy would find an error missed by that seasoned team. Nor was there truly any reason for an associate trader to concern himself with administrative details, except that Shan insisted, explaining, with a sweep that drew all eyes to the Master Trader's amethyst on his hand, that there was enough knowledge in the wide universe that Gordy never need fear learning too much.

Immersed in checks and cross-checks, he did not hear the light step behind him, and he started badly at the sudden hail.

"Well met, young Gordon! How do you go on today?"

Gordy's fingers jammed home three keys at once, eliciting a peevish *beep* as he spun in the chair, blood mantling his cheeks. "Oh," he said quellingly. "Hi."

The slender, dark-haired gentleman performed a bow as exquisite as his clothing; to eyes unused to the nuances of such things, the movement was a confection of graceful delight. "Your enthusiasm does you credit. Indeed, the invariable warmth of your greetings has ever been numbered among my chiefest joys in our kinship."

Sure it has, Gordy thought. He came out of the chair slowly, towering over the other man like a mountain over a molehill, and solemnly bowed the bow between Clanmembers.

"Forgive me, kinsman," he said, the High Liaden words only slightly edged in Terran accent, "for the attention to my work that hid your approach and may have cloaked my greeting in less than cordiality. You must by this time in our association have the measure of my admiration for you."

"Oh, very good," Pat Rin murmured, dark eyes gleaming. "Quite nearly a hit, I believe. Well done, young Gordon."

Gordy ground his teeth, keeping face and voice smooth with an effort that became less with each trade deal he negotiated. "How may I serve you, sir?"

"I seek your foster father, child. Is he within the house? Or must I languish upon Lady Mendoza's doorstep for a sight of him, like all the rest of the world?"

Priscilla would have you arrested for vagrancy, Gordy thought savagely, while he politely inclined his head. "He was just up the hall, speaking to Jeeves."

Pat Rin sighed delicately and flicked a wholly imaginary speck of dust from a moss-green sleeve, rings glittering on shapely fingers. "Speaking to the robot? But Shan will speak to anything, won't he? I've noted it time and again."

"Shall I fetch him for you, sir? It would take but a—"

"Pat Rin! Well met, cousin, how do you go on?"

Gordy spun toward the door, face wreathed in disbelief.

Pat Rin laughed his soft, malicious laugh and performed another beautiful, sarcastic bow. "Kinsman. I am exceptionally well. How do you find yourself?"

"I leave that to Priscilla," Shan said, smiling vaguely and impartially on Gordy, Pat Rin, and Lady Pounce. "Morning isn't my best time, and if I had to spend half of it finding myself—well, you appreciate, cousin, I'd be in a fair way to getting nothing else done at all."

Pat Rin frowned at the rush of Terran but answered competently in the same tongue. "You see me here on your word. How may yos'Phelium serve yos'Galan?"

The silver eye sharpened. "yos'Phelium? Have you taken up Thodelm's melant'i?"

"Certainly not," Pat Rin said, dropping his eyes to watch the play of light among his rings. "But you see, cousin, we of Line yos'Phelium find ourselves without a lord these several years, so that we grow accustomed to coming to Korval's First Speaker for resolution of matters belonging more properly to the Line."

"A complaint, in fact."

"An observation. You are yourself Thodelm yos'Galan. Would you run to the First Speaker with every up and down of your close kin?"

Shan blinked, icicle-sharp eyes melting back to blandness. "Well, things are a bit confused these days, cousin, admit it. Korval has shrunk to a handful; the Nadelm fends the Ring from his finger; the lines of administration are crossed and recrossed a dozen times over." He smiled. "We muddle on."

"While Nadelm Korval remains missing, and the Clan does its least to discover him."

Shan said nothing.

Pat Rin shrugged and looked up from admiring his rings. "One hears rumors, as one goes about. All the world notes the continued absence of Val Con yos'Phelium. Many remark upon yos'Galan's complaisance. They recall that Korval passes the Ring from pilot to pilot. They recall that Shan yos'Galan wears the badge of a master pilot." He dropped his eyes again and concluded softly, "While Pat Rin yos'Phelium is no pilot at all, nor ever shall he be one."

The silence stretched. Gordy watched Shan's face, but saw only vagueness there.

"Rumor is a dangerous song to heed," Shan commented. "But none of this bears on my need to see you, cousin! I wonder about your trip."

Pat Rin actually blinked. "My trip?"

"Exactly! Weren't you planning a jaunt to Philomen soon, for a bit of rest from your labors?"

"Yes. My plans are firm, in fact."

"Fine, fine, excellent! You'll be wanting a pilot, I know, and it—"

"It happens that I employ an adequate pilot, kinsman. My thanks for your kind thought."

"Yes, but you see, we have at hand a more than adequate pilot—and you need not be out of pocket an additional tenth cantra! Korval will balance any difference between payscales." He raised his glass and sipped. "The man requires occupation, kinsman! Surely you wouldn't deny him work to pass the time away?"

Pat Rin considered him out of thoughtful dark eyes, and Shan bore the scrutiny patiently, seeing anew how much his cousin resembled Val Con: the same glossy dark hair, level brows, and firm mouth.

"So," Pat Rin murmured. "And what am I to do with my new pilot when we reach Philomen? Shoot him?"

"Well, certainly that's up to you," Shan said, "but I've no reason to expect his service will be as bad as that." He raised his glass. "The First Speaker strongly suggests that he enter your employ and remain there—oh, six Standard months should be more than sufficient."

The smaller man bowed. "Of course it must always be my most ardent wish to obey the First Speaker's word."

"Yes," Shan drawled. "I'd heard that."

Pat Rin laughed. "Rumor sings dangerous songs, as I have only recently been reminded. Understand that nothing would induce me to doubt you, but I yearn to hear the First Speaker's wishes from her very lips. Might she be available to speak with me?"

"I believe she's alone in the study. Shall I have Jeeves escort you?"

"Thank you, but I know the way." He bowed farewell. "Kinsman. I think I will not see you again before *Dutiful Passage* leaves us. Fare you well. You also, young Gordon." He was gone, mincing daintily in his fancy boots.

Gordy let his breath go in a explosive *pough!*, spun toward his foster father, and hesitated.

"Yes?"

"Is Pat Rin—in love—with Cousin Nova?"

Shan shook his head. "No . . . No, I don't think Pat Rin's in love with anyone."

"Except himself!"

Surprisingly, the response was another headshake. "Not at all."

Gordy flung out his hands, startling Lady Pounce into opening her eyes. "Then why's he *like* that?"

"Well," Shan said thoughtfully, swirling the dregs of his wine, "I suppose that, like most of us, he's not finished yet. Have you checked these equations?"

Gordy flushed. "I'll be done in fifteen minutes."

"Fine. I'll be back then. We'll be going up to the *Passage* tomorrow morning for the last checks; we've got departure scheduled for Solcintra sunrise, Treslan Seconday."

"I'll have to tell Karea good-bye . . ."

"Yes, of course." Shan sighed. "Finish your equations, Gordy." And he was abruptly gone, closing the door behind him.

Shan touched the PLAY key and leaned back, eyes closed, to listen again to Val Con's recorded message to Edger.

"I greet you, brother, and thank you for the lives of myself and the youngest of your sisters. I am to say to you these things, which are true: We are alive and have been well treated, having received food, a place to sleep, and medical aid. I regret that the ship of the Clan has continued its voyage without us. It was undamaged when it left us and should achieve its destination as planned, as it kept course without fail during the seven seasons of its labor."

There was a small pause, then Val Con finished, "I am also to say that we will be returned our knives and given a ship in which in continue our travels. My thanks to you again, brother, for your care of two of your Clan who are foolish and hasty."

A Korval ship had already been dispatched to the coordinates indicated in Val Con's message. Exact figures relating to the distance a ship of the Clutch would have traveled in "seven seasons of labor" had been included in the hodge-podge of information that made up the balance of Cheever McFarland's delivery. The possibility had to be covered, of course, but Shan felt no optimism that Korval's ship would find Val Con and his lifemate anywhere near those coords.

The tape hissed briefly, and then the other voice came in, bright, clear, singsonging its nonsense as if there was nothing in all the worlds to fear:

"Hi, Edger. Everything's fine. Wish you were here. Love to the family and see you soon."

The tape hummed, clicked, and rewound noisily before the machine shut off.

"I like her," Shan said to the dim and empty study. "But, gods, brother, the Juntavas?" The agreement between the intergalactic mob and Korval stretched back generations: You don't touch mine; I don't touch yours. Simple, effective, efficient. "Why didn't you tell them who you are? They would have dropped Korval Himself and his Lady like so many hot potatoes . . ."

Chilled, he considered an alternate scenario. Val Con reveals himself. The Juntavas, horrified beyond reason by their act, knowing a balancing of accounts with Korval would ruin both, simply cut two throats, leave two bodies drifting . . .

"Gods!" He snapped to his feet, covering the room in five long strides, to stare out at the twilit garden, where the fountain caught the sun's last rays, transmuting light to emeralds.

Memory provided a boy's high voice, half-pleading: "But there *isn't* a Delm Korval really, is there, Shan? Just a made-up person—it could as easily be you as me." And he heard his own voice, laughing in reply: "Oh, no! *You're* the Korval, denubia! I don't want to be Delm."

"But you *could* be, couldn't you?" the boy Val Con demanded in memory, and Shan turned cold in the present and whispered, "Only if you die, denubia." He shook himself, hard.

"They're alive," he whispered, willing his hands to unclench and bringing his heartbeat down with a Healer's stern discipline. "You have that on the best authority. Do strive for some sense, Shan."

And there were two to find now. Even if Val Con . . . His lifemate must be found and brought back to the Clan, for if they did not have a Delm, they might yet have a Delmae. Nova saw that, thank the gods. Korval ships Jumped in a dozen directions that long afternoon, seeking news, any news, of Val Con yos'Phelium or Miri Robertson. Lifemates will hold together, Shan told himself, staring at the shadows growing from the trees toward the house. Find one and we find both.

Sighing, he shook himself free of his thoughts and slipped away from the house of yos'Galan to go home at last to Priscilla.

VANDAR

SPRINGBREEZE FARM

She was never going to get it right.

The minute she thought she had command of a word it slipped away, unmoored by a dozen or more others. It was all she could do to remember the name of the dog, never mind the word for its species. And all morning Zhena Trelu had been in a waspish mood, yelling and pushing at her when she did not understand. Which was mostly.

After the third such incident, she had twisted away from the old woman's grasp and run, screen door slamming behind her.

Flinging herself to the ground beside the scruffy little

flower patch that marked the edge of Zhena Trelu's property, Miri scrubbed her hands over her face and tried to calm her jangling nerves.

"This ain't like you, Robertson," she muttered. But that didn't help at all.

Her head hurt. She reached up and pulled the braid loose; unweaving it slowly, she ran shaking fingers through the crackling mass, mightily resisting the urge to yank it out in handfuls, and hunched over, staring at her hands and just breathing.

She found she was staring at her calloused trigger finger. What business did her hands have baking sweet things? Why should she have to sit and listen to endless repetitions of the names of the powders, granules, and dried leaves that went into food? She did not intend to be a bake-cook.

Worse was all that zhena-and-zamir stuff. Why should Miri be asked first whenever Zhena Trelu wanted Val Con to do something? Since when was he Miri's trooper? But no, there were rules, and one of them was that a zhena—wife? mistress? lady? lover?—could tell *her* zamir what to do, and he, perforce, would do it. What kind of partner was that?

They had figured out that Zhena Trelu owned the house and lived zamirless. They had gotten across that they were looking for a place to stay, and she had supplied some story for herself that Val Con was slowly getting down. But there! Barely a week had passed and Val Con could hold a conversation with the zhena while Miri's head hurt more and more . . .

She wanted to shoot, dammit—a little plinking would calm her down. But Val Con had not seemed to think too much of that and after some thought she could see why: They were guests here, wherever here was, and it just wouldn't be good form to fill somebody's sacred tree all full of pellet holes.

"Hello, Meri," he murmured from her side.

"My *name*," she gritted out, not lifting her head, "is Miri." There was a small pause. "So it is."

She took one more deep breath and managed to raise her head and face him. "Sorry. Bad mood."

·

"I heard." He smiled slightly. "Zhena Trelu tells me you are a 'bad-tempered brat.' What is that, I wonder?"

She tried to smile back and was fairly certain that the effort was a failure. "Whatever it is, it ain't nice. I messed up something she was teaching me to bake. Told me to put in *pickles* and I put in *milk*. Or the other way around. *I* don't know . . ."

He frowned. "It must have been *milk* and not *pickles*. *Milk* is the white liquid we drink, isn't it?"

"I don't know. Told you I didn't know. Every time I think I know what something means, got it all lined up in my head with what it means in Terran, she hits me with forty-seven *more*—" She flung her hands out in exasperation. "I ain't never gonna catch up at this rate!"

"Cha'trez . . ." He tipped his head. "Why are you trying to match these words and Terran words? Surely that will only confuse matters. Perhaps if you waited until you have this language firmly before attempting to compile a lexicon, it would go better. For now, it might be best to simply learn the tongue, as you were taught in school."

"I didn't *go* to school!" she snapped, hearing the rising edge to her own voice.

Val Con frowned. "What?"

"I said," she repeated with awful clarity, "that I didn't go to school. Ever. In my whole life. Accazi?" Her head was throbbing; she bent her face down and jammed her fingers through her hair.

"No." His hands were on her wrists, insisting that she lower her hands. She allowed it, but kept her head bent, eyes on the ground, and heard him sigh.

"Miri, don't run from me. Please. I don't understand, and I would like you to explain."

"You don't understand?" She was on her feet, wrists yanked free—and he was up, too, hands loose, face wary and watchful.

"You don't *understand?* Ain't anything to understand—it's all real simple. On Surebleak, if you paid the school tax, you went to school. You didn't pay the tax, you didn't go to school. With me so far? My parents were broke—you *understand* broke, or do I gotta *explain* that, too? Real broke. Bad broke. So broke they could about come up with enough money every month to fool the landlord into thinking someday he'd collect the whole rent. And, while we're at it, there were rats—you *understand* rats?—and my mother was sick all the time and whenever we *did* get some money Robertson would come home, drink it all up or snort it all down, smack us both around—" She caught her breath, horrified to hear how close it sounded to a sob.

"So I didn't go to school," she finished tonelessly. "My mother taught me how to read; and when I joined Liz's unit she beat Trade and basic math into my head. Don't need a fancy education to get by in the Merc. Guess that's why I never learned the right way to learn a language. Doing the best I can. Sorry it ain't good enough."

Val Con was standing very still, eyes on her face, his own features holding such a scramble of expression that she sat down—hard—and clamped her jaw against the sudden surge of despair.

Now you've done it, you prize loobelli, she told herself, and swallowed hard, waiting for him to turn and go.

"Miri." He was on his knees before her, hand outstretched, but not touching.

"You understand now?" Her voice was a husky whisper; his face swam, unreadable, before her eyes.

"Yes." He moved his hand slowly, keeping it plainly in sight as if she were some wild thing he wished not to frighten, and gently stroked his fingers down the line of her jaw. "I am sorry, cha'trez. I was stupid."

The tears spilled over. "No, *I'm* stupid. Told you so."

"You did," he agreed. "And I wish you will soon stop feeling it is necessary to lie to me." He brushed as her wet cheeks with his fingers. "There is a great difference between education and intelligence, Miri. You are not stupid. Normally." He offered her the slightest of smiles. "And—normally—I am not stupid. But everyone makes mistakes, I am told."

Her lips twitched. "I heard that."

"Good." He sat back on his heels, eyes serious on her face. "Having now made our mistakes, let us consider what may best be done to rectify them." One brow slid up. "Does your head hurt very badly?"

She blinked. "Who said anything about my head hurting?"

"I still get a headache when I try to translate from one language to another," he said. "Speak to me in any tongue I know, and I will answer in that tongue. Ask me what a word in one language means in another, and it may take me hours to decide." He paused to push the hair out of his eyes. "Will you do something for me, cha'trez?"

"Do my best.

"That will suffice," he murmured, reminding her so forcefully of Edger that she laughed. He glanced at her from under his lashes before adding his own grin. "Are you comfortable here? Would you prefer to go inside?"

"I'm fine," she said hastily, visions of Zhena Trelu dancing in her aching head. She crossed her legs and tried to look alert. "What's the job?"

Val Con was rummaging in his pouch. "It is only to help me think more properly about the best way for you to learn this tongue . . ." His hand moved sharply, and her eyes followed the movement, seeing that he had flung several objects to the ground.

"Close your eyes!" he snapped, and she did, instantly. He slipped two fingers under her chin and raised her head until her closed eyes were directed to a point slightly over his head.

"Keep your eyes closed," he said more gently, "and tell me what you saw just now on the ground."

Her brows twitched. "Starting nearest you and moving east: credit card—metallic orange with three skinny blue stripes—covering one corner is a wholebit. Then there's a flat white pebble the size of two bits together, a cantra-piece—obverse: the linked stars. Nearest me is the ship's key; there's a stylus next to that, then a short wire twisted like a corkscrew; a piece of paper with writing on it—don't know what language, but it looks like your hand—then back to the credit card." She paused, then nodded. "That's it."

There was a silence, lengthening.

After a time she said, almost hesitantly, "Val Con?"

"Yes."

"Can I open my eyes?"

"Yes."

She found him looking at her closely, the expression on his face a mix of amusement, wonder, and—anger? Before she could be sure, it was gone; he was lifting a brow and nodding downward.

She glanced at the jumbled arrangement and grinned, the ache in her head suddenly less acute. "Didn't miss one. Thought I'd be outta practice."

The second brow rose to join the first. "Dumb, Miri?"

"But there ain't anything to that!" she protested, genuinely startled. "It's a gag—a memory trick. Anybody can learn it— got nothing to do with brains."

"I see. A useful gag, eh?" He scooped the stuff up and dumped it haphazardly into his pouch. "How long can you retain it?"

"Depends. That batch'll probably fade out by the end of the day, unless you want me to remember it longer. Better tell me now if you do, though, 'cause I've gotta—" She moved her hands in one of her shapeless gestures. "It's kinda like putting a sticker on the memory, so I remember not to forget it."

"I see," he murmured again, apparently finding nothing the least confusing in this explanation. "Can you do the same with sounds? Put a tag on them so you do not forget?"

She shook her head. "It works better if I can see what I'm supposed to remember—either a picture, or a pattern, or written down." She bit her lip. "That's why I'm having so much trouble with this gibberish? 'Cause I can't tag sounds? Can't figure out how it looks?" She seemed inclined to blame herself severely.

Val Con shook his head, smiling. "Most people pay more attention to one set of—input—than the others. I, for instance, happen to key to sound. I rarely forget a piece of music I've heard, or a word. It seems a natural inclination: For some reason I decided that sounds were more important than anything else." His smile widened. "And so, when I became a cadet I suffered through hours of remedial work until I finally learned to tag a visual pattern and call it back."

He shifted, staring sightlessly at the scraggly grass between them. Miri waited, aware that she was tensing up again; she jumped half a foot when he moved his head to look at her.

Concern flickered over his face, and he leaned forward, grasping her arms lightly. "Cha'trez?" He moved his fingers, lightly massaging. "So *tense,* Miri. What is wrong?"

She shifted, not sure if she wanted to escape his touch. "Zhena Trelu—" she began.

"Will wait. She was upset when she spoke to me, and I think it might be good for her to have some quiet time, as well." He sat close to her on the grass and took her hand in his.

For some reason, that increased the tension. "Why're you doing that?" she snapped.

"It gives me joy to touch you," he said softly. "Shall I not?"

Yes, she wanted to yell, you should not! You should bloody well *go* if you're going and before things get any worse, or . . .

"I'm scared," she told him, finally identifying the emotion.

"It is not comfortable to be afraid," Val Con allowed gently. "Do you know what it is that frightens you? It may be something we can resolve."

She took a deep breath, fingers tightening around his. "I'm afraid of being stuck here—by myself."

"Ah." His eyes were troubled. "Will I abandon you, Miri?"

"How do I know what you'll do? Month ago I'd never clapped eyes on you. It'd make a hell of a lot more sense for you to get out on your own, though, wouldn't it? Be able to learn faster, move around more, settle in quicker, better. You're a Scout; I ain't nothing—"

"No . . . Miri." He lay a light finger across her lips. "I am not a Scout. Not now. Now I am a man who is trying—with the help of his partner and his friend—to insure that a long and joyful life will be possible together. A partner who," he added, mouth twisting slightly, "is afraid that he will run from her."

There did not seem to be anything to say to that, and the silence grew taut between them.

"Unless," Val Con murmured, "I am being sent away?"

She jerked as if he had slapped her. "No!"

"Good," he said, squeezing her fingers. "Because I am not certain that I would behave—with honor—in such a case." One brow slid up. "I would be lonely, too, do you think?" He sighed as he read the answer in her face. "Ah, *I* do not get lonely . . ."

Miri looked down at their entwined fingers, took a deep breath, and looked up. "Val Con?"

"Yes."

She took another breath. "I'm new at all this stuff. Not just the Scout-type things—*all* of it. Being partners. Being married. Never had a partner. Never wanted one." She tried a smile and caught the glimmer of his, answering. "Takes some getting used to," she concluded. "I'm sorry—"

But what she was sorry for was drowned in a bark of welcome as Borril hove into view. He was with them in a thrice, flopping to his side and *whuffing,* yellow eyes rolling in anticipation of a fine session of ear-pulling.

Miri and Val Con exchanged glances and began to laugh.

"Dog," Val Con said, yanking hard on a ridiculous ear, "I venture to say you were well indulged before we came here. But now that you have three pairs of hands to command, you've become insupportable . . ."

VANDAR

SPRINGBREEZE FARM

Val Con entered the room with unnatural scuffling to avoid startling the aging woman, and bowed when she looked up.

"Zhena Trelu?"

She smiled, relief washing her face. "Cory," she said, using the short form, as she had been doing since their second day with her. He had raised a brow at the first usage but had not protested, and Cory he had become.

"Did you find the child?" she asked him. "Is she all calmed down? I'm sorry I upset her—likely I was a bit sharp myself—but that girl has the wind's own temper with her!"

The man's brows pulled together slightly as he moved farther into the room. "Only noise," he said in his laborious Benish. "Like Borril. Sees something, maybe bad—makes noise. Maybe bad something goes away . . ." He perched on the arm of Jerry's reading chair, eyes intent.

Zhena Trelu sniffed. "Bad! Meri knows I'm not going to hurt her."

Cory moved his shoulders. "Here, things are not home. Miri is—" He sighed sharply, tipping his hands out toward her in a gesture she had come to know well the last five days.

"She's homesick, you mean. Misses her home." She drank down rest of her tea and set the cup aside. "Of course she is, poor child. I'll try to be more patient with her, Cory. You tell her that for me, will you?"

"Yes." But still he waited, watching her.

"What else? Are you hungry? I made you some sandwiches—they're on the kitchen table. You know where the milk is."

From the floor at her feet Borril gave vent to a heartrending groan. Cory laughed, then looked up again.

"Zhena Trelu. I ask—for Miri. Is there in your house—these . . ."

He swept a slender hand at the book-covered wall—Jerrel's books, mostly; dusty since his death. "For childs?"

"Children," she corrected, "Might have a few around from when Granic—my son—was a little boy. Why?"

"For Miri," he said. "To learn the words."

"Books to help her learn words?" she repeated. "But you're doing so well!"

"For Miri, Zhena Trelu," Cory told her for the third time.

She sighed. "You're a patient boy. All right, I'll look around and see if I still have any of Granic's old books."

He tipped his head. "Soon, Zhena Trelu?"

"Well, I—" She bridled, staring at him. He met her eyes calmly, his own a clear and bottomless green.

After a moment, Zhena Trelu sighed and pushed carefully

out of her chair. "All right, Cory," she said, with a touch of acid. "Soon."

After supper, Zhena Trelu left the two of them to clean up and went to pursue Granic's old storybook collection through the attic, grumbling audibly as she went up the skinny stairs.

Miri ran water into the sink and started to wash while Val Con cleared the table. She turned her head to smile at him. "I feel better," she said, which was not quite a lie. She *did* feel better—a little. The headache was gone, which was a big plus; but she was still as jumpy as a Merc without kynak.

Val Con finished the glass he had been drying and set it aside. "After we are done with this, if you like, I can show you a way to make living here—easier, perhaps."

She looked at him doubtfully, not sure that she really needed to learn something *else* right now; and he tipped his head, catching her eyes on his.

"I promise not to give you a headache," he said solemnly. She gave a wan grin. "Okay," she said. "What the hell."

Brrrinngg!

Miri whirled, ready to charge, staring at the black box on the opposite wall. Until that moment it had always been silent.

It repeated its shrill noise, and Val Con had his hand on it; then he was lifting the top part away and bringing it to his ear.

"Zhena Trelu's house," he said carefully in Benish.

A pause filled with tiny crackles, then a woman's voice spoke, high-pitched in amazement. "What? Who is that? Where's Estra?"

Val Con sighed gently. "Zhena Trelu's house," he repeated clearly. "Cory. Attic."

There was another pause on the line, and he turned to look at Miri, standing tense by the sink. He wrinkled his nose, which made her laugh, and then the voice on the phone was spouting more questions.

"Cory? What are you doing there, Cory? Where are you from?" The amazement had been replaced by avaricious curiosity.

Gossip, Val Con thought darkly and withheld another sigh. "Work. Home. Who is *that?*"

"What!" the voice exclaimed, though it apparently did not expect to be answered, because it rushed right on. "This is Athna Brigsbee. You tell Estra that I'm on the phone and want to talk to her right away."

"Stay," he said, as if she were Borril, and let the receiver down to dangle by its cord. Leisurely he went down the long hallway, up the stairs, and to the thin attic stairway.

"Zhena Trelu?"

There was a thump and a rustle from above. "What?"

"Athna Brigsbee on the phone to talk to you right away."

"Wind take the woman!" Zhena Trelu grumped, and Val Con grinned. "Tell her to hold on, Cory. I'll be there soon."

"Yes." And he was gone, soundless, down the stairs and back to the kitchen.

"Hold on," he told Athna Brigsbee. "Zhena Trelu is here soon." He let the receiver back down without waiting for an answer, picked up his towel, and began drying the mountain of clean dishes Miri had produced.

By the time Zhena Trelu reached the dangling receiver, it was making indignant noises, which the two diligent workers at the sink seemed not to hear.

"Young man? Young man! Pick up this phone, young man! Just what do you think—"

"Hello, Athna," Zhena Trelu said, unable to resist a grin at Cory, who raised a brow and continued drying dishes.

"Estra? Well, thank goodness! I was terrified. That rude man . . . Who *is* he, Estra? I asked, of course . . ."

I just bet you did, Zhena Trelu thought. "Cory and his zhena are helping me out around the place. You know it's been threatening to fall down around my ears these last couple winters. Thought I'd get everything all lined up and then maybe sell it, come spring." She stopped, surprised at herself.

"Well, that's lovely for you, dear," Athna Brigsbee said. "I know how hard it's been for you to keep everything up since poor Jerrel passed on." Zhena Trelu gritted her teeth: Jerry and Athna had not been the best of friends.

"But *tell* me about them, Estra," the voice in her ear continued. "Where are they from? I asked Cory, but all he said was 'home.'" She gave a shrill little laugh.

Good for you, Cory, Zhena Trelu thought. "They don't speak Benish very well. They're refugees—survivors of that volcano and earthquake they had over in Porlint last year."

"But, Estra," Zhena Brigsbee protested, "when I talked about how we should all get together and *do* something about those poor people right after the disaster you were—well, I won't mince words. You were *cold,* Estra. And now to take *two* refugees into your house—and they don't even speak the language!"

There was a pause that Zhena Trelu spitefully refused to fill, then Athna took up her thread again, voice lowered. "Are you *sure* they're married, Estra? The stories I've heard! People taking refugees into their homes who turn out to be thieves, or murderers . . ."

"Meri and Cory aren't thieves," Zhena Trelu snapped. "And I sincerely doubt they're murderers. Just a young married couple that happened to need help the same time I needed help, so we're helping each other." She took a breath, trying to force the irritation down. "Athna, I really am going to have to go."

"Of course! But we *must* get together—say on Artas? I'll bring a nice scuppin salad and some brownies, and the four of us can have a lovely dinner and a nice talk—it's been such a long time, Estra! Well, I won't keep you any longer—I'll see you on Artas, for dinner. Take care of yourself, dear." The line went dead, leaving Zhena Trelu gasping in outrage.

Athna Brigsbee was coming to visit in two days? There was no stopping her, of course. That sharp nose smelled gossip, and she would not rest until she ferreted out every bit of information possible about Cory and Meri and then did her best to make that information known throughout Gylles and the neighboring county.

Zhena Trelu returned the receiver to its hook, turned toward the sink—and gasped as she saw the young couple as a stranger would see them.

Meri was putting away pans while Cory finished the drying, both dressed in the tight-fitting leather garments that were the only clothes they owned. As Zhena Trelu watched,

Meri picked up the heavy iron skillet and bent to put it into the oven. The zhena tried to imagine the expression on Athna Brigsbee's face, were she presented with such a spectacle during her visit, and was almost tempted to allow the situation to continue.

"Meri," she said, shaking herself and moving toward the stove and the tea kettle. "Cory."

They turned to look at her, the girl drifting closer to the man's side, eyes great and gray in her thin face.

"Winter's coming," Zhena Trelu said, trying to talk slowly enough for Meri to understand, "and you're going to need warmer clothes. We'll go to town tomorrow and buy you something nice. Better clothes," she added, as she saw Cory's irrepressible eyebrow slide upward.

"Zhena Trelu," he murmured. "Buy is—" He tipped his hands out. "We not buy, maybe."

She frowned at him. "You don't have any money to buy clothes, is that it?" She shook her head, feigning irritation. "All the work you two have been doing around this place? Did you think you were working for nothing, Cory?"

"Dinner," Meri said unexpectedly. "Supper. Bed."

"For the little bit the pair of you eat," the older woman informed her with feeling, "I got the best end of *that* bargain. I owe you a few clothes—couple jackets, maybe. That should make us even for what you've done so far, all right?"

Meri looked at her husband, who moved his shoulders in that foreign gesture of his and bowed slightly. "Thank you, Zhena Trelu."

"You're welcome," she said, unaccountably touched.

Cory reached out and took the girl's hand, and the two of them slipped out of the kitchen, leaving only a soft "Good night" drifting behind them.

"Good night, children," Zhena Trelu said quietly, and turned to run water into the kettle.

"You should be as comfortable as possible," Val Con told Miri softly. "Later, you will be able to do this at any time, but to learn it is better to be at ease." He sat cross-legged in the middle of the double bed and smiled at her. "Perhaps you should unbraid your hair and take your boots off. Take off all of your clothes, if you will feel better so."

Miri grinned as she unbraided her hair. "I'd hate to tempt you like that."

"I," he said austerely, "am above such things. It is not for you to think that Scouts might be human."

She made the bow of student to teacher, hamming it, eyes very round. "Forgive me, Commander, I'll remember."

"Do so," he directed. Then he grinned. "I shall endeavor to keep my thoughts pure."

She shook her hair and combed rapid fingers through it, then sat on the wall-bench and yanked off her boots before shedding the rest of her clothes. "Now what?"

He patted the bed at his side. "Come lie down."

She lay on her back, eyes tight on his face, right hand fisted between her breasts.

"You are comfortable?" he asked. "Not cold? It is better if you put your arms at your sides and let your hands relax." He reached to brush the clinging copper threads from her cheeks; his fingers touched her lips lightly. "I promise you, cha'trez, this is a good thing, pretty and friendly—not at all frightening. Even I was able to learn it the first time."

She gave a gurgle of laughter and composed herself as he had suggested.

"Good," Val Con murmured, noting how tense her muscles still were. "Now I will tell you what will happen, then I will show you the way, and then I will ask that you repeat the process by yourself while I watch. All right?"

"Okay." Her eyes were on his, and he folded his hands on his knees, making no effort to break that link between them.

"The name of this technique," he said softly, "is 'The Rainbow.' It is a way of relaxing mind and body so that one may improve concentration and think—more rightly. People who are tense and confused make mistakes. And tension and confusion leach joy from life, which is a thing to be avoided. We should strive for more joy, not less—and that is what the Rainbow is for." He found his voice taking on the proper rhythm, found himself speaking the same words he had heard from Clonak ter'Meulen, all those years before.

"What you must do," he told Miri, "is picture the colors of

the rainbow, one by one: red, orange, yellow, green, blue, purple, violet; and use the—key—of each color to relax more deeply. By the time you reach the end of the rainbow you will feel very nice indeed: warm and comfortable, perhaps a little as if you were floating. You will then walk down the stairway and through the door. That is what will happen." He lifted a brow. "Shall we continue?"

Miri was frowning "You're gonna hypnotize me?"

"No. I help you relax. Each person's Rainbow is unique. I may show you the way because of the superficial similarity of the color structure. But your Rainbow is *yours,* cha'trez. There is no danger. If you should become frightened or un-comfortable—or simply wish to go no further—you need only open your eyes. It is *your* will that commands, not mine."

"Got it." She closed her eyes, then opened them with a sigh. Her left hand had curled into a fist while he was talking, and she flexed it open before looking back at him with a ragged grin. "Well, let's give it a spin and see what comes up."

"All right." He smiled. "Close your eyes now, Miri, and breathe deeply. Try not to think of anything specific, but let the thoughts flutter by, unconsidered . . ." He closed his own eyes briefly, feeling for the proper rhythm and words. Wily old man, Clonak ter'Meulen, he thought; I wonder where you are now.

"Miri," he began gently. "Please visualize the color red. Hold it before your mind's eye. Tell me when you have it firm."

"Now," she said instantly.

"Good. Hold it; let it fill your head, pushing away all those little, half-formed thoughts. Let there be only red. There is only red. Warm, happy red, filling your thoughts entirely.

"Now," he said after a moment, "let the red flow down through your body, starting at the top of your head, warming and relaxing you—down through your face, your throat, your shoulders—warm, friendly, relaxing red . . ."

And so he took her through the Rainbow, slowly, gently, watching the tension ease out of her, her face soften, her breathing slow. He reminded her at yellow and again at purple, as Clonak had once reminded him, that she might open her eyes and return, should she so desire, but she did not choose that path.

"You are now concentrating on the color violet," he said softly. "The end of the Rainbow. How do you feel, cha'trez?"

"Nice," she murmured, voice slightly fuzzy. "Warm and kind of—cloudy-feeling. Safe." She smiled a little. "I'm glad we're closer here."

He tipped a brow at that but replied gently, "I am glad, also. Look about you now, Miri. Do you see the stairway?"

"Standing on the top stair," she told him, voice entirely unsurprised. "It goes down a way."

"Will it make you feel—unsafe—to walk down?"

"No," she said unhesitatingly. "Should I?"

"If *you* wish to, Miri."

"Okay." A slight pause, then she said, "Val Con?"

"Yes."

"There's a door."

"So?" he murmured. "What sort of door?"

"Old-time door—all shiny, dark-brown wood and a big brass knob. There's a keyhole as big as my fist."

"Why not go in? Or would you rather return now?"

"I'd rather go in," she said definitely. "But I don't have a key to fit this beast—"

"Perhaps in your pouch," he suggested softly.

"Naw, I don't have a key like—" Her brows twitched over closed eyes. "I'll be damned."

There was a longish pause before she said again, "Val Con?" Wonder and excitement filled her voice.

"Yes, cha'trez."

"It's a *library,*" she breathed. "You never *saw* so many books—tapes and bound—and a desk and a chair—big and soft—candles—little knickknack things and—uh-oh."

"What is wrong?" He expended the effort necessary to keep his voice smooth.

"I'm in trouble, boss—there's a Belansium planetscape in here."

He grinned. "I do not think you need worry. Does the room please you?"

"Please—it's *wonderful!* Is yours like this?"

"Everyone's room is different," he told her gently, firmly refusing to consider the shambles his own must be in, if it still existed at all. "I am happy that you are happy."

He paused, then decided on a departure from Clonak's technique. "Miri?"

"Yo."

"May I give you a gift?"

Her brows contracted slightly. "A gift? Why?"

He winced. "It gives me joy to do so," he said very gently. "Will you allow it?"

"Yes."

"Thank you," he said seriously. "Look on the seat of your chair. Do you see the book there? Not a large book—very thin, in fact. Bound, with paper pages . . ."

"Here it is!" After a moment she went on, hesitantly. "Val Con? It's—it's beautiful. You sure you want to give it to *me?*"

He extended a hand, stopping just short of touching her near-sleeping face. "I wish it," he said gently, "with all my heart." He paused. "Listen, now, and I will tell you about this book. You will see that each of the pages is blank, except for the first four, where I have written something for you."

"Yes."

"Good. The first page, that says 'Sleep,' does it not?"

"Yes," she agreed once more.

"And the next," he continued, "says 'Study;' the third, 'Relax;' and the fourth, 'Return.' Is that correct?"

"Exactly correct."

"Very good. Now, what you may do, whenever you come to your library, is look at this book and choose what you will do. If you choose to sleep, you need only open to that page, concentrate on the word there—and you will sleep. If you wish to allow your mind to review and integrate the day's affairs—or if you wish to work on a particular problem—you will open to the page marked 'Study,' concentrate on the word, and your mind will be ready to learn.

"If you find yourself growing tense, you might wish to go to your library and regard 'Relax.' And, if you wish to return to the world outside your room, you need only bring your attention to the fourth page, and you will awaken." He waited a moment to let it all sink in.

"Miri, please open your gift to the page on which I have written 'Return.' Concentrate on it . . ."

She took a sudden sharper breath, then her eyes flickered open, and she smiled at him, very gently.

He smiled back. "Hello, Miri."

"Hi." She stretched, catlike, her smile widening to a grin as she extended a hand and touched his scarred cheek. "You're beautiful."

He raised a brow. "I am happy that I please you," he murmured. "How do you feel?"

"Wonderful. This gimmick might not help me talk to Zhena Trelu, but if I feel this relaxed every time I go down and come back, we're up."

"But it will help you talk to Zhena Trelu. If you choose to do so, you may go to your library and concentrate on 'Study' and 'Sleep.' Then you will be able to assign your attention to sorting and making sense of all that has come to pass—today, for instance—while your body and your waking mind rest. Tomorrow you will then have access to all of today's data, not just a jumbled mess that you have no time to sort through."

"If you say so." Her brows twitched together in a frown. "Where'd you learn this gag?"

He unfolded his legs and stretched out beside her, head pillowed on an arm, eyes level with hers. "It is a Scout thing. A man named Clonak ter'Meulen taught me, when my uncle hired him to make Shan a master pilot."

"Your uncle hired a *Scout* to teach your cousin to pilot?"

"Oh, no—Shan had been a pilot for years! He merely required tutoring to attain his master's rank, and Uncle Er Thom would settle for no less. As for hiring a Scout . . ." He moved his shoulders. "Clonak desired passage; my uncle desired his son to have the best tutor available. So a bargain was struck."

"And he just taught you this Rainbow thing on the side?"

"Of his kindness. He had known my father, you see, and he was much taken with Shan and me. I achieved my third class that trip, under his training." He stroked her cheek lightly. "Will you do a thing for me now?"

"Do my best."

He smiled. "Will you go through the exercise again, while I watch? And when you achieve your library, would you assign your concentration to 'Sleep'? The past days have been very hard for you—I am sorry that I did not understand *how* hard, so that we could have resolved this sooner. And tomorrow we are to go to town and buy clothes, which may prove trying for us all . . ."

Miri laughed and laid her lips firmly against his; he felt her fingers in his hair, and a quickening of his own blood. When she leaned back, the laughter was still in her eyes. "*Sure* you want me to go to sleep?"

"Alas," he murmured, half smiling in regret and admiration.

"Slave driver." But she rolled onto her back and closed her eyes. In a little while, the rhythm of her breathing told him that she was asleep; and in an even shorter while, he followed her.

DUTIFUL PASSAGE

LIAD ORBIT

Priscilla took off her shirt and laid it neatly on the bed, then stretched with casual sensuality and bent to remove her boots. The soft belt with its cleverly worked silver buckle was next, followed by the dark blue trousers.

Unencumbered, she stretched again and crossed the first mate's quarters to the wide, cloth-covered chair. She curled into it like a cat, which reminded her of Dablin, so that she smiled for a moment before closing her eyes and beginning the discipline that erased all expression from her face.

The discipline progressed: breathing deepened; heartbeat

slowed until it was a distant boom coming at long intervals, like an ocean beyond the hills; body temperature dropped four degrees. When she was satisfied that those functions had stabilized and would remain steady until the body itself failed of hunger or trauma, Priscilla withdrew her attention to her place of safety, admitted the prayer that would keep her whole on such a chancy venture, opened the door between her Self and that which was not her Self—and went forth.

Sounds, dazzling patterns, seductive perfumes: the *Passage* and all within it suddenly experienced with only the inner senses. There: Shan on the bridge. There: Lina in the common room. There: Gordy in the trader's room; Rusty at the comm; Ken Rik, Calypso, BillyJo, Vilt . . . Priscilla touched each, acknowledged all—and let them go.

The *Passage,* with its din of familiarity and love, dropped away, and she was alone in the noisy outside. She disallowed the clamor of strangers, brought up the template of the aura she sought, and focused on it, stretching awareness until her Self was barely more than a webbing of moth antennae, listening, quivering, straining far and farther . . .

It was at the point that Self was strained to the thinnest, when the thread that anchored her to the *Passage,* to the body, was at the limit of its elasticity, that she heard/sensed/saw it.

A glimmer, no more. A hint of familiarity; a bare taste of acerbic sweetness . . .

Awareness contracted as Self rushed toward the hint, unsubtle in desire; everything focused on the pattern growing in her senses, intent on contact, so that it was not until the last instant that she recognized the subpattern of one protected within deep meditation.

Aboard the *Passage* the body cried out, awareness and Self expanding toward dissolution as she struggled to absorb the psychic impact, scrambling even then for the shredding lifeline, clawing her way back, awareness a shivering knot of pain within the fire-shot network of Self—and plummeting into the body at last, heavy as a stone.

She cried out again as the pain ate along nerve and sinew, heartbeat stuttering, respiration a gasping mess, body soaked in sweat, and it was hot, hot, too hot—

Cool.

"Shan!" That cry was no less desperate, for all he was Healer and strong in his skill. "Shan, no!"

Cool enveloped her, leaching the heat and stifling the agony. She collapsed into it as if into his arms, and opened herself utterly, allowing him to cool even the memory of the pain, letting it vanish out of knowledge as heart rhythm steadied and breathing smoothed . . . She sighed and drifted, thinking of nothing.

"Priscilla."

It was with no common effort that she opened her eyes and looked into his face, vaguely surprised to find that she was indeed lying in his arms.

"No more, Priscilla." Face and voice were stern; exhausted witch-sense brought her the echo of his terror. She thought about smiling, and perhaps she even did.

"I saw Val Con."

His pattern changed too subtly for her to read. "Where?"

She moved her head. "It doesn't work that way, love. There aren't any directions when you go—spirit-walking. He's alive . . . strong . . . Meditating—playing, perhaps. I should have remembered how the music rings around him when he plays . . . That's what got me in trouble. Rushing in before I looked close. Wooly-headed as Anthora."

"I don't recall that Anthora has ever put herself in quite so much danger in her checks on my brother—or on any of the rest of us. Understand me—no more. You will not endanger yourself searching for my renegade of a brother, who is, incidentally, quite capable of taking care of himself." His arms tightened fractionally, and she had no trouble reading the shift in his pattern that time. "I can't afford to lose you, Priscilla; have some sense."

There was no talking to him, not with the fright he had just had—she saw that clearly, exhausted as she was. She smiled once more and lifted a hand to his stark cheek. "Of course, dear," she murmured. And slept.

STARSHIP CLARION,
ALLIED TO CAPTAIN ROBERT CHEN-JACOBS

TAKING ORBIT ABOUT THE
WORLD NAMED KAGO

The trip had been hasty and wondrous; the captain of the Terran vessel in which Sheather and his T'carais traveled was a gracious individual with an understanding nearly as bright as that of Val Con yos'Phelium Scout. He was a treasure, was Captain Chen-Jacobs, and Sheather had lovingly subscribed him to memory, knowing already how much might be learned from those hasty persons of the Clans of Men.

Consider that his T'carais, known to men as Edger, claimed untold wisdoms acquired from his adopted brother, that same Val Con yos'Phelium Scout—and the T'carais had a memory both long and rich. Indeed, only see what Sheather himself had learned, through their last brief meeting with the brother of the T'carais and the lifemate of that brother. Another treasure entirely was Miri Robertson; and Sheather dwelled often upon the honed brightness of her, to his wider appreciation of what was.

"Four days from Lufkit to this place," Edger said beside him.

Sheather blinked solemnly. "The Clans of Men and the ways of those Clans are hasty indeed, brother. And yet I find myself—exhilarated—by their speediness, touched by the valiance of their striving."

"Do you so?" The T'carais considered him with care.

There was that in the voice of the T'carais which brought to mind vividly one's own position as a mere Seventh Shell;

yet Sheather did not efface himself. "I find myself," he said instead, "looking at this action or another of an individual with the eyes of our new sister. It is a difficult endeavor, and one that I perhaps undertake imperfectly, yet I say to you, brother, that a certain—correctness—exists, though the view must be both hasty and imperfect." He foundered somewhat under the unwavering regard of his T'carais and the eldest of his brothers. "No doubt there is much thought yet required."

"No doubt," Edger responded calmly. "Honor me, brother, with your further thoughts upon this subject, when you have considered more widely."

"Certainly, brother."

"Your pardons, Most Wise." Captain Chen-Jacobs bowed deeply, and Sheather, seeing as his new sister might see, understood that the man was distressed.

His eldest brother, with what resources must be available to the one who was both T'carais and Edger for the Clan, had achieved the same understanding. "My pardon you do not need, for you have done us no harm," he assured the man in a booming voice. "But I perceive that you are uneasy and hope that ill news has not found you."

"Ill news?" The captain spread his hands, palms up, in a variation of the gesture favored by Val Con yos'Phelium Scout. "Who can tell? But you spoke of a pressing need to raise Shaltren when you boarded my ship, and I said that I would try to make arrangements for a connection from Kago."

Edger bent luminous eyes upon the man's face. "And have you not done so?"

"Wisdom, I have. But you spoke of haste, and I'm afraid the arrangements I've made are insufficient to your need."

Edger waited, eyes glowing.

"Understand, Wisdoms, that respectable ships do not ordinarily go to Shaltren. I have, in fact, located one. Its name is *Skeedaddle,* and the captain has said she will add you both to her passenger list."

"Thus far there is only amiable news, Robert Chen-Jacobs. Acquaint us with your trouble."

The man sighed heavily and shook his head, though what

he denied was more than Sheather could find, even with the assistance of his sister's sight.

"My trouble is for you, Wisdoms. *Skeedaddle* and Captain Rolanni are willing to take you to Shaltren. But they do not leave for thirty days."

There was a silence, short for Clutch, long for a human. "It may be possible," Edger said, "to hire a ship and a pilot for the purpose of taking us to Shaltren. We shall investigate this possibility. For I confess to you, Robert Chen-Jacobs, that I am not entirely easy with human speediness and the rate at which events may sometimes take place. It is perhaps true that thirty days is too many to wait, in this instance." He turned his head. "What think you, young brother?"

Startled, Sheather blinked. "I?" He was aware of a conviction that thirty days was far, far too long and offered that information to his T'carais, adding diffidently, "It is what I perceive, brother, with the understanding I have of our sister's perception. The T'carais . . ."

But the T'carais, in a most unClutch-like manner, had turned back to Captain Chen-Jacobs. "My kinsman and I are grateful for your efforts, but I, too, feel that thirty days are too many to simply wait upon transportation, no matter how respectable. We shall find another way." He extended a three-fingered hand and inclined his head. "You have done well for us, Robert Chen-Jacobs. We are grateful."

The man hesitated fractionally before putting his hand into Edger's. "I'm sorry I couldn't be of more help. If there's anything else I can do . . ."

"You have done what was asked of you, and it may be yet that we shall utilize what you have wrought. But we must explore this other possibility. In the affairs of men, days are most often of the essence."

LIAD

ENVOLIMA CITY

Tyl Von sig'Alda sat in an office overlooking Envolima Spaceport, frowning at the screen before him. The bowl at his right hand had long since ceased to steam; the spicy scent cloyed, irritated for an instant, then was whisked away by the air-cleaning system.

Thirteen.

No other clan owned as many ships; indeed, Korval might be said to hoard the things. Tradeships, yachts, retired Scout ships, miners, intrasystem garbage scows—if it was a ship and came into Korval hands, there it remained until the care of men could no longer keep it spaceworthy. Never in the memory of the longest Rememberer had any of Korval loosed a vessel of their own will, excepting, perhaps, the very ship of the Migration.

Thirteen was a mote from such a fleet, yet even Korval could not afford to scatter ships like handfuls of seed throughout the galaxy.

That an exodus of thirteen ships occurred mere days after Korval-in-Trust's inquiry for Val Con yos'Phelium was—disturbing.

Of the five major tradeships, only *Dutiful Passage* remained about Liad; so it seemed half-breed yos'Galan was immune to whatever orders had sent lesser captains scrambling to file Change of Departures and ring their crews back from abruptly shortened leaves.

Well, and Korval ever moved to the necessities of its own madness, to Liad's gain, mostwise. Though of course that was never its primary object. Korval served the interests of Korval; it merely happened that its interest ranged widely. So widely that one Terran encyclopedia had labeled Korval

"Liad's ruling House," likening its Delm to a king. And to individuals of mere Terran understanding that must seem to be the way of it.

Tyl Von sig'Alda touched the keypad, banishing the tale of ships. The next file was even less satisfactory, and frequent viewing had failed to sweeten the contents. Oh, it started well enough, with verification of Val Con yos'Phelium's most recent mission successfully completed: The Second Quadrant leader of the Terran Party, one Kelmont Jaeger, was dead, according to plan; precisely as ordered.

Well done, sig'Alda allowed, and sighed as the file scrolled on.

He was viewing now his own efforts at tracking the missing agent, looking, as he had countless times before, for that flaw in his reasoning; that glaring error in his conclusion that had led the commander to assign him this thrice-hopeless task. Even the verification of the Loop and the report he had given while under the drug had left the commander unmoved. Agent Tyl Von sig'Alda was assigned the project of ascertaining *without doubt* the whereabouts and condition of Val Con yos'Phelium.

Agents, as sig'Alda knew, were expendable. Yet the commander insisted on being certain that any unaccounted for had indeed been expended and neither captured nor subverted, though surely Loop and Option guarded against either . . .

sig'Alda sighed in sharp irritation. He had reached the point where it was a matter of retracing Val Con yos'Phelium's steps, thoughts, and conclusions. His office was cluttered with records of yos'Phelium's past missions—for his search, he had been granted ultimate clearance. He had requisitioned and attained yos'Phelium's Scout files; had listened to them over and over, until the man's quiet voice and precise phrasing seemed likely to haunt the few hours of sleep he allowed himself.

And still there was no clue.

Certain matters were obvious: both sanctioned escape routes had remained unused at mission end, and a ship lay empty at Lufkit Prime Station, doing nothing more than collecting berthing fees. Past missions illustrated yos'Phelium's resourcefulness: as had been the case in previous missions, alternatives to prepared and rehearsed situations had existed. This time the alternatives appeared to have failed, yet the data in hand were certainly too few to marshal as incontestable.

Further, he found that he was perforce made to study Korval itself. As much as the Department taught—and had demonstrated!—that the agent might safely be removed from the Clan to more ardently pursue Liad's own needs, it seemed clear from the records that an unquantified but significant portion of yos'Phelium's success was from the genes and mad genius of Clan Korval—which suddenly included the Department of the Interior among its ranging interests.

Thirteen ships sent forth from Korval. What did they know? He scrolled through the list again. As he watched, the screen shivered; then the list re-formed with yet another name appended: *Dutiful Passage*.

VANDAR

SPRINGBREEZE FARM AND ENVIRONS

Val Con awoke chilly and discontented. Not only was Miri's head not on his shoulder, but body-sense told him that she was not even in bed, though he did detect some faint rustlings from across the room, which could just as easily be mice as his wife.

Irritably, he opened his eyes.

She was standing before the mirror across the room, fully clothed except for her belt, totally absorbed in arranging her hair. As he watched, she finished mooring the elaborate knot on the right side of her head and took her hands gingerly away. Satisfied that her hair was firmly anchored, she rummaged among the objects on the table below and came up with a slender, polished stick—the knife he had given her in

Econsey, little more than a month earlier. The blade they had been wed by.

Miri flicked the knife open, closed, then thrust it through the center of the knot. She shook her head several times, hard, but hair and blade remained steadfast.

"Very nice," Val Con remarked. "Shall we be festive when we go to town, then?"

She grinned at him in the mirror. "Morning," she said, coming over to sit on the side of the bed. "I don't know 'bout festive, but I did notice Zhena Trelu don't wear a belt or a pouch. Which probably means we're not gonna be able to wear ours after we get these new clothes she's so hot for. An' I just wouldn't feel right without some kind of weapon—been a soldier too long, I guess." She shrugged.

He lifted an eyebrow. "Not too bad, for someone who is stupid."

"Bastard." But she was grinning, "Thought you told me Liadens were polite."

"Formality," he said, pausing to stretch, "must never be confused with courtesy." He rolled to his side, closer to her. "How are you this morning, cha'trez?"

"Really fine," she said seriously, and he read the truth of that in the clearness of her eyes and the looseness of the muscles in her face and body. "Rainbow's good to know," she added, and bent her head in self-conscious formality. "Thank you."

"You're welcome. I am only sorry that I did not realize sooner—I was not watching well . . ." You could not have been watching at all, he told himself bitterly, to allow her to come to such a pass.

But Miri had tipped her head, the line of a frown deepening between her brows. "You got other things to do, doncha? Can't always be watching me. An' I could've told you, couldn't I? Wasn't that I thought you wouldn't help; just didn't think there was anything you could do." She smiled apologetically. "Never been married before. Hard to get the hang of asking for help."

He put his hand over hers where it lay upon the bed. "We will learn together. I've never been married before, either."

"Yeah, you said that." She was still frowning. "Why not?"

"Scouts rarely take lifemates," he murmured. "One should enter into at least one contract-marriage—however, I did not choose to do so."

"But why not?" she persisted, watching him closely.

He rounded his eyes at her. "I was waiting for *you,* Miri." She laughed and squeezed his fingers. "Okay, you win . . ." she began, then her eyes fell on the sun-lit window and she leapt up. "Holy Panth, look at the time! I gotta feed those damn birds or Zhena Trelu'll fuse. Boss, start breakfast, okay? I'm *starved* . . ." And then she was at the door, hand on the knob.

"I am owed!" Val Con cried, surprising himself at least as much as her.

Miri spun. "Huh?"

He threw back the covers, slid out of bed, and began pulling on his clothes. "I am owed," he repeated. "I awaken and my wife is not at my side; I confess feelings of astonishing magnitude—and am disbelieved. I am ordered about. All this," he concluded, dragging his shirt over his head and glaring at her, "without so much as a kiss. I am deeply wronged."

"Oh." She came back across the room and stopped before him, studying his face. He was clowning—she had seen the glint of mischief in the green eyes—yet there seemed an undercurrent of serious intent in his attitude.

"So, how do I pay up?"

He gave it consideration. "I believe," he said, after a time, "that a kiss would do much toward balance."

"Right. Just so happens I've got a kiss on me. Is Terran currency okay?" She came closer, and his hands settled about her waist as she ran her hands up his arms to his shoulders and looked up into his bright eyes.

He smiled. "Terran currency is perfectly acceptable." He bent his head to collect.

Zhena Trelu followed the unaccustomed odor from the door of her bedroom to the kitchen and stopped, staring.

The biggest iron skillet was on the burner over a low flame, a generous handful of pungent bulbroot already starting to brown in the center. Cory was at the counter, grating cheese right from the block; several scuppin eggs, two sprigs of parsley, the milk pitcher, and a mixing bowl sat to hand, along with a knife and the remains of the bulbroot. The teapot was already steaming.

Meri, egg basket in hand, was on her way to the door; she turned, placed the basket on the floor, went to the stove, and poured out a cup of tea, which she took to the table, smiling.

"Good morning, Zhena Trelu," she said clearly. Then she was gone, the door banging behind her.

Cory looked up front his grating and grinned. "Good morning, Zhena Trelu."

"Good morning, yourself," she muttered, more than a little put out by all the activity. They were fixing a meal at *this* hour? Normally, they each had a cup of tea to start the day and then went about the chores until dinner. She sipped tea and frowned at the man's narrow back. "Cory?"

He turned, cheese in hand. "Yes, Zhena Trelu?"

"Why's Meri got her hair all done up like that? Looks—" It looked outlandish. is what it looked. Barbaric. "Different."

Cory moved his shoulders, smiling a little. "For town."

"For town? She doesn't have to fix her hair different for town. The braid will be fine."

One brow slid up. "It is for town, Zhena Trelu," he repeated. "Miri works hard."

And that, the old woman thought, taking another sip as he turned back to his cooking, would appear to be that. Well, and what business was it of hers if the two of them chose to go into town looking as if they had just escaped from the circus?

"It's just that," she told Cory's back, "this hairstyle doesn't make her look very pretty." And when one was as plain as Meri was in the first place, poor child . . .

Cory had turned around again, both eyebrows up. "Zhena Trelu? *Pretty* is?"

"Eh?" She set her cup down and pointed at the vase of sweelims on the table. "The flowers are pretty, Cory."

"Ah." He reached to the sink and showed her a pink-and-cream cup Granic's wife had made, a lovely thing, airy and smooth. "Pretty, this?"

"Yes," she agreed. "The cup's pretty. Very pretty."

He contemplated it for a moment before returning it with great care to the sink. Thoughtfully, he cracked eggs into the bowl, added milk, parslee, and grated cheese, then whipped it all together with a fork. After pouring the stuff into the skillet and adjusting the heat, he set the bowl in the sink and ran water into it.

"Borril," he asked over the water's noise, "is pretty?"

Zhena Trelu gave a crow of surprised laughter. "No. Cory, Borril is *not* pretty. Borril is—" But just then the outside door was pushed open and Meri marched in, carrying a basket containing three large eggs, the unlovely Borril at her heels.

"Pretty," Cory said, grinning at her.

Meri blinked incomprehension. "Pretty?"

He took the basket and put it on the counter, conducted her with ceremony to the table, and gestured to the flowers with a flourish. "Flowers are pretty," he said solemnly.

Meri bowed slightly to the sweelims. "Pretty flowers."

Hand under her elbow, Cory guided her back to the sink, where he held up the pink-and-cream cup. "The cup is *very* pretty."

She lifted a slender finger and ran it lightly down the glazed surface. "*Very* pretty."

Setting the cup down, he slid his arm around her waist and turned her to face the dog, which was curled up and yawning on the rug.

"Borril," he said, affecting to speak into her ear but talking loudly enough for Zhena Trelu to hear, "is *not* pretty."

Meri laughed.

Cory hugged her, then looked over her head at Zhena Trelu, who thought she knew what was coming.

"Miri is pretty."

Meri returned the hug and stepped back, raising a hand to his scarred cheek. "*Very* pretty, you," she said, and then she was at the pantry, tucking eggs away as Cory drifted back to the stove and poured tea.

Meri brought the cups to the table, but paused at the cupboard and glanced over her shoulder. "Zhena Trelu? You eat? Good eggs."

Zhena Trelu stopped on the edge of refusal. They might

have a point, at that. Shopping was pretty tiring; it might be best to start off with a little something in the stomach.

"I'll have just a bit," she said, managing a sour smile. "Thank you very much."

Three plates were delivered to Cory at the stove. Meri pulled bread, jam, and butter from various keepsafes, brought them to the table, and returned flicker-quick—or so it seemed to the woman watching—with silverware and napkins. Pulling the bread to her, she cut off three quick, even slices and handed one to Zhena Trelu.

Cory and the plates arrived. He gave Zhena Trelu hers, put Meri's down at her place, and slid into his own seat. Accepting a piece of bread, he began to eat.

In a moment Meri had joined him, eating with every evidence of enjoyment.

Zhena Trelu picked up her fork and considered her plate. The eggs did not look like proper eggs at all—all scrambled up and smelling of cheese and spices. Gingerly, she took a smidgen and tasted it.

Odd, but not awful. She had another smidgen, and then a larger one—and suddenly discovered that her plate was empty.

A deep sigh brought her attention to Meri, who was sitting back in her chair, grinning, teacup cradled in her hands.

"Thank you," she said to Cory. "*Very* good eggs."

Zhena Trelu added her approval. "Yes, thank you, Cory. You're a good cook." A thought struck her. "Is that what you used to do to make money at home?"

There was a pause during which Cory leisurely finished his bread and butter and washed it down with a swallow of tea. Zhena Trelu had begun to despair of an answer when he tipped his head.

"I eat. I cook."

That was almost as bad as no answer, when she thought about it. But it did raise another point that had better get firmly settled before Athna Brigsbee started bullying and terrifying them with her questions. "Cory, where are you from?"

He rested his eyes on hers. "Home."

Zhena Trelu sighed. "Yes, Cory. But where *is* home?"

He gestured, waving a slender hand toward the east and little upward—the direction of Fornem's Gap.

Zhena Trelu sighed again. "All right, Cory, we'll do it this way. If someone asks you where you're from, you tell them 'Porlint.' We don't get many refugees up this way, but stranger things have happened, especially if you got yourselves turned around somehow and came through the gap."

Cory finished his tea and glanced at his wife. "Home is Porlint," he told her, and pointed a severe forefinger. "Where are you from?"

Meri blinked. "Porlint," she said meekly, then grinned. *"Cory."*

"Bad-tempered brat," he responded, but she only laughed and got up to clear the table.

The truck started up at the first hint from starter switch and key. Zhena Trelu nodded to herself in satisfaction and leaned across to open the passenger's door. Thin as the two of them were, she figured that they would all three be able to fit on the single bench seat.

The door swung wide, and Cory pulled himself into the cab. The girl followed immediately, standing poised on the ledge, gray eyes wary.

"If she's gotta move her arms to drive this thing, maybe you better not sit so close," she said seriously to Val Con. "If you don't mind, I can sit on your lap or something—give her room to operate." She grinned. "Thing looks as unsafe as this does, I don't wanna do anything 'bout adding to the other side's odds."

"You may be right," he murmured, taking note of various levers and foot pedals. "It is never wise to crowd the pilot." He shifted closer to the door, and Miri sat on his lap, settling sweetly in.

"No!" Zhena Trelu snapped.

Startled, Miri looked down into Val Con's eyes. "Wrongo, boss. *Now* what, do you think?"

"We shall attempt to ascertain." He turned his attention to the frowning old woman. "No?" he repeated in Benish. "Bad?"

Zhena Trelu stopped herself from making the first remark that occurred to her and reminded herself that they were foreigners, with wind-knew-what notions. For that matter, there had been her own son's zhena—stormy-tempered and wild to a fault, yet biddable enough with Granic and pathetically eager to do her best for him.

She sighed. "It's *good* that you children love each other. Very pretty. It's good to touch each other. But in town some people might not understand, if they saw Meri sitting there like a—well, never mind. When you're at home, you can touch each other and hug and that's *fine*. But when you're out with people—in town—you have to be *respectable*." She paused, wondering how much of her lecture was making sense to either of them. One of Cory's eyebrows was out of alignment with the other, but his eyes were serious on her face. Meri was watching her, too, the line of a frown just visible between her brows.

"Refugees already have a bad name," Zhena Trelu continued. "You don't want people in town maybe not hiring you when you go to get a job, because they think you don't know how to behave, now do you? Especially you, Cory: a zamir as trusted and responsible as you are—well, you have to always be sure to bring honor to your zhena, and not let her do things that will make people think poorly of her.

"So, Meri, you get up now and let Cory slide over here next to me . . . All right; sit down, Meri, and close the door."

Once everyone was settled to her satisfaction, she put the truck in gear and turned her full attention to driving.

Miri sighed and leaned carefully back into the seat—and discovered Val Con's arm already there. She nestled closer to his side, and the arm curved more tightly around her waist.

"Sneak," she muttered.

"But such a *nice* sneak. Did you receive the impression that we are rude, yet not fatally so? If there is need, perhaps we could yet hold each other's hand."

Miri raised her eyebrows. "In case I get scared, you mean."

"Or I."

She snorted.

Val Con looked at her. "What an extraordinary person I

am," he murmured. "Never afraid, or lonely, or in need of laughter. Or a touch. I am quite overcome by my superiority."

She winced at the bitter note underlying the smooth voice, at the trouble shadowing his bright green eyes, and she recalled the urgency of his tears. Carefully she reached down to squeeze his fingers and summoned up a disrespectful grin.

"Yeah, well, I wouldn't be all that impressed. First of all, you gotta remember how hard it is to get a straight story out of you. Person could die of old age before she figures out the right question. You *manage* people—quiet about it—just don't treat 'no' like an answer. And the gods help whoever's there, you ever let that temper of yours off the leash." She gave him a thoughtful look. "Kinda like to be around to take notes, though—you sure got a way with words. Be useful, I ever wanna go back into the sergeant business."

He laughed, his arm tightening around her briefly. "I am chastised."

Then the truck swung uncertainly into a wider way, rattled over metal tracks, and raggedly negotiated a curve, coming upon an amazing structure: an open house in the middle of the road!

"A wooden tunnel?" Miri demanded.

"Hush," Val Con said.

And like Scout and soldier they watched the rest of the way to town, taking careful note of distance, direction, and terrain.

VANDAR

GYLLES

Brillit's Emporium stood two stories tall in the very center of town, directly across from the many-windowed tower and just up the street from the little blue build-

ing. It faced an oval of sere vegetation set in the middle of the
road—the so-called town green.

Zhena Trelu herded her charges across the street and up the
steps to Brillit's front door, muttering under her breath as she
saw Mrythis Wibecker come out of the glazing shop and stare
at them. In less than ten breaths it would be all over town that
Estra Trelu was here with her pet refugees. If there was one
gossip in Gylles worse than Athna Brigsbee . . .

Corvill and Meri hesitated on the threshold, and Zhena
Trelu gave each a firm push in the small of the back, pro-
pelling them into the dim, sawdusty interior.

"Ever look forward to a day," Miri murmured to Val Con,
"when you won't get shoved around?"

Val Con's shoulders jerked, but he managed not to laugh.

Zhena Trelu took the lead, quick-marching them down
aisles lined with gizmos and tantalizing gadgets which her
charges would have liked to examine in more detail, to the
foot of a wide stairway. She peered carefully in both directions before beginning the ascent, for all the worlds like a
Merc expecting to see enemies bursting from the brush on
either side.

Nothing of the sort happened, however, and she waved
them ahead of her. Obeying the gesture, they climbed the
stairs and waited while she made her more laborious way up
and stood for a moment to catch her breath.

"All right, children; here we are. We'll get Cory settled
first." And she marched off to the right, the pair of them trailing behind.

"She likes you best," Miri told her partner.

"Untrue," he returned. "She merely wishes to have me out
of the way in order to spend more time with you."

"Estra! It's been a time, hasn't it? How are you?" The
speaker was a plump, balding man a little taller than Zhena
Trelu. He was wearing a gray jacket to match his gray
trousers and a white shirt and a dark-blue neck-string. He
was standing at the mouth of an aisle lined with racks of
clothes.

Miri blinked. Clothes? And no valet in sight. How was one
supposed to figure out which of all those clothes was the

correct fit? Unless that was what that bald guy did. Gods, she thought. What a job.

Zhena Trelu was talking about them. "Porlum, this is Cory. Him and his zhena are doing some work around the place for me, and it looks like they'll be staying the winter. Thought it was high time for them to be having proper work clothes."

Porlum considered the man in the dark leather slacks and vest. A little under average height, but nothing to be unduly concerned with. The slenderness of his build might be more of a problem. Still, work clothes? He smiled at the smaller man, who did not return the courtesy, and nodded to Zhena Trelu. "I'm certain we'll come up with something suitable. Good, warm shirts and durable pants, of course. How many? And will you want him to have a set of—ah, dress clothes, also?"

Zhena Trelu frowned. "Three, four shirts, I think; couple of work pants—and a jacket, too, Porlum. Shoes . . ." She glanced at the high black boots on Cory's feet and sighed. "Work boots. I think we'll let the dress clothes go this time."

"As you say, Estra," the man agreed. "If zamir will come this way?"

"You go with Porlum, Cory," the old woman instructed. "He'll make sure you get the right things. Meri and I will meet you back here when we've gotten some things for her." She clamped her fingers around the girl's wrist and pulled her along.

Miri threw a glance over her shoulder in time to see Val Con disappearing down a clothes-lined aisle. As she watched, he ducked back to the end and waved, vanishing again immediately.

Grinning, Miri let herself be propelled farther into the store, to a place lined with clothes different from the clothes displayed in the area where they had left Val Con. A cadaverous woman with unlikely black hair, unlikelier red cheeks, and a thin, dissatisfied mouth looked at Miri, and her mouth turned sharply downward. She made no attempt to intercept Zhena Trelu, who peered about until Miri yanked on her sleeve and pointed.

"There you are, Salissa," Zhena Trelu said with a distinct lack of warmth. "This is Meri. She's been helping me out on the farm, and it's time she was getting some proper work clothes."

"I should think so!" Salissa sniffed. She turned to Miri. "Where did you come up with those—things—you're wearing? You look perfectly outlandish."

"Of course she looks outlandish," Zhena Trelu snapped. "She's a foreigner! *I* know she needs clothes—that's why we're here! Good, warm clothes, Salissa; the kind she can work in. And don't bother trying to talk to her much. She can't understand more than one word in ten."

She turned to Miri. "Meri, you go with Salissa, now. She'll find you some nice, warm clothes to work in. I'm going to buy some things for myself, and then I'll come back for you and we'll go find Cory."

With a sinking feeling in her stomach, Miri watched the old woman walk away, then squared her shoulders and turned around to glare at Salissa.

The small man had a mind of his own. He insisted on being shown the different grades of work shirts, subjecting each to close inspection, and finally deciding on the soft wool-and-julam blend—by far the warmest and most durable, in Porlum's opinion. Not that it was solicited.

The customer's stringent standards were also applied to trousers and work boots, though he deferred to Porlum in the matters of size and fit, as was proper, and allowed socks and a belt to be suggested.

In all particulars, however, was Cory's own taste followed—from the plain, rather than plaid, work shirts, to the tough black trousers. The jacket he chose was stuffed with hoyper feathers—a good, warm, well-crafted garment that because of its odd, greenish-gray color had languished on the racks. The small man grinned when he saw it and pulled it on immediately.

Porlum studied the effect and nodded. The jacket fit well; the deep pockets and hood were just the thing for winter, and the off-color brought out the amazing green of the customer's eyes. He sighed. It was a pity Estra had not thought dress clothes required.

Cory was standing quite still, head tipped as if listening, then pointed at the pile on the counter—three shirts, a pair of pants, socks, and the peculiar clothing he had worn into the store. "I come back for this," he said, and was gone.

Val Con paused to consider the scene before him. Miri—dressed in something he was fairly certain Miri should never be dressed in—was having a disagreement with a black-haired woman. Zhena Trelu was standing to one side, apparently trying to resolve the situation by keeping Miri silent long enough for the other woman to prevail.

He walked forward.

"*Bad* is," Miri was telling the black-haired woman with a great deal of passion. "Not warm! Say Zhena Trelu *warm*—"

"With that hair and those freckles," the other woman cut in, "you'd better think about looking pretty! Isn't it worth being a little chilly, knowing you look pretty, instead of like a—a tomboy?"

"Now, Salissa," Zhena Trelu said. "She doesn't understand. And Meri, if you'll just let Salissa show you some more clothes—"

"No more clothes," Miri announced with decision. "Bad clothes. *My* clothes," she told Salissa clearly, "are pretty!"

"Those things you wore in here?" the saleswoman demanded. "Well, I suppose they are, if your idea of pretty is looking loose and—*hoydenish* and—"

"You will not," a quiet voice said, cutting across her rising tirade, "say those words to this zhena."

Salissa stared. A man was abruptly at the side of the red-haired woman, his green eyes resting blandly upon the saleswoman's face.

Those eyes regarded her for what felt like long minutes, before he spoke again. "You understand my words?"

She licked her lips. "Yes."

"Good," the man said, no particular inflection in his soft voice. He turned to the red-haired woman. "Cha'trez?"

Miri raised her hands in exasperation and looked down at herself. "Zhena Trelu say warm," she said, sticking to Benish. "Warm this not. Not pretty." She smiled a little. "Borril."

His lips twitched as he considered the garment. The bright yellow shirt was long-sleeved, to be sure, but made out of some flimsy material that would barely be adequate on the warmest day they had yet encountered on this world. The skirt was not quite as thin, but ruffled and furbelowed—impossible to work in.

He shook his head and turned to the old woman. "Zhena Trelu? Miri is—right? This is not warm. It is not pretty. There are clothes like Miri's clothes here?"

"I should say *not*." Salissa sniffed with rather more assurance than she felt.

The green eyes flicked to her and ran—slowly and with deliberate insult—down her length and back to her face. He shrugged and turned back to Zhena Trelu. "There are other stores."

"What?" She gaped at him. "For wind's sake . . . Yes, there's another store. But this is the *best* store, Cory."

For a moment, she thought he would insist; then he moved his shoulders in that odd not-shrug of his and sighed.

"Zhena Trelu, you will—make sure Miri gets right clothes. Cha'trez, you want?"

She grinned and waved a slim hand at his new finery. "Warm. Work in . . ." She laid a hand on his chest, ostensibly to touch his shirt. "Soft."

He tipped an eyebrow at the old woman. "This is right? Not bad? *Respectable?*"

"There are women's clothes like the ones you're wearing. But, Cory, she ought to have at least one dress!"

His brows twitched together. "Dress? Dress clothes? No dress clothes."

Zhena Trelu sighed. "All right, Cory. Meri, come with me, dear . . .

But Miri tarried a moment longer to inspect his jacket. "Pretty," she admired, grinning at him. He grinned back.

"Meri!" called Zhena Trelu, and Miri laughed and ran off.

Having led the girl to the small section containing trousers and man-styled shirts for women, Zhena Trelu found that she had very little else to do. Miri's brief sojourn with Salissa had taught her the trick of the racks, and her quick eye had picked out the single recurring symbol on every item the saleswoman had chosen for her. She chose four shirts: pale blue, indigo, black-and-white check, and the palest of pale yellows.

Zhena Trelu approved those choices, allowing that they fit well enough, though there was a brief tussle over the snugness of the chosen trousers. That argument was put to rest when the girl tried on the pair Zhena Trelu thrust at her, buttoned them, and let go.

Effortlessly, they slid from waist to hip, where they hovered, apparently poised on the brink of further descent.

Zhena Trelu sighed and agreed that the others would have to do. When they left the dressing room, they found Cory leaning against the nearest end rack, holding something over one arm. When he saw Meri, he straightened, approving the light-blue shirt and indigo slacks with a grin.

"Very pretty." Stepping forward, he offered her a jacket that was the twin of his own, except that it was dark blue and several sizes smaller.

The girl's eyes widened, and she carefully put her armload of clothes on the floor. Cory helped her into the jacket as if she were a queen and the coat silk-lined fur instead of waterproof cotton stuffed with feathers. She pushed her hands deep into the pockets, fastened the front all the way to the throat, pulled the hood up to almost—but not quite—cover that outrageous hairdo, then ran her fingers over the sleeve and felt the thickness of the lining.

Cory took her by the shoulders and turned her to the mirror. She studied their reflection for a long time.

"Thank you for pretty—jacket?" she said, catching his eyes in the glass. She smiled a little. "Not Borril, us."

"Not Borril," he agreed, returning her smile, his fingers tightening slightly on her shoulders. "Very pretty us."

Then he loosed her and bent to pick up the abandoned clothing. Straightening, he smiled at the quiet old woman.

"Porlum will—make up—ticket? For all at once," he said, and went off without further ado, Meri at his side.

After a moment, Zhena Trelu followed.

•   •   •

They had just reached the sidewalk, Cory and Meri carrying between them the paper parcels containing their new clothes, as well as the cardboard box into which Porlum had carefully packed their foreign clothing, when disaster struck.

"Estra! Well, for goodness sake, if this isn't a surprise!" Athna Brigsbee cried, crossing the street with a wide smile on her face and her hand extended in welcome.

Resigning herself to the inevitable, Zhena Trelu forced a smile. "It's nice to see you, Athna," she managed, but so feebly that Cory, frowning, shot a look at her from under his lashes.

Characteristically, Athna Brigsbee did not notice. She seized Zhena Trelu's hand and wrung it until the bones protested before turning her voracious smile on the two slender figures standing patiently to one side.

"This must be Meri and Cory!" she surmised brightly, and Miri heard Val Con sigh. "Estra, the funniest thing! I just happened to run into Mrythis Wibecker a few moments ago in Jarvill's, and she said she'd seen you going into Brillit's with two *men!* She really should wear those glasses Dr. Lorm prescribed—but, my dear! so vain . . ." She turned her attention back to the refugees and their obviously new clothes.

"It's very kind of Zhena Trelu to buy you clothes," she said, speaking quite loudly. "You're both very grateful, aren't you? And you'll work twice as hard to pay for them."

"They've already earned their clothes," Zhena Trelu said firmly. "They work plenty hard already—I'm not sure I could bear up under it if they worked any harder." She turned to her charges. "Why don't you children go put the packages in the truck? No use carrying them with us to the library."

"Yes, Zhena Trelu," Cory said, and moved off at once. After a fractional pause, Meri followed.

"My dear," Athna said, not waiting until they were out of earshot. "What a very plain girl! And so surly! I know foreigners have all sorts of notions, but Estra, she can't be more than sixteen!"

Miri glanced at Val Con, noting the frown and the slight stiffness in his shoulders. "What's up?"

He glanced at her, lips relaxing into a faint smile. "That horrid woman . . ."

"Her?" She jerked her chin in the direction of the two old women. "Don't pay her no mind. All hot to hear the latest bad 'bout anybody. Ain't worth getting riled about. Waste of time." She slanted a look at him. "Like that dope of a woman in the store. Tough on her, weren't you? Took her down four pegs—counted 'em. Trouble is, she was only up three."

He grinned, then sobered. "She should not have spoken to you so." Pausing, he considered the street, judged it safe to cross to the truck, and stepped off the curb.

"Really," he continued. "She should not speak to anyone so. Perhaps I have taught her a lesson she will take to heart."

Miri studied the side of his face for a moment. "Gets hard, being treated like a complete know-nothing all the time, don't it?"

He reached up to yank on the truck's door handle and grinned at her, shoulders and face loose once more. "Indeed it does." The door did not open and he pulled again. "Locked."

Miri set her packages on the ground. "I'll get the key from Zhena Trelu," she began, but he shook his head.

"That should not be necessary." He reached into his pocket and pulled out a thin, flexible wire. Balancing on the foot-ledge, he played with wire and keyhole for a bare moment, then nodded and hauled down on the handle.

The door came open with a *pop*.

Grinning, he jumped to the ground, letting the door swing wide behind him, and began to put packages on the bench seat.

Miri shook her head at him. "Lazy."

When all the parcels were stowed, he slammed the door closed, solemnly checking to be sure the lock had caught. "For it would be very bad," he told Miri, offering her his hand, "if our new clothes were stolen by some desperate criminal."

She slid her hand into his. "What next? Back to Zhena Trelu and Badnews Berta?"

"Not just yet," he said, glancing around. "They seem deep

in conversation—and I would like an opportunity to see what is here. Zhena Trelu rushes us about . . ."

"So, we go for a walk," she said, moving with him away from Brillit's and the two figures on the front walk. "How long you figure us for Zhena Trelu's, boss?"

He considered it. "I think we must stay the winter to balance the debt properly." He glanced at her. "Our work has not paid for these clothes, cha'trez."

"Didn't think it had," she said, untroubled. "We stay the winter and pay on our account. Then what?"

"It is also to be hoped that the winter will allow us opportunity to improve our command of Benish, as well as learn to read and write," Val Con continued. "Then we should be able to leave here and seek out a city, if that pleases you. It is generally true that cities offer a wider range of tasks to be performed for wages—whatever wages may consist of here. It may be that we already possess skills that will make it possible for us to be—independent."

"And not get shoved around." Miri sighed. "Sounds great. If I start slacking off on my lessons, you remind me it's so I don't need to be shoved any more, okay? I'll pick right up again."

He tipped his head. "Does it bother you so much? I do not think she means it ill."

She laughed softly. "Naw. It's just been a lot of years since anybody dared shove me. And now this old lady I could bust in half with one hand—" she stopped suddenly. "What in the name of bright blue chosemkis is *that?*"

They wandered over to the window containing the object in question, Val Con's brows pulled slightly together, Miri's eyes wide.

The thing was rectangular in shape and made of some shiny substance that appeared to be metal. The front was glassed in, giving a view of a multitude of coils, wires, and tubes. There were knobs on the top and sides, a piece of thin metal tubing extending from the back, and more knobs under the glass. The whole affair was garlanded with red, yellow, and blue streamers.

"I haven't the faintest notion," Val Con confessed. "A device of some kind, certainly. But what it may be meant to do—or not do . . ." he shrugged. "We can find the store-keeper and ask."

But that proved impossible. The shop door was locked, and a large piece of paper bearing hand-drawn symbols was attached to the inside of the window.

Miri sighed sharply. "We gotta learn how to read. This whole damn world's passing us by."

"In the fullness of time," he said, managing by some trick of his soft voice to evoke Edger's boom. "All things cannot happen at once."

The door to the next shop was open, and from it drifted music. *Real* music, Miri realized. The sound of someone actually playing an instrument, not the recorded music Zhena Trelu listened to on her radio every evening.

Val Con stopped, head tipped, face intent. Miri stood quietly at his side, watching him and listening to the sounds. It was nice, she decided; something like a guitar, but softer, unamplified.

The piece came to an end, and her partner sighed, very softly, and looked at her. "Miri . . ."

"Sure," she said, and squeezed his hand. "Let's go in. Why not?"

"**And** did you hear, Estra, about those horrid Bassilan rebels? Landed on the coast, not two hundred miles from here! Claiming sanctuary, just because our king had made some treaties with their barbaric Tomak years and years ago! Well, of course, the king said no, but do you believe it? The report is they're moving inland. They might even get to Gylles!"

"Poppycock," Zhena Trelu said, looking around uneasily. "The king's militia will have that bunch of troublemakers rounded up in wind's time. Just a bunch of common criminals, that's all they are. As if the king would stand for an invasion, even if Bentrill hasn't been to war since people stopped using bows and arrows and wearing hides."

"Well, perhaps you're right, dear," Zhena Brigsbee conceded sadly. "But, still, Estra, what if some got away!"

But Zhena Trelu was staring down Main Street, looking hard for two short, slender figures.

VANDAR

GYLLES

Hakan Meltz looked up from his guitar and smiled at the two blurry figures in the doorway.

"Hi, there," he said in the casual way that was the despair of his father, the proprietor of the shop in which Hakan sat playing the guitar. His father did not allow guitar-playing in the store—except, of course, if one were demonstrating the instrument's properties to a potential buyer. Happily for Hakan, his father was currently in the capital, attending the king's assembly as alderman for the town of Gylles.

Hakan smiled again as the two figures moved farther into the shop and into the range of his shortsighted eyes.

The woman was toy-tiny, yet there was adult assurance about the set of her shoulders and the straightness with which the large gray eyes regarded him. She returned his smile with a thoroughly friendly grin, holding comfortably onto her companion's hand. The man lacked two inches of Hakan's height, twenty of his pounds, and all of his mustache. He wore his dark hair long for a man, and the line of a recent scar marred one smooth cheek. Smiling, he raised his free hand and indicated the instrument Hakan held.

"Very pretty," he said softly, the words accented in a way that tickled the other's ear. "It is?"

"This?" Hakan offered the instrument, and the shorter man slid his hand out of the woman's to take it. "It's a twelve-string guitar."

"Twelve-string guitar," the man murmured, turning it around and over. He righted it and tried a sweep across the strings with his long fingers, laughing softly at the discord he produced. He placed the fingers of his left hand carefully on the neck, tried another sweep, and nodded as if better satisfied. Working slowly, using a combination of strumming and plucking, he managed to pull a melody line out of the guitar while Hakan watched in growing puzzlement.

The guitar was strange to the man—that much seemed certain. But he worked with it as if he had once played something similar and knew what to expect of wood and gut.

The man came to himself with a start, glancing up with a smile of apology. "Forgive me," he said, handing the instrument back with obvious reluctance, fingers lingering on the neck. "It has been long," he said, as if to explain. "I am—" He frowned and moved his hands in what Hakan thought might be exasperation. "It is to be hungry," he concluded, head tipped as if he were unsure that he would be properly understood.

But if there was one thing Hakan did understand it was the hunger for making music. "Lost your piece?" he asked, somehow certain that only catastrophe would have separated this individual from whatever it was he played. He put the guitar aside and stood, waving his hand to indicate the rows of musical instruments. "What's your specialty?" he began, feeling an impulse his father was certain to bewail rising within him. "Maybe we can work out a—"

From the back of the shop, the woman—forgotten in the music—called something out, emphasizing it with three musical keys pushed at random.

The man's brows shot up, and he looked at Hakan, eyes intensely green. "That?"

"Piano," Hakan told him. "You play *piano?*" But the man was already gone, heading toward the back of the store.

It was apparent that the man did play piano—or something so close to piano that it made little difference. He spent a few moments exploring the instrument, eyebrows lifting as he discovered foot pedals; running his fingers up and down the keyboard, he located true C, sharps, flats, and scales. Then his fingers moved, half-joking, it seemed to Hakan, and produced a tinkling little tune reminiscent of cool summer evenings playing hide-'n-seek.

His hands shifted, up-board and down, calling forth less

childlike music. The woman leaning against the piano's side laughed softly and sang a line in a weird, chopping language, and the man grinned and moved his hands again, playing a clear intro riff.

The woman grinned at Hakan, straightened, and began to sing. He stood rock-still until the song was done, then dove across the room for his guitar.

It was thus that Kem Darnill found them some time later: Hakan painstakingly working out the melody; the piano correcting him now and then. Setting her books on the counter, she went quietly toward the threesome, trying not to disturb the music making.

The man at the piano looked up and smiled at her. "Hakan," he murmured.

"Hmm?" Hakan looked up, caught the other's nod, and turned his head.

"Kemmy!" He was on his feet, his smile a warmth she could feel. Sliding his hand into hers, he brought her forward.

"Kemmy, this is Cory and Miri. Cory plays piano, and Miri sings. Amazing stuff—you never heard anything like it. I've never heard anything like it, anyhow." He grinned at the pair on the piano bench. "This," he announced proudly, "is my fiancée, Kem."

Kem felt herself blush but managed a smile at the two strangers. Cory smiled and inclined his head in a formal little gesture; Miri grinned at her.

"Hi," Miri said. Her accent made Kem blink. Still, they seemed nice enough, and they were musicians . . .

"Oh, goodness!" she said suddenly, leaning forward. "Cory and Meri?"

"Cory," the man agreed, tipping his head.

"Miri," the woman said.

"Zhena Trelu's looking for both of you," Kem told them. "She's awful worried—thinks you've gotten lost or something." She hesitated, remembering that Zhena Trelu had said that they did not speak much Benish.

But the woman—Miri?—had turned to her companion with an expression of comic woe on her face. "Zhena Trelu!" she cried. "*Bad* us!" And she dropped her head against his arm, shoulders shaking.

Cory grinned and patted her gently on the back. Then he sighed and looked down at the piano, raising his hand and letting it fall to his knee.

"I don't get it," Hakan said, looking from Kem to his two new friends.

"They're staying with Zhena Trelu," Kem explained rapidly. "Helping her out around the farm. She brought them into town today to get winter clothes, and they wandered off—and that rattlepated Athna Brigsbee's out there calling them thieves and worse!"

"But that's great!" Hakan cried, turning to the other man. "Cory, listen to me—Zhena Trelu's got a piano! Real nice one—a hundred times better than this piece of junk," he added, with a fine disregard for the basic precepts of business.

Cory's brows pulled together, and he shook his head. "Zhena Trelu? No piano, Hakan."

Miri shifted at his side, murmuring something in a language that jarred on Kem's ears. Cory glanced at her and then at Hakan.

"There is a place—" He stopped, frowning, then sighed. Carefully he lifted his hands, wove the slim fingers together, and held the knot out to Hakan, one eyebrow up.

"Locked? A locked room, maybe?" Hakan looked at Kem, who could only shrug. "That makes sense. It was her zamir's piano, Cory. He had it set up in a room by itself. Could be she locked the room when he died—ought to let you play it, though. Regular sport, old Zhena Trelu. You just ask her about it, and I'm sure—"

"Hakan—" Cory was holding his hands out as if to stop Hakan's enthusiasm. "Too many words, Hakan."

"Ah, wind—I forgot." He turned back to Kem. "What were you supposed to do with them, once you found them?"

"They were supposed to be going to the library. Zhena Trelu went there, in case the two of them got ahead of schedule. I was supposed to take them to her, if I ran into them." She giggled. "I guess this qualifies as running into them."

"Well, then that's simple," Hakan decided, waving at the two foreigners. "Let's get ourselves down to the library. *I'll* ask Zhena Trelu for you, Cory."

"What about the store?" Kem demanded, vowing that nothing would prevent her from witnessing the expression on Athna Brigsbee's face when Zhena Trelu's charges were restored to her.

But Hakan was already turning the Open/Closed sign to the Closed side and pulling the key from his pocket.

"All for one," he said, waving them out the door with a flourish.

"And one for all," Kem said, laughing.

Hakan locked the door and turned up the street, slipping one hand into Kem's and the other into Miri's, as a child might. Hand-linked and laughing, the four of them began to run.

LIAD

TREALLA FANTROL

THAT INFORMATION IS RESTRICTED.

Nova had swept the screen clear and entered a second, more potent, ID before the cat lounging by the keyboard had time to blink.

There was perhaps a heartbeat of hesitation, then the response from Central Information:

THAT INFORMATION IS RESTRICTED.

Nova swore, though perhaps not as violently as she might have. "Restricted from the Council of Clans! Who dares it?"

Neither cat nor screen ventured an opinion, and after a moment of frowning thought, she reached for the keyboard once more.

Central took rather more time with the new request, but finally the letters began to appear, one by one, as if the computer itself was perplexed by the answer it had to give.

UNIVERSAL ACCESS OVERRIDE. REQUESTS REMANDED
TO JAE'LABA STATION. ACCESS DENIED.

"So." Here at last, was the germ of something.

STATIONMAP, she demanded of Central. There was no hesitation at all. The screen flowered interconnecting lines, varicolored rhombi marking primary, secondary, and tertiary stations.

Nova paused, considering the flashing bit of purple that denoted the station at Jelaza Kazone. Korval's Own House, with Korval's own tricks up its sleeve, age upon age, Cantra to Daav . . .

"Not yet," she whispered, and touched QUERY.

JAE'LABA LOCATION?

In the upper left-hand corner a tertiary indicator glowed a brighter gold and began to pulse.

"As simple as that?" She was Liaden and mistrusted simplicity. She was of Korval and smelled a trap. And yet . . .

DETAIL, she commanded; and watched the indicator enlarge as another map grew about it, showing the familiar outline of Solcintra. A building took shape, enclosing the pulsing gold, and a legend appeared at the base of the screen.

SCOUT HEADQUARTERS.

"But Val Con's a Scout, after all," Anthora said reasonably a short time later.

"They denied him!" Nova cried, breaking the pattern of her pacing to face her sister. "Assigned to the Department of the Interior, they said! And information about the Department of the Interior is restricted—to my code and to the Council of Clans."

"Oh." Anthora bent to the desk, offering a finger for its occupant to sniff. "Good day, Lord Merlin."

Nova swallowed a sigh. She should have known better than to open such a discussion with Anthora, but Shan was gone with the *Passage,* and she was further robbed of Pat Rin's caustic intelligence . . .

"If a station is in a place," Anthora asked, rubbing Merlin's ears, "must it mean that it belongs to the owners of the place?"

Nova froze. "No. No, of course not. But—the Scouts . . ."

"Scouts are not gods," the wooly-headed baby of the family commented. "Val Con said Scouts spend a great deal of time mucking about in the mud and running afoul of custom." She looked up. "It's a simple thing to shunt information from one terminal to another. Even simpler to hide information an honest user would have no reason to look for, then dump what's hidden, with no one the wiser. A tertiary station? Who would trouble to invade something so unimportant? Who would think to look for tampering?"

The idea took simplicity and snarled it with a hundred knots, basing all on the honor of Liad's Scouts. It supposed an enemy more dangerous than an unrecorded organization disinclined to answer questions. Nova sat on the arm of a chair, staring at her sister with wondering violet eyes. The theory appealed, yes. It appealed mightily.

"The Scouts," Anthora continued, "have no reason to lie. Were our brother eklykt'i—were he even dead!—these things have come to those of Korval in the past, have they not? And the Scouts sent word, just as to any other."

"Truth." The melant'i of the Scouts was not in doubt. It was more possible to consider a new and secret enemy than to consider that the Scouts might have lied. "They say what they know. It worries me that they may not know all. It worries me more that this Department of the Interior has its eyes upon us while we are blind to them." She closed her eyes while Anthora bent to scratch Merlin under the chin, and for several minutes his purrs were the only sound heard in the room.

Then Nova snapped to her feet, brushed past sister and cat, and leaned to the keyboard.

"What do you, sister?"

"Whoever they are, they must have money. Mr. dea'Gauss may— Good day, Sor Dal. Has Mr. dea'Gauss leisure to speak?"

"I will ascertain, Eldema. One moment."

Somewhat less than a moment later the wait-signal cleared

to show the old gentleman himself. He inclined his head respectfully. "Lady Nova."

"Mr. dea'Gauss. It's good of you to leave your work to speak to me." She followed the form with well-hidden impatience, mustering one of her thin smiles.

"I am always at Korval's service, your ladyship. How may I assist you?"

Gods, Nova thought. What can it portend that Mr. dea'-Gauss becomes brusque? She moved a hand in acknowledgment of truth spoken and looked into the old dark eyes. "I desire information regarding the business we spoke of earlier, sir. Its funding and its expenditures. I desire this urgently."

The old eyes did not flicker. "Your ladyship is wise to check all contingencies before committing her resources. I shall see to it."

"My thanks to you, sir."

"Line dea'Gauss serves Korval," he said calmly. "Now as ever. With your ladyship's permission?"

"Of course."

The screen went blank.

"Mr. dea'Gauss is worried," Anthora said at her shoulder.

Nova glanced over. "You can read over comm lines?"

She looked surprised and thoughtful. "I don't think so . . . But I didn't need to, just now. It was obvious."

This from one who barely noticed rain from sun! Nova hesitated over a question and, Anthora-like, the other plucked it out of air and gave answer.

"Shannie told me to help you. Not," she added with a sniff, "that he had to. And before he left he said I must pay close attention to—things—and not be backward about speaking my thoughts. He said that there are often several ways to look at something, and I mustn't assume that because I've seen one or even two ways that you've seen the same ways. He said you need to see as much as possible, to keep Korval safe."

"Did he? I'm in debt for his concern."

"Don't be angry at Shannie, sister. He'll be searching, too, you know. And he has Priscilla with him. I taught her how to see Val Con." Her brow wrinkled slightly. "At least, she can't see him very clearly—and I'm not at all sure she sees him the same way I do. And it tires her, I think. But she has—a sense—of him. And of his lady. She'll be able to tell if the *Passage* comes near them."

"Will she?" Nova tried to catch her mental breath. It was often thus with Anthora, who took such abilities as easily as sight and hearing, even though the very language had to be bent and twisted in order for her to speak of them. "And can you—see—Val Con with his lady now? Are they well?"

Anthora nodded vigorously. "Val Con's more Val Con than he's been for—oh, a long time! And his lady is very bright."

She spoke with such clear approval that Nova found herself comforted a little.

"I'm going for a walk before Prime," Anthora said softly. "Come with me, do."

A walk? With Val Con yet missing, even though he was "more Val Con than he'd been"—and gods alone knew what that meant! Had he been ill? What was she thinking of, that supposed lifemate, that she was so careless of him?

"Sister . . ." Anthora slid her arms about Nova's waist in a wholly unexpected hug. "He is well. More—I believe him happy. We search; we do what we might, as well as we might. Val Con would never grudge you an hour's pleasure when there is nothing more for you to do."

Nova hugged back, cuddling the warmth of her sister's body against her. "Truth . . ." She stood away, summoning the second smile in an hour. "Let us go for a walk, then. The day does seem fair."

LIAD

TREALLA FANTROL

The house was too empty.

Nova sighed. The information in front of her was important, or it would not be on her screen. Mr. dea'Gauss was not in the habit of bothering her with trifles. Yet the house was too empty: the children, by her own order, taken by their tutors to the Port for half a day's holiday; Anthora gone with the twins to visit Lady yo'Lanna ... There was no one to claim her attention, no reason to make a decision immediately. The words on the screen not yet urgent enough to—

She blinked at the carpet, which was not blue enough by half, and what was that tiny screen doing *there* on the desk, when only that moment she had been looking at the large, amber colored—

"No!"

Nova pushed back at the Memory, half-sick with the effort to separate the room *she* knew from that other—long gone, changed, changed again—knowing even as she thought that it was useless if the time was come. Dismay rode briefly over loathing; dismay of the power that the past generations of Korval women had over her. Edger had addressed her as "She Who Remembers;" she wondered—and then was certain—if Val Con had explained her "talent" of reliving the memories of those long dead. Loathing rose again and she pushed at the Memory, hard.

The Memory expanded, the long-ago room taking on more and more substance, as the room *now* faded.

Nova recalled her own past with guilt, wondering which of her decisions or experiences might be forced on some unsuspecting child or unwelcoming grandmother—

Vertigo overtook her; she clutched at the table, then

squared her shoulders and walked to the couch. She sat with
unaccustomed heaviness, half expecting the thing to be nothing more than a Memory-phantom, substantial and actual to
all but her body.

Carefully, striving to put bitterness and loathing and dismay all aside, she took a deep breath—and another, began
the relaxing sequence the Healers had given her . . .

And it was there, as searing as her memory of the argument with Shan.

A Liaden youth, hair clipped tight in a style dating him
hundreds of years in the past, was arguing. She knew him,
ached to grant him his demand, yet denied him, nonetheless.

"Yes, Ker Lin, I did hear you. I believe *you* have not heard
me. I am not speaking as your aunt in this. I am speaking as
Delm!"

In the part of her mind shielded by the Healer's magic,
Nova recalled the name, recalled a much older face from the
portrait gallery at Jelaza Kazone—Ker Lin yos'Phelium,
seven hundred and twelve years dead.

His face went rigid. "I hear the Delm," he said, courtesy
thinly sheathing his anger. "I request the Delm listen once
again."

What was this, after all? Ker Lin's Delm at that age must
have been old Renoka yos'Phelium.

A flash of impatience was recalled, and a flare of almost
feral love, before she gave him haughty leave. "You may
speak. But you must offer more or different information,
boy! I grow weary of hearing your 'musts!' "

Eyes. Gods and demons, what eyes the child had! Silver
bright, shining, hypnotic—and the will!

"I have Seen that I shall join the Scouts in the spring," he
said, with some fair semblance of calm. "I shall not wed until
after my third mission."

"And I say you will do so now! I will see a yos'Phelium
contract-wed into yo'—"

"Silence!" He gestured, and her voice choked in her throat;
her bones rocked with the force of the command, and her
blood chilled. She stood, moving as if against strong wind,
found the energy needful to shake off his will, and glared

down at him, the one of all of them who would be Delm . . .
ah, yes, if he lived so long!

"Defend your actions!" she ordered, the High Tongue
crackling with the force of her own will. "Defend, or be
gone!"

His face lost some of its luster, it seemed, within a moment, to grow old and to fall away almost into the face of the
child he had been, with tears at the corners of his eyes; then
his eyes—only silver—were sad.

"If you will insist," he said, and she tried to tell herself it
was merely halfling dignity she heard in his voice. "I have
said that I have Seen what will happen, and I am taught not
to foretell to others—"

"The melant'i of the situation, Ker Lin! We are alone: If
you had done this in public, I would have had to send you
away at once! I shall need to know."

Suddenly he looked defeated and small, and then, in an instant, he became a man.

"You will see a yos'Phelium contract-wed into yo'Hala,"
he said very quietly. "The child shall come to yos'Phelium,
and the alliance thus formed will last for many, many years.
I shall join the Scouts, and after my third mission I shall lifemate. Later I will be Delm."

Renoka bowed to that, believing all, because already she
had believed half. "And in this present case, my wise? Who
shall fulfill the contract with yo'Hala in your stead?"

"You, my aunt and Delm."

Blank astonishment was recalled, along with the beginning
of a suspicion. "You know that Tan El yo'Lanna has my
promise to wed him, when *Zipper* is next in port."

The eyes were silver ice; she thought she saw pity and
knew, but would not allow herself to know. Selfishly she
made him say it.

"Tell me, Ker Lin."

"Let be!" Pain roughened his voice, not command; but she
was pitiless in her own pain.

"You are required!"

He bowed, then, very, very gently. "Aunt Renoka, forgive
me." He paused, then looked at her straightly. "*Zipper's* drive
failed in the outer arm. The cargo has been orbited, and news

of its location will come to me when I am Delm." He paused and sighed. "The attempt to restart the drive was catastrophic. Dan Art yos'Galan alone has survived."

He bowed again, with all the love and care he could fit into the gesture, and left quietly.

"Let be!" Renoka cried out to the echoing room. "Let be!"

She called up flight schedules and requested docking information, angrily scrubbing at the tears that would neither stop nor take on urgency. The silver eyes—she sighed and cried the harder.

Alone in the house, Renoka looked over the blue carpet, waiting. After a while someone—not Ker Lin—came to tell her that Dan Art yos'Galan was rescued. She was already dressed in mourning when they arrived.

Nova opened her eyes and saw the proper furniture and the amber screen; she reached up and angrily scrubbed the tears from her face.

What had she touched? What had she done that demanded that Memory?

She glanced at the material on the screen: a list of proposed alliances and known wedding negotiations. With a clarity she mistrusted she heard Ker Lin's voice.

"Let be!"

She swept her hand across the controls savagely.

"Jeeves!" she yelled into the air. "Jeeves, bring me some tea!" The robot arrived in seconds, bulky engine to a train of three cats.

"Tea and company, I'm afraid, Miss Nova." Jeeves set the service down on the low table by the window, poured, and stepped back.

Nova bent down to pick up the middle cat, a sorry mop of varicolored stripes named Kifer. He began to purr and knead immediately, and Nova rubbed her face in his outrageously, wonderfully soft fur.

"Let them stay," she said to the robot. "I can use some company just now."

LIAD

ENVOLIMA CITY

Tyl Von sig'Alda sat in the quarters assigned him
and frowned at the graph hung over the desk. Several spe-
cialists had provided the uniform opinion that the coils of the
ruined ship where yos'Phelium and the female had been
stranded might have been coaxed to provide one Jump, given
an individual with the knowledge and the will. The computer
took his opinions as fact and constructed a portrait of the
Jump-sites so attainable.

Records rendered a portrait of Val Con yos'Phelium as a
man of will and wide knowledge, from a Clan that valued
ships and the lore of ships above all else. It was utterly con-
ceivable that he had demanded and received of the tired coils
one last effort, that he was already on some world or other,
evading debriefing or striving valiantly to win home.

The female . . . He fingered the report recently acquired
from several highly confidential sources. The female was
negligible; a mere Terran mercenary, lacking education or
any other discipline besides her skill at arms. True it was that
she had survived the disaster of Klamath; also true was the
fact that she had spent months afterward in rehabilitative
therapy for the abuse of the substance Lethecronaxion—
Cloud, as so many Terrans called it, kin to the drug utilized
by the Department to induce its agents to complete recall.

The function of Cloud, however, was to inhibit memory.
sig'Alda experienced shadowy revulsion. The female was a
brute; a killer addicted to a drug that wiped her yesterdays
from experience as quickly as she lived them. How came Val
Con yos'Phelium to travel with such a one?

If she were a tool . . . He ran the odds, consciously adding pertinent factors from yos'Phelium's record and data gained during training.

.8

Well within the realm of possibility, then, that the female was but a convenient tool, held in check by her dependence upon the drug—and upon the supplier of the drug.

So then: The mission on Lufkit had gone well enough of itself, but something unknowable had gone amiss between its completion and the time Val Con yos'Phelium was to rendezvous with his transport home. Sometime after the completion of his mission and before the firefight between Lufkit police and members of the local chapter of Juntavas—substantiated in several popular newspapers from Lufkit—Val Con yos'Phelium had acquired the services of Miri Robertson, retired mercenary and former bodyguard.

Suppose that yos'Phelium had understood the situation to be worsening. Suppose further that he acknowledged sleep a physiological necessity. It would certainly be prudent, in a case where one expected disaster around every corner, to engage something to guard one's sleep. Chance had provided something well versed in guarding and competent with her weapons—and the solution had worked: Circumstances showed as much.

Provided with a solution that had answered so admirably in one instance—and perhaps yet unsure of what might await him—yos'Phelium takes the female with him aboard the Clutch ship. She is competent in her brutish way, and even loyal—he, of course, having taken care to provide himself with a supply of Lethecronaxion beforehand.

sig'Alda ran the odds once more.

.8

Well enough. The female was but a tool to yos'Phelium's hand—provided by chance, honed by necessity. He had been foolish to suspect anything else. What other use had a well-trained agent for a bitch Terran, after all?

Reasoning reconstructed to satisfactory tolerance, sig'Alda pulled the keyboard toward him, beginning to plot the coordinates of the planets on the graph that hung over the desk. Several of the worlds represented there were Interdicted. However, the duties of Scouts took them to many strange orbits, including those about Interdicted Worlds. Best he consider any reports the Scouts had on files regarding those particular Forbiddens before he made further plans.

VANDAR

SPRINGBREEZE FARM

Zhena Trelu left her boarders to clear up the sup-per dishes and made her way down the hall, key clenched tight in her hand, second thoughts buzzing in her head. The Meltz boy would be here soon, to tune Jerry's piano, just as she had said he could. Except now she was not so sure.

She paused at the door, looking from key to lock, telling herself hopefully that three years was a long time, telling herself that maybe the key did not work anymore, after all this time . . .

Undecided, she fidgeted with the key; then, with a sharp head-shake, she clenched her fingers, her hand moving toward the pocket of her apron.

Behind her she heard a noise.

She jerked around—and there was Meri, gray eyes huge in her pointed face, one hand tentatively extended. "Zhena Trelu, please. Cory play yes."

It was said in the mildest possible tone, but the old woman clutched at the spark of resentment the words ignited, using that warmth to chase away the cold confusion.

"Why in wind should he?" she demanded, knowing it was unreasonable, but not caring. *Hers* was the loss, and how should that—that *child*, her husband standing healthy at her side, presume to judge . . . "You two are supposed to be working for me, not taking over my house! Telling me what to do. That's Jerry's piano! Nobody ever touched it but him. *Nobody.* And I should just hand it over to some—*foreigner* I first laid eyes on three weeks ago? Why? Like as not, the pair of you're only out to rob me—"

No!" The girl's voice cut passionately across the stream of nonsense. "Good Cory! *Patient* Cory! Works hard—fixes— helps. Helps you. Helps me. Who helps Cory?" She flung her hands out, and Zhena Trelu saw the shine of tears in the gray eyes. "Zhena Trelu. *Please*. Cory play yes."

And what good, the old woman thought suddenly, sanely, was a piano to a dead man? She closed her eyes, feeling suddenly close to tears herself. Jerrel Trelu had been a kind man; no one should go hungry for music in his zhena's house.

Slowly she opened her fingers around the key, turned back, and fumbled a moment with the lock before twisting the knob and pushing the door wide.

"Thank you, Zhena Trelu," Meri whispered behind her; but when she turned back, the girl was gone.

The piano was badly in need of tuning. Hakan worked carefully, Cory at his elbow, watching everything he did. On the doublechair to the right of the instrument, Miri and Kem had their heads together over a book. Kem's cool voice occasionally reached Hakan—she seemed to be teaching Miri the alphabet.

Zhena Trelu sat in the single chair on the other side of the lamp, ostensibly reading, but Cory, looking at her now and then from under long lashes, thought she had not turned a page since sitting down.

The tuning finally done, Hakan closed the case and waved Cory toward the keyboard, grinning. But the slighter man hesitated, then drifted soundlessly over to stand before the old woman and her book.

"Zhena Trelu," he said softly, and she looked up, frowning.

Slowly, with full pomp, he made her the bow of one who acknowledges an unpayable debt. "Thank you, Zhena Trelu. Very."

She sniffed. "Just don't you let me find you shirking your work and coming in here to play, hear me? Work comes first."

"Yes, Zhena Trelu." He smiled. "I will work."

She sniffed again, mindful of three pairs of young eyes on her. "Well, what're you waiting for? *You* were the one who wanted to play." She flicked her hand toward the piano. "So, *play.*"

He grinned and moved back to the instrument, slid onto the bench, and ran his fingers up and down the keys. Then he began to play, straightly and without flourish, the main line of the piece Hakan had been running through his guitar, three days past.

Hakan gave a shout and grabbed his guitar, taking up the weaving minor thread.

In the doublechair, Miri and Kem set aside the book to listen to the music. In the single chair, Zhena Trelu sat rapt.

In the manner of such things, one song led to another. At some point during the evening, wine was opened and poured; and, in the manner of *those* things, was found too soon to be gone. A little time later Zhena Trelu excused herself with a yawn and went upstairs to her bedroom, waving aside an offer of an escort from Kem and Meri.

Her departure brought Hakan to an awareness of the hour, and he and Kem bundled themselves together, eliciting promises from their new friends to come to supper on Marin evening and making arrangements for Hakan to pick them up.

When the taillights of Hakan's car had finally faded, Miri leaned back against Val Con with a sigh. "Boss, I think I'm drunk."

She heard him laugh softly and felt his fingers tighten where they rested on her shoulders. "I am afraid that I am also drunk, cha'trez."

"Couple of saps," she judged, turning around and grinning up at him. "*One* of us is supposed to stay sober to carry the other one home and get 'em in bed. Now what?"

He appeared to consider the problem while he laid his arm about her waist and drew her into the hallway. "I suppose," he said, locking the door with great care, "that we must then carry each other."

"Okay," Miri agreed, sliding her arm around his waist.

Leaning on each other, they gained their bedroom without mishap.

It was not yet dawn when Val Con drifted awake. He kept his eyes closed, feeling Miri pressed tightly against his side, her head on his shoulder, one arm flung across his chest. He was conscious first of a warm contentment; then he heard the song.

Though "heard" was not precisely the correct word; nor was "song." Cautiously, eyes still closed, he sought the song that was heard only within his head and found it, a thing of surpassing brightness and warmth, singing blithely to itself—and tasting strongly of hunch.

He regarded it for some time, remembering the old tales, knowing what it must be, joy building within him.

The gods make you a gift, he told himself gently.

And the part of him that was Korval replied: As it should be. The gods owe much.

Alive-and-well, sang the song-that-was-not-a-song from its joylit corner of his self. *Miri-alive. Miri-well.*

Fear surfaced for a moment as he recalled the man he now was. But then he recalled that his lifemate had shown no wizardly skills at all, so might not be able to hear him—and the fear was vanquished.

He moved a little in the predawn, curling around the woman beside him, burying his face in the cloud of her hair. Warm within, warm without, Val Con slid back into sleep.

VANDAR

SPRINGBREEZE FARM

Val Con sat at the piano, letting his fingers roam randomly over the keys. The sound of Zhena Trelu's radio

reached him from down the hall, and somewhere close by
Borril groaned and shifted. He wondered where Miri was and
moved his attention for the briefest of instants to the song of
her and its joyous message: *Alive-and-well, alive-and-
well . . .*

Lips relaxing into a smile, Val Con turned his attention to
the notes he played, ear snagging on a series of three that recalled the piece he and Hakan had been working on the previous night. Shaking his head, he ran lightly through the
song, then returned to the beginning, playing in earnest.

Best you practice, he told himself with mock sternness. If
Hakan succeeds in getting the two of us a job playing music,
you must be ready and able.

He was unsure of the likelihood of such work, but Hakan
hardly spoke of anything else. It seemed there was a fair of
some type looming, and Hakan's heart was set upon the two
of them playing in one of the exhibition halls. The wages, in
Hakan's estimation, were barely less than a joke—in fact, he
had suggested that Cory keep the whole sum himself, since
Zhena Trelu did not see fit to provide either of her charges
with pocketpaper. No, one was given to understand that the
sole reason for playing—besides the playing itself—was the
exposure. All the world, in Hakan's eyes, attended the Winterfair at Gylles.

A soundless something called him from his reflections, and
he glanced up to see Miri hesitating in the doorway. He let
his fingers slow on the keys and smiled at her. "Hello, Miri."

"Hi." Her answering smile was apologetic. "I didn't mean
to bother you. Left my book."

"It's no bother," he said, watching her go gracefully
across the room to the doublechair. She had taken to wearing her hair loose of late, which he found pleased him
greatly. It seemed they both considered this world—this
place—a sanctuary.

Miri had found her book and was turning to go.

"You might stay," he said, wishing she would. "Unless my
playing will disturb you?"

She grinned. "Naw. Thought *I'd* bother *you.*"

"It's no bother," he repeated gently. "I would be pleased if
you'd stay."

"Rather listen to you than Zhena Trelu's radio stories any day," she said, curling promptly into the doublechair and opening the book.

"High praise," he murmured, and grinned when she laughed. His fingers touched the keys, and he began to play once more.

He moved from song to song, working through the list of eleven that made up their scanty repertoire. The music had his whole attention, though now and then he heard a small sound as Miri turned a page.

The last of the eleven was a slippery thing requiring sharply curtailed ripples from the keyboard, as well as a jagged staircase of mismatched notes reaching toward an impossible crescendo. Such a line would have been bad enough on an omnichora, yet some demented creativity had thought it suitable for an instrument as clumsy as the piano . . .

Sighing at his failure yet again to realize the line's potential, he glanced up and saw Miri curled in the chair, head bent over her book, lamplight glittering over the red wealth of her hair.

Unbidden, his fingers moved on the keys, building a line like laughter, like something lovely and wild half-seen, poised to fly away. His other hand shifted and found the undercurrent of strength, of constancy and surprising courage. The two lines melded, became one, separated for a time, and rejoined, each making the other whole. His fingers found an end of it too soon, and he glanced up, aware that the volume of his playing had increased.

Miri was smiling. "That was pretty," she said. "What was it?"

He returned her smile. "You."

"Me?" Her disbelief was apparent.

"Certainly, you," he returned matter-of-factly. "Listen." He moved his hands again, picking out a limping, aged phrase, frail without fragility, predictable and obstinate.

"Zhena Trelu," he murmured, aware that Miri had left her chair and was drawing closer.

Shifting again, he played a bump-and-tumble bass line, and she immediately laughed and cried out, "Borril!"

"None other," he said, grinning, caught up in the game.

Gods, it had been years since he had indulged in such foolery!

Fingers touched keys, and Miri stirred. "Kem."

"Correct again," he said, sliding down the bench to make room for her to sit beside him. Hands at the top of the scale, he ran through a chaos of high-pitched chords, sharps and flats mixed indiscriminately. "And Hakan, of course . . ."

She chuckled and sat on the edge of the bench, careful, it seemed, not to touch him.

He tipped his head and began a foghorn melody, running a not-quite-correct underline interspersed here and there with a hasty flutter of sound from the higher end of the board.

"Edger," Miri said, and he nodded.

Her ear was excellent: He ran through the short list of their mutual acquaintances, and she named each unfailingly, though one made her crow with laughter even as she protested, "Oh, no! Poor Jason!"

His hands shifted again, building a solidly balanced, stately top-line, the undermelody as uncompromising as stone, except—did Miri detect the faintest hint of laughter? Of—informality? If it existed, it was a very ghost. Val Con's fingers had stopped, and the last note vibrated into stillness before she shook her head.

"Got me there. Don't think I know him."

"Her," he corrected. "My sister Nova."

"Pleasure, I'm sure," Miri said with a certain lack of enthusiasm. "Hope I never do anything to make her mad."

He laughed softly and began another line, this one gentle, relaxed, almost absurdly good-natured—until one heard the steel beneath the surface, sharp as any blade. "Shan," he murmured, then moved his hands once more.

The new tune was like a glitter of dark snowflakes seen briefly in the glare of a lightning bolt, like kittens giving each other chase upon waking. "Anthora," he said.

He sat back and inclined his head slightly. "Clan Korval," he told her. He reached to cover the keyboard.

Miri's hand on his sleeve stopped him. "Somebody missing, ain't there?"

He lifted an eyebrow.

"Val Con?" Miri asked. "Seems to me I heard he was Second Speaker."

"Ah, well," he said. "Val Con." His fingers dropped carelessly to the keys, playing a quick ripple of sound in the midrange that was merely an echo of his murmuring voice; then his hands lifted and brought the cover gently down into place.

"Oh," Miri said.

He turned to look at her and noticing the tension in the small muscles around her eyes. "Cha'trez? What is wrong?"

She frowned and moved her shoulders slightly, as if to shrug the problem away. "I—it's stupid, I guess. Just seems like you try to hide yourself from me, or something."

"Do I?" He turned on the bench to face her fully. "I am your friend. And your partner. And your lifemate. Do I not please you, Miri?"

"Please?" She looked surprised, then shifted sharply to sit astride the bench and looked him fully in the face. Her own was wide open, so that he knew the answer before she spoke it.

"I love you so much it hurts. So much I try not to think about it, 'cause I get scared." She clamped her jaw.

He extended a hand and stroked her cheek. "Such a large present, cha'trez, for someone you do not know." He tipped his head. "And you knew me well enough, did you not, to intercede with Zhena Trelu so I might have use of this piano?"

"How'd you know that?" She was regarding him with some suspicion. He stroked her cheek again, moving his fingers to trace the curve of her brows.

"Zhena Trelu told me; so I would know for certain how well I was loved." He ran his fingers down the line of her jaw. "You are so beautiful . . ." There was an ache of wonder in his voice.

She reached up to brush the hair from his eyes. "Val Con?" There was a pause while she searched his face and eyes; he felt as if she were searching his soul and held his breath, afraid. "You love me," she said finally and very softly, as if the discovery were a new one.

"Miri," he said suddenly, shifting into the most intimate of modes, nearly singing the Low Liaden words, "you are my wisdom and my laughter, the song of my heart, my home. Best-loved friend; wife and lover . . ."

She did not understand; the words meant nothing to her, though he saw her following the song of his voice. Almost sharply, he brought both hands up and ran his fingers into her hair, holding her so her eyes had to look into his. Consciously keeping his voice pitched for intimate speech, he reached for the hopelessly inadequate Terran words.

"I love you, Miri; you are my joy."

Releasing her, he sat back and was conscious of intense pleasure when she moved her hand to take his.

"Lifemates means what it says?" she asked, smiling at him just a little.

He raised a brow. "What else would it mean?"

"Just checking." She stood, pulling him with her. "Let's go to bed. Betcha it's after midnight . . ."

DUTIFUL PASSAGE

"Priscilla," Lina inquired with the straight-forwardness of friendship, "is this wise?"

The other woman looked up from unbuckling her belt, her slim brows arched in surprise. "It's necessary," she said, and laid the belt smoothly aside.

Lina stifled a sigh. Believing in necessity, Priscilla would pursue her mad course, whether her friend consented to watch or no.

"Perhaps it might wait," she ventured, watching Priscilla slip her trousers off and fold them neatly atop her shirt, "until Shan is on the ship? He only trades until local dusk, Priscilla. Surely time is not of such—"

Lina had suspected all along that this enterprise had none of Shan yos'Galan's smile—which boded not so well for Lina Faaldom, if she had to seek him out to say "Old friend, your heart slipped away while I watched her; and the way of her going is such that a Healer may neither follow nor find . . ."

The bed shifted slightly as Priscilla lay down and smiled up at her friend. "I'm not in any danger, Lina. You'll be with me, after all."

The smaller woman laughed. "Yes, assuredly! The mouse shall guard the lion."

Priscilla nodded, quite serious. "Who better? You will watch closely and not rush into danger, as another lion might; and so keep yourself safe and able to assist." She smiled again, softly. "Wise Lina."

"Pah!" Lina banished flattery with a flick of a tiny hand. "Well, and if you must, you might as well—and quickly."

"Yes. You have the Words I gave you?"

"Of course." *Priscilla!* Lina was to cry, if there came a hint that things were not as they should be. *Priscilla, come home!* Heart-words, Priscilla had named them, saying that she would hear that phrase and return, no matter how far the distance.

The ways of the dramliz are wondrous, indeed, Lina thought, and clutched the heartwords tightly in memory.

Beside her, Priscilla's breathing had slowed and deepened, the pulse in her throat beating with alarming slowness. Healer-sense showed the pattern she recognized as Priscilla Mendoza pulled in upon itself, so dense it seemed that even outer eyes must see it.

And as she watched, that strangely dense pattern began to rise, until inner eyes placed it above the sleeping body; then even farther above, rising toward the cabin's ceiling, trailing behind it in a single thread no thicker than a strand of silk. Rising still, it faded through the ceiling and was lost to all Lina's sight.

The clamor of the galaxy was easier to ignore than it had been the last time. No sooner was the template in place than the aura it represented was found, flaring among the multitudes of lesser lights like a nova amid mere stars.

She approached slowly, mindful of the lesson that haste had taught her, traveling a time that could not be measured over a distance that seemed at once very great and no more than a roll from one side to another to embrace one who lay beside her.

Suddenly she was very close. Cautiously she opened a path from herself to him—and very nearly recoiled.

Temple training saved her from that error; her own necessity drew her close again, to examine what was there.

Protections. The boy she had known had encompassed no such walls and ramparts, though he had been adept enough at shielding himself. But even at that, with him awake, as he was now, and she with the need and the Aspect upon her, there should have been yet the small ways in, where one might enter and leave a seed-thought, to grow to suggestion and then into dream and so be absorbed into consciousness.

Disconcerted, she brought template against pattern, thinking that she had somehow erred in her urgency—but no. There could not be two such, matching, edge on edge, protected or wide open. And witch-sense brought her a bare hint of the passion that had previously overflowed him, burning still, but deep within, a bonfire at the heart of a citadel.

Val Con! She hurled his name, hoping for a crack in those protections, perhaps even a recognition.

He heard her, of that much was she certain, but the walls stood firm. Almost she turned to leave, defeated—and saw then, with witch eyes, the bridge.

A sturdy structure, built with more honesty than skill, vanishing into the very heart of the tightly guarded place that Val Con yos'Phelium had inexplicably become and stretching away to—where?

Cautiously she followed the bridge back, marveling at its flexibility and strength, then found the source and marveled anew.

The pattern shone, life-passion licking through the gridwork even though consciousness was at the moment disengaged. Priscilla bent her attention closer and discovered the sleeper's core lightly locked behind doors while the rest remained open to any with eyes to see. She sensed a bit of lambent shine, which might indicate witch-sense; the bridge argued power, even as it showed an architect untrained. Had she been in her body, Priscilla might have smiled. She had found lifemate, and a fitting receptacle for her message.

Taking care not to disturb the other's slumber or cast the slightest quiver onto the bridge, Priscilla placed the thought-seed within the sleeping pattern and withdrew a little way to watch. Only when she was certain that neither the sleeping nor the wakeful had been disturbed by her action did she loose her hold upon the place and follow her mooring line home.

VANDAR

SPRINGBREEZE FARM

Val Con slipped out of bed and silently pulled on his clothes. He stood over Miri for a time, studying her face in the crisp moonlight, unaccountably delighted that the small, satisfied smile still lingered on her mouth. Gently he tucked the covers around her, fingertips barely brushing the tumble of copper silk, then turned and went like moon-shadow across the room and out into the hall.

He paused briefly in the lower hall, decided against the piano, and continued on to the kitchen where Borril moaned but did not wake as the man took his jacket from its peg.

Just beyond the scuppin house he paused again, breath frosting on the air. Energy tingled through him, head-top to toe-tips: the excitement of making music coupled with the exuberance of making love, of being loved. He stretched high on his toes, arms flung out toward the meager stars. Tonight, tonight he could fly.

Or nearly so. On the verge of soaring, he brought his arms down and stood looking quietly at the sky, thinking of a ship.

Of his own will and heart, he had brought forbidden tech-nology to an Interdicted World and left it, barely concealed, no more than three miles from habitation. Though it was coil-dead, ransacked—even the distress beacon dead—he should have sent it into orbit and oblivion the moment they had been safe on-world, rather than trying to reconcile Scout-conscience with bone-deep need.

He had no means to repair the ship, no excuse for the madness of keeping it by. It was only that it went hard against the heart to lose such a resource, even though reasoned thought showed it to be no use to him. From the very first—from Cantra forward—Korval had kept the ships that came to it. Thirty-one generations of yos'Pheliums had led Korval, gathering ships as they could, obeying Cantra's law. And to Val Con, of the Line Direct, seventh to bear the name—to Val Con yos'Phelium fell the task of sending a ship to certain death and acknowledging to his heart that he and his lifemate were stranded on a forbidden world, Clan-reft, and likely to eventually die here.

Homesickness swept through him, sudden and shocking: He recalled the library at Jelaza Kazone, the long row of identically bound Diaries. He remembered even more vividly Uncle Er Thom's office at Trealla Fantrol, his uncle seated at the desk, head bent over some work, fair hair gleaming in the scented firelight; remembered his own rooms, gray Merlin lounging on the window seat, blinking yellow eyes against the midmorning sun; Shan laughing and talking; Nova so solemn; Anthora; Padi; Pat Rin . . .

Out of the near-dawn he heard a sound, as if someone inexpressibly far away had cried his name. He spun, every sense straining; heard the echo die and nothing more.

After a time, he turned back toward the house, carrying home-memories like a dull ache behind his heart.

Miri woke as he opened the door; she grinned up at him and stretched with very evident enjoyment. "Morning."

"Good morning, cha'trez." He sat carefully on the edge of the bed and held out a mug. "Would you like some tea?"

"Why not?" She wriggled into a sitting position against the pillows and took the mug, the coverlet falling away from one slight breast. "Umm—nice," she said, sipping. "And thanks."

"You're welcome."

"Yeah. You're up early."

"A touch of performance exhilaration." He smiled. "Even with the exercise that followed I found I needed no more than a nap."

She laughed, shaking her head and hiding the breast behind a curtain of hair. "And here I thought I wore you out!" Her expression changed abruptly and she sipped her tea. "Had a dream, boss."

"So?" he murmured, watching her face closely from beneath long lashes. "Tell me."

"Funniest thing about it," she said slowly, "is that it was so real, like I knew the people. Like they were—family."

"Dreams are very odd," he offered when a moment had passed and she had not spoken further. "Perhaps these are people you have seen somewhere before, even in passing."

"Naw," she said hesitantly. Then, with complete surety, she repeated, "No. I'd remember a pair like this one, no matter how short a sight I'd had." She closed her eyes, brows drawn in concentration. "They were in a—it looked like a ship's bridge, but *big*—and they were standing together, shoulder to shoulder. She's a little taller than he is—black hair, all curly, black eyes, and pale—beautiful, boss; that's the only word for her. And him—white hair, but not old; light eyes; brown skin; big hands—holding a wineglass; wearing a purple ring . . . They said—" Her brows twitched, and he watched her breathlessly. "*Somebody* said, 'We're looking for you. Help us.'" She sighed. "So damn *real*."

"Priscilla," he breathed.

She opened her eyes. "Huh?"

"The people you described," he managed, fighting against hope and terror. "The white-haired man is my brother Shan; the woman is Priscilla Mendoza, who is—ah, she is first mate, say—on *Dutiful Passage,* which my brother captains."

There was silence between them for a moment, then a careful: "Val Con?"

"Yes."

"How'd your people get in my head?"

He hesitated, then reached out and took her hand. "Priscilla is of the dramliz—a wizard, Miri. I— Outside, I thought I heard someone call to me, but— Perhaps it was beyond her skill to leave a message in a waking mind, and so she chose the mind of my lifemate."

"Yeah, but how'd she know that, boss?"

He looked at her helplessly. "Miri, I am not dramliz. How would I know?"

"Right." She stroked his cheek, brushing the hair from his eyes. "It's okay, boss, honest." Her fingers trembled. "Why're we scared?"

"They are looking for us," he whispered. "They will put themselves in danger. The Department of the Interior—gods, my Clan . . ." And the ship was useless, useless . . .

"We must start for Liad today," she thought she heard him say. "Or we must warn them away."

Miri stared. Then, moving carefully against the miasma of fear and sorrow and guilt, she set the mug aside, threw her arms around him, and held tight.

SHALTREN

CESSILEE

Grom Trogar stood before the starmap, absently fingering this gem and that: Shaltren's diamond, Talitha's niken, Foruner's topaz, Jelban's rosella. It was a magnificent map, with each one of the worlds that bowed to the might of the Juntavas—to the word of Grom Trogar—designated by a jewel produced by that world and tithed to the chairman.

He extended a broad forefinger to touch again the flashing blue-and-gold niken, then drew it back, frowning, as the receptionist's pretty voice came over the speaker.

"Mr. Chairman?"

"Yes?" he snapped.

"I'm sorry to bother you, sir," she said breathlessly. "But there are two, umm, *individuals* here to see you. They say their business is urgent. I—they don't have an appointment, sir, but they said they'd wait."

"Did they?" He considered the speaker stud, glowing bright red in the gloom of his office. "But we aren't that discourteous, are we? Please send these—individuals—in."

There was a pause and a half gasped "Yes, sir." Grom Trogar smiled as he strolled back to his desk.

Grom Trogar frowned at the two large individuals before him, even knowing that they, unlike most, could see his expression quite clearly in the dimness of his office. The knowledge titillated, adding a new dimension to a game long grown predictable.

"A Scout, Aged Ones?" he said. "Of Miri Robertson I am aware. I have urgent need to speak with her; less urgent need, I will admit, to see her dead. Though that will suffice."

"But of a Scout," he continued thoughtfully, "and the threat brought against this other member of your Clan—I am adrift in ignorance. I will investigate the matter thoroughly, and I promise you that it will go quite badly with Justin Hostro if he has failed to file a complete report."

"And the report Justin Hostro has already filed, Grom Trogar?" Edger rumbled politely. "Does it make mention of my kin in any way?"

"Merely that he had Miri Robertson in his hand, and that he allowed her to slip away. He begged forgiveness for his clumsiness and accepted the fine with good grace." He parted his lips in what passed for his smile. "Now I am shown the why of this uncharacteristic meekness. I am indebted, Aged Ones."

"Perhaps," the smaller of the two visitors suggested, "your indebtedness will allow you to call back your decree concerning our sister? She is young and very hasty, but it is in my heart that she has done nothing to warrant her name cried outlaw. Certainly she deserves no untimely death."

Trogar shrugged with a touch of impatience, and the larger visitor took up the discussion.

"It may very well be true that you are wronged in some

smaller way, Grom Trogar. Name the offense, and let us as Elders decide upon the injury price."

The man sighed, deeply and regretfully. Really, the game was going quite well. "Aged Ones, I am sincerely grieved. But the truth is that there is no price that will buy my vengeance where Miri Robertson is concerned. She has slain many of my best fighters—individuals I will be hard-pressed to replace. My organization is left in a position of vulnerability—because of Miri Robertson.

"Further, she dared ally herself with Sire Baldwin, who was himself outlawed for crimes committed against m—the Juntavas. That she aided and abetted his escape from justice is inarguable. That she herself is privy to much of the information Baldwin stole from this organization must be a logical certainty. Information is a dangerous thing, Aged Ones. I cannot ignore the possibility that dangerous information is abroad, held in hands not fit to grasp it."

He sighed again. "Understand that I will do my utmost to see that this Scout goes unharmed, should he still be at her side when she is taken. And that is a great deal, Aged Ones. Surely you recall that the Scouts have been less than kind to my people over the years and years? Vagrants, they call us, and gypsies. They hound us from gatherplace to gatherplace, branding us thieves and jackals, hangers-on of Yxtrang, deadly danger to holy Liad. In the usual course of things, you must know that if he lay dying at my feet and I held in my hand the cup of water that would save him, I would upend the cup and laugh as he expired." He shook his head, too unfamiliar with the persons to whom he spoke to read the signs of outrage.

"But these are not ordinary times, Aged Ones," he went on. "Nor am I an ordinary man. I am Chairman of the Juntavas, and I have said to you that I am indebted. Here is how I shall pay: When Miri Robertson is taken, should the Scout still be with her, and if it is within the realm of what is possible, he shall go free. Of course, He Who Watches, who has been threatened by one in our employ, need fear nothing more from the Juntavas." He inclined his head.

"You have made a good bargain: When you entered, the lives of three were potentially forfeit. Now that we have spoken, you regain the lives of two." Grom Trogar rose from behind the steel-and-crystal desk and bowed briskly. "Be satisfied, Aged Ones. In your eyes Miri Robertson will soon be dead in any case—is it not so? What matter that I recover what is mine before she is gone? Good day."

"You are," the one called Edger said, "in error. The day has not thus far been good. I hold forth some hope, however, that it may improve. You have said much that is hurtful to me, as the brother of my brother and my sister. You have behaved in a manner—Elder to Elder—that I find distressing in the extreme. Even, Grom Trogar—were it not in the poorest possible taste—I would say that you have lied to me." He held up one large, three-fingered hand. "Understand that I have not said this. Only, did courtesy permit, that I would do so." He moved his head so that he might gaze at his kinsman, who stood at his right hand. "What think you, brother?"

"I think, T'carais," Sheather said with a certain hasty care, "that Elder Grom Trogar has perhaps spoken before all facts have been laid before him by the members of his Clan most conversant with the affair. This would perhaps lend his words a certain air of—glibness, T'carais—that might make one think he is lying. It is true that we have learned from our brother that humans break truth differently, so one may say what one does not believe and yet know it for a truth."

"There is," Edger conceded, "much in what you have said. Do you make recommendation as to our next step, brother? You would honor me by speaking what is in your heart."

Sheather inclined his head, considered for a moment the bright blade that was his sister, and spoke, finally, with some measure of *her* understanding of the way in which the worlds of Men turned. "T'carais, it comes to me that Grom Trogar knows not with whom he deals. A demonstration is perhaps in order, before we depart to allow him time to gather his facts and rethink the words he has said."

"I have heard," Edger said. He was still for a time, his luminous eyes on the man who stood so quietly behind the desk. Carefully he considered his brother's thought, perceiving its intent and origin. Even in its hastiness, he found it good.

"Grom Trogar," he said.

"Yes, Aged One? Is there a further service I might perform for you?"

"You have heard the words of my brother, Grom Trogar. I find myself in agreement with him. We shall school you, that you may not suffer by your ignorance of the worth of the Knife Clan of Middle River. Then we shall leave you for a time, that you might make inquiries and acquire facts. We will return to speak further with you in five Standard days. Now, attend me."

Edger closed his huge eyes briefly, opened them—and sang.

One note, held to the edge of endurance. Another. And a third.

The miraldine conference table shivered, acquired spider-webs of cracks, then crumbled and fell in on itself, a glittering pile of rubble and dust.

Grom Trogar heard someone cursing fluently, disbelievingly, in the tongue of his youth; recognizing his own voice, he silenced it.

"Understand," Edger said, "that this is the simplest of the songs I might sing you, Grom Trogar. I chose it because its simplicity was sufficient for a demonstration, yet leaves more complex crystalline structures—as those which are part of your communication devices—unharmed. I am sorry that some of the gems in yon piece of artwork have also suffered." He motioned to his brother, Sheather, and inclined his head in the manner of Men, "Keep you well, Grom Trogar. We shall return in five days."

Moving with a quickness astonishing in persons so large, they crossed the room, striding over the crumbled table, and passed through the door. Grom Trogar saw his hand twitch toward the desk key that would forbid them exit, clenched it and let them go.

Slowly he moved to the shattered remains of the table, bent, and picked up a jagged blue shard. Holding it cupped, so that the sharp edges pricked his palm, he went over to the fabulous illustration of Juntavas might, in which each of one hundred and four worlds was marked by a flashing gem.

He was not really surprised to see that only thirty-one remained.

LIAD ORBIT

Scout Lieutenant Shadia Ne'Zame was unhappy.

"A whole blasted *year* on Liad," she grumbled to herself while the pilot part of her mind got on with the commonplaces of board calibration, vector analysis, coord check, and velocity match.

"I'm certain it's very nice that the Clan now has a fine healthy daughter to replace me, if and when my luck runs out," she continued, relishing the feel of the tantrum, "but I do think a year of my life is excessive. Stupid custom anyway, contract-marriage. Archaic. We have the technology; why not just have the Speakers negotiate among themselves for the genes and then grow the damn kids in jars? Let everyone else get on with things."

The board stuttered, then steadied: coords locked in. Her eyes flicked to the peripherals, anticipating the glow of the aqua go-stud indicating Tower's permission to depart.

Instead, the orange lit, concurrent with a muted chime.

Her right forefinger touched the connect. "Ne'Zame."

"Lieutenant Shadia? Delight of my night, were you going to leave without farewell? My heart is broken. Belike I'll die of it."

In spite of herself she grinned. "Clonak ter'Meulen, you hoary fraud."

"No one knows me like you, my sweet, my chernubia. My heart is at your feet, battered as it is. Care for my daughter, swear, do I die of your cruelty."

"Clonak, your daughter's older than I am!"

"Does that mean she needs no care? But I grow maudlin. No doubt I'll survive the damage, though I shall never altogether recover."

"I'm trembling in shame," she told him, though in fact it was repressed mirth. "Is there a purpose to this tying up of the airwaves and delay of my departure, or did you merely wish to chat?"

"Ah, the advantages of honored senility! But, yes, now that you bring it to mind, there was a reason for the call. When you complete your assignment, child, report to Auxiliary Headquarters on Nev'lorn and place yourself at the disposal of the commander there."

She sighed. "I suppose you have that in some sort of official form?"

"Transmission completed and locked to your filecomp. Will I see you again, Night's Delight?"

"How do I know? Are you going to be on Nev'lorn in a relumma?"

"For you, even Nev'lorn."

She laughed. "Farewell, Clonak. May your broken heart soon mend!"

"Farewell, Lieutenant Shadia. I doubt it. Clearance coming through—now. Jump at will, and the luck be with you!"

"And with you, old friend." She cut the connection, slapped the go-stud, and hit the sequence: *Jump!*

Leaning back in her chair, she blinked at the Jump-grayed screens and caught herself on the edge of a reminiscent chuckle.

An entire year on Liad, she thought, resuming her tirade. And then what? Return to the Scouts, ready—eager—to go out again; wanting nothing better than to fling myself out into the vast Uncharted, for the glory of Liad and a much-needed rest . . .

"Scout Lieutenant, First In, Shadia Ne'Zame," her orders had read, "upon return to active duty will, for the next three months Standard, occupy herself with observation of Interdicted Planets (list appended), tagging for pickup any and all flotsam of a possibly technological nature, listening and noting significant cultural advances or declines . . ."

"The *garbage run?*" she had demanded of the captain behind the desk.

He had shrugged elaborately. "Somebody has to do it." His comm had chimed then, and he had turned away, leaving Shadia to stew and finally walk away. Orders were orders, after all . . .

And now Clonak ter'Meulen and his sheer nonsense, with orders to report to Aux 'quarters when the garbage run was finished. Faint hint of some action there. Shadia allowed herself a smile and wondered if he would be on Nev'lorn, after all.

SHALTREN

CESSILEE

"Aged Ones, I regret most deeply that I have found no cause to change my opinion." There was no artwork upon the walls here, and the conference table was of unadorned steel. Grom Trogar folded his hands upon the cold surface and met the eyes of the one called Edger.

"I see," that person boomed gravely. "And have you gathered further facts, Grom Trogar? Have you spoken with Justin Hostro, your kinsman, and demanded of him a fuller accounting?"

"I have all the information I require from Justin Hostro. I repeat that the decision of the Juntavas remains unchanged."

The words clashed upon Sheather's ears like crystal crying out under intolerable stress, and at his side, the T'carais sighed, most gently.

"In that wise, I, T'carais of the Knife Clan of Middle River, demand to be heard by the full council of Elders of Clan Juntavas. Satisfaction has not been gained; our talks describe circles, encompassing nothing. The lives of my sister and my brother, brief or long, are of far too much importance to hang upon your whim."

Grom Trogar smiled. "Aged One, you speak at this moment to the highest authority possible within the Juntavas. There is no Council of Elders: My voice speaks the final law." He spread his hands flat on the cold tabletop. "You have no recourse."

There was a pause, very brief, as Clutch measure such things.

"Grom Trogar," Edger said, and Sheather blinked in solemn amazement at the patience that the hastiest of their Clan could bring to bear, "it appears you consider us fools. Am I an eggling, to believe that a Clan which spans worlds has at its nexus one individual, whose solitary judgment—"

The intercom chimed overhead, and the receptionist's light, hasty voice skated above Edger's bass rumble. "Mr. Trogar? I am sorry to disturb you, sir, but the delegation from Stelubia has arrived."

"Thank you." Grom Trogar pushed back from the table and bowed with heartfelt irony to the two Clutch members, who were much worse than children. Oh, much worse than fools! "Aged Ones—indulge me. This business is quite urgent and will be but a matter of moments. Pray remain here, and we will continue our discussions when I return."

He was gone then, as if their permission were assured, the door opening and closing behind him with a snap.

The spirit of his sister rising in his heart, Sheather rose, went to the door, laid his hand against the mechanism, and then took it away. "Brother, the door is locked."

"Yes," the T'carais said, with great sadness. "I felt that it might be."

VANDAR

SPRINGBREEZE FARM

"What a beautiful morning!" Zhena Trelu exclaimed in surprise. The sun glittered, achingly bright, off the snow on the scuppin-house roof; the sky was cloudless and deeply blue; the iced shrubbery shivered in the very slightest of breezes. Such a day was a gift in midwinter.

Zhena Trelu pulled on a heavy sweater and a skirt instead

of the trousers she usually wore around the house, combed her hair, and left the bedroom with a positive spring in her step, already compiling a list in her head.

Meri and Corvill were in the kitchen ahead of her, usual; Cory was seated in a chair, shoulders hunched, as his wife worked on his hair with comb and scissors.

"Sit up!" she said in Benish as Zhena Trelu went across to the stove for a cup of tea. "How can I see what to do when you hunch? I should cut your head off, yes?"

"My hair is fine," Cory protested weakly.

Meri snorted. "Very fine. So fine you don't see to play." She bent until her nose nearly touched his. "You look like Borril," she whispered loudly.

"No!" Cory recoiled in mock horror.

The girl stepped back, eyeing him consideringly. "No," she agreed finally. "Borril's much prettier." She came close again and put a small hand under his chin, coaxing his head up. "I promise it not hurt. I do it very fast."

Sighing, he allowed his head to be raised, though he screwed his eyes shut with exaggerated tightness. Grinning, Meri wielded comb and scissors, trimming the lock that fell across his forehead back to touch the straight brows. A few more deft snips took care of the ragged sides, though she left his hair long enough to cover his ears, to Zhena Trelu's dissatisfaction. It really ought to have been another two inches shorter; and a mustache would have been a great improvement.

Meri stepped back, nodded, and moved a hand to rumple his thick, shiny mop. "I think you live."

He opened his eyes and raised his hands to feel his new haircut. Meri leaned across the table and yanked the toaster toward him.

"Look!" she directed. "Honorable, I am. My word is good." Cory regarded his reflection in the toaster's side, then looked up with a grin. "Thank you, cha'trez. Not Borril now?"

"Very pretty now," she assured him, smiling, and moved across the room to put the scissors and comb away inside the dish closet. "Good morning, Zhena Trelu."

"Good morning, Meri." She sipped her tea, eyes on the

beautiful, bright day outside the kitchen window. "Children," she said, "a day like this needs to be used. I'm going in to town to pick up some supplies, maybe stop at the library . . . There's some stuff it sure will be nice to have, when the weather turns serious." She brought her gaze back to the kitchen and the two young people before her. "Cory, I'm going to need you to carry things."

"Yes, Zhena Trelu," he murmured, setting the toaster carefully back in its accustomed place.

She sipped tea, knowing that her next words would disappoint Meri. The child did love books. But the truck had a limited amount of space, and the list in her head had grown to alarming proportions. Her shopping trip had begun to look like an all-day affair.

"Meri, dear, I'm afraid you'll have to stay home this time. There won't be enough room in the truck." Not looking at the girl, Zhena Trelu hurried on. "You tell Cory what you want from the library, all right? And if the two of you need anything else." She finished her tea and set the cup in the sink to be washed. "I'll be ready to leave in a couple minutes, Cory." She went off down the hall to get paper and pencil.

Miri looked at her husband. "She really does like you best."

"Not so," he replied, standing and stretching. "It is only the labor of my muscle-bound body she desires. *You* she perceives as intellectual." He bowed profoundly. "What will you have from the library, O sage?"

She grinned. "Oh, you know, whatever looks good—oops!" She brought fingers to her forehead. "Nearly forgot. You better take back the ones I got last time." She was already on her way out of the kitchen.

Grinning, he wandered over to the stove and poured himself a cup of tea. Miri's reading habits were amazing: science, gardening, murder mysteries, poetry—he had forgotten half the subjects covered by the last batch of books she had foraged. She had read each with serious concentration; gods alone knew how she managed to keep track of it all. His own tendency was to pick one or two subjects at a time and read through the levels available until he felt himself to have a clear fundamental understanding of the principles involved.

Fiction had been a pleasure of his youth, sharply curtailed by school and then by duty.

He turned as she came back into the room, arms full of books, including the six he had borrowed. "You forgot!"

He sighed. "Forgive me, cha'trez. But *you* forget how very old I am—memory is the first to go, I am told."

She laughed, dumping the collection on the table, then turned and looked at him seriously. "You need gloves, boss. Tell Zhena Trelu so, okay? She wants you to fetch and carry, your hands oughta be warm."

"And you?" he asked. "I do not recall that you have gloves."

"I'll keep," she began. But Zhena Trelu was already calling down the hall for Cory to come along.

Sighing, he poured out the last of his tea and set the cup in the sink. He pulled his jacket from its peg and shrugged it on as he came back to Miri's side. Seriously he measured her fingers against his own before dropping a kiss on her palm.

"I will see what may be done," he said. "Keep well, cha'trez—and mind you protect Borril from strangers."

She laughed and hugged him as the truck's asthmatic horn wheezed peevishly at the back stairs. Val Con gathered up the books and dashed out the back door, letting it slam behind him.

Miri drifted to the window and watched the truck make its careful way down the drive and turn cautiously into the road. Borril groaned from his rug by the stove—the only sound in the house.

"Work to do, Robertson," she said against the silence. Then she smiled. Zhena Trelu was gone; there was no reason that the radio in the parlor should not be turned up as loud as possible.

Encouraged by that thought, she made her soundless way down the hall. Kneeling on the ottoman, she turned the control until it clicked and waited for the machine to warm up.

The announcer's voice gabbled into existence, and Miri strained her ears for the sense of it. Something about—Bassilans? and armies? The professional whine of the newsman's voice, along with the crackle of static, defeated her. She twisted the numbered dial: Voices talking. Voices singing.

Voices, voices—music. She stopped turning the dial and listened. Music, indeed, and of a variety that could claim kinship with the type of music Hakan made. Good enough, she decided, and upped the volume.

Then she was on her way back to the kitchen, rolling up her sleeves in anticipation of washing the dishes.

Zhena Trelu drove with precision unmarred by confidence. The last snow had been some days earlier, and the road was clear. There were, however, occasional patches of ice on the surface, and Zhena Trelu navigated the truck over each as if one wrong breath would buy them disaster.

Val Con considered the side of her face, decided that talking would only make her more nervous, and directed his attention to the day.

It *was* fine, though very cold, and he was briefly, intensely, grateful for the warmth of the clothing he wore. Liad was a warm place, after all, though he had been on worlds far chillier than Gylles in midwinter, and he found he preferred being warm to being cold.

The truck slowed; apparently Zhena Trelu was even more distrustful of the covered bridge than of the occasionally icy road. He hardly blamed her. The wooden structure rattled and groaned unnervingly, no matter what the season, seeming to threaten imminent collapse. But, once again, the truck made safe passage and, beyond the bridge, leapt ahead at nearly twenty-five miles an hour.

Val Con shifted on the seat squinting as a sunbeam, deflected by an icicle, stabbed into his eyes. On a rise to the right, a cluster of cows grazed the scant, winter grass; though they looked even less like the animals he had learned, as a child, to call "cows" than Borril looked like a dog.

Comehome.

Startled, he considered the thought. Go home? But surely—

Home. The thought was insistent, strongly flavored with hunch. *Dangerathome.*

The breath caught in his throat then, and he sent his awareness to touch the spot that still sang, untroubled: *Alive-and-well . . .*

And yet his hunch; always played, never in error: *Danger. Dangerathome.*

Zhena Trelu turned the truck onto Main Street, and Val Con forced himself to breathe deeply, to consider both messages dispassionately. It was true that one could be in danger and yet be alive—be well.

The truck pulled to the curb, and Zhena Trelu turned off the switch and removed the keys.

"Zhena Trelu," he said quickly, almost breathlessly. "We must go home. Now."

She stared at him. "We just got here. There's a lot to do before we go home." Her face softened somewhat. "Meri's all right, Cory. Like as not, she's pleased to have the house to herself for the day."

"Meri is all right," he agreed, keeping his voice even and firm. "But there is danger at home, and she must not face it alone."

The old lady's face grew stern. "Poppycock," she decided, opening her door.

"Zhena Trelu," he began again, strongly tempted merely to take the keys from her.

"No!" she snapped, getting out of the truck and glaring at him from street level. "Now stop wasting my time, Cory. The faster we get everything done, the faster we'll be able to go home." She slammed the door.

Wincing at the sound, Val Con worked the handle on his side, slid to the ground, and closed the door gently. Turning left, he began to run.

"Cory!" Zhena Trelu yelled at his fleeing heck. "Corvill Robersun, come back here this instant!" But he gave no sign that he heard.

Zhena Trelu stood for a moment, bosom heaving, anger warring with worry. It was not really like him, she acknowledged, to just run off like that. Anger flared.

"What do you know what's like him or not?" she grumbled to herself. "Let him run all the way home. Teach him a lesson."

So saying, she turned her back on the truck and the man

who was running away and marched across the street to Brillit's.

Tomat Meltz looked up when the entrance bell rang and frowned at the short, long-haired foreigner his son had taken up with.

"Hakan!" the little man called, with no regard at all for the proper way to behave in a place of business. "Hakan, are you here?"

"See here, young man," Zamir Meltz began in his best speech-before-Assembly voice.

"Cory?" Hakan appeared out of the back room like a conjuring trick, mustached face glowing. He held his hands out. "Cory, I was just trying to call—*we got the job!*"

"What?" The little man brushed this aside with a frown. "Just trying to call—who answered?"

"Huh?" Hakan blinked, joy diminishing visibly. "Nobody answered, Cory. You're here, aren't you?"

"Miri." It was nearly a whisper. "Miri is home alone." He looked up sharply and found his friend frowning at him in puzzlement.

"Hakan, please . . ." He extended a hand and grabbed the other's sleeve. "There—I feel that there is danger at home. Miri is alone. Hakan—drive me home."

The pause was less than a heartbeat. "Right. Let's go." Hakan dived back into the storeroom and reemerged seconds later, car keys in one hand, jacket in the other. The little man was already pulling the outside door open.

"Hakan!" Tomat Meltz snapped. "Just where do you think you're going? You're paid to help in this store, and the business day has just begun. If you think you can go running off on some—on some *skevitt chase*—"

"See you later, Dad," Hakan called as he charged through the door on his friend's heels. "I'm going to drive Cory home."

Tomat Meltz stood staring at the place where his son had been, then shook himself and walked carefully over to the door. He opened it to the roar of acceleration: Hakan was driving Cory home.

Zamir Meltz closed the door, walked back to the counter, and resumed his accounting. He was smiling, just a little.

SHALTREN

CESSILEE

The Stelubia Delegation were not sufficiently impressed. Worse, they had apparently begun preliminary negotiations with that upstart of an O'Hand, who thought himself so safe in his rat's nest on Daphyd. Well, let him continue to think so yet a while; a lesson would shortly be forthcoming. But first Stelubia had to be secured.

Grom Trogar smiled and settled his dark glasses more firmly on his nose, aware of the comforting pressure of the weapon against his ribs, beneath his jacket.

"It is true," he acknowledged thoughtfully, "that the Juntavas has many detractors, all busily crying out that our power is failing, that even now we are ripe for the plucking. You will have noticed, I am certain, that the few attempts to pluck us have been checked, the ringleaders . . . punished." He smiled again, though none of the other six around the table joined him.

"It will perhaps be instructive for you to consider the individuals now held by the Juntavas, awaiting our disposal. I offer this instruction because it would sadden me, gentles, most deeply, if you were tricked into making a decision of alliance that might prove—painful—to all parties concerned."

He touched the appropriate disk on the panel before him, and the large screen to his left lit, showing the interior of the specially reinforced metal room with its metal table and chairs, in which was—

Nothing else at all.

Grow Trogar gaped. The proportions of the hole in the farther wall were quite modest, considering the size of the largest of the two escapees—a sharp-edged rectangle showing a glimpse of the hallway beyond. The steel sheet that had once been part of the wall had been pulled to one side and laid upon the floor, as if those who had cut it away had expended some care to insure that none would trip over it and injure themselves.

He was on his feet, moving through the door of his office and sweeping past the receptionist's desk. Tricked! They had tricked him! Well, it would be their last trick. A sad pity, indeed, that a being might reach the exalted age of eight or nine hundred Standards and yet be unable to recognize a man who will not be bested.

He did not have to go far to find them. At the main hall, he stopped, staring while the two of them sauntered forward, apparently intending to leave by the front entrance, as if they were not already dead.

Grom Trogar strode up to them, planted his legs wide, and glared, secure in the knowledge of the weapon that rode against his heart.

"Stupid reptiles!" he cried, oblivious to the six who had followed him out of his office; oblivious, as well, to the others summoned by the alarm system: security guards, unit managers, emergency personnel. "So you value your lives as little as that! You come onto my planet, into my city, dare to bargain with *me* for the lives of a Terran bitch and a Liaden Scout! You repudiate my judgment, question my power! You have greatly overstepped, Aged Ones. And now we shall see the price to be paid."

"Grom Trogar," the one called Edger rumbled, "you are obviously in a haste so great that it is harmful. You do not understand the meaning of the words you speak. We will allow you time to compose yourself and call together a Council of Elders, then we shall return to talk further. In reason and calmness—"

"Silence!" the man roared, riding his rage like a fire-crested wave. Was he a child to be so instructed? No! He was Grom Trogar, the ultimate voice of the mightiest network of power and wealth in all the galaxy!

"This ceases to be amusing, Aged One. Know that there is no Council of Elders to heed your ridiculous bargains, nor shall I create such a thing to placate you. Know also that the entire Juntavas shall be charged with hunting down Miri Robertson and your filthy, murdering Scout of a brother. And when they are found, I promise you that it will take them quite a long time to die. It will be amusing, I think, to have a Scout beg me for death. Almost as amusing as it will be to kill you, Aged One. This feud is between you and me—and you cannot win it."

Sheather shifted, perceived his brother's sign, and regained stillness, though there was something pricking him to attention that made his hand long for his blade . . .

"Grom Trogar," Edger repeated, "you are in harmful haste. Perhaps you are even ill. You cannot mean that you desire a personal feud between you and me. Consider yourself; consider what the blades of Middle River have already wrought within this place. A duel between us two is sheerest folly. Reconsider your words. We will return in some days and have calmer speech." He inclined his head and turned aside, meaning to detour around the man.

The weapon flared as Grom Trogar brought it from beneath his jacket; it hummed as he thumbed it to life and brought it up, aiming for the vulnerable spot, where neck met shoulder armor.

It is true that the members of the Clutch are often slow. But not *always* slow. Grom Trogar screamed once before his body understood that it was dead and slumped to the floor beside the evil, humming thing, his blood already pooling about it.

Edger turned to look long at his brother Sheather, then turned again to study the pitiful, soft man impaled upon the glowing crystal blade and the gun humming to itself in the growing pool of red.

Not a sound came from the humans all around.

"What say you, brother?" Edger asked gently.

Sheather bowed his head. "In defense of the T'carais I did strike. The weapon—the weapon, brother! It was no clean thing he sought, decided between two, with honor, with justice. Only to slay . . ." His sister's voice whispered in his heart; he stopped himself and raised his head to look into the eyes of his T'carais and his eldest brother. "If I have been in error, I do accept the penalty. Strike surely, brother!"

As T'carais, Edger made the sign of negation; as eldest brother, he added the sign of honored esteem. "Retrieve your blade. The blow was rightly dealt, in defense of T'carais and Clan." He raised his luminous eyes to the still-silent, watching humans.

"As for the weapon . . ." Edger sang a song consisting of seven notes, three of which human ears were not capable of hearing.

Grom Trogar's blood steamed where it pooled about the weapon as the power pack ruptured, leaked energy. There was a *flash!* of pinpoint light, a *snap!* of sound—and the weapon was molten metal, mixing with liquid red.

Finally, from the humans all about came a stir, a sound— a drawing close together and a drawing a little apart. One stepped forward to bow.

"I am called Sambra Reallen, Chairman Pro Tem," she said softly. "How may I serve you, Aged Ones?"

VANDAR

SPRINGBREEZE FARM

Hakan drove with the same casual intensity that characterized his guitar-playing. His eyes and hands worked together, and Val Con found that portion of himself which measured such things gauging the other man's reaction times.

They were approaching a patch of ice that had caused Zhena Trelu so much anxiety on the way in, but Hakan did not even seem to notice that it was there. They were over and past it, with only the barest hint of instantly corrected skid.

Pilot material, this one, Val Con thought.

"Hakan," he said quietly. "I have said there is danger at home. Maybe it is not only danger for Miri; I do not know.

It could be danger for you, too. I think that we should stop before . . ."

Hakan slowed the car, changed gears before they were fully out of the dipping curve, and accelerated again, shaking his head. "Not to worry. I said I'd take you home, didn't I? I'll help you, too. You say there's trouble, and I *believe* it— you've got such feeling about things." He glanced over, smiling. "I never had a chance to play with anybody who catches things so quickly—not just the notes, but the full spirit of the music. I think you live life that way, too. So I think you *know* that something's wrong."

Val Con frowned. "I have just said that I *don't* know," he reminded softly, but Hakan cut him off with a wave of his hand.

"Look, if Miri's hurt herself somehow, I had the medic course when I was in the militia. And I was in the volunteer fire department until the politics bored me out of it. I can help, whatever trouble."

"And will you take orders from me?" Val Con asked. "Will you do as I say, without talking, if there is a big danger?"

"You're the boss," Hakan said. Val Con clamped his mouth on a gasp. The other glanced at him. "You'd help me, wouldn't you? If it was Kem?"

"Yes . . ."

"Well, there you are," Hakan said.

Val Con rolled down the window in the door, letting the sharp air wash against his face, then reached out and touched that special place in his mind: *Alive-and-well.*

The covered bridge loomed—then quickly they were through it, boards rattling and car shaking, at a pace Zhena Trelu would have considered sheerest folly.

"You have been in the militia," Val Con murmured. "Have you been to war?"

"No. Hasn't been a war in these parts for a long, long time. I helped out after the explosion at the fireworks factory in Carnady, though. Folks said that was a lot like a war."

Val Con shifted, growing uneasier as the farm came closer. His mind was demanding reactions from him—*weapons, fight,* even *kill*—and he took a deep breath, consciously imposing calm while he took inventory. Edger's blade rode secure in his sleeve. He bent and slipped the throwing blade from the top of his work boot.

If Hakan noticed the knife, he said nothing.

"Do you have any weapons at all, Hakan?"

"You're really serious, huh? Yeah. I got a half-and-half there in the back, somewhere under everything."

Val Con turned in his seat, groping among guitar cases and sheet music.

A half-and-half, it turned out, was a large-bore weapon with a small-bore weapon overtop.

"It isn't much." Hakan's voice was unusually serious. "I've got a few shot shells, and there should be plenty of—"

"Explosives?" Val Con demanded, eyeing the shell meant for the larger bore.

Hakan choked a laugh. "No, *shot* shells—for birds and varmints at close range. The rifle has more range, but it's only for plinking, really . . . though I guess you could hurt somebody."

Val Con hefted it, understood the loading and firing. "Recoil?"

"Well, the shot . . ."

Stupid thing, Val Con thought. "Keep it for you," he said to Hakan.

They heard a sound: something uncommon over the sound of car and wind.

"Slow down," Val Con murmured, but Hakan had already done so.

The sound came again.

"Guns!" Hakan snapped, jamming the speed back on.

"Rapid-firing guns. Hakan, this may be very bad. You will listen, and you will do as I say. When we are close to the house. I will get out. If you see that I go no closer, or if I wave at you—go back to Gylles! Go back, but burn the bridge behind you. *Burn* it, Hakan, and tell the people that there is war here!"

They topped the last small hill, and Hakan cut the power to the engine, letting the car drift through the little clump of trees and into the farmyard.

Val Con finished loading the half-and-half, flipped the safety off, and laid it on the seat.

Four bodies in dirty uniforms lay in a group before the porch; two had been shot in the back.

Hakan gripped the gun, his good-natured face grim and a trifle pale. "Miri?"

"In the house, I think," Val Con said. He was gone in an instant, slipping noiselessly from the passenger seat and closing the door without a sound.

Hakan put the car in gear, let it drift back the few yards to the road, and pulled the keys out of the ignition. Guns clattered, shockingly close, and he froze, but the sound died away to nothing. Cautiously he opened the glovebox under the driver's seat and took out his militia cap.

The cap firmly on his head, it occurred to him to wonder if a militia corporal and a knife-wielding foreigner would be enough to stop an invasion force.

Then he thought what Cory must have thought: Miri's in there! Car keys in pocket, half-and-half held ready, the militia began to infiltrate.

Val Con stood invisibly in the shaded underbrush that Zhena Trelu called shrubbery, listening. From the house came the sound of voices speaking excitedly in an unknown language; nearer at hand was a whimpering noise. Blade in hand, he moved toward the smaller sound.

A bloody bundle of cloth—*No!* His eyes closed in protest, even as he reached for the glowing part within: *Alive-and-well, alive-and-well.* He let the song and the brightness have his attention for a full minute before putting it aside.

Viewed through calmer eyes, the bundle was fur, not cloth: Borril lay wedged between a thickly needled bush and the side of the house. His tail beat raggedly against the ground; his bloody head was propped against the wall.

Val Con fingered his throwing blade, keeping very still; he heard the voices of many men from inside the house and the sound of gunfire, close. Hesitantly, almost retching in revulsion, he reached into his own mind, located the switch he had never wanted to use again, and thought the Thought . . .

He receded from himself, fear burning away like fog as he gained the distance taught by the instructors of agents. His current mission was not some remotely patriotic killing of an anti-Liaden fanatic: his mission was to save Miri. He struggled mentally to open that walled-off portion of his mind, then nearly reeled as the programs ran his thoughts, stretching and erasing him . . .

> STATEMENT OF MISSION OBJECTIVE: Preserve Miri
> Robertson from attacking military forces and drive
> forces from base.
> LIMITATIONS: None
> MISSION PRIORITY: Ultimate
> ACCEPTABLE DAMAGE TO AGENT: Priority Override
> PAIN THRESHOLD: Disallow
> FULL AUTOMATIC: Yes
> ANALYSIS LOOP: Chance of Mission Success: .37
> GO: Go

In the initial training, each phase had taken hours to fulfill, then minutes, then seconds. Now it was simply the time it took to make the decision, to think the Thought: PRIORITY GOAL ACCEPTED.

He was more than pilot-fast, more than mercenary-accurate, more than berserker-deadly. He was again fully an Agent of Change. He blinked.

Dog and bush blurred just slightly out of focus; Val Con blinked again—yes. The creature before him had a good chance of survival, if it managed to live through the firefight. The wounds were not themselves mortal, though extended loss of blood could kill it. Alive or dead, it was not essential to the mission.

He slipped away, angling toward the house and the low window that looked out from the so-called formal dining room. Glass glittered in shards on the earth before him; the window frame itself was smashed and twisted. A soldier, his neck broken, lay just inside the room.

Analysis indicated that the kill had been made by Miri Robertson. Val Con went through the twisted frame; he heard a sound as his feet touched the floor; he spun and threw.

The guard moved before he died, making quite a bit of noise as blood welled into his throat.

"Kwtel?" a voice called from the next room.

Val Con ran to the body, pulled the clumsy sidearm from the dead grasp, found the safety switch, though he did not know if it was engaged or not, jerked the blade free, and spun to face the door.

"Kwtel?" the voice demanded again, louder and accompanied by the sound of several pairs of heavy boots moving across carpeted floors.

The first soldier's head came through the doorway.

Click!

That one, too, died by blade, but he fell before another, who was armed and began to fire instantly.

Val Con dove for the scant cover of the wooden dining table, yanked the safety to the proper notch and fired, shuddering with the recoil.

Screaming, the enemy dropped to the floor, hands at his face. Val Con fired again, and the noise stopped.

He damned himself briefly for poor shooting. Chance of Personal Survival showed as unknown for the action, seventy-five percent for the next minute. From the floor above came the sound of many feet, then a short burst of gunfire.

Retrieving his knife, he slipped down the hallway. The radio in the front parlor was playing, loud in the shocking stillness.

The kitchen was empty. He was turning to go when a familiar electrical *click* sent him diving across the room to snatch the receiver up before the bell sounded.

"Hello? This is Athna Brigsbee—"

"Shut up!" he snapped. "Emergency and danger! Send—"

"Cory? Will you tell me what's going on? I never, in—"

"Shut up, Brigsbee! Call army; call militia—enemy invasion!" As he spoke, the ugly sound of heavy automatic weapons began outside the house, answered by an odd *snap-snap-snap* barely louder than a pellet pistol.

"Invaders? Invaders! Oh, my word! Cory—where's Estra?"

"Estra okay, Miri missing. You call police—army. I go."

He let the phone down to dangle from its wire and, after momentary consideration, cut the outside wire.

From high in the house came four measured shots and, a moment later, three more.

Miri! Very faintly Val Con was aware of relief, then he was moving back toward the dining room.

The handgun held only three more shots, and he hefted one of the fallen long-arms. It was dirty, corroded in several spots, and had only seven rounds in the magazine. He thought he would be lucky if it worked at all; and the recoil might slow him.

A volley of shots sounded from upstairs, a high-pitched keening riding above: the Gyrfalks' battle cry!

More shots from upstairs; the rumble of booted feet, running; voices, shouting; pounding— Val Con was moving, taking the stairs three at a time, lugging the stupid weapons with him.

At the top of the stair was a crowd of soldiers, their backs toward him, watching the one who had apparently just broken in the attic door.

The heavy rifle was up and firing at the backs of heads— he managed three shots before the gun jammed, and he brought the pistol up to kill three more.

A shot was fired wildly from the left. Val Con dodged, cuffed the soldier heavily across the face with the spent pistol, and stepped to the next, knife out.

The confined space made it hard for the remaining soldiers to react. Behind, all they saw was smoke and the surging motions of someone demented.

One of the enemies dropped his weapon. Another followed suit, speaking sounds that might have meant surrender. Val Con found a soldier with a gun in his hand and killed him with a blade thrust. He looked for more, but saw only weak weaponless creatures, cowering before him.

From the attic came several more measured shots, then surrender sounds there, as well, and the Gyrfalks' keen.

Val Con lunged forward, snatched up a fallen weapon, and held it on the six survivors as he worked his way to the base of the attic stairs.

"Friend?" The word was in Terran, the voice husky and familiar.

Val Con hesitated, groping for a switch that slid from his mind-grip, and located an adequate response. "Cha'trez."

They heard another burst of gunfire outside. Hakan? Was Hakan there?

Down the attic stairs came a red-haired woman, pushing several unarmed enemies before her. She carried a well-oiled, wood-clad rifle; a stickknife of Liaden Scout issue was thrust through her belt.

She shoved her prisoners among his six and came to his side, looking worriedly into his face. "What took you so long?"

There was a sudden racket outside, punctuated by the sound of automatic guns.

"Guard them!" Val Con snapped, and rushed off, running silently down the stairs.

Miri stood very still, then looked at her prisoners and asked them very plainly, in Terran, "*Now* where's he gone to?"

Her tone must have sounded extremely threatening; they backed as a shivering group into Zhena Trelu's upstairs parlor, one of them tenderly helping the boy with the smashed nose and swollen eye.

Miri sat on the arm of the sewing chair, rifle ready across her knees. Her prisoners sat carefully on the floor and avoided looking at her.

"We won, I guess," she said, after a time and to no one in particular. "Hot damn."

LIAD

Dispassion. Control. Calculation. Success.

Tyl Von sig'Alda reviewed those concepts as he walked to the conference room. No hint of anything other than confidence escaped him; the occasional agent he passed registered no sign of doubt; the underlings and clerks averted their eyes, in the usual deference to an Agent of Change.

He had spent two days writing the report that outlined his reasoning, his deductions, the probabilities cited by his Loop, and his suggested course of action.

A bare quarter-shift after he had submitted it, he had received orders to attend the upcoming meeting. He had three days, then, to wait inside the deep complex, the underground control center that would one day be the command post for a galaxy. Three days to reconsider and to seek his own errors, while the Department moved deliberately on with the Plan.

The problem: the Terran female. The other problem: yos'Phelium himself.

The Loop flickered, indicating that he would reach the conference room within fifteen seconds of his targeted time.

He had been thorough, he assured himself; the report had been dispassionate. Calculating. Controlled.

Success . . . The door was before him.

Opening the door was proof enough of success.

The room was arranged for a working meeting: enough chairs but no more, an erasable board with supplies, and people waiting—for *him*. There was no interrupted conversation, no surprise.

The commander was there; his presence explained the careful scheduling of the meeting. The three others were his weapons master from first training, the shift biomed specialist, and the exotic pharmaceuticals specialist.

One chair remained empty. Tyl Von sig'Alda bowed to the room and sat down. Five chairs for the table with five equal sides—an eloquent statement of the meeting's melant'i. All who sat there were met as experts, to teach and learn equally.

"Agent," the commander said gravely. "Your report has been read and analyzed. Additional factors beyond your prior scope of operation and information have been considered. We meet to synthesize an entirely appropriate response to the situation. The Department takes this matter to be of the utmost seriousness."

sig'Alda bowed his head in acknowledgment. Not merely important, but of the utmost seriousness . . . He touched the

Loop; accessed the program allowing concentration on all
levels.

"We concur in your assessment that yos'Phelium's genes
and Clan environment have contributed to his success as an
agent—and to the current uncertainties. Clan Korval tends
toward maverick. That they are Liaden is more accident than
intent. That they are a success cannot be denied. You have
seen the files: They search for yos'Phelium even as we speak.
More, Korval begins to meddle in our affairs—the First
Speaker mentions us all too frequently in public conversations; subtle inquiries arise in strange places.

"We have considered eliminating the current leader, Nova
yos'Galan. The house is tainted with Terran blood—" The
commander paused and looked around the small table. "Actions reducing the leadership of Korval have occurred in the
past. The timing of a new trimming must be weighed carefully. We do not, for example, know why they pursue their
kin so ardently. Is it merely 'Clan business'? Is there a deeper
plan? Do they intend to supplant us in controlling Liad's interests in space? Of all the Clans, only Korval might mount a
respectable military threat against Liad without allies."

sig'Alda found the weight of the commander's eyes upon
him alone.

"Understand that Val Con yos'Phelium's recruitment as an
Agent was a five-year program requiring expenditure of several operatives, as well as much cost. His usefulness to the
Department extends among many lines of action, not the
least of which has been his extreme effectiveness in carrying
out assignments on our behalf. That he leaves Korval in the
hands of a half-blooded merchant family we intended, eventually, to exploit.

"Therefore, every contingency you mentioned in your report, and many others, have been analyzed. The possibility
that Clan Korval might attempt to reclaim yos'Phelium and
secure him as Delm—that alone—would make our search
worthwhile. His knowledge must not fall into half-blood
hands. He must not be subverted to use what he has learned
from us—for the preservation of Liad!—for the sole gain of
Clan Korval. His abilities . . . Tyl Von sig'Alda, this will be
your most important assignment as an Agent of Change. You

will locate and return Agent yos'Phelium to us. If he is dead, you will bring us a body, bones, witnesses."

The commander had named him! He nearly missed the bow to the biomed specialist. That man began at once.

"The working model assumes you will locate yos'Phelium and be required to secure him physically. To do so you must be aware of certain factors." The man stood, grabbed up a point-writer, and began marking on the message surface.

"Your information package contains complete graphs. The overview is this: One, Korval seems purposefully aimed at achieving speed and accuracy of reflex in its members. Only a pilot may become Delm; Delm's genes are those most likely to be passed on.

"Our tests show that, under normal circumstances, yos'Phelium's response time is a measurable three to four percent faster than yours. In certain high-stress situations tested during training his responses were another two percent faster yet. You, of course, have continued to train and have a newer implementation of the Probability Loop—we project that, effectively, you are his equal. Lack of vitamins, isolation, depression, injuries—your report indicates he received combat damage—such factors suggest an advantage to you, should he need to be reminded of his loyalties. We give you charts, as I mentioned. Also—" The biomed man nodded across the table.

"At the commander's urging we have considered other possibilities," the pharmacist said, "and have developed a new design of perceptual stimulants. These enhance the ability of the brain to process information received from the senses, thus increasing the ability of the agent to respond rapidly and efficiently to outside stimuli."

She frowned severely at sig'Alda. "These stimulants are not to be used during Jump; they should not be used at a rate of more than six doses per Standard day. Note that only under extreme emergency conditions should you take three doses together. Take one if you consider action likely, another if action is imminent or carries a high risk factor.

"A muscle-tone enhancer will also be supplied: See me, it is an implant." With that, the pharmacist fell silent.

The commander spoke almost softly. "Your analysis of

Val Con yos'Phelium's actions during recent events, Agent sig'Alda, is inconclusive in the extreme. We have gained no insight into the reasons or the circumstances contributing to yos'Phelium's use of the Terran mercenary. Others, however, have studied the mercenary with care."

sig'Alda felt the rebuke keenly, understanding that he might have followed his original urge to discover more.

The commander's pause was brief—enough to emphasize, not enough to require an answer. "Therapy records indicate a difficult case," he went on. "The Terran escaped from reha-bilitative isolation several times during the course of treat-ment, and the doctor's final report reads merely: 'Subject no longer chemically dependent upon Lethecronaxion.' Our analysis of this phrasing indicates continued psychological dependence. This offers opportunity for manipulation."

The pharmacist touched a pocket and brought out several small, plastic bags containing an ivory-colored powder.

"This bag," she said, holding it out to him, "has a red dot on the seal. It is standard Lethecronaxion inasmuch as any drug of this kind is standard—of extremely high quality. Therapy records indicate the subject had a tendency to syn-ergize this, ah, *Cloud,* with alcohol, thus becoming forget-ful and intractable at once. The dose here is adequate for a large Terran male; the addict will be familiar with ingestion techniques."

sig'Alda was aware of uneasiness and touched the Loop for calm. Addicts . . . His dislike faded under the Loop exer-cise, and he once more gave the specialist full attention.

"This bag has a blue dot." She handed it to him. "It has the same overall weight, a double-strength dose of Cloud, and a time-release double dose of something you are well familiar with: MemStim."

sig'Alda smiled at the blue dot. Of course!

"Yes," the pharmacist said, apparently pleased with his ap-proval. "Agents use MemStim while reporting to aid the exact recall of events. This particular mix also contains a dis-inhibitor and an experimental receptor flush-and-bind." The pharmacist dared a smile of her own. "I designed the packets several days ago. Tests on subjects of the approximate mass of the Terran show interesting effects.

"Initial effect is unremarkable to Lethecronaxion: all memory older than a few hours, and, later, memory older than a few minutes, becomes uncertain, clouded—hence the vernacular designation. At the time release, the flush was nearly instantaneous, throwing the subjects from complete cloud-effect to a deep MemStim state. The beauty of the flush-and-bind system is that it ties the MemStim to those receptors most affected by the Lethecronaxion. An addict—or, for that matter, anyone who takes MemStim—has trained receptor sites; in the case of a Cloud user, these sites are most likely to be triggers to painful memories, else why cloud them?" The pharmacist paused, glanced at the commander, and received a wave that indicated she should continue.

"Thus the subjects went from total repression of unwanted memories to a total and enhanced recall. Depending on the amount of alcohol and disinhibitor in their systems, subjects recalled their memories to the point of reexperience. Variously, subjects attempted suicide, became delirious, bit and clawed at themselves, or were otherwise incoherent for periods exceeding half a Standard day. I expect that when the receptor-stimulus time is reached—that is, when another fix is required—there will be another period of disorder."

sig'Alda placed the packets carefully into his belt. The Loop showed a ten-percent gain in Chance of Mission Success, stipulating the opportunity to introduce the mixed drugs to the Terran.

The commander bowed to the drug expert, then toward the weapons man, who began to speak.

"We've run an analysis on yos'Phelium's mission reports and compared it with known events in the recent unreported mission. We have the following guidelines and comparisons." He took a breath, fixed his eyes on a spot above sig'Alda's head, and began.

"First, we have uncovered a bias. The Department had been taking advantage of yos'Phelium's ability to operate close to his targets. This consideration figured in his last mission—terminating an upper-level Terran agent in a bombproofed building. A more carefully factored reading shows that Agent yos'Phelium has a tendency to use a knife or other bladed weapon far more frequently than would have been expected from his training. This affinity leaves him vulnerable to middistance pacification by projectile weapons. He has a good-to-excellent rating with pellet weapons, but Agent sig'Alda's rating is within the margin of error."

The weapons master deigned to meet sig'Alda's eyes. "You," he said calmly, "will take extra practice with a variety of weapons before leaving. You will be equal to yos' Phelium at his best. We have tapes of his practices, and a competition program will be constructed for your practice sessions." He paused and redirected his eyes to a point above sig'Alda's head. "Given Agent yos'Phelium's tendency toward bladed weapons, it is suggested that Agent sig'Alda wear flexi-mesh."

The commander bowed to the three experts. "Your reports are most useful."

The dismissal was clear, and they all rose. sig'Alda stood, as well, but at a glance from the commander he sat again as the experts left the room. Dispassion, control, he repeated to himself.

"Your desire to pursue your mission immediately is appreciated, sig'Alda," the commander said. "You will consider yourself to be on mission now; you will leave this building only to leave the planet under orders. I will now address a resource with which you cannot be familiar."

The commander stood, went to the door, and set the portal locks. Then glancing at a wrist device, he rotated in place.

sig'Alda felt confusion and astonishment. The commander was checking for a spy, here, within the heart of the Department?

The commander returned and sat, hand on table so that the wrist-warn could be seen clearly by both.

"You are among our most excellent agents," he said. "And the one we seek is also among our most excellent agents. Understand this completely and explicitly: Your mission is to find Val Con yos'Phelium and return with him. If he is dead you will provide explicit and complete proof. If you find him alive and he refuses, in spite of all your best persuasions, to return—then you will bring explicit and complete proof that he is dead. His head will do for proof; or several portions of his spinal column."

sig'Alda blinked.

"Yes. I give you precedence. Do you understand?"

"Yes." sig'Alda bowed. "yos'Phelium is to return, even if under extreme compulsion."

"Exactly. We must not, at this juncture in the Plan, allow any Clan an opportunity to question our goals or to subvert our information. Now—extreme compulsion takes several forms. Death is but one of them.

"You have heard it mentioned that your training came after yos'Phelium's. Certain safeguards available to you are not available to him. You, for example, may go into 'Hold'; keeping yourself and your mind closed to outside interference until brought back by a special command issued by myself. This avoids the possibility of interrogation. Earlier implementations were not as secure, nor were they self-activated.

"There is a set sequence of phrase and echo built into Agent yos'Phelium's Loop. When you present the beginning of the sequence, he will respond—he must. If you continue, he must continue. At the conclusion of this sequence, yos'Phelium will be as a tractable imbecile: He will follow orders without question."

The commander glanced at the wrist telltale, then back at the rapt sig'Alda. "You will be the third person to know this sequence. You will not, under any circumstances, divulge or discuss this with anyone but myself or my successor. Do you understand?"

"Yes, Commander."

"Good. Tyl Von sig'Alda clare try qwit—"

He blinked. The phrase had not quite made sense.

The commander was smiling. "All is well, Tyl Von. When the sequence is needed, it is yours by repeating yos'Phelium's name, and then 'clare try qwit glass fer.'"

The commander extended a hand. In it was a small blue pin in the shape of a Liaden glow-gull in full flight.

"You are my deputy, Tyl Von sig'Alda. You may not fail." The agent took the badge of trust and bowed, momentarily touching the commander's cold hand. There was nothing to say.

VANDAR

HELLIN'S SURCEASE

Val Con settled comfortably in the chair, leaned his head back, closed his eyes, and consciously discounted the sounds being made in other parts of the house by Hakan and his father. He checked heartbeat and respiration and found both within the tolerances for physical relaxation. The Loop was quiet—there was nothing, after all, to calculate, the mission being three days done—and his mind was clear. His status was that of an agent in excellent overall condition.

Deliberately, maintaining calm, he sought the switch level and the switch.

He noted resistance, a flicker that might have been Loop-phenomenon, and a slight acceleration of respiration.

Patiently, he brought his breathing back down and called the logic grid to prime consciousness:

The mission is done. There is no need for the agent to be on constant standby. The switch exists and has tested well in initial action. There is no reason to suspect that it will fail in another instance.

Resistance faded. Val Con achieved the switch level almost immediately and perceived the thing he had constructed within himself on Edger's ship, using the L'apeleka exercises Edger had taught him. He withdrew his whole attention to the switch level, concentrating only on the switch, then reached forth—

Heart rate spiked and he was half out of the chair, gripping the arm rests, gasping, eyes open but seeing inward, where the loop reported Chance of Mission Success at .03.

"Cory?"

He was fully out of the chair at that, spinning to face the

intruder, heart stuttering back to normality, CMS fading from his inner eye.

Hakan was holding two mugs, steam gently curling from each. He held one out. "Want some tea?"

"Thank you." Val Con took the thing, slid back into his chair, and looked up at the younger man, seeing trouble in the soft blue eyes.

"Can I talk to you, Cory? About—about what happened."

The battle. Val Con inclined his head, and a measure of relief seemed to enter Hakan's face as he sat on the chair opposite. He stared into his mug.

"The newssheets say we're heroes," the musician said.

That was not new information; the four royal princes who had come over during the last three days to shake their hands had said the same thing, as had the commander of the militia mop-up squadron. Val Con waited.

Hakan looked up, mustache drooping, eyes as sharp as nearsightedness would allow. "Do you feel like a hero, Cory?"

Val Con sighed gently. "Hakan, how do I know?"

"Right," Hakan's gaze dropped to the mug again. "I feel rotten. I—" Then he looked up again, and it seemed that his eyes were filled with tears. "I killed three men. *Three*." He turned to look at the window, voice dropping. "How many did you kill?"

Memory provided an exact tally. "More than three." Val Con sipped his tea. "You did well. Hakan, you did your duty. Besides the three dead, you wounded many and kept them from fighting. Remember that you were armed with only a gun for hunting—"

"That's it!" The other man's face was alight with passion. "That's it exactly! I felt like I was *hunting,* not . . . The one guy, he was—running through the brush, and I knew he was going to have to jump the stream and I just waited for him, Cory. Played him like he was a stag; and when he jumped, I—" His voice cracked, but his passion impelled him to finish. "He jumped and I killed him; and then I was on to the next guy—and I never felt anything, except that *that* was taken care of . . ."

A cool head in battle and the reactions of a pilot. Corrective surgery for the myopia and a bit of training, and he might well have been an adequate agent. Val Con sipped tea.

"You were in the militia. Did they tell you that you might need to kill in battle?" He paused. "You own a gun to hunt with. You say you have hunted and killed before."

"But not a *man*," Hakan whispered. "I'd never killed a man before, Cory."

"Ah." Val Con considered the reddish depths of his tea. Why does he come to me? he wondered irritably. And he answered himself in the next breath: You were the Agent in Charge. To whom else would he go?

"It is—sad," he began slowly, eyes still turned down, "that men must be killed in battle. It would be better if no person ever—needed—to kill another person." He sighed, groping after concepts that should not be so tenuous, beliefs that had no strength of conviction, though he knew, somewhere very deep within himself, that he believed them with a passion that shadowed Hakan's grief. "The thing you did—the man who jumped and died. That man carried a—a big gun—a *heavy-automatic*. Is that right?"

"You saw him? Yeah, he was carrying a thalich gun. I used one once, in the militia. Thing can really tear up a target."

"So. Think about that man, with that gun, and one more man to guard his back—think about that man on Main Street in Gylles." He glanced up, saw that Hakan was looking vaguely ill, and pushed the point home. "One man, one gun—how many would *he* have killed? People who were unarmed, who were not soldiers, or—children, shopkeepers. Zhena Trelu. Kem."

He leaned forward and touched the other man's arm. Such a gesture seemed required. "You did well, Hakan. I can see no way in which you could have done better, after you decided to disobey me and stay."

Hakan actually grinned, though the expression was a little wobbly around the edges. "Well, what could I do? Miri was in there, and you go walking up to the house, just as cool—with a *knife*, for—I thought at least I could, you know, create a diversion. Keep the guys who were outside busy, so they didn't decide to go in the house. Give you and Miri a chance to get out alive."

"You achieved your goal. You lived through the battle. You have found abilities inside you that you did not know were there. All of this is good, Hakan."

Val Con shifted uncertainly. "You asked me—I have never met a hero. I don't know what a hero feels like. I think that it doesn't matter how *many* men you kill. I think that only animals kill without sadness, even when there is no choice except to kill. I think—you have not been playing your guitar, Hakan. When I have been—troubled—before, I found it was—good—to play music. To let the music help—sort out what has happened."

"Neither one of us has been playing," Hakan agreed. "Might be a good idea—" He made a determined effort, and the grin this time was much better. "There's still Winterfair to practice for, you know." He tipped his head. "My father's got a council meeting tonight. I'll invite Kem over for dinner, and we can practice after, okay?"

Practice? Music? Panic was noted; was contained. "All right . . ."

Hakan was looking at him sharply. "Maybe we could slide by and pick up Miri, too. Bet she's ready to go bats, being cooped up in a house with Zhena Trelu and Zhena Brigsbee."

Miri? Something else was added to the panic and quickly suppressed. "I don't think so, Hakan, thank you."

There was a pause, the expression on the younger man's face unreadable. "Well, okay, man. If you change your mind, though . . ."

"Thank you, Hakan."

THE WIDE UNIVERSE

The courier ship flashed into existence at the edge of the system, broadcasting on all frequencies, then skipping back into hyperspace on the third repetition of its message.

On Philomen, Cheever McFarland blinked at the radio and then at his employer. "Relative of yours?"

Pat Rin yos'Phelium turned a bland face toward him, brown eyes depthless and unreadable. "yos'Phelium is kin to yos'Phelium, certainly. You will have this matter here corrected in how soon a time?"

Cheever thought strenuously. "If I do it right, she'll be ready to go round midnight. But I can cut a few corners and get us out sooner."

Pat Rin raised elegant eyebrows. "I anticipate no need for haste, Pilot. Continue with your work." At the exit hatch he turned and bowed, very slightly. "Please."

The hatch cycled and he was gone.

Half a quadrant away, Shadia Ne'Zame snapped upright in the pilot's chair, slapped the tracer into action, got a line on the ship—and lost it as she vanished into Jump.

"Master Class piloting there, Shadia," she told herself, "which you could well emulate. Now, what's to do?"

She tapped the log for the recording, frowning.

Neu'lorn's quarters absorbed the message, even as two of the Guard dropped out of formation and shot after the courier. Halfway across the Access, the interloper faded, along with one Guard ship. The other executed a showy tumble and headed back to her post.

"Lost him," a cheerful young voice reported to Master Com. "But Cha Lor had him dead on."

Clonak ter'Meulen logged the response and replayed the courier ship's message. He was still frowning when his shift-mate came to relieve him.

"Broadbeam just caught, Cap'n." Rusty handed over a sheet of hardcopy with a slight forward tilt of his portly body. "Thought you'd want to see it."

"Bowing, Rusty? Lina must be teaching you manners."

"She tries, off and on." The other man was watching him

closely, concern evident in face and pattern. Shan rustled the sheet and looked down.

> ATTENTION ATTENTION ATTENTION. ALL JUNTAVAS EM-
> PLOYEES, SUPPORTERS, DEPENDENTS, ALLIES SHALL FROM
> RECEIPT OF THIS MESSAGE FORWARD RENDER ASSISTANCE,
> AID, AND COMFORT TO SERGEANT MIRI ROBERTSON, CITI-
> ZEN OF TERRA, AND SCOUT COMMANDER VAL CON
> YOS'PHELIUM, CITIZEN OF LIAD; REDIVERTING, WHERE
> NECESSARY, YOUR OWN ACTIVITIES. REPEAT: AID AND
> COMFORT TO MIRI ROBERTSON AND/OR VAL CON YOS'PHE-
> LIUM IMPERATIVE, PRIORITY HIGHEST.
>   MESSAGE REPEATS . . .

"How lovely to have a Clutch Turtle with one's interest at heart," Shan murmured around the cold feeling in his stomach. He looked up and smiled into Rusty's worried eyes. "Pin-beam a copy to my sister if you please, Rusty."

"Yessir." He hesitated, then blurted, "Is everything okay?"

"Everything's okay," Shan said, as if he were comforting a child. "The Juntavas have taken my brother and his lady under their wing—which you must admit is far superior to having them hunt you from one corner of the galaxy to the other."

"Sure . . ." Hesitancy was plain in the round, uncomplicated face.

Shan gripped Rusty's arm. "Old friend. My brother has gotten himself into a bit of a scrape." He rattled the paper. "This appears to balance the matter."

"So everything's fine," the other summed up, hope glittering bright.

"Everything is fine," Shan said, and wondered, as he watched Rusty walk away, if that was a lie or the truth.

VANDAR

– HELLIN'S SURCEASE

"But that's—" Kem turned around in the passen-ger's seat and stared at him. "Hakan, Cory and Miri are *married*. How can she be staying with Zhena Trelu and letting Cory stay with you?"

Hakan shrugged. "Militia captain split us up that way and told us to stay available. I don't think he realized they were married—and Cory just muttered something about her being safe now." He cast his mind back with an effort. "Don't think Miri liked it too much myself."

"I should think not." Kem eyed her fiancé worriedly, decided that talking about something was better than allowing him to lapse into another un-Hakanish silence, and put forward the idea that they might make a detour and pick Miri up before going home. "They'll *have* to talk to each other then."

"I asked Cory if I should swing over and get Miri. He said it wasn't a good time." Peering through the thickening snow, Hakan carefully slowed the car to turn into Berner's Lane. "Leave it alone, Kemmy," he said hesitantly. "Cory's pretty tense and I—it does things to you, being in a battle. He'll know what he needs to do—and what he doesn't."

"All right," Kem said softly as Hakan pulled into the drive and cut the motor. He sat for a moment, hands curled around the wheel, staring out at the blur of snow and gray sky.

"Kem?" he said. Then he turned rapidly, strong fingers closing lightly around her wrist. "Kemmy, I missed you."

"I missed you, too, Hakan." She hesitated, scandalized but certain that the time was right for telling truths. "I never want us to have to be apart again."

His face relaxed, his smile almost as bright as she remembered, and then he was serious again. "We've got a lot of things to talk about. But tonight—let's just be with each other tonight, all right?"

"All right. I'd like that." She smiled, and he cleared his throat awkwardly.

"Well . . . Let's go in and see what kind of mess Cory's made out of dinner."

Cory had made a work of art out of dinner, transforming everyday meat and vegetables into exotic viands, subtly spiced and astounding. Hakan contributed a bottle of wine from his father's fall pressing, and matters progressed as well as they could for a young lady with two virtually silent gentlemen as dinner companions.

Cory accepted compliments on his cooking with a slight smile and a formal bow of the head; he was predictably evasive about where he had learned the skill and fell silent the moment Kem ran out of questions.

Hakan loosened up a bit with the wine, and by the time the after-dinner fruit was eaten and the dishes were stacked neatly in the sink, he was very nearly the Hakan she knew. The phone call from Zamir Meltz informing his son and guest that he would be staying in Gylles that evening, rather than brave the growing snowstorm, seemed to restore him completely. He grinned at Kem. "Looks like you're snowed in too, honey. If you want to be."

"Hakan!" She jerked her head toward Cory, but the smaller man seemed absorbed in rinsing off the soup bowls.

Hakan's grin widened. "Hey, Cory—leave that stuff for tomorrow, man; we'll all three pitch in after breakfast. We got some practicing to do now! Winterfair's coming fast."

Cory turned, and Kem saw the worry on his scarred face. "Hakan—"

But Hakan had grabbed her hand and was hustling her down the hall to the parlor, whistling as he went.

Cory drifted soundlessly into the room as Hakan was tuning his guitar.

"Pull up a stool, my man, and get that keyboard smokin'."

"Hakan—" Cory began again, but he was interrupted by a quick staccato riff and a wide grin.

"What's the matter? Forget how to play?"

"No . . ."

"Well then, what're you waiting for?" The guitar went into a complicated arabesque of chords, and after a moment Cory went to the piano, slid onto the bench, and put the cover up.

He sat with his hands poised over the keyboard for so long that Kem thought he would refuse to play after all. Then, very carefully, as if he expected an explosion instead of music, he touched the keys and ran a soft set of scales.

From the guitar came the unmistakable intro riff to "Bylee's Beat." There was the slightest of hesitations before the piano took up its line.

Kem leaned back in her chair, eyes on the side of Hakan's face, preparing to lean back into the music. Hakan's frown and the protest of her own ears were simultaneous.

Disbelieving, she turned to stare at Cory. Notes were issuing obediently forth from the piano, correct and in proper time. Technically, Kem realized, the piece was probably perfect; even the crazy zigzag of sound that always made Cory shake his head was fully accomplished, without flaw.

But it was not *Cory's* music. There was no joy, no impetuosity, no subtle undertones. It was as if a music box were playing, rather than the musician she knew Cory to be.

Kem shifted in her chair, thought of going to the piano and making him stop, then paused and tipped her head as she caught some other sound there, under the sounds of piano and guitar.

Carefully, seeing that Hakan's frown had deepened, Kem got up to answer the door.

A very small person stood in the pool of yellow porch light, hood pulled back and red hair frosted with snow.

"Miri, for wind's sake! You're half frozen!" Kem caught her friend's arm and pulled her inside, peering toward the driveway as she did. She saw no car, no tire tracks. "How did you get here?"

"I walked," Miri said matter-of-factly.

Kem stared at her. "From Brigsbee's? In this? Miri—"

Miri shrugged. "I come to see Cory."

"Yes, but, love, you could have called us! Hakan would

have come to get you. Give me that jacket—you're soaked! What in wind possessed you?"

"I come to see Cory," Miri repeated, and leaned forward to hug her. "Don't fuss, Kem! The walk is not long. And where I come from, it snows like this—oh, often!" She winced suddenly, her head turning toward the open parlor door.

"Hakan and Cory are practicing," Kem began weakly, but the other woman had spun back, gray eyes huge.

"He don't play like that!"

Kem moved her hands helplessly and noticed again the snow in her friend's hair. "Go in there by the fire," she ordered, glad of a problem she could solve. "I'll bring you some hot tea and whiskey. You'll be lucky not to get the very *brute* of a cold."

Miri smiled faintly and went toward the parlor, moving with a silent grace that rivaled Cory's own. Kem watched her for a moment, then headed down the hall to the kitchen.

Cory's hands went flat on the keys, ending soulless perfection in discord. Relieved, Hakan brought his palm against the strings and looked up.

His friend was staring at the door, with no particular expression on his face. Hakan turned to look.

Miri stood in the center of the double doorway, eyes only for the man at the piano. She stood there for a long moment; then she shifted, moved her eyes, and smiled warmly.

"Hakan." She came across to him with her small hands held out. "I don't get a chance to thank you for your help. Brave you were. Very a friend." She slid her hands into his and bent to kiss his cheek. "Thank you," she said again, straightening. Then she tipped her head, smile fading.

"Hakan, I come to see Cory. Talk, we must. It is your house, and I am sorry to—impose? This room, another room? With a door that closes? You can lend us that?"

"This room," he told her. "No imposition—that's what friends are for." He squinted at her to verify that the braid wrapped around her head *was* wet. "We better get you dry, though. You'll catch pneumonia or something."

"Kem brings tea, and the fire is good here. Soon I will dry. Thank you, Hakan, again. You are a good friend."

That was definitely a dismissal. Hakan rose and started for

the door, guitar in hand. Grinning at Cory as he passed the piano, though the other did not seem to see, he almost bumped into Kem.

She set a large mug on the low table near the fire. "You drink every drop, now," she told Miri sternly. "We can't have you getting sick." She turned and went out, pulling the double doors firmly shut behind her.

Val Con had turned on the bench; he sat with his back to the piano. "Hello, Miri."

"Hi." She came to stand before him, noting with dread the blandness of his face and feeling stiff with more than cold.

"I ain't gonna keep you long," she said abruptly. "Just wanted to hear you say it, okay? So I *know*."

He considered her warily. "Say it?"

"Yeah," she said harshly. "Say it. Figure it's pretty clear— you sending me off with the old ladies and then no word. Little surprised—didn't think that was your style. Thought you'd tell me straight. Something like 'Miri, go away.' She took a breath, eyes on his face. "That's what I came to hear."

Dismay was noted and overridden as the Loop flashed into existence, extrapolating a CMS of approximately .96, with the removal of the woman from the equation. His lips parted; they were dry, and he licked them.

Miri drifted a step closer, hands clearly in view, stance specifically nonthreatening.

"It's real simple," she said softly. "Like this: 'Miri, go away.'" There was a small silence before she leaned forward, her eyes holding his. "It ain't like I never heard it before."

Tension was building; he attended it briefly, found no specific source, and discounted it. He licked his lips again.

"Miri—" His voice choked out, tension increasing to a level that could not be ignored. He experienced a confusion of purpose; was unable to separate personal desire from the requirements of the mission.

The woman before him leaned closer. "That's a start. Two more to go."

"Why?" The word came out of the confusion, lashed with tension, so that it was nearly a shout.

"You want me to go away," she said. And then, very softly, she asked, "Don't you?"

Did he? What *did* he want? Surely nothing akin to what she supposed. Surely whatever he wanted was not a thing so deadly that the mere desiring of it should leave him sick and shaken. He cast his mind back, fighting the screaming tension. Once, certainly, he had wanted something . . .

"I want—" He heard his own voice from a singing distance. "I want to speak to my brother. Three years—four— and I sent him no word; never went home. Never dared go home—he would see! He would ask questions; he would probe and—endanger himself—Zerkam'ka . . . kinslayer . . ." His hands were cold, and he was shaking.

"Val Con."

She was holding his shoulders; he should not allow her to hold his shoulders. She was dangerous; she was Miri . . .

"Boss." Her fingers brushed the hair from his eyes and touched his cheek. "Your brother's safe, Val Con. You never went home."

"But I *wanted* to!" he cried. "Shan—" He reached out and cupped her face in icy, shaking hands. "You do the same— ask questions, put yourself in danger. Miri . . ." He took his hands away, seeing what must be done for her, as once he had done it for Shan. "Miri, run."

"No sense to it," she said with shocking calm. "You're real fast, boss. Catch me in a second." She touched his cheek again, then put both hands on his shoulders, fingers kneading. "Stiff as a board. You sleep since the fight?"

"A little . . ."

"Thought so. You and Hakan look like a couple zombies."

"Hakan told me he had never killed a man before," he said, not sure what it had to do with anything.

"Hell . . ." The small fingers continued their massage, soothing in a way that transcended the mere physical. "I tell you what, boss—they shouldn't let civilians have guns."

"And they should not let soldiers have agents," he said almost drowsily. "Miri—"

"I don't wanna hear 'run' outta you any more tonight, accazi? I don't know if you know it, but there's a *blizzard* going on out there. Already walked five miles in it—I sure ain't running nowhere in it."

One hand left his shoulder, cupped his chin, and lifted it until his eyes looked into hers. "Boss, what's going on?"

"I—" The Loop flashed, predicting disaster, an adrenaline surge snapped him toward his feet while something unnamed kept him nailed there, eyes looking into hers, trying to find words in Terran or Trade, words that would let her understand what had happened and the peril she was in. "I cannot—locate—the—the switch."

"Switch?" She frowned in incomprehension.

"Switch." He paused, groping after more proper words. Switch? Not precise. Key? No. Pattern of thinking? Closer, but Terran would mangle it beyond sense.

Gods, what a language! he thought savagely. It's impossible to explain anything in it!

He did not know he had spoken the thought aloud, until he heard her say, softly, "Yeah, but I don't think they did it that way on purpose, do you? Probably just the best anybody could come up with on the spur of the moment, and they thought they'd get back and sharpen it up later . . ." She looked closely into his eyes and moved her hand to stroke his cheek. "Can you give me just the broad outlines? We get you outta this jam, then I'll learn Low Liaden. Deal?"

Impossibly, he smiled—*truly* smiled. She saw his eyes light with joy as his mouth curved, and for just a moment she thought they had done it. Then the moment was gone and she was seeing him still, but through the other one—the agent one—as if she were seeing him through bars.

He closed his eyes, and she felt the effort he was making as if it were her own. She bit her lip and did not dare to move, barely dared to breathe, until he opened his eyes again.

"When we were on Edger's ship, I left you for a time to dance *L'apeleka* and relearn the—proper—way to think."

She nodded, watching with fascination as his hand rose—painfully slowly, fighting his own muscles all the way—and curved around hers where it rested on his shoulder. She squeezed his fingers and thought she felt a slight response.

"What I did then . . ." he said slowly. "Understand that I—gathered up all that was—that I felt was—wrong—and put it

into one small . . . closet, Miri. A closet in my mind. I put a—
a lock on the closet. Then I put the key in my pouch and pre-
tended the closet did not exist." He paused and took a breath,
his fingers exerting pressure on hers. "Another way: I had
cornered the genie, so I found a bottle, shoved him inside,
and firmly corked the mouth."

"And when the army attacked, the genie got loose."

"No," he said. "No. *I* opened the door—threw the switch.
My choice. The lock was secure."

"Why?"

Why, indeed? He struggled for the memory itself, brushing
aside datum she would scorn as meaningless.

"I was afraid," he achieved after several minutes. "I—you
were in the house; there was danger. Many hostile people
were between us, and I did not know what to do. I—*wanted*
you to be safe, and I knew I would have to be—efficient and
very quick. So I—" His fingers were gripping hers tightly,
but if she was in pain she gave no sign. "I am not naturally
good at killing people, Miri."

She blinked, then grinned. "Not the kind of thing folks
usually apologize for." She paused. "So, you figured you'd
go in, wipe out the enemy, shut off this switch thing, and
everything'd be goomeky, right? 'Cept you can't find the bottle, and the genie's bigger'n you remembered."

"I—" Scout understanding signaled acceptance of the sim-
ile, and he inclined his head. "Something alike, yes."

"Hope it's close enough." She frowned. "You're caught up
in this—ah, hell—this *master program* they imposed at spy
school, and it won't let you find your gimmick for getting
out. Pattern's a mess—you ain't sleeping—getting jumpier
and more confused . . . Master program'd rather have you
dead than have itself shut off again, boss." There was silence
then. "You outsmarted it once with *L'apeleka.* Done any
lately?"

"There is no room . . ."

"We'll find you room." She gnawed her lip, considering.
"Okay, here's what: Lie down on the rug next to that fire, run
through the Rainbow, and get inside your room. Once you're
there, you can get yourself some rest, and I'll go rent the
local gym."

"No . . ."

She went very still, eyes sharp. "No? Why not?"

"I—the militia captain was here to speak to me. His unit will be sweeping the gap, and he wanted whatever information I could give, since we so recently came that way." He hesitated. "They will find the ship, Miri. It is not so well hidden that a concerted search will miss it. I must go and send it away."

"That a fact."

"Yes." And it was, though not the fact he had intended— had *wanted*—to put forth.

"When were you planning on leaving?" Her voice was almost casual, belied only by the sharpness of her eyes.

"Tomorrow, after dawn. A single person can easily outmarch a unit. I would reach the ship in late morning, send it away, and be back with Hakan by evening."

"Simple," she agreed. "No need for you to go, though, boss. *L'apeleka's* more important. I'll get rid of the ship."

"You are not a pilot, Miri."

"Did I say I was? Shut up—I'm thinking."

Thought took no more than a dozen heartbeats; she squeezed his fingers gently. "I need to move around a little. You gonna be okay?"

"I will be okay."

She hesitated, staring into his eyes, then sighed and slipped away. At the sideboard she yanked drawers open and made a satisfied sound as she extracted a pencil and a sheaf of papers.

Kneeling next to the piano bench, she sketched with utter concentration for perhaps sixty seconds, then leaned back and pointed. "Here's what the board looked like when we left. You show mc what it's gotta look like to lift."

He knelt, feeling the warmth of her body like a torch against his side, and considered what she had drawn.

The rendition was precise. Drawing a line beneath it, he sketched the pertinent instruments and the settings they had to achieve to engage the magnetics and initiate lift.

She studied it, frowning slightly, then nodded once. "Can do." Wadding the paper into a ball, she threw it into the heart of the fire. "Taken care of. Lie down on the rug and close your eyes."

"No."

"Now what?"

"Miri—" The unburdening came like a dam bursting; he sat suddenly on the worn rug and her face blurred before his tearing eyes. "On Edger's ship, when I was caught— 'battleshock,' you said—but I was caught in the Rainbow. I needed to relax so badly; reached for the best way, the safest way . . . a Scout thing, Miri, I swear it to you! Made myself vulnerable and this other—arms proficiency program— imposed itself—trapped me . . . Nothing is safe—they teach you that. And it's true—the only truth they tell. Miri, I dare not . . ."

She moved, wrapping her arms around him, and he should have fought, but instead he bowed his head, pushing his face into the soft hollow of her neck, and heard her say, "All right . . . all right, kid. Val Con, Val Con, listen. Are you listening to me?"

Face against her flesh, he nodded.

"Good. Now you're gonna have to trust me, okay? I been at your back, ain't that true?"

"Yes."

"Okay. We're gonna get you down to your safe place— your room. I'll be with you every step of the way. You see anything scary, you sing out, and I'll get you out of it." Her arms tightened around him, fiercely. "Nobody's gonna trap you again, boss—an' you get my word on that one."

Her grip loosened; he was pushed gently away and found himself confronting a pair of very serious, gray eyes. "Lie down, Val Con. Please."

It might work. Something so very far away within him that he barely noted its input was screaming, clamoring, demanding that he do as she said; the Loops, for a wonder, were quiescent.

Slowly he gained his feet, approached the fire, and lay down on his back, arms loose at his sides. Miri, sitting beside him, grinned and saw the ghost of the ghost of his smile in return.

"Okay," she said, schooling her voice to that tone of

friendly firmness she used in the most desperate battle situations. "Close your eyes and take a deep, deep breath." She took one herself, eyes only on his face.

"Now, visualize the color red . . ."

When they were at violet, the end of the Rainbow, she asked, "Do you see the stairway, Val Con?"

"Yes," he said softly. "The stairway is—still there."

"And are you okay?" she asked, hearing the slight hesitation. "Not frightened? Not threatened?"

"I am—well."

"Then do you choose to walk down the stairs?"

There was a small pause, then he said, "The door is also still in place." There was a hint of wonder in his voice.

"Will you open the door?" Miri asked. "Go inside?"

"In a moment . . ."

She drew a careful breath. "Val Con? Is something wrong? Maybe I can help you."

"Not—wrong. It is only that I have not been—inside—since . . . Miri," he said suddenly.

"Yo."

"Thank you—is it only 'thank you'? Nothing more? Cha'trez, thank you for loving me—for loving me so *well*."

"I ain't done yet," she said, managing to keep her voice pitched right. "But you're welcome. You going inside, or you gonna stand around on the landing all night?"

His lips curved in a smile. "Inside . . ." And there was silence. Miri sat, short nails scoring her palm, eyes glued to his face, teeth drilling into her lower lip so she would not shout and break the web.

"Miri?" It was a whisper. Then it came again, louder. "Miri!"

"Right here." And what to do if something *was* wrong? After all that bluff about not letting anything hurt him . . .

But the expression on his face was joy, and when he spoke again he nearly sang the words. "Miri, it's still here! Still whole. *They never got inside!*"

"You happy?" she asked inanely against the beat of her own rising joy, not quite understanding what was happening.

It almost seemed as if he would laugh. "Let us not overstate the case . . . A moment." There was a long silence. "I will sleep now," he said then, "and key myself to begin *L'apeleka* tomorrow. A large space, cha'trez, if you can. If not, I will dance outside."

"And put Hakan to all the trouble of explaining to the neighbors that you were okay yesterday and then just went bang off your head? I'll find you something with a roof over it. And don't worry about the ship. Good as in orbit already."

"Yes, Miri."

"Bastard." Grinning in spite of herself, she rose and stood looking down at him for a moment.

His chest rose and fell with the rhythm of deep relaxation, his body limp, his face looking years younger—a boy's face, fast asleep.

Cautiously she inspected the new pattern inside her head and was able, after several moments, to be satisfied. It was not nearly as screwy as it had been earlier in the day, when she had made the decision to hike over and talk to him, face to face. Maybe it'll work, Robertson, she thought, and went silently across the room and out the door, taking care that it was shut tightly behind her.

VANDAR

HELLIN'S SURCEASE

Hakan, looking up as Miri came into the kitchen, lay a muting palm on the strings and set the guitar aside.

"How's Cory?" he asked, voice almost soft.

"Better," she told him, dropping into the chair Kem pulled out for her. "I think better. He's—asleep."

"Good," Hakan murmured. He leaned forward slightly to peer into her face. "Porlint isn't a cold place, Miri. It's near the equator, so it hardly ever snows."

She blinked, then she bowed her head with a touch of Cory's formality. "Thank you, Hakan. I'll try to remember."

"That's all right." He eased back a little. "Do the two of you want to go back to Zhena Brigsbee's? I can drive you."

"Tomorrow," Kem amended softly.

Miri flickered forward and touched his hand, flashing a smile to the other woman. "Hakan, thank you again. But it would be better . . . Do you know a place—a big, empty place—Cory could use for five days—six? If you do, he should go there. Me, I need to be someplace else tomorrow, and then I go back to Zhena Brigsbee."

At Hakan's distinctly blank look, Miri bit her lip and tried again. "The battle is not easy for Cory—he only comes because I need him . . ."

"Cory was in Gylles! How did he know you needed him? Came running in to the store, asking me to take him home . . ."

She was aware of a strong desire for a slug of kynak, a quiet room, and a book; instead she took a deep mental breath. "You and Kem are together long enough, you will know when something is not right with the other one."

"That's right, honey," Kem said. "But why does Cory need a big, empty place? If he's depressed from the battle, wouldn't it be better for him to be with you?"

"Not until he—" She sighed, hearing the echo of Val Con's voice, snapping with frustration: . . . *You can't explain anything in it!* "He must—exercise so body and thoughts run together . . ."

She flung her hands out, silently damning the tears that were filling her eyes again. "Hakan, I don't explain so good, and I'm sorry—you and Cory have to fight, and it is my fault!"

"Your fault? A troop of Bassilan rebels walks in on you and it's your fault? Miri—"

"Honey, it *isn't* your fault—" Kem started, but Miri cut them both off.

"My fault! Because one of them kicks the door down, comes in, and points his rifle at me. Borril jumps, and the man hits him with the rifle; Borril jumps again, and I take the rifle away—shoot the man—and another man comes, so I shoot him—I am stupid, you see? I think they are bandits—

maybe five, maybe six—the rifle, it is bad—rust, not oiled. I think I can stay and fight—"

"Stay and fight?" Hakan demanded. "Against six armed men?"

"Hakan, if there are six, already I take two—problem is not bad. But the third man—he doesn't come to find his friends. This one has a—a big gun—and I see him set it up and I see others behind him and I know I am stupid and there is no way to run. I have this bad rifle. I have my knife, but I am not Cory, who is good with knives. I am worried—Cory comes and he brings you—neither one a soldier! My fault, Hakan. I should have taken Borril and run away."

"Cory killed a lot of people, Miri—and I killed some, too."

"Three, Cory said." She frowned. "Hakan, why do you have a gun?"

"Huh?" He blinked. "I—well, it's a hunting gun, for—"

"Hunting? Why do you hunt? There are no stores? You don't make enough money to buy food?"

"Well, but—"

"You had no business shooting at those men with such a gun!" she cried. Catching the flare of pain on his face, she snapped forward to grab his shoulders. "Hakan, you were very brave—maybe you save my life. In battle, who can tell? You learn something now. You learn you can kill people. You learn how you feel about it." She leaned back, loosing his shoulders. "Maybe you should give away your gun."

"What about you?" His voice was husky, his expression still half aggrieved.

"Me? For a long time I am a soldier, Hakan. Soldiers don't break down doors and shoot people. Soldiers come, say they have taken the area, ask people to leave, and give escort, if the enemy is near." She shrugged. "People sometimes think bullets don't go through doors. Think their house won't burn—I don't know what people think." She shook her head. "You and Cory are not soldiers. You know how you feel. You hear how Cory played."

"Bad . . ."

"Like a machine," Kem added, and Miri nodded.

"This is why he needs a place—to be alone and to exercise. Please, Hakan—do you know? Kem? Anyplace, as long as no one goes there."

There was a long silence, and she despaired of their help. Then, Kem said softly, "Hakan? What about the barn?"

He considered the suggestion, his nearsighted gaze on nothing in particular. "Could work—it's sound, and we've still got the stove in there from when that crazy tourist was using the place as a studio." He nodded. "We'll do it. Cory can exercise in the barn till he grows a long, gray beard."

Relieved, Miri almost laughed. "Nothing takes that long. Tomorrow I show him where, then I do my errand and go back to Zhena Brigsbee." She looked at Kem. "If Zhena Trelu calls, you can—tell her something? I ask for a lot . . ."

Kem smiled. "I can cover you for a day, honey. Don't worry."

The tears came yet again, so she saw her friends through a sparkling kaleidoscope. "Thank you," she said, getting shakily to her feet. "Thank you both."

She was halfway across the kitchen when Hakan's voice stopped her.

"Miri?"

Now what? she wondered and turned back. "Hakan."

His expression was calmer, and he held Kem's hand as if he meant it, but his eyes were very puzzled. "Where are you really from, honey? In Porlint—"

"In Porlint," she interrupted tiredly, "little girls are not soldiers. I know, Hakan. Good night."

In a moment, the doorway was empty. They heard nothing for the short space it took her to walk the length of the hall, then only the sound of the parlor door, opening and closing behind her.

VANDAR

FORNEM'S GAP

"That looks like it, Robertson. Hit the timer and go."

Her hand hesitated over the last toggle, though, and she spun away from the board with a curse and took two steps before stopping to stare at Val Con's map all around her.

"Gods." Crossing her legs and sitting in the middle of it, she touched a duct-tape mountain, then picked up a paper spaceship. One world. One world to spend the rest of her life on, when she had once had her choice of hundreds . . .

"You're stuck, Robertson. Face facts and quit belly-achin'. I don't know what's got into you lately—turning into a damn watering can. You think it's tough here? What about Val Con? Grows up on Liad, goes for First-In Scout—been places; done things—got a family; misses his brother. Hear him kvetch?"

She sat for a little while longer, staring sightlessly at the map and thinking about Liz, about Jase and Suzuki and a dozen or so others. Thought about Skel—and there was no sense at all to that, because Skel was long dead and rotted on Klamath. If Klamath was still around.

"There's worse places, Robertson. Get moving."

Slowly she levered to her feet, moved to the board, and checked it one last time before setting the timer, sealing her jacket, and running for the exit.

She rolled out of the emergency hatch, spinning as she landed, then pitched the ship's key into the narrowing slit and skittered away in the knee-deep snow, heading for a downhill clump of scrub.

Ground, snow, and brush shivered; there was a grating, subaural scream, and Miri dove, twisting around to see—and the ship was already twenty feet up, heading straight into the cloud-cast sky.

She watched until it was nothing but a glint of hidden sunlight on scarred metal; watched until it was nothing at all. Watched until her eyes ached and she came to herself because the tears had frozen and were burning her cheeks.

She scrubbed them away with cold-reddened hands. Then, rigidly ignoring the gone feeling in her belly, she turned and marched back toward Gylles.

Body reported cold and darkness growing beyond closed eyes. The inner sentinel assigned to monitor outer conditions allowed the body to burn more calories, to generate more heat. The dark was of no account.

He danced: beat, breath, thought, movement, without division; only Self and the attributes of Self, thus named: Val Con yos'Phelium Scout, Artist of the Ephemeral, Slayer of the Eldest Dragon, Knife Clan of Middle River's Spring Spawn of Farmer Greentrees of the Spearmaker's Den, Tough Guy.

He had passed through the three most elementary Doors, taken the designated rest, and approached finally the fourth Door, *B'enelcaratak,* the Place of Celebrating Fragments.

He drew yet again upon his name and focused his celebration, his understanding, upon that special portion: Tough Guy.

There was a flare of bright warmth, perceived wholly, as name brought forth celebration of she who had named. He lived the joy, tears running unremarked from behind shielding lashes, and the dance changed to exultation of so sharp a blade, so bright a flame, so unlooked-for a lifemate—so beloved a friend.

The dance came back upon itself, joy constant, and he moved close to the Door, opened his understanding to the fragment of his name—and cried aloud, eyes opening to darkness, body shuddering, joy dissolved in an acid torrent of self-loathing.

He gained minimal control; he pushed his body to the stove in the corner and forced his hands to pick up wood and stack it in a pattern drawn of skill belonging to a man he once had been.

Hunching over the fire, he strove to warm his body while the coldness raging within filled his mouth with the taste of copper and his soul with despair.

"Miri." He put his hands toward the flames and spoke to her as if she stood there, in the shadow behind the stove. "This other—it is very strong, Miri—and I am not very strong at all. I tricked you—made you lifemate to a man who does not exist. Ah, gods . . ." His voice grew ragged with horror. "Gods, the things I have done!"

Being made over to somebody else's specs—that's dying, ain't it?

He froze, listening to her with memory's sharp ears.

Master program'd rather have you dead than have itself shut off again, boss.

How many tricks had they planted to turn himself against himself? To be sure that he would keep to the Department— or die rather than break free?

He had beaten them once—on Edger's ship. Had beaten them with one shard of certainty caught and held from the confusion of four years' divorce from his soul: They lied.

Of his own will, he had shattered the gain of that dance upon Edger's ship, but he held still that shard of truth. It was a beginning, though not the beginning he had thought to make. Humanlike, he had flung himself headlong into *L'apeleka* before all proper thought had been taken. He smiled ruefully at the darkness beyond the stove.

"The dance will be long," he said softly. "Cha'trez, do you wait for me . . ."

THE GARBAGE RUN

Pre-entry sounded. Shadia woke and cycled the pilot's chair to vertical, dragging the safety webbing into place with one smooth motion, eyes already sweeping the board. She registered the go-pattern, signaled pilot readiness, and brought up the screens, and the Scout ship phased gently into normal space.

Hanging in her forward screen was a midsize planet—one of three in the system, the only one habitable. Planet I-2796-893-44—Vandar, according to the locals—Interdicted and Off-Limits to Galactic Trade and Contact by Reason of Social Underdevelopment.

Sighing, she kicked in the log—and sighed again as the legend INITIATE DESIGNATED APPROACH scrolled across the bottom of the prime screen. More for something to do than because she doubted the ability of ship automatics, she slapped the board to manual and rolled smartly into the designated spiral.

"As if," she grumbled in Vimdiac, the tongue in which she most commonly talked to herself, "they have anything remotely strong enough to see me. Ah well, Shadia—consider it a bit of piloting practice, though the problem's hardly knotty. Hah! Getting a trifle overwise, are we? And just how precisely can you overlay the route, my braggart?"

For the next little while she busied herself with matching the designated approach point for point. In second aux screen, the blue of ship's approach ruthlessly overlaid the black route, while Shadia hummed in contented concentration.

"A cantra says you'll miss the pace at orbit entry; you were ever a— What by the children of Kamchek is *that?*"

It glinted in the light of the yellow sun as its orbit brought it from behind the world. Mid-orbit and holding. Shadia upped mag, directed the sensors, and very nearly snapped at the computer. The second aux screen showed ship's approach steady on the route.

A vessel, the computer reported, as if intuition had not told her that seconds earlier. Coil-dead, the sensors added, and the computer provided an image to aux three, delineating an orbit in strong decay. Life-form readings were uncompromisingly flat—not so much as a flea was alive on that ship, though sensors indicated a functioning support system.

Shadia punched Navcomp, remembered the board was on manual, and ran the calculation in her head, plotting the intersection of the route and the derelict. Velocity adjusted, sensors and scanners kicked to the top, the Scout ship moved in.

Her ship hung within seconds of the empty vessel. She had pulled the files: The ship was without Liaden reference marks, and the two numbers—a seven and an eleven connected by a dash, with the homeport apparently blotted out by a dab of paint—brought nothing up on the screen.

The damage the ship had endured was obvious: scars, scrapes, and bright metal-splashes, as if it had gone through a meteor swarm at speed with no screens. The longer she stared at it, the more she expected it to act as a ship should, to roll or orient, to acknowledge the presence of another ship.

The good news, if there was any, was the lack of major leaks. The spectroscope showed no untoward gas cloud, no signs that the ship had been opened to vacuum.

The bad news was the location, confirming again the need for the garbage run. Damn! The last time someone had found something around a proscribed world they had spent three years tracking everything down and filling out reports.

For a moment she considered forgetting that she had seen the thing, knowing full well that eventually her tapes would be audited and someone would spot it.

"Damn book!" she muttered. "Page 437, Paragraph 4: Report before boarding any suspicious or unauthorized vessel in a proscribed zone."

Unwillingly she punched up the coords for the nearest report bounce and powered up the emergency pin-beam. She hit the switch that would broadcast her sensor readings on the side band, all the while cursing her luck.

Some time later, she stood on the bridge of the derelict, frowning at the map on the floor. The yacht had fallen to Yxtrang—anyone with eyes could mark the signs—yet Yxtrang did not commonly take time from a raid to engage in meticulous cartography. Nor would one expect them, with an unprotected world at their feet, to delay even a heartbeat in the mapping of an expedition.

Shadia crouched, as if closer proximity would uncover rhyme—she did not expect reason—and finger-traced the familiar symbol for river.

Certainly Yxtrang, whatever their unknowable needs, would not use Liaden symbology on their map.

And certainly, she thought, eyeing the thing with new understanding, they would never map just so, as a Scout might map, taking time and infinite care, forcing hints of information from the yacht's pitiful scans and incorporating them into a body of fact that might be studied and known. The computer on such a vessel would never have had the capacity for the task, even assuming the ship had been undamaged at the time of mapping . . .

"Someone gone eklykt'i." Shadia sat back on her heels. Such things happened. Scouts tended to drop out of sight, to go native on some world they may have found and failed to report—or on any world that suited them better than stuffy, stifling Liad. It was not inconceivable that someone had found Vandar just to his taste.

She considered it, eyes on the map. The unknown Scout raises Vandar—leave for a moment the questions of why he might arrive in something as incongruous as a mere private yacht and in such ignorance of his world of choice that he must squander days in mapping and deciding. He arrives, we say, and in time descends to the planet surface, perhaps programming the yacht for an outbound course—or an inbound course, Shadia thought abruptly. Best to sink the thing in the sun and be done with it.

The empty yacht, then, is apprehended in its course by Yxtrang, who strip it and tag it for salvage.

"And leave it harmlessly in orbit around an inhabited world? Come now, Shadia!"

She sighed sharply and snapped to her feet. The facts were that a derelict yacht had no business about Vandar—never mind how it had gotten there. Her duty was clear, at least. Surface scans showed no disruptions such as an invading force of Yxtrang might engender, nor was she authorized to search out one gone eklykt'i. Speculation could be put aside for a later time. It would help fill the remaining hours of the garbage run.

She ran the hand sensors around, recording whatever details mere human eyes might miss. It was possible that she was stranding someone there—but that was their lookout, not hers. Besides, the way the orbit was canted, the ship was not good for much more than a few hundred days. Might as well finish the job properly.

Purposefully she turned to the board, flipped toggles, and initiated overrides, brows rising briefly as the Statcomp reported several mandatory energy governors missing entirely; she cycled the magnetics until the whine hurt her ears, fed all available energy, including life support, into one critical cell, and ran for the door.

She hit the pilot's chair and slapped toggles, not bothering with webbing, then jerked the Scout ship away in a dizzying roll, hands flashing over a board yellow-lit with warnings, building velocity at an alarming rate, blurring impossibly into Jump. Behind her, the derelict yacht exploded, raining daytime meteors onto the world below.

VANDAR

SPRINGBREEZE FARM

Dawn was three hours away when a shadow de-
tached itself from the others clustered about the scuppin
house and made its way soundlessly across the crusty snow
to the base of the kitchen steps. At the top of the flight, the
door swung open on newly oiled hinges, and a second
shadow—shorter, more slender—leaned out, yellow light
spilling from the room behind and gleaming off a wealth of
copper hair.

"Morning," she said, as if she could see him plainly,
though the light did not reach nearly so far. "You coming in
or not?"

"Good morning," he murmured, drifting silently up the
stairs. At the landing he paused and smiled and made his
bow. "I would very much like to come in, please, Miri."

"Good thing." She grinned and slipped back into the room.
"Breakfast's almost ready. Thought I'd have to give your half
to the dog."

"Am I late?" he asked closing the door and unfastening his
jacket. From the rug in the corner, Borril thumped his tail and
gave a groan of welcome.

"Not late," Miri said from the stove. "I guess you're just
right on time."

He grinned, hung his jacket on the peg between her blue
one and Zhena Trelu's disreputable plaid, and bent to yank on
Borril's ears. "Hello, dog. So you survived, did you? Quite
the hero—the newssheets told your story most movingly."

Borril groaned loudly and dove sideways onto his head,
rolling an ecstatic yellow eye.

Val Con laughed, reached out to grab the blunt snout, and
gave a brisk shake. "Shameless creature. I've come home

only to pull on your ridiculous ears, I suppose. Yes, I see the splint. Your own fault for breaking the leg in the first place. Surely you might have managed things better than that?"

The dog answered with another soulful groan, which squeezed off into a sigh as the man rose and moved toward the stove.

Miri glanced up and pointed a brisk finger at the cup steaming on the counter. "You walk all the way from Hakan's, boss?"

He curved cold hands gratefully about the teacup and bent his face into the fragrant steam. "It is quite lovely tonight—very clear. It is true there are not so many stars in this system, but I think tonight one might have counted each." He sipped carefully. "I was not so patient, alas."

"Could've stayed till morning," Miri said, doing efficient things with spatula and skillet while Val Con sniffed appreciatively. "Hakan would've brought you on his way into town."

He raised a brow. "But, you see, I wished to speak to my wife tonight, and I am very much afraid that Hakan was abed by the time my necessity had made itself known."

"There's the phone . . ."

Val Con laughed. "Inadequate." He went to the dish closet and pulled out silverware and napkins. "Would you like the plates over there?"

"Yeah . . ." she said, attention almost fully on the task at hand. Val Con divided knives, forks, spoons, and napkins—yellow for her, blue for him—carried the plates to the counter, and poured a second cup of tea. He took both cups to the table and returned to rummage in the icebox for bread and butter.

"Breakfast," Miri announced, bringing the plates to the table. "Hope you're hungry."

"Not quite ready to expire," he said, slipping into a chair and picking up the fork.

Miri grinned and attacked her own meal, surprised at her sudden hunger.

There was a sigh from her right; she glanced up to find him smiling at her. "It tastes wonderful, cha'trez; thank you. I was afraid I would have to eat my coat, you see."

She laughed and reached to pick up her cup, then shook her head at him. "Zhena Trelu thinks you run off. Wants me to call the cops and have you brought to justice."

"A rogue," he told his plate, with deep sorrow. "A man without honor." He glanced at her from under his lashes. "You did not believe this?"

She blinked. "No."

"Progress," he informed the plate, stabbing a forkful of breakfast. "Good."

The green eyes were back on her before she could frame a fitting reply. "Has Zhena Trelu brought you more clothes, cha'trez? The shirt is very nice."

She shook her head. "Funny thing—people from all over Bentrill have been sending us clothes, and books and—ah, hell, I don't even know what half the stuff is. Money. Lots of money, seems like. Zhena Trelu was trying to tell me how much we own right now, but I don't think I got it straight. Bunch of stuff for you piled up in the music room—" She slammed to a halt, catching the frozen look in his eyes.

"A bounty?" he asked quietly, fork forgotten in his hand. "For the soldiers we killed?"

Oh. Yxtrang took bounty; Liadens counted coup.

"I don't think it's a *bounty,*" she said carefully. "The way Kem explained it is people think we're heroes and are—grateful to us for stopping the army when we did. Would've been ugly, if they'd gotten into Gylles." She paused, biting her lip. "The stuff's for balance, I think, 'cause people feel like they owe the three of us something for doing them a favor."

"I see," he murmured, and returned his attention to breakfast.

She finished her own, savoring the taste, happy just to have him there, quiet and companionable. Tentatively she reached inside and touched the pattern-place in her head—and nearly dropped her fork.

The pattern shone. It glittered. It *scintillated.* She forced her inner eye to follow the interlockings and branching-aways—and felt the wholeness and the rightness and the warmth of it like joy in her own heart.

She drew a shaky breath, unaware that he was watching until he said her name.

"Yo." She withdrew from the pattern-place with a little wrench.

"What are you thinking, Miri?"

"I—" She blinked. "Where's the genie, boss?"

"Ah." He leaned back in his chair, eyes on her face. "Subsumed, I think you would say; his powers taken and his vision destroyed."

"And it's not gonna happen again? You gotta fight again, you won't get stuck?" She shrugged, eyes bright. "Scariest thing I ever saw in my life, when that thing went haywire. I was looking right at it! One second, it's fine; next second, it's totally nuts."

"I am sorry," he said, "that you were frightened. And, no; I will not get trapped again. There is nothing left to be trapped within—only Val Con, the things he knows and the abilities he possesses."

She frowned. "The Loop?"

"Exists," he said calmly. "It is, after all, an ability I have— to observe and to render odds." He saw the shadow cross her face and leaned forward, hand outstretched. "Miri."

Slowly she slid her fingers into his. "Val Con?"

"Yes," he assured her, very gently. "Who else? Are you frightened, Miri? I—"

But she was shaking her head, eyes half closed as she touched the pattern inside her head. "Not scared. The pattern's—it's *right*. Not quite the same as it was—but it's okay."

He drew a breath, but she was suddenly wide-eyed and smiling as she squeezed his fingers. "Where'd you come up with the notion of genies, anyhow? Thought that was homegrown Terran stuff."

"So it is," he said, leaning back and releasing her hand. "But my foster mother was Terran, remember? And she told us stories. One had to do with a man who had found a bottle on a beach. He pulled out the cork and a genie emerged, bowing low and proclaiming indebtedness. He offered to perform three services, as balance for the debt."

"Sounds like the standard line," Miri agreed, watching his

face. "Can't trust 'em, though. Genies are a very slippery bunch."

"So it seemed. But it must be said that the fellow who had found the bottle was not among the wisest of individuals." He picked up his teacup. "I was enraptured by the tale—it took strong hold of my mind, and I found myself considering how I might have managed the thing, were it to happen that a genie owed *me* three services." He smiled, eyes glinting in what she recognized as mischief.

"After much thought, I felt I had a plan which was foolproof. I was, after all, six years old—and very wise for my age. All that remained was to obtain a bottle containing a genie." He laughed a little and set his cup down. "So, I took myself to my uncle's wine cellar—"

"Oh, no," Miri breathed, eyes round.

"Oh, but yes," he assured her. "It was perhaps not *quite* wise of me to have chosen a time for this search when my uncle was at home. Though I still do not understand why he made such a fuss. It was not as if I had failed to recork the bottles that contained only wine . . ."

She was laughing, head tipped back on her slim neck. "And he let you live?"

"It was," he admitted, "a near thing."

Her shoulders jerked with more laughter, and she wiped at her cheeks with unsteady fingers. His eyes followed the motion, and feeling absurdly shy, she held her hand out to him.

He smiled gently at the silver snake curving about her finger, blue gem held firmly in its jaws. "I am happy that you choose to wear it again, cha'trez. Thank you."

She shrugged, dropping her eyes. "It was hard to wear it and work around here—afraid I was going to break it or lose it. King's carpenters, or whoever they were, did such a bang-up job of putting this place back together, there ain't nothing left to do but feed the scuppins." She glanced up, half smiling. "We're out of a job, boss."

"We shall find another, then." He lifted a brow. "What pattern?"

When she hesitated, he leaned forward, remembering old fears. "Does it hurt you, cha'trez?"

"Hurt?" She shook her head. "Naw, it's—nice. Mostly, it's

nice," she corrected herself. "When you went all bats there during the battle, then it wasn't so nice, but it didn't hurt, even then. It was just—wrong." She bit her lip, looking at him worriedly. "Val Con, aren't you doing it? I was sure—it *feels* like you!"

Her shoulders were starting to tense, puzzlement giving way to alarm. He pushed his chair back, captured her hand, and coaxed her onto his lap. Straddling his knees, she looked into his eyes.

"Boss, it's *gotta* be you. I knew you were in trouble. Knew it! *Saw* it. Left you alone for three horrible days, like a certified pingdoogle, figurin' you'd pull out—"

"Miri. *Miri*—don't, cha'trez . . ." He ran light fingers down her face, trying to stroke away the lines of pain. "Please, Miri—it was not your failing."

She closed her eyes and drew a deep breath.

"Miri?"

"I'm okay." She opened her eyes to prove it, and Val Con smiled, very slightly.

"Good." He paused briefly. "Let us say that it is me," he began, feeling for the proper way to arrange the bulky Terran words. "It truly does not distress you? I am happy if that is so. I was afraid that you would be able to—hear—and that it would hurt you."

"Why?" She frowned, eyes sharpening. "No, wait—you've got a pattern for me in your head? Does it hurt *you?*"

"Not a pattern," he said gently. "A song. I like it very much. It is—a comfort."

There was silence for a heartbeat or two. "Val Con?" she said then.

"Yes."

"What is it? If you're not doing it, but it's you . . ." She shook her head. "I don't think I get it."

"I am trying, cha'trez—it is not so easy, in Terran." She shifted, and he smiled. "I am not blaming you, Miri. It is only that what I must explain is a Liaden thing. Did you speak Low Liaden, the name itself would tell you about the thing. In Terran, I must try to bend the words—though not so far, eh? Or they will be nonsense."

"Okay." She reached down and wove their fingers together, then looked up. "Go."

"Let us," he said, after a moment, "see if it will make sense this way: What you have in your head—what I have in mine—is a fragment of empathy. You, for me. I, for you. 'Alive-and-well,' my song seems to say. Also, I found tonight, it is directional. When I set out from Hakan's, I walked toward Zhena Brigsbee's house; then I thought to touch my song of you and found you had come back here." He smiled. "Perhaps that is why I was almost late for breakfast. How did you know I was coming?"

She shrugged, eyes on his. "I—ah, damn!—I felt you homing, I guess. Whatever that means." She frowned. "And I knew when you were in trouble."

"Yes. And I shall know if you are hurt, or in great distress. I think that, over time, one might become more skilled at reading the nuances." He sighed. "Not a good explanation, at all. Does it suffice you?"

"Gimme a century or two . . . Val Con?"

"Yes."

"Do all lifemates have this empathy thing? That's why you married me? 'Cause you could hear this song, or whatever?"

He shook his head "It is not a thing that is often given—" he began, silently damning the futility of trying to fully share the wonder. "And I have not been able to hear you for very long—certainly not before we came here. In the very old days I think that this was something more, that lifemates were, indeed, understood to be people who had become—joined. I—the tale goes that—again, in the old days, when such things were more common—those so joined became as—one person. Ah, that is wrong! That the thoughts flowed back and forth, one to the other, without need for words. That there was sharing—" He broke off, shaking his head sharply. "Cha'trez, I am very stupid."

"Naw, it's just a goofy idea. No sober Terran'd believe you." She thought for a moment. "This sharing stuff—that gonna happen to us?"

"I do not think so. After all, we are only ordinary people, not wizards in the full flush of our powers."

"Right." She sighed, stared intently at nothing, then grinned. "Guess I'll have to learn Low Liaden real soon."

"I would like that," he told her, holding her hand tightly. "Do you truly wish to learn?"

"Yes!" she said with unexpected passion, gray eyes blazing.

Breath suddenly caught in his throat, and his brows snapped together.

"What's up?"

"It is—a strange thing, Miri. I have only just thought." He smiled, though she was not sure of the expression in his eyes. "If I had not been recruited by the Department of the Interior, I would have had no cause to be on Lufkit at all, nor would I have walked down a certain alley at such a time . . ." *And all my life, he thought, I would have awakened unwarm, not understanding that I missed the weight of a certain head upon my shoulder; grown ever more silent, unable to know that I listened for the sound of one voice laughing at my side. In the old days, it was told that one had been able to call, searching for the beloved one had yet to know . . .*

"Now that's crazy, whatever language you say it in," Miri was snapping. "Better you'd stayed a Scout and been lightyears away from Lufkit than had everybody and his first cousin messing around inside your head, hurting you—" She snapped it off, appalled again by the easy tears.

He bent forward to lay his lips against hers, meaning only to comfort her, but he felt the passion flare and stood, cradling her in his arms.

"What the hell do you think you're doing?" she demanded.

"Holding you." He was laughing softly. "Shall I put you down?"

"Naw. Just trying to remember the last time somebody picked me up and lived." She closed her eyes, apparently engaged in a mental tally. "Been a while," she said presently. "I must have been ten or so."

"Not such a while, then," he said. "Five or six years?"

"More like eighteen or nineteen." She snorted. "Softsoaper."

He raised a brow, eyes traveling the short length of her. "So many?" he asked earnestly.

"At least so many."

He brought his gaze back to her face. "But—when shall you grow tall?"

She laughed. "Just as soon as you do. You gonna stand around and hold me all night?"

"There is merit to the suggestion," he allowed, "but I think instead that we should go to bed."

"You do, huh? I ain't tired."

"Good."

DUTIFUL PASSAGE

She went without anyone to guard her body, but the way was known and she had relearned caution. Time enough had passed for the seed to grow into consciousness. Time and past to have gone for an answer.

The familiar aura flared; she traveled the time required and knew that she need travel no farther.

Cautiously she opened an inner path and found herself again confronted with that bewildering array of defenses. Expanding the path, she discovered him at the core: asleep, at peace, shimmering slightly with the faint violet glow indicative of lust energetically expended.

There he lay, and there she saw him, and for all of that he was as unreachable as if she had never found him at all. Priscilla experienced a strong desire to grab his shoulders and shake him awake, demanding to know what under the smile of the Goddess had possessed him to build such a citadel around his soul. Had she been in body, she might even have done so.

As it was, she imposed Serenity upon herself and turned her attention to the bridge, stark and beautiful, and followed it to the scintillant pattern of the lifemate.

Once again that one was asleep, soul locked lightly behind a single portal. Priscilla allowed the shape and flavor of that barrier to grow before her inner eye and saw suddenly and with surety a large, wooden door, keyhole ornate with shining metal, wood gleaming with age and loving care.

She expended will, came close enough to try the latch— and paused to allow the landing to solidify about her.

The lifemate thought with extreme care, Priscilla understood suddenly, and formed her analogs with a firmness approaching physical solidity. A landing was necessary to accommodate the door, and a landing had thus been crafted; it would be discourteous to accost the door outside of context.

It was at the very instant that the landing came into itself, just a moment before she narrowed her attention to accommodate only the latch, that she perceived sitting on the floor just outside the door: a package.

Priscilla brought her concentration to bear, discerned the familiar yellow-and-black stripes of the Galactic Parcel Service, and found further a lading slip filled out in a round, clear hand:

> *For Priscilla Mendoza only.*
> *Sign here:* _____

Laughter almost destroyed concentration and sent her on her way home with neither package nor contact.

Sternly she embraced Serenity, then considered the analog minutely before signing her name, tearing the top slip away, and tucking it securely between handle and latch. She paused then and performed the action that, in body, would have been the laying of a hand in benediction upon the door.

"Goddess love you, sister."

Obedient to the other's necessity, she bent, picked up the package, and turned at last to go home.

ORBIT

INTERDICTED WORLD I-2796-893-44

Tyl Von sig'Alda studied the planet below him with fanatic precision. He measured magnetic fields, tracked weather patterns, and located likely volcanic faults and tectonic features. He compared the star's light constant against Scout files, compared once again the computer model against the actuality, and knew within a tolerance even the commander must accept that he was very near his quarry at last.

His information so far was excellent; the Scout was to be commended for the accuracy of her report. The cloud of debris orbiting the third planet had proved to contain a high quantity of isotopes and alloys not yet discovered in nature.

There were identifiable fragments collected on the second day—a metallic screw of Terran standards and a ceramic nimlet used in adaptive purification systems were the first things recognized—and more on the third.

The Loop showed him a percentage verging on certainty that he had found the remains of Val Con yos'Phelium's escape vessel.

Satisfied, sig'Alda assigned to the computer the tedious task of backtracking the cloud to a common origin and turned his attention to radio transmissions.

He was not much disappointed when the study of transmission frequencies, strength, and patterns showed no obvious sign of a call for help from the world below. It was not to be expected that a former Scout would announce himself as an extraplanetary and demand entry to the most powerful transmitters on the planet.

Dutifully sig'Alda called up the first of the four "survival models" the Department had provided.

The first assumed that yos'Phelium wished to remove himself from the planet with the utmost speed and cared not into which hands he fell—Scout, agent, rogue, or trader. That reflected the "average survivor" model, and sig'Alda did not think such would be the case. Nevertheless, he had the computer check for the model: voice broadcasts in Trade, Liaden, or Terran in standard galactic frequencies; Trade-code broadcasts superimposed on planetary broadcasts; and sideband broadcasts using planetary frequencies in either code or voice.

The second—his own choice, based on exhaustive studies of the man—was the "informed survivor" model. It presumed discretion: one would not broadcast indiscriminately in galactic language from a planet under interdiction. Instead, any broadcast would be on Scout or Departmental frequencies, with a slight possibility that it might also be on a private Korval frequency. Code or timed bursts would be used to attract attention to the proper frequency, at which point the listener would respond, creating a dialog and an opportunity for a brief exchange in code or voice.

The third was the "intentional survivor" concept, and the key to it was that yos'Phelium had *chosen* this world in particular. He would be waiting, according to that model, for a message, or for a particular time or event—or he had chosen what the Scouts dignified as eklykt'i—to be among the Unreturned. In that circumstance he would need to be tracked and found and, perhaps, persuaded, which was not a task sig'Alda contemplated with any degree of eagerness.

The fourth was the "victim of circumstance" model, and sig'Alda gave it the least credence of all: the submodels had yos'Phelium dead or hopelessly wandering a savage world. sig'Alda grimaced. As likely *he* would wander about doing nothing as would yos'Phelium—even more likely, according to the Loop. After all, yos'Phelium had been a Scout commander, a man with a gift for evaluating worlds, for learning languages, and for prospering in alien environments.

The computer having provided a target continent—that with the heaviest overlaying of smog, to sig'Alda's sighing dismay—he went through the files obtained from Scout headquarters, found the appropriate language, and slid it into the sleep learner. In a few hours he would know the names of the mountains and seas, the right way to hold a cup of tea, and the political system as it was at last report.

Setting the computer to wake him if it discovered a match of any the four survival models, Tyl Von sig'Alda relaxed into trance began to learn.

A command of the local tongue failed to soothe his loathing for things not Liaden. The language reported by the Scouts was without subtlety. Unless one was of the elite, there was little to distinguish oneself from others; it was difficult to proclaim precedence or authority—and slightly more difficult for males than for females.

The society itself was bucolic. While one could insult others, it was not a culture where an accidental insult was likely to result in a blood feud or even a fistfight.

The Scouts had indicated that the rate of change was unspectacular, though they had warned that local technology was reaching the Suarez point, the point at which technological advance might become the focus of three or four generations of society, society itself becoming fragmented until the growth was assimilated.

The sleep tapes had also given him a look at the food, which was uniformly off-putting. He could look forward to the flesh of game animals in many areas, as well as fruits and vegetables that would be old by the time he ate them, the world's shipping systems being woefully underdeveloped.

sig'Alda sighed. The creatures there—aside from his quarry—were barely sentient, by any thinking person's standards. Their goals were limited by their backwardness, their vision shortsighted, by testimony of their language and culture—the whole world populated by faulty genes.

There were times when the Scouts, with their insistence on independence for such "developing" worlds, produced nothing but ugliness and waste. Were Liadens merely put in charge there the world would quickly become productive and useful. Once the Department was able to arrange things properly, such waste would be eliminated.

In the meantime, Tyl Von sig'Alda studied the files on local costume, confirmed that at least there was no need to change his skin tone or have the autodoc graft on a beard. He brightened at the thought that yos'Phelium would also not be changing—or hiding—his appearance much.

He studied also the computer grid, ran probability checks, and finally targeted his first search-site: a large, industrial city on the southern shore of the bottle-shaped continent. All he knew of yos'Phelium indicated that he would establish his headquarters in such a place, which was what pitiful vanguard of technology so backward a world could muster. From that point, yos'Phelium would have access to the world's most powerful transmitter; would have quick access to new innovations; would be able, if need be, to influence a group of locals to do his bidding and serve his ends. Also, the climate was somewhat warmer than the second-choice site, farther north.

Well satisfied with his choice, the Loop showing a CMS of .45 and a CPS of .76, Tyl Von sig'Alda prepared to invade Vandar.

DUTIFUL PASSAGE

"Good evening, Priscilla. Delightful to see you return."

She fumbled, found the mechanism, and opened her eyes. "Shan."

"How kind of you to recall. Perhaps after a moment you'll also recall that you promised to cease exposing yourself to this danger." His eyes were silver ice, his pattern a webwork of fury and terror.

"What in *hell* were you doing?" he snapped, terror rising even above anger.

What had she been doing? She struggled, squirming further into her body—and memory returned with a burst of half-hysterical laughter.

"Priscilla . . ." He was out of the chair, gripping her arms, shaking her where she lay on the bed. "Priscilla!"

"I was—Mother love her!—I had to pick up a package!" She grappled with the laughter, hiccuped into sense and stared up into his eyes. "I have a message from your brother."

Face and pattern went very still. "Indeed."

"Actually," she amended, slipping from between his hands and sitting cross-legged in the middle of the bed, "I have a package from your brother's lifemate. I assume it holds a message."

"But not from Val Con himself."

Impossible to read all the nuance there. She shook her head. "Val Con has—many protections. I tried twice—awake and asleep—and couldn't reach him. I—" She met his eyes squarely. "Some time ago, I went soul-walking and left a message with the lifemate: an image of you, an image of me, and the message, 'We are looking for you. Help us,' loaded with familiarity, family-caring." She paused, then added softly, "Lina kept watch over my body."

"Did she? What a gift it is to have friends."

She winced. "Shan—"

He waved a big hand and sat suddenly beside her on the bed. "Never mind. You'll have told Lina necessity existed, which it certainly does. For Korval." He looked at her, and the anger was gone completely, the terror fading fast. "Your melant'i is very difficult, Priscilla. Forgive me."

"Lifemates," she said, hearing the Seer-cadence echoing in the words, "are heart-known. He is my brother, too."

"A theory Nova would be just as happy not to entertain. But we are drifting from the subject of your package." He sighed, and she felt him working, shifting internal balances; wondering, she saw him sculpt intuitive understanding and shadowy theory into a clearly recognizable seed-thought.

Healers are not taught such things, she thought. She wondered, not for the first time, if years of close association had sharpened and altered both of their talents.

"Perhaps I can understand how you might leave a message with my brother's lady," Shan was saying, turning his construct over in his mind. "But I cannot for my heart see how she could have left you a package!"

Priscilla grinned. "You've had training, love; and she hasn't had any. She doesn't know it's impossible to leave packages in your mind for pickup." Laughter escaped again. "And she seems to have left it, and I seem to have brought it away—so I suppose it's not impossible, after all!"

"Brought it away . . ." He glanced around the room, eyebrows up. "You tell me you have this package with you."

"Oh, yes." She touched it within herself, reading the lading slip and seeing the angular slant of her own signature.

"Might I see it, Priscilla? Understand that I would never doubt you—"

"Of course." She laid her hand over his, then heard his sharp intake of breath as his inner eyes perceived it.

"Priscilla?"

"Yes?"

"It's dusty."

"It's been sitting on a landing for weeks, awaiting pickup; and she does tend to be extremely concrete in her thinking," Priscilla said with delight. "Entirely unschooled, but very strong-willed."

"Val Con's lifemate could hardly be anything but strong-willed, if she was to survive the mating," he murmured. "The tag says this is for you alone."

"We can open it together, if you like." She sensed his passionate agreement, opened the packet, and nearly laughed again.

Carefully, striving to recall exactly how physical hands would manage it, she unfolded the single sheet of yellow paper; she caught a wordless rush of something from Shan as the two flat-pix clipped to the top were uncovered.

The first showed a man, dark hair indifferently cut, the line of a scar slanting shockingly across one lean, golden cheek, green eyes lit with joy, wide mouth curved in pleasure. The entire image glowed bright, as if with some inner brilliance, and Priscilla felt her throat tighten with that reflected love.

The second picture was less sharp, less bright: merely a redhaired woman, freckles sprinkled across a small nose; gray eyes direct in a willful, intelligent face.

Priscilla heard Shan sigh, but was too enmeshed in her own perceptions to read the echo of his.

Deliberately she turned her attention to the body of the letter, finding again the round, painstakingly clear hand, apparently written in bright purple ink.

> *We're okay. Clan Korval in danger. Don't talk to Interior Department. Go to Edger if things get bad. Ship coil-blown—world restricted. Tell Shan: Access Grid seven-aught-three \Trimex:Veldrad. Repeat: Access Grid 703 \Trimex:Veldrad. Love to all.*

Priscilla opened her eyes and saw Shan staring at her.

"Well," he said, and she was not fooled by the light note in his voice, "we seem to have done everything wrong! Not only has my sister had at least one delightful conversation with the Department of the Interior, but Edger has come to us! And there's no mention of the Juntavas, did you notice, Priscilla? As if that were no trouble at all."

He slipped his hand away from hers and rubbed the tip of his nose. "They're okay, she says—and Val Con looks worn to the bone. Got that scar in a brawl, I daresay—or a crash . . ." He sighed. "Access Grid 703, is it? Well, let us see."

But ship's comp, queried, took far too long to respond to the code, and when it did, the information was not satisfactory:

ADDRESS ON LIAD PRIME.

Shan sighed again and shook his head, and Priscilla felt his bone-deep worry as if it were her own. "It looks like we send it to Nova, my love," he said. "And await events. Gods, how I hate to await events!" He took her hand and smiled at her, wanly but with good intent.

"She looks quite sensible, doesn't she?"

Miri woke in the lightening gray of dawn, shifted up on one elbow, and lightly touched his scar.

He opened his eyes, mouth curving lazily into a smile. "Cha'trez . . ."

"Hi." She stroked the hair back from his face, then bent and kissed his forehead. "Letter's gone, boss."

"Ah." He reached up and pulled her back down beside him. "That is good, then."

LIAD

TREALLA FANTROL

"Ready, Miss," Jeeves said from just behind her shoulder. But still she sat, her fingers poised above the keyboard, chewing her lip in most unNova-like hesitation.

It was not, she told herself firmly, the *way* they had gotten the message. After all, Korval had produced its share of dramliz over the generations, including her own sister, Anthora. It was rather, Nova thought suddenly, that she feared Access Grid 703 itself. Which was of course nonsense and not, in any case, to be allowed to come before duty and the best survival of the Clan.

Deliberately she opened a channel and fed in the address. "Instantaneous download, Jeeves," she murmured, though he had already reported ready. And she read:

OBJECTIVES AND GUIDANCE

THE AGENT WILL RECALL FROM TRAINING THAT ALLE-
GIANCE TO A SINGLE CLAN IS ADDICTION TO AN OUTDATED
AND LIFE-THREATENING PHILOSOPHY. FOR CENTURIES
HAVE THE CLANS, EACH PURSUING THEIR OWN NECESSITY,
STIFLED LIAD, ENTRAPPING INTELLIGENT PERSONS IN A
FALLACIOUS EMOTIONAL WEBWORK AND SO DENYING THE
CHILDREN OF LIAD THEIR RIGHTFUL PLACE AMONG THE
STARS.

THE FRUIT OF THIS NONSURVIVALIST WAY OF LIFE IS
NOW CLEAR: TERRA SEEKS TO OVERPOWER AND ANNIHI-
LATE US. WORKING FOR THEIR OWN PETTY INTERESTS,
SEVERAL CLANS HAVE ALLOWED LIADEN BLOOD TO BE-

COME DILUTED AND HAVE GRANTED THESE HALF-BREEDS
FULL RIGHTS. IT IS WELL-KNOWN THAT TERRA PROMOTES
THOSE MATCHES, WHILE IT SEEKS TO BEST LIAD ON ALL
OTHER FRONTS, AS WELL. IN VIEW OF THIS THREAT, IT IS
THE PART OF THE INTELLIGENT PERSON TO FORSWEAR AL-
LEGIANCE TO CLAN AND, INSTEAD, TO ALLY HIMSELF WITH
LIAD, THROUGH THIS DEPARTMENT.

IT IS THE PRIME OBJECTIVE OF THIS DEPARTMENT TO ES-
TABLISH THE SUPREMACY OF LIAD AND TRUE LIADENS. TO
ACCOMPLISH THIS——

The image on the screen shivered, broke apart, and went blank.

"What!" Nova cried around the pain in her heart. She
reached for the keys, noting the channel still wide open.

REPORT FOR DEBRIEFING.

"Yes, certainly," she muttered, and ran quick fingers over
the board: RETURN FILE.

REPORT FOR DEBRIEFING, her correspondent insisted, and
added an explanation: COMMANDER'S ORDERS.

RETURN FILE, Nova reiterated. "Jeeves! Disengage."

"Disengaged, Miss."

FILE WILL BE RETURNED AFTER DEBRIEFING. YOU WILL
REPORT IMMEDIATELY. ACKNOWLEDGE.

MESSAGE ACKNOWLEDGED, Nova typed rapidly. RE-
GRET CANNOT REPORT. APOLOGIES TO COMMANDER. FILE
NOT REQUIRED THAT URGENTLY.

There was hesitation then, as if her correspondent perhaps
knew Val Con well enough to recognize the authenticity of
that reply. Nova glanced down, saw the open-channel light
still glowing, and folded her hands in her lap.

REMAIN AT CURRENT LOCATION, the message came
then. ESCORT WILL BE PROVIDED.

The channel light went dark.

NEV'LORN HEADQUARTERS

"**Come now, Shadia,**" she **muttered to herself in** Vimdiac. "What can be hunting you in Auxiliary Headquarters?" The hairs at her nape refused to settle properly down, and she added jocularly, "Besides Clonak ter'Meulen, I mean."

No good. The part of her concerned with keeping her alive in conditions where she might well *be* hunted kept her hackles up, and against all sense she found herself scanning the dock as she crossed the strip and turned toward the duty desk.

Half a dozen steps was all it took to convince her. Too many techs in sight, or too few; eyes turned toward her that had no need to note her passage. Her mouth tasted of adrenaline, and she began to scan the strip in earnest, looking for a face that she recognized. Looking for a friend.

She saw him coming toward her, his lined face bemused and slightly simian, his light brown eyes bland; beneath his snub of a nose he wore a most unLiaden mustache.

She almost shouted to him, but the unease and the training stilled the urge. Whatever was wrong, it was to be survived. Survival hinged on ignoring them, on allowing them to think she thought nothing amiss—whoever, she added to herself wryly, *they* were.

She increased her pace then, as the plan took shape, and nearly ran the last little distance between them, hurtling straight into his arms. Raising her hands to his startled face, she sang out in the mode used between those most intimate, "Clonak, I am all joy to see you!"

Surprise flickered in the taffy eyes, then his arms tightened convincingly about her and he bent his head for her kiss. "Well, now, Night's Delight; and of course I am all joy to see you!"

•   •   •

He had caught the look in her eyes and knew that she had understood already that something was amiss. Quick, oh, very quick, Shadia! He released her on the thought, the warmth of the embrace fading instantly as his eyes caught the pattern he had been hoping against.

"And now, my dear, I'm afraid we must return momentarily to your ship." He placed a light hand on her back and felt the resistance melt immediately. Bright girl!

"And what a trip you've had, eh, Shadia? A chance to sleep, to pine away for—"

He chattered on, fitting in, "There, three on the left, two on the right," as if it were a part of the chatter. The pattern had coalesced into purpose: They were moving to cut Shadia and himself off from the ship!

"How bad?" she mumbled, looking brightly at him and matching his rapid walk.

"I need a liftoff, oh, fifteen seconds after we hit the ladder."

"We'll kill someone!"

"Give a five-second warning. If you prefer, I'll lift it!"

"'S'mine."

"Right," he said as they touched the edge of the hotpad.

The sound of rapid steps was heard, too close—breaking into a run as Shadia's hands touched the hatch.

Chonak caught the belt she flung at him, grabbed the first pistol that came to hand, and fired a flare into the hotpad.

Alarms screamed; he slammed the seal even as the ship's emergency blast warning gonged across the lift zone. His last sight of the base was of several people standing straight up, frozen, while others more knowledgeable ran and dove for cover.

"Now!"

He grabbed the seat as the blast warning ceased and nearly fell across it as lift began.

"Lose me that way," he muttered under his breath as he groped his way into the copilot's chair.

"Nine seconds," Shadia snapped.

"Oh. Good. Let's listen to the comm, eh?"

The comm was a nearly unintelligible mix of yelling, pleading, and demanding. Emergency channels crackled; within seconds there were reports of five injured, several seriously.

"Ne'Zame, report in! Do not orbit; repeat, do not orbit. Cut and return to base immediately!"

The ship was accelerating rapidly. Clonak felt crushed by the weight, but managed to get his hand to his lips in the age-old sign for silence.

Ground Control demanded action, and suddenly Orbital Control was getting into the act, too.

"What is it?" Shadia demanded finally, keeping the ship on manual.

"Department of the Interior. No way to warn you . . ." His breath came in gasps. It had been years, perhaps decades, since he had flown like this.

"Should I back off?" she asked, concern evident.

"Fly it!"

She flew it well. He watched her hands and eyes: She would do. She had the reactions.

"Prepare to Jump," he gasped.

"We're in atmosphere!"

"Just be ready. Anywhere. As soon as we're free—"

No wasted motion. Good. No panic. Better.

"Ne'Zame, orbit and standby for boarding. This is the Department of the Interior. Orbit and standby for boarding!"

Shadia threw a glance at him. Clonak smiled.

"Better?" she asked.

"Rainbow," he said succinctly. "Forgive me, child—there was no way to get to you sooner. It wasn't until I saw those techs—all out of position—that I *knew*. Department of the Interior—been getting into our records; detaching our people— set up Nev'lorn 'quarters to hold them at bay, and *damned* if they didn't follow us here! They must think we don't know it—they must think we're fools, Shadia . . ."

"Ne'Zame!" the comm snapped. "Orbit and open, or we'll board by force! Who authorized this unfiled flight—"

Clonak reached out and tapped the button.

"This is Clonak ter'Meulen," he said calmly. "*I* have

authorized this unfiled flight. Administrative Override is in force."

"We do not recognize your authority, ter'Meulen. Ne'Zame has been detached to this Department! Orbit and open!"

Ship screens were full of ordinary traffic and, as the ship rose, they began to track the trajectories of the orbiting ships, the crawl of the suborbital transports, the— There was no sound. The lights were bright yellow.

Clonak glanced at Shadia, smiling.

She grimaced. "Intercept alert. My screen three."

"I had no doubt. Three ships on screen three. One of the warship class. What would have happened if you'd have been asleep?"

"I know, I know. I'm supposed to have that on audio, too, but it just gets so useless in the meteor . . ."

"Not to worry, my lovely. We need a Jump-ready status."

"Ready as I can be. We've still got too much pressure—"

"Right. Where's the moon? Ah. Let me give you the orbit."

Shadia stared at him. "Without the comp?"

"Of course without the comp! They're reading every bit they can! They may be able to pick up our control codes."

Clonak forgot about the residual ache in his chest, forgot about the meaning of the three dots bearing down on their tiny scout craft, forgot about the people—the enemies?— dead or dying at the dock. Reading from the screen, he computed the orbit they were to achieve and began to dictate it, watching the course board with half an eye.

"Pressure's down." Shadia said, all business. "Can they make that reassignment stick? Will you get in trouble?"

He called out six more numbers before answering. "I'm already in trouble—and so are you. Department of the Interior's been sharking about for information on you ever since you made contact with the ship out on Vandar. Collected the beam report, I suppose. Your bad luck, Shadia."

"What comes of following the book. Damn!"

The ship shuddered; Shadia hit buttons and read numbers off to herself. "Laser carrying a charge beam. Close. What do we do?"

"Start to roll—just like you're going to orbit. When I say *now,* we Jump. Instantly."

"Clonak, that could kill us this close in!"

"*They'll* kill us, my dear. They will. Jump when I say."

She cleared a screen and watched the gravity wells of the moon and Nev'lorn and the minor blips of the other ships. "You got it."

The ship shuddered again; she switched to a backup board without hesitation. "Charged all hell out of my circuits!"

Alarms, both sound and light, came to life.

"They've fired. Rockets," she said quietly.

"Right."

Her hands went to buttons microseconds after the automatics had done the job: all shields up.

"What's going to happen to Nev'lorn?" she asked suddenly.

"It'll be empty within minutes, I suspect. Project Orange will go into effect, and with any luck at all the Department of the Interior will get a nasty—"

Flash!

Blinding light exploded inside the ship, sparks bouncing across the walls.

"Kill my ship, you clanless—" She stopped with her finger on the switch. "Liadens. Clonak, what should I do? They're Liadens! How can I return fire, even with this popgun?"

"Administrative Override, my dear. I order you—as Chief of Pilot Security—to react as occasion demands. You have one half-minute before we Jump."

Her hands flew over the board; the ship tumbled with the program, its self-defense rockets spewing suddenly, hopelessly, across space, toward the destroyer bearing rapidly down on it.

Flaaassshhh!

Again boards were blown; again she hit the circuit overrides.

There was another strike, and the ship protested—there was a high-pitched scream of air . . .

"Breached!" she cried.

"Now, Shadia."

Her hands continued their motion—a last firing in defense,

in rebellion; they skipped in a single motion to the bright red button and slapped it, hard.

The enemy's charge hit as she hit the button—and the ship began to come apart as they jumped.

LIAD

TREALLA FANTROL

The Memory was hard upon her, and Nova sought to relax into it as the Healers had taught her, trying to forget how much she hated her talent, how much she had always hated it—how helpless she was against the rising of its tide.

This Memory had belonged to one called Bindrea yos'Phelium. An ancient Memory—Trealla Fantrol had not yet been built when Bindrea was alive—but for all of that potent and quite impatient. Nova had had a brisk tussle at the outset for control of the landcar, managing to keep it in her hands only by driving much faster than she would have preferred, no matter what the emergency.

It was madness to go so quickly, no matter how well she knew the road. She shrugged to herself. All that she did was madness just now.

The children would be off-planet already, as well as Cousin Kareen yos'Phelium and Mr. dea'Gauss' heir. The old gentleman himself had refused evacuation.

"But the danger, sir!" Nova had protested, squandering moments of her own escape time.

"I am quite safe, Lady Nova," he had returned calmly. "Word has been left for the Accountant's Guild in my name, should anything untoward befall me."

"The Accountant's Guild?" she had demanded, while that minute and another slipped away.

"Exactly. It is to be hoped that the—persons—in question are canny enough to ask themselves what would happen should every accountant in Solcintra step away from their computers at once." He had smiled coolly. "Also, I have set inquiries about in the business of Korval. It is only proper that I be here to receive the answers."

"As you will, then, sir," she had said and cut the connection with scant courtesy, for the Memory crashed full-blown into consciousness then; time was suddenly far too short and even the use of a secured line was none too wise for so long a time.

Anthora had also refused to go, and time had fled so quickly that there was nothing left for Nova but to give a fierce hug, laying cheek against cheek, and go, leaving a sister—a member of the Line Direct—alone in the empty vault of their home.

Quite right, Bindrea's Memory interrupted. *Can't leave the Tree unguarded. Can't leave the Clan without representation. Might want to come back. Gods damn you, girl, drive! Is it your life you're saving or a game?*

Nova gunned the car, which seemed to pacify the Memory, then turned back again to her tally of madness.

Word had been sent to Shan and to Pat Rin; and to Shan had also gone a transcript of the Department of the Interior's Objectives. Nova shuddered. That Val Con owed those people duty—Val Con, who had been raised as a brother to his half-Terran cousins, who had called a Terran woman 'Mother,' who was a *Scout,* and who, by all reports received, had chosen to share his life with a woman who counted herself Terran.

Madness was everywhere, not the least of it having to do with the First Speaker of Clan Korval haring away from her Line House mere minutes ahead of those who must be deemed assassins—or worse.

The landcar swerved, took the curve into Jelaza Kazone's drive badly, straightened, then accelerated, seemingly straight for the Tree itself, which was impossibly tall and no comfort to her at all, though before it had always been so.

She roared into the front court and never slowed as Bindrea's Memory sent her charging toward a serviceway between two garages.

The serviceway ended before an outbuilding of the old

style, built of rough-hewn red stone. Nova killed the car's power, fumbled with the door catch—and Bindrea was with her fully, moving her out of the car and sending her at a dead run across the thin court to the outbuilding's door.

It was Bindrea who slapped two locks—the first visible at shoulder height; the second invisible by her knee—and Bindrea who was relieved to see that the sleek little two-seater was still where she had left it.

It was Nova who slammed the hatch, fed power to the coils, cycled the magnetics, and began the test cycle. She called up the course computer and began to plot evasive maneuvers, drawing on what she knew of the planetary defense screen. Fingers moved so rapidly that it hardly mattered who controlled them; she locked the plan in; seeing a flicker of green light at the edge of vision, she frowned at the non-standard readout.

No worry, Bindrea's Memory assured her. *We're just interfacing with the world-net. Jelaza Kazone was the first defense base. We stayed tied in—unofficially—after they set it up permanently. That's the way it was when I was Delm. Any Delm who let that liaison lapse would've been a damn fool or worse. In my day, yos'Phelium didn't grow fools that benighted.*

The little ship reported ready, and Nova slapped the "Go" sequence, webbing in belatedly as her craft accelerated smoothly across the lawn and lifted effortlessly, its nose angled toward the blue-green sky of evening.

In Liad Defense Station Five, Pequi pel'Manda swore and hit reset. Her screen wavered and solidified, showing static gray, and she punched up the auxilliary boards, swearing some more as the screen kept to gray—and then shimmered into normality. Across the top margin was the legend: POWER OUT-AGE, MICROSTATION 392. SELF-CHECK POSITIVE. RESET.

Sighing, Pequi reset the board again and settled down to scan the small part of the planetary defense screen that was the responsibility of Station Five.

LIAD

TREALLA FANTROL

Agent-in-Charge Rel Vad Yoltak laid his hand against the annunciator. The five additional agents making up the mission team scattered as ordered, and Yoltak imagined they might be laughing at him. For which he could not in justice blame them.

Six—two of them experienced off-planet agents—sent to bring away one man! It was laughable. That the Line House they were sent to for pickup showed none of the bustle and busyness of an inhabited house only lent spice to the joke.

He paused. The Loop suggested a 22 percent probability that he would meet resistance there: Abnormal conditions noted.

Yoltak put his hand against the bell again.

The door opened a crack, then swung abruptly wider, revealing a dark-haired woman with extraordinarily light blue eyes, unattractively full at breast and hip, and perhaps even a shade too tall. She was dressed in house-tunic and soft boots, and just behind her stood a towering monstrosity of a robot.

"Yes?" the woman said, smiling at him brightly. Her eyes moved after a heartbeat, scanning the guest yard, looking directly at each of the half-dozen of them, even yos'Rida crouching, well out of view, behind the armored car. The Loop could not read the meaning of that: Abnormal condition noted.

Rel Vad Yoltak bowed slightly. "We are here," he said in the mode of Command, "for Val Con yos'Phelium."

"Are you?" The light eyes widened innocently. "Then I regret to inform you, sir, that he has not been here for several relumma. Leave your name, do, and I shall deliver it to him when he returns."

Yoltak frowned; the tactical radio in his ear sounded a minute tone, informing him that all team hand weapons but his own were now armed.

"We have been reliably informed that Val Con yos'Phelium was here not more than an hour ago," he told the woman in the doorway imperiously. "We have urgent business with him regarding his duty to the Department of the Interior."

The smooth brow knit slightly, and the wide eyes became shadowed. "Department of the Interior?" she wondered, then shook her head, Terran-wise.

Yoltak ground his teeth. "You will," he informed her sharply, "surrender Val Con yos'Phelium to us, or we will enter and retrieve him."

"No," Anthora said softly. "No, I really don't think so, sir."

Behind him, one of the company shifted to lay her hand on the butt of the gun riding her hip—and cried out, snatching her hand away from metal suddenly grown too hot to touch.

The flash missed Yoltak by bare millimeters; his face still warmed to it. The Loop rendered odds approaching surety that the robot was armed: Abnormal condition noted.

"Weapons are not allowed to be drawn within the borders of Korval's valley," Anthora said quietly. "Please do remember it. The next reminder will not be as gentle."

Yoltak moved his right hand, intending to signal the charge—and found himself halted by an extraordinary pair of silver eyes.

"Rel Vad Yoltak," she said experimentally, though he had not told her his name. "How strange of you to think you might walk into this house at your will. I am quite sure that Line Yoltak does not at all look to Korval. I may be wrong, of course, but it seems to me that Yoltak belongs to Clan Simesta and takes guidance from Derani scl'Mindruyk, who is Delm."

"What if it does?" he snapped, still in the Command mode.

Anthora sighed. "Why only, if it does, then you are sadly lost, sir, and must make haste to Solcintra-city. You will be able to find a shuttle there, I am sure, to take you to Chonselta, which is your Clan's seat, if you have such need to enter a Clanhouse. *This* is Trealla Fantrol, yos'Galan's Line

House, and the seat of Korval's First Speaker. You are—forgive me—neither welcome nor invited here."

"We are not concerned with Clans! I have said that we are here for Val Con yos'Phelium. We do not leave without him."

"And I, Anthora yos'Galan, have said that Val Con yos'Phelium has not been here for quite some time. Forgive me yet again that I send you forth unfulfilled." Steel glinted in the deep velvet voice, though the eyes remained as guileless as always. "You were allowed within our homeplace because it was not certain that you were a threat. Now that you have made threats, the house recognizes you as—undesirable." She glanced at the monster behind her. "Jeeves."

"Working, Miss Anthora. The representatives of the Department of the Interior have four minutes to gain the valley access road before Trealla Fantrol takes further action to protect itself."

Rel Vad Yoltak moved one step toward the half-breed bitch in the doorway—and found himself suddenly flung backward down the curving stairs, though no one had touched him! He snatched at his weapon, and the Loop countermanded the reaction so forcefully that his arm muscles spasmed. Exposed as he was, touching that gun could mean death: Abnormal condition noted.

"Three minutes and one-half," Anthora yos'Galan snapped as he came to his knees on the stairs. "I would move my folk with all due speed, were I you, Rel Vad Yoltak. Not," she added as an afterthought, "that it is my part to give a person of another Clan advice of any kind."

In the driveway, the car came suddenly to life, motor snarling. One of the agents lunged toward it, got into the driver's seat, and tried to kill the power. The car roared louder, bucking against the brake.

Yoltak's Loop gave the CMS as .15 and offered no information as to how their car's emergency remote had been subverted. Nowhere yet was there any sign of another human—only that woman with her icy, Terran-tainted manners and the monster, hand-built robot. The Loop indicated a .85 probability that yos'Phelium *had* been in the house, accessing Departmental files. The probability that he was *still* inside—and commanding this farce—went steadily down, though it remained well within the boundaries of what was possible.

Yoltak brought up his reserve of Loop energy and invested it in control of the Command mode.

"I *command* Val Con yos'Phelium to return to his superiors at the Department of the Interior!" With all that energy feeding it, the nuance should have been strong and nearly overpowering; instead Yoltak sounded like a schoolboy, even to his own ears.

A trace of some emotion flickered across the woman's face; his Loop read it as rage. She then seemed to peer into the far distance before returning her gaze to him.

"None of Korval is now under the dominion of the Department of the Interior," she said with a surety so sincere that his Loop read it as incontrovertible fact. "And you cannot shout hard enough or long enough to Command me. Time passes. Rapidly."

Her eyes sharpened, bright silver and scathingly intent.

"Run, Rel Vad Yoltak," she told him. "You are outmatched, your position weak, your numbers observed. Run! And do not come here again."

Yoltak gasped, his Loop flickering as if each word she spoke struck it directly, and saw that his Chance of Personal Survival was falling rapidly.

Heart stuttering, training fragmented and useless, Rel Vad Yoltak took her advice. The car was already moving as he flung himself into it. The Loop was unreadable in its gyrations, except for one recurring message: Abnormal condition noted.

VANDAR

WINTERFAIR

Zhena Brigsbee was a hero.

The king said so, giving a pat little speech about her presence of mind during a national emergency. Then he waved at the colorless zhena standing at attention on his right, who obediently stepped forward and carefully pinned a gaudy bronze medal on Zhena Brigsbee's heroic bosom and stepped back while the older woman turned pink and fluttered and said, "your Majesty" and "Wind's sake" until one of the other people from the king's entourage guided her back to her seat.

Miri smothered a yawn. Borril was a hero, too, with a shiny medal attached to his new red collar. On the whole, she thought, the dog had behaved much better than Zhena B. Which just went to show that breeding did tell.

Zhena Trelu's name was called by the man with the list. She walked straight up the aisle to the king's chair with her fragile, no-nonsense stride and curtseyed briefly. Miri wrinkled her nose: Catch *her* performing any such shines in front of a roomful of people!

The king was much nicer to Zhena Trelu than he had been to Zhena Brigsbee, and Miri's opinion of him rose an erg or two. He did not give her any plastic clap-trap about how strong and upstanding she had been; just apologized, in a voice that sounded sincere, for letting her house get torn to shreds and hoped that the repair job was satisfactory. He did not wait for an answer to that but swept on, his voice taking on a note that somehow reminded Miri of Val Con in his snitzy mood, announcing that the house was thereby proclaimed a national monument, with Estra Trelu as its caretaker and administrator, which position she would hold for the rest of her life, drawing an annual salary of 5,892 speldron. The upkeep of house and furnishings was, of course, the responsibility of the Crown, as were the salaries and upkeep of the militia squad that was to be the all-hours, around-the-year guard.

The king gestured, and the colorless zhena stepped forward to offer Zhena Trelu a rolled tube of paper tied with a white ribbon. "Your charter," she said in a loud, colorless whisper.

The old woman stood still a moment, tube held between her palms. Then she said, firmly, "Thank you, your Majesty," made another of those stupid, dipping bows, and walked back to her seat.

Miri felt like applauding. Instead, she looked over at her partner, who smiled and squeezed her fingers.

"Nervous, Miri?" he asked in soft Benish.

She blinked. "What of?"

His shoulders jerked, and she opened her mouth to remind him that they had promised Kem that they would be dignified, which probably meant not laughing in public.

"Will Hakan Meltz please stand forward," the man with the list ordered. "Will Meri and Corvill Robersun stand forward."

Val Con squeezed her hand again and slid his fingers away as he stepped into the aisle. She followed, wondering at the size of the crowd that had turned out for the giving of medals and proclaiming of heroes. Val Con reached the edge of the cleared circle, paused until she gained his side, and they walked the rest of the way together.

Hakan was before the king's chair, bowing low and managing it more creditably than Miri would have expected. He straightened and was moved to one side by the colorless zhena, who motioned to Val Con.

The Liaden stepped forward, Miri right beside him, then stopped and bowed the bow between equals, graceful and brief.

Miri blinked—*equals?*—and reproduced the bow to an inch. Straightening, she saw the colorless zhena staring at her, seemingly about to speak, a bright blotch of color decorating each pale cheek. At a wave from the king, the woman swallowed her words and stepped back, her face still registering shock.

"For extraordinary service to the Kingdom of Bentrill," the king said in the more regal of his voices, "it is hereby declared that Hakan Meltz, Meri Robersun, and Corvill Robersun are Heroes of the Realm. As such they are entitled to and shall receive a sum of money equal to the present value of a quarterweight of hontoles.

"In addition to this, Meri and Corvill Robersun, natives of Porlint, are made by this decree Citizens of Bentrill." He stopped, brown eyes vague, apparently having forgotten the next part.

Good, Miri thought. No medals. I wonder what's a hontoles? She shot a quick glance at Hakan's face and noted the slightly glazed look around the blue eyes. Could be we're rich, she theorized. Whatever that means.

The king had remembered the rest of his lines.

"On behalf of the people of the nation of Bentrill, I wish to thank each of you for your valor and your courage in the thwarting of this danger to our realm. To this I add my personal gratitude and beg you to understand that my audience room is open to you at a moment's notice." He smiled vaguely and waved at the colorless zhena.

Hakan got his medal first—twice as large as Zhena Brigsbee's, or even Borril's—and made of bright gilt. He was also given a pouch, which crackled when he took it.

Val Con was next. The look Miri slanted sideways showed his face smooth and formal, his shoulders level. He stared past the woman pinning the medal to the front of his new white shirt and took the crinkly pouch without deigning to look down.

The zhena approached Miri with wariness not untouched with outrage. Resisting the temptation to stick her tongue out, Miri adopted Val Con's strategy instead. Fixing her eyes on a point just over the woman's shoulder, she failed to notice the affixing of the medal and acknowledged the pouch only by the finger-twitch necessary to keep it in hand.

The zhena stepped back to her place by the king's chair, and Miri sighed softly. *That* was over . . .

"Meri Robersun, Corvill Robersun: Raise your right hands," the list-keeper boomed.

What? But Val Con had already raised his hand to the height of shoulder, so she shifted her pouch to the other hand and did the same.

The king levered out of his chair and came forward, a plump, homely man with sad brown eyes and graying brown hair.

"With the power vested in me as sovereign of this State of Bentrill I do hereby give you the oath." He paused to raise his own hand, and when he spoke again, his voice was vibrantly clear.

"Do you, Meri Robersun, Corvill Robersun, swear to uphold the laws of this land, obey the king's lawgivers, respect the king's sovereignty, and fight, if called upon, to defend this country from invasion or rebellion?"

There was a short pause, then Val Con's voice replied quietly, "Yes."

The king's eyes moved.

"Yes," Miri assured him.

He smiled. "I do hereby declare you sworn citizens of Bentrill, having all rights and obligations pertaining thereto." He smiled again. "You may lower your hands. Come forward now."

They did, side by side and silent. The king extended his right hand and touched Miri on the right shoulder, then repeated the gesture for Val Con.

"My personal thanks, as well. This was not your country; you did not have to fight. You could as easily have run away and allowed the invasion force to proceed into Gylles. Bentrill is proud to add such people to her citizenry. If all goes as it should, neither you nor any other citizen of Bentrill will ever find it necessary to fight again. War is brutal and, thankfully, not common. But we must always be prepared." He smiled again, but this time it did not reach his eyes. "Thank you."

He turned and sat down. Val Con bowed, Miri bowed, and Hakan bowed, then they, too, returned to their seats.

DUTIFUL PASSAGE

He sat in the dimness of her quarters, screenglow limning stark cheekbones and kissing frosty hair with gold.

Priscilla shivered, though the air was not cold. She shivered because the inner warmth she knew as Shan was gone and all her attempts to read him slid off a cool, mirroring shield—the Wall, he called it, behind which a Healer might retreat to rest and regroup.

And to hide.

She could pull him out of it, of course—she was that strong. But it was not a thing that was done, to strip another of his protections and rout him from his safe place, simply because one was cold and alone and frightened in his absence.

"Shan?"

Nothing. He sat and stared at the screen and barely seemed to breathe.

Priscilla went quickly forward and laid her hand on his shoulder. "Shan."

He started, then caught himself and deliberately leaned back, head against her hip. "Good evening, Priscilla."

"What is it?" she demanded, desperately wanting to scan him, yet determined not to try it.

He waved a hand screenward. "A message from the First Speaker, to the point, as always."

She frowned at the amber letters. "Plan B? What does that mean?"

He sighed, and she felt the tightness of the shoulder muscles under her fingers.

"Plan B . . ." He paused, then continued, very carefully. "It means that the *Dutiful Passage* is from this moment forward acknowledged to be exclusively on the business of Clan Korval. It means that we unship our weapons and free ourselves of cargo. It means that other Korval ships, where possible, will take over parts of our route."

He shifted, then stilled. "It means that Korval is in deadly danger, that the First Speaker has evacuated the Clan from Liad; that the Nadelm may be untrustworthy; that my brother—*my brother!*" His voice broke, and he bowed his head, muscles bunching as Priscilla grabbed and shook.

"Shan, your brother is well!"

He craned his head to look into her face and raised a hand to her cheek. "Is he?"

"You know it." She stared at him, reading the anguish in his eyes and face. "We could both go," she offered tentatively, knowing that she was just strong enough to carry him so far, "and you could read him yourself. He might hear your thoughts more clearly than mine."

He gave a gasp of laughter. "And expose captain and first mate to unknown danger when we are poised on the edge of a war? Later, Priscilla—and send that we find them in body before."

"We will find them," she said, hearing a certain deepening of her voice.

Shan heard it, too. "A prophecy, Priscilla? We'll hope it's as true as the others you've given."

He leaned forward sharply, clearing the screen with a handsweep, spun in the chair, and stood, facing her. "Call an assembly of the crew for Second Hour; attendance mandatory; lattice-crew to attend via comm."

"Yes, Captain." She bowed obedience and respect.

He smiled then and shook his head, his Wall shimmering and resolidifying. "I love you, Priscilla."

DUTIFUL PASSAGE

They had shed cargo at Arsdred; more at Ragg-town; still more at Wellsend, so they came into Krisko orbit lean and sleek, more like a cruiser in outline than a tradeship.

They had shed crew, as well. A few went because their Clan did not enjoy a sufficiently close relationship with Korval; others, because they were too important to Line and House to be put into the way of another Clan's danger. Most stayed—Terrans with shrugs for incomprehensible Liaden politics—though the captain had urged all to leave.

Priscilla had stayed, and Gordy, though Shan's urging in that quarter had approached actual commands; and she sighed now as she walked toward the captain's office. Shan himself had taught her the subtleties of melant'i, so she was alive to the knowledge that, while the captain might order her, Shan could not. And the captain would not order her gone: she was far too valuable a first mate. That did not, of course, mean that Shan had to like it.

She laid her hand upon the palm-plate, and his door slid open; he glanced up from his screen as she came into the room.

"Good day, Priscilla."

"Good day, Captain."

His mouth quirked, his pattern registering a certain wistfulness. "Still angry with me, love?"

She came forward and held out her hand—and nearly sagged in relief when he took it. "I thought you were angry with me."

"Only terrified for you," he said, and she read the truth of that deep within him. "It would seem to be my time to be terrified for those I hold dear." He pointed at the screen. "I have a pin-beam from Anthora."

"Is she well?" Priscilla asked, wondering at several new

resonances within him, at a loss to ascribe them place or purpose in the matrix of the man she loved.

"Well?" Shan laughed shortly. "She reports repelling invaders from Trealla Fantrol's very door and begs my permission, as her Thodelm, to activate the primary defense screens—which she confesses she has already done. She also lets me know, most properly, that she and several of the cats plan to relocate to Jelaza Kazone for a time."

Priscilla sank to the arm of a chair, staring at him. "Anthora is still on Liad? But I thought—"

"That all were safely away? So did I. But my sister informs me that she has stayed to guard the Tree," he said with no little bitterness.

The Tree—the living symbol of Korval's greatness, hundreds of years old, a quarter-mile high and still growing. Priscilla forced her mind to work, to consider the use of symbology and the political advantage of leaving a caretaker in residence. Liadens had a long history of subtle politics, and she knew from her days in Temple the power of a long-held, potent symbol. She glanced up to find Shan watching her closely.

"Jelaza Kazone," she said slowly, feeling her way, "is the Delm's Own House—the original Clan House, you'd said. And Val Con once told me that the older parts are underground, so it's probably better fortified than Trealla Fantrol. If Anthora's purpose in remaining is to guard the tree, it makes good sense for her to be with it, at Jelaza Kazone."

"So she says," he replied dryly, and she caught a flare of something bright and hard and potent before it was skillfully leashed and subsumed within the rest of his pattern.

"In light of my sister's report of invaders with murderous intent," he said after a moment, "the captain has a task for the first mate."

She inclined her head and awaited the captain's instruction, dread coming seemingly from nowhere and lodging deep in her stomach.

"You will present the captain's compliments to Cargo Master yo'Lanna," Shan said softly, "and ask him to attend me here immediately. You will then yourself attach the four pods to be delivered at fifteen-oh-six, one to each of the prime articulation points, and lock them into place. Screen readout will indicate when the automatic system has meshed with the main computer. You will then return to me here."

"Weapons pods." She stared at him, the dread turning to fear. "The *Passage* has weapons, Shan—"

"It will now have its full complement." He shifted, avoiding her eyes, though he did not shield his inner self, for which she thanked the Goddess. "Anthora reports assassins calling at the front door, Priscilla. What would you have me do?"

He sighed sharply when she did not answer and raised his eyes to hers. "We are on the business of Clan Korval, as you heard me explain before the crew and privately. You see now what it means—what it can mean." He leaned forward, hand extended, light glittering off the Master Trader's ring. "We are at war, Priscilla! Or may be, soon. *Will* you go to safety?"

"Safety?" She shook her head, ignoring his hand. "The weapons—here. But you only just received Anthora's 'beam. You came here to load weapons."

"No." He sat back and rubbed the tip of his nose. "Priscilla, Korval is an old Clan and a wealthy one. We have warehouses everywhere. There are several weapons caches. It happens that Krisko houses one." He paused, then added, with a peculiar shimmer deep within his pattern, "By the luck."

"All right." She slid to her feet and bowed. "The first mate goes to fulfill the captain's orders."

She was two steps toward the door before he called her; she turned to find him standing before the desk, both hands held out to her.

"Paranoia, Priscilla—is that the right word? Korval . . ." He hesitated. "For centuries, since Cantra yos'Phelium brought the escape ship to Liad, the Delms of Korval have acted and implemented policy for *Korval alone*. We gather ships, for escape, for battle. We gather money, power, influence. Only a pilot may be Delm. We breed for pilots, Priscilla! To give the greatest chance of successful escape to the greatest number of Korval, should necessity arise. Renegades, even the most proper of us."

She came back to him, extending lines of comfort and love that went unacknowledged in his urgency to tell her.

"And you," he said, catching her hands and staring into her eyes. "Protect the Tree, you said, as if you had heard it from birth, as we did . . ." He shook his head. "Cantra yos'Phelium swore an oath to protect the Tree—Liad exists because a mad outlaw needed a safe place for a dead man's plant! Jelaza Kazone—Jela's Fulfillment! Generations dead and still Jela's damn Tree—" He dropped her hands and stepped back, outwardly calm, though she still read the tearing urgency within.

"Do you know what the captain's prime mandate is, should the ship be breached or need to be abandoned?" he asked.

"No." She projected calm, forcefully, swallowing amazement as he batted it aside as easily as a kitten batting away a ball.

"I'm to go to a certain safe place and remove the stasis box therein, taking it with me to safety. If it should happen that there is no room in the escape pod for the captain, he should hand over the stasis box to another and secure that person's oath to stand guard over the box until one of Korval should come and relieve him of it." Shan tipped his head. "Guess what's in the box, Priscilla."

She did not have to guess. "Seedlings."

"Seedlings." He nodded. "Every Korval ship has a stasis box; every captain has the same mandate. The *Passage,* as Korval's flagship, carries, in addition, several cans of seeds, as well as cloned genetic material, in the storage hold of each escape pod."

He reached forward and cupped her face in his big hands. "Priscilla, by the gods—by your own Goddess—go to safety. I beg you."

"I love you," she said, and saw the tears start to his eyes, just before he closed them and dropped his hands. She reached to touch his face. "Shan?"

The silver eyes opened, reflecting the exhaustion she read in his spirit. "Yes, Priscilla?"

"The captain gave me instructions. I—is it still required that I fulfill them?"

"Yes." He hesitated, then took her hand and looked closely into her eyes. "Understand that you are chosen, Priscilla,

rather than Ken Rik—even though Line yo'Lanna and Clan
Justus are both closely allied with us—because it is a more
proper use of melant'i that one of Korval set the weapons in
place and make us ready to meet necessity." He paused, and
it was just possible to read his love through her own astonished joy. "With your permission, I will explain this to Ken
Rik. I'll meet you in the cafeteria on the next hour, and we'll
announce our lifemating to the crew."

She forced herself into Serenity and regarded him dispassionately. "This is for protection, of course."

"Of course," Shan said with a glimmer of his usual humor.
"But don't, I pray you, Priscilla, ask me whether it's yours or
mine."

VANDAR

WINTERFAIR

The chill in the air was not entirely due to the
weather. Even Hakan felt it: the stares and glares, the change
in conversational tone when they entered an area.

For the most part the huge room was busy. Lamps and candles were everywhere, illuminating people cheerfully working their way toward the exhibitions and competitions that
would follow the fair's opening march. There was a darker
corner at the back of the practice hall, toward which Cory
seemed bent. As they circled, Hakan occasionally exchanged
words with friends, and there was hesitation in the greetings,
an awkwardness in the banter.

Hakan's burden of guitar cases and song books, no larger
than Cory's, grew heavier as they got closer to the far corner.
"Cory, it's pretty dim back here!"

"So much the better," the small man said with half a grin.
"This way everyone will watch someone else and not steal
the tunes we play."

Hakan frowned, then jerked his head about as someone rolled out a quick, bright riff of a song they had been practicing. "Yeah, I see what you mean. But—I feel like we're exiled back here!"

Cory carefully put down his load of cases and music.

"It may be better, Hakan," he said finally. "We are different from all these others. We are—what would you say?—the gust that breaks the branch. Everyone here knows who we are. I know only you; you know only a few."

Hakan felt his cheeks flush. "Do they really think that way?" he demanded. "Do they think the King's Court will choose us because of . . ."

"Hero," Cory said succinctly, and Hakan flushed deeper. "We play at a handicap, alone or together."

"It's not fair!" Hakan muttered, suddenly seeing a dozen faces turned in their direction, a hand pointing them out, a huddle of curious youngsters . . .

Crash!

There was mild laughter nearby as Cory slowly extricated himself from the bench he had fallen over.

Hakan rushed to his side. "Are you all right, man? You never trip!"

"Ah," Cory said mildly. "Do you mean I am not perfect?"

Hakan looked at hint sharply. "You've done this before, haven't you?"

"I've never been to a Winterfair, Hakan; how could I?"

"Damn it, Cory, you play more games than a fall breeze in the leaves! You've played before—in competition!"

Cory smiled, gave Hakan a brotherly pat on the wrist, and turned his back to open an instrument case. He spoke softly, nearly to himself. "Hakan, I know competition. I know I play well. Here? How do I know? In Gylles I only know how you play . . . and I enjoy working with your music. But now we are not so great—and now perhaps your friends will talk with you if you see them without me."

Hakan grinned. "You're really devious!"

Cory shrugged. "I hope you have the old strings I asked you to save. We should practice with them—for a while . . ."

Hakan laughed, opening his mandolette case. "Until they all break?"

"Exactly!" the smaller man said, pulling out a guitar.
"Exactly."

***

The fairgrounds were a marvel to Miri. Tucked into a valley
with a large hill sealing the windward side, the place was
built entirely of timber. The permanent buildings and the
many raised walkways were of wood, and over both the Av-
enue of Artists and the Parade were tall wooden frames sup-
porting taut canvas to help keep out the snow and wind while
still letting in light and air.

Some of the fair events took place away from the structures: the downhill sled races, the woodcutting champi-
onships, and the team sled-drags. Clearly, though, the focus
was the fairgrounds and the wooden structures.

"Kem, this is like there is two Gylles! One for all the time,
and one for the fair!"

Kem laughed. "Of course! The fair is something special—
it brings in a lot of money each year, but you can't hold it in
town. People come from all over the country! Look over
there—that pole now, that's for . . ."

Without missing a step Miri noted its location, ignoring
Kem's explanation of the obvious: a radio tower higher than
the pennant poles.

"Why don't I see that before?" she asked, pausing to stare.

"They bring it in by train—the King's Voice goes to all the
big events. There's even a chance that Hakan and Cory could
be on radio all over Bentrill if they win the competition!"

"And the electric?" Miri demanded. "I see no wires!"

Kem looked at her in surprise. "I don't know—I think they
use the train for the electric."

"Do they?" Miri said, and headed that way, purpose in her
small stride. Kem gaped for a moment and then followed,
hoping that her friend was not going to do anything rash.

***

Val Con and Miri said good night to Hakan quietly, careful
not to wake Kem, who was asleep against his shoulder.

"Drive well, my friend," Val Con said, and Hakan grinned.

"No fear." His grin widened. "Oh, man, we were great!"

Val Con laughed gently. "Yes, Hakan. Drive carefully. Sleep well. Good night."

They stood on the porch and waved until the taillights were lost at the end of the drive, then slipped inside, moving down the dark hallway and up the steps in utter silence. Zhena Trelu had left the fair soon after Hakan and Cory had finished their first set, claiming exhaustion; it would be less than wise to wake her at this advanced hour of the night.

Miri lay down on the bed with a deep sigh. Val Con sat on the edge, eyes smiling.

"Did you have a good time, cha'trez?"

"Wonderful. This thing goes on for another week? I'll be spoiled for doing anything that looks like work!"

He was laughing. She snapped her fingers and twisted to sit up, digging into the deep pocket of her skirt.

"Almost forgot, boss. I got—" She hesitated, suddenly shy. "I got a present for you."

"A present? Will it explode, I wonder? Is that why you're sitting so far away?"

She grinned and slid closer, until her hip was against his, then offered him the blue plush box.

He took it in his long fingers, found the catch, and opened it. Miri, watching his face closely, saw his expression go from pleased expectation to smiling delight.

"A 'jiliata," he murmured, inclining his head to the silver dragon on its black cord. "I salute you." He looked up, green eyes glowing. "Lisamia keshoc, cha'trez."

She smiled and answered in her still-careful Low Liaden. "You are welcome, Val Con-husband. It gives me joy to give you joy."

He laughed and hugged her. "Spoken with the accent of Solcintra!" He offered the box. "Will you put it on?"

She slipped the necklace from its nesting place, ran the soft cord through her fingers, and slid it around his neck, twisting the intricate clasp shut. "There you go."

He raised his head, smiling, then lifted a brow at the look he surprised on her face. "Is there something wrong?"

"Not wrong." She touched his face, her hand fluttering from cheek to brow to lips. "Right." She grinned. "Punch drunk—fair drunk. Gods."

There was a small silence; her hand fell away, and she shifted a little, recalling a question from much earlier in the day. "We rich now, boss?"

He laughed lightly. "We have been rich for some time now, you and I. Today they merely gave us some money."

It was her turn to laugh; she squeezed his hand tightly. "We got you out of there kind of late—I meant to ask if they told you 'bout the station?"

"Station?" His brows furled. "The Winter Train?"

"Nah. The one they call the King's Voice. The radio station."

His eyes sharpened. "Ah! That is it! I thought the King's Voice was like the King's Eyes or—a representative of the king."

She shook her head. "Nope. It's a portable radio station, tower and all. Goes all 'round the country. Uses a generator in one of the trains."

"I must see it." It was almost hunger she felt coming through the pattern in her head. "I must see the transmitter!"

She nodded and fumbled in the pocket of her skirt. "Thought you would. Here we go: four passes, special deal for hero types. Had a time talking 'em loose. Thought Kem was gonna disown me."

Val Con hugged her tightly. "Miri, Miri. Things come together! Soon we'll leave for Laxaco—the city where flying machines are ordinary and they have radio factories. We may be on our way home soon—or at least in contact."

"Promise me something," she said earnestly.

He moved back a bit. "What should I promise?"

"That we'll finish out this fair before you drag us away to the smog!"

He grinned. "Of course! We stay to the end of the party!"

She hugged him back then, for a long time.

VANDAR

WINTERFAIR

The icy gray clouds flowed through Fornem's Gap, relentlessly driven by the stiff, oceanic breeze. Miri glared at them without result, while Val Con leaned against the front porch rail at her side, watching six of the king's honor guard march up the lane from their temporary camp. He sighed lightly at the two cars farther down the lane: sightseers, looking over the battleground.

From the lane came a familiar roar, closely followed by Hakan's car, green and red fair-ribbons snapping smartly in the breeze. The driver's side window was down despite the cold, and Hakan's voice—but not his words—could be heard long before the car stopped.

"I said," he repeated breathlessly, "that we've got some bad news and some good news!"

"Bad news first," Miri said firmly as she opened the back door and started packing in the picnic lunch, picnic dinner, and snacks Zhena Trelu insisted on sending with them.

"Always," Val Con agreed.

"Right. The bad news is that Capstone Trio won't be coming in for the fair after all. They've all come down with pneumonia or something—the radio man called Kem's mother last night to tell her they'd need to come up with a replacement."

Miri shrugged. "Bad news like that beats the wind out of something serious!"

Hakan barely flushed. "Well, you haven't heard them, so you don't know—and I was going to get to meet them!"

Val Con finished stowing the extra blankets Zhena Trelu had sent and slid close to Hakan on the bench seat, keeping a wary eye on the large hot mug perched precariously next to the driver. "Then," he said, "you may tell us the good news."

"Right," Hakan said again. "The good news is that they've decided—the fair governors—to have a contest for the slot the Capstones would have been in. It'll be open to any trio!"

Miri snuggled in next to Val Con and slammed the door shut as the car began to accelerate.

Val Con stared straight ahead as Hakan shifted and looked at the two of them.

"Well?" he demanded.

"Well what?" Miri asked, then began shaking her head. "No. No. No chance. No way. I don't stand in front—"

Val Con was laughing, eyes straight ahead.

"Miri, I've heard you sing—you're terrific!" Hakan said. "We've got a great chance of winning. All we need to do is come up with a good name—already have a couple for you to think about—and practice today after the duo competition." He glanced at her face. "Look, you don't even have to sing all that much if—"

"No!" Miri exclaimed. In Terran, punctuated by an elbow in Val Con's side, she said, "Stop laughing, you devil!"

But Val Con continued to chuckle, ducking to let the argument bounce back and forth over his head, all the way to the fair.

Miri grumpily folded the newspapers under her arm as they left the practice room and headed for the competition hall. The problem was not listening to Val Con and Hakan practice. It was listening to the people around them, hearing the remarks—and collecting the papers. The two men were in a world only peripherally connected to Vandar, mumbling about song order and such like, oblivious to the points and the stares and the papers.

They were yesterday's papers, mostly, each with accounts of the battle, and four of the five, including the *King's Press,* featured photographs taken at the awards ceremony. The other paper had sketches that were barely recognizable—and which tipped her annoyance into anger, for the one of Val Con made the scar the most prominent feature on his face.

It was not snowing yet, which was some comfort, Miri thought. She shook her head. Somehow it had been settled that she would sing with them the next day, and she could not even blame the decision on Val Con, who had merely laughed throughout the whole argument. She still needed to come up with a name, though, having rejected out of hand Hakan's favorites: the Gap Trio, the Zhena Robersun Trio, and the Springbreeze Farm Trio.

"Wind'll take these things," she grumbled in Terran. "And I'm damned if I—"

Karooom!

"Wow! It's going to snow now!" Hakan cried. Then he stopped, abruptly realizing that his friends stood rooted in their tracks, heads craned skyward.

Miri's eyes were on one spot in the overcast; she moved her head ever so slightly, following the sound.

"What's the matter?" Hakan demanded, puzzled. "It's only thunder—"

"Hush!" Cory snapped.

Hakan listened, too. True, it had been a rather sudden bit of thunder; there was a distinct but distant rumble trailing away to the northeast and Fornem's Gap.

"That's funny," he said a moment later. "It sounds like the thunder there is echoing against the wind!"

Miri said something in the language she and Cory sometimes used between themselves. She said it three times, progressively louder, as if casting an incantation. "Sonic boom. Sonic boom. Sonic boom."

Cory answered in the same language, moved his shoulders in that foreign way of his, and finished with the same words. "Sonic boom."

He sighed. "Do you always have this kind of thunder, Hakan? So isolated? No flash of lightning?"

"Well, we get thunder in snowstorms a few times a year— usually means it's going to be a big one. But I think I still hear that—you don't think it's a windtwist, do you? We haven't had one of those since I was a baby!"

"No, I think not, friend. Probably just a squall. I have heard this thunder once or twice—at home—and so has Miri, but we have heard nothing like it here."

The sound faded out; the conversations of the crowd around picked up, and in moments the isolated, far-rumbling thunder was stored away as a strange memory from the Winterfair.

"There!" Hakan said as they arrived at the competition hall. "It was the first cloud breaking its ice!"

He pointed to a gray curtain moving down the side of the mountain, obscuring all behind it.

"Just like Surebleak," Miri said in unenthusiastic Terran. "Except there's too many happy people around. And some idiot skypilot who don't know the local limits!"

"Cha'trez, we don't know that. After all, there is an active Benish aviation industry."

"Yeah? I'll tell you what. You prove that was homegrown or natural, and I'll take the next ten watch details we come up with!"

"Ah, but what if we are done with watches?"

She grinned. "Always wanna hedge your bet, doncha, Liaden?"

"Come on!" Hakan said, grabbing Cory's arm. "They're posting the competition order!"

Grinning, they made appropriate haste.

VANDAR

WINTERFAIR

The snow pelted Miri as she wandered through the double-flapped cloth door, cold bit her nostrils, clearing them instantly of the scent of a thousand humans.

Hakan and Cory were scheduled after the next group. Miri grappled with the name once again, struggling to avoid "Hakan and Cory and Miri" or, as Hakan had also suggested, "Miri and Hakan and Cory." She sighed. Hakan's musical talent was balanced by inability to choose a name with a snap to it.

Despite the snow—or because of it—the fair outside the performance hall was lively. The sleds that had been sitting idly in the fields were in full use, ferrying families to and fro; the hill in the distance was masked by the white stuff. The braziers spotted here and there were well tended, and Miri moved slowly toward one, trying not to step on a child.

As a Merc, she had never had much to do with children; certainly she had never developed the amazing talent Val Con had demonstrated yesterday, of being able to talk and patiently answer questions. The man seemed to actually *like* kids!

Good thing, too, Miri thought, 'cause they were *every*-where. One was at that very moment angling toward the brazier, followed by a shorter version, both with coats carelessly unfastened and hoods hanging down their backs. They stood in front of the fire and turned their faces into the snow, giggling, until the taller of the two spotted her beside them and smiled.

"Good fair, zhena."

"Good fair, zama," she answered, feeling her mouth curve into a smile. "Button your coats before you go sledding."

The smaller one gave a crow of laughter. "We *been* sledding," he told her. "*Now* we go eat!"

"Good choice," Miri said, and they laughed, waving as they moved away from the fire.

Miri moved down the snow-covered path, admiring the true whiteness of the snow, so unlike the gray precipitation of Surebleak. Kids could be happy here—

She broke the thought off, ears straining against the muffling of the snow, against the soft whisper of flakes striking her coat.

It *was* there! From above the clouds came a thrumming, lurking noise, the sound of a modern craft, hovering.

Fair noise overwhelmed the sound, and for a moment she doubted herself. Then it came again—the kind of sound she had hoped and prayed and cursed for when Klamath had come apart around them, freezing them, frying them, killing them . . . She banished the memory and ran through the Rainbow's sequence so quickly that the colors blurred into a wheel before her mind's eye.

The thrumming sound came again—louder, it seemed— and she turned, resolved to run to Val Con, to bring him out to listen.

What for, Robertson? she asked herself derisively. What's he gonna do about it? Yell? You need a radio, quicktime.

Damn. A radio right here, and no way to send a message! There had to be a way . . .

A man came around the corner of the hall, shrouded in snow and blinded by it. She dodged, blinking up at the huge-ness of him, and called out of happier memories, out of hope. "Jason? Edger?"

He stopped, taking shape out of the snow and smiling down at her. "Zhena?"

Miri laughed and apologized. "In the snow I mistake you for someone I know."

"Easy to do when the snow winds come!" he boomed good-naturedly. "Good fair!" He was gone then, leaving warmth behind amid the confusion.

A gong banged in the distance and was echoed by others— the new hour was starting. She rushed into the hall, a name for the trio on her lips.

Hakan and Val Con were still setting up. Miri moved to a front-row bench and instantly felt Val Con's gaze on her. She smiled, adding quick flutter of hand-talk—Old Trade—that said "Need to talk later." His wave and smile reassured her.

Val Con sat briefly at the piano before the introduction, testing it. He would be playing backup on the guitar in some of the songs, but in the others he would play melody while Hakan sang. A few touches of the instrument assured him; he nodded to someone off-stage, and a white-haired woman in fur boots walked to centerstage amid the stomping of feet and whistling from the audience.

"Next on the program is a new duo. Hakan, of course, is known to many of us; his partner Cory is a recent addition to our area, and we'll all get a chance to hear them right now!"

The music started instantly, and the audience chuckled as

the emcee hurried off stage. Hakan waited until she had actually made the wings before he began to sing.

Miri relaxed. So far, no one had mentioned that Hakan and Cory were heroes. She sat back and listened extra hard, studying the music. The Snow Wind Trio was going to have to be damn good to get on the radio.

The applause died away, and Miri went toward the stage to join the small group at the bottom of the steps. She sighed. If the number of stage-side fans and the volume of applause meant anything, then Hakan and Cory were not the hit they had hoped to be.

Hakan stopped to talk with some friends, and Miri smiled wanly at her husband, surprised at the amount of joy in him.

He swung an arm around her waist and hugged her tight, laughing at raised eyebrows.

"So we are not traditional enough, we two?" he asked in Benish.

"Looks that way, boss," she replied in Terran.

He slanted a bright green glance at her face. "A problem, cha'trez?"

She shrugged and pulled him with her toward the back of the hall. They found seats on the aisle near the door-flaps and settled down just as the next group signaled that they were ready and the emcee came on stage.

"Problem or solution, I don't know," she said carefully. She turned to look him full in the face. "Someone's sitting upstairs, doing circles over the clouds. Not transport class. Say, an unbaffled ship or an out-and-out jet—can't tell with all this other noise. But doing a loiter."

"Ah," he said, and she clamped down hard on the need to ask him what "Ah" meant this time.

"Thing is," she said instead, "I know how to get their attention. If you want to."

Val Con raised an eyebrow, waiting.

"All we got to do," she said, as if she was not certain that he had already thought of it himself, "is get on the radio. This trio gig of Hakan's . . . If you and me can sing something in Terran or Liaden—a round, maybe—one part in Benish, one in Terran, one in Liaden." She saw his frown. "Know it's against the rules, boss, but I can't figure it otherwise. Unless you want to hijack the station!"

"Inefficient, hijacking a station. And you think your idiot sky-pilot will be listening?"

"What the hell do you think she's doing? Way it makes sense is they were doing the frequency scan, like you and me did, homed in on the radio like a beacon, and now they're circling, trying to decide if it's worth a stop."

He nodded. "You were wasted as a sergeant, Miri. You might have been a—"

"Hey! Cory! Miri! Somebody wants us to teach them our playing style!" Hakan called, arriving with two young women and a shy man in tow.

Val Con smiled vaguely at the group; Miri's smile contained a touch of frost.

"Hakan, it is to be flattered," she said more sharply than she had intended. "But us—we need to practice. We must be better!"

Hakan looked crestfallen, his exuberance lost in a mumble.

One of the young women bustled forward and nodded to Miri, as if to an equal. "I am Zhena Wrand. After you have practiced—and played—Hakan tells me you may compete tomorrow—after that, we will work with you! There is a new feel to what Hakan and Cory do. Not revolutionary, mind. But new, not as hide-bound. All these traditionals want nothing more than to hear exactly what they heard last year! You watch and see who wins—a traditional band! Next year, though, I—we—will be so good they can't ignore us!" With that she turned, lifted a hand to her friends, and stalked away.

Hakan stared after them strangely, then his eyes lighted as Kem arrived.

"Hakan and Cory—you did fine!" She smiled, tucking her hand into Hakan's.

"At least some people think so!" Hakan said, pointedly glancing at Miri.

Val Con began to say something, but Miri put her hand out, silencing him.

"Hakan?" she said very seriously. "Do you still want a

trio?" His face actually paled. "Of course, Miri," he stammered. "I didn't mean—"

"Quiet," she ordered, and Val Con bent his head to hide his smile.

"If we have a trio, we do it right," Miri announced. "First, the name. The name should be 'Snow Wind Trio,' unless another—"

"No, that's good. Real good!" Hakan smiled at Kem, tightening his grip on her hand as Miri continued.

"Fine. We settle that much. Now." She pointed back and forth between Val Con and Hakan. "You two, you work good together. Me? I sing some. Mostly before I sing at parties, not on stage. And these is bests—the best groups in Bentrill! We have to be very, very and traditional—like that zhena said—or different! So different they can't compare. We don't have time to be all traditional. So—we practice being different!"

Miri turned to the other woman suddenly. "Listen, Kem, this fair—it might not be much fun for you. If we do good we can make a name—establish ourselves like Hakan wants to. But we need him to practice hard right now!"

Kem laughed, holding up a hand. "Miri, don't worry. Hakan is happiest when he's doing his music. If you and Cory can help make the music work—I couldn't ask for more."

She grabbed Miri's hand and gave it a squeeze. "I'll help, honey. I'll bring food, applaud, chase people away, whatever you need. All right?"

"All right." Miri looked at them all and smiled. "Zhena Trelu sends all this food. You help us eat it and we talk—then practice."

She led the way into the snow at such a determined pace that it took Val Con a moment to catch up and put his hand in hers.

VANDAR

SPRINGBREEZE FARM

Hell with it, Miri decided and tapped him on the shoulder. "Val Con?"

He stirred. "You are not asleep?"

"Nah. You ain't either."

"No. Adrenaline."

"Hmmph. Thought you could sleep anytime anywhere." She moved closer and slipped an arm loosely around his waist. "For that matter, thought I could, too. Tried to use the Rainbow, but I keep getting off track."

He backed into her, sighing. "I am not certain. My hunch is you are correct about this ship and its interest. But there are other matters, and the Loop—"

"What in the hell can that thing have to say about it?" she demanded. "If the Loop lets you see through clouds maybe it'd help."

He was silent for a moment before turning to face her.

"The Loop," he said with emphasis, "indicates that contacting a spaceship is beneficial only if we have plans to leave this planet. Have we such plans?"

She shifted irritably. "Why ask me?"

"We are lifemates, Miri," he said softly. "I ask to know. I ask because it is not so bad a place, really, and because life could be pleasant here. No Juntavas, no Department of the Interior . . ."

Trust him to see her second thoughts. She was silent for some time, trying to work it through.

"Well," she said eventually. "You got plans. Gotta keep an eye on that family of yours. Got stuff to say to your brother. Got stuff to say to Edger. And I might get bored of singing for my supper in a couple years . . ."

"Then we have such plans," he said. "In order to leave this world we should make earliest contact with a means of doing so—even the Juntavas or the Department. This is contraindicated if the ship belongs to Yxtrang; yet they would hardly wait, circling a single outpost, when there is a whole world to plunder. The chance of it being Yxtrang is something under one percent, by the way."

"What chance that it's Edger?" she asked hopefully.

"Less than ten percent—closer to nine."

"Mmmpf. Lots of percents left, huh? What's the odds mean, if you gotta use that thing?"

Val Con stroked her arm gently. "The odds are twenty-four percent that we have a Scout overhead; thirty percent chance that it is a smuggler, perhaps coming to see what has happened to his associates. There is a smaller chance that it is an accidental discovery, and the odds of it being the Juntavas are rather slim."

She shook her head in the dark. "You wanna boil it down for me? Long day, long night . . ."

"The largest chance," Val Con said, trying to phrase things as vaguely as possible yet give her the essential information, "is that it is someone directly looking for us—slightly better that it's the Department of the Interior than a Korval ship. The politics of either are hard to measure at this distance."

"Depending on what your brother decided to do with that computer code. Which I still don't know was a good idea."

"They had to be warned," he said mildly.

Miri snorted. "Tell me, then: All that Scout blood in your family—not to mention your grandma the smuggler—what's the chances of them coming into an Interdicted World, breaking the sound barrier and probably every aviation law on the books?"

Out of the darkness came a sigh. "Rhetorically? Not high."

"Look at the damn thing, Liaden. What's it say?"

He sighed again, then suddenly gave a low laugh. "It says that despite it all, it is only estimating. If it happens that an Yxtrang general wanted to have a holiday shoot, then all the Loop's numbers mean that, as unlikely as the event is, it could still happen."

"Great," Miri said. "Did I ever tell you about the time I needed to roll five sevens in a row to stay out of trouble?"

"Did you?"

"No. Rolled four."

"Ah—and then?"

"I had some trouble."

Val Con grinned in the dark. "Shall I ask more?"

"Later." She touched his cheek. "Basically what you're telling me is that if we're planning on going through with these shenanigans we're likely to have trouble. And if we don't, trouble might find us anyway."

"Will," he corrected, reaching out. He pulled her close and kissed her ear gently. "Cha'trez, let us talk the Rainbow together tonight. My hunch is that *we* are trouble; events flow roughly around us because we seize every opportunity."

"Carpe diem," she muttered, and laughed. "We seize the day. Sometimes, the day seizes back!"

He laughed with her and reached to touch the barely seen, much-beloved face. "True. Let us now seize a Rainbow. Red is the color of physical relaxation . . ."

Eventually they slept soundly.

MCGEE ORBIT

The message hit them as they hit orbit. His boss had been sitting in the co-pilot's seat since it had, staring at the screen and frowning. The couple of glances Cheever had been able to spare for the message board during the orbiting drill had not shown anything that seemed to warrant Pat Rin yos'Phelium's frown; a couple of lines of Liaden characters and a rendering of a dragon flying over a tree at the end of it all; like a seal.

"Right, then, Tower," he said into the mike. "Landing time acknowledged and recorded. Thanks." He checked the board once more, nodded, and leaned back in the chair, wondering what was going on.

"Pilot McFarland."

He straightened. "Yessir."

Pat Rin was still staring at the screen, one hand idly toying with the blue stone in his left ear. "I offer you the opportunity to leave my employ, Pilot—and at once."

Cheever goggled. "You're firing me?"

"Did I say it?" Pat Rin snapped. Abruptly he turned the chair around, so that Cheever could see his face. "Forgive me, Pilot," he said more carefully. "I am in every way satisfied with your service. I offer a letter of reference stating so, and a continuance of your pay until you may locate another employer."

"I'm doing the job, but you're gettin' rid of me," Cheever repeated, brow rumpled in perplexity. "Why?"

For a minute he thought the little dandy was going to go all high and holy on him, tell him to shut up and pack up.

But Pat Rin hesitated, then sighed. "Circumstances sometimes overtake one, Pilot. In my—business—one schools oneself to accept reversals and to use them to future advantage." Once again the slim fingers adjusted the blue earring. "Circumstances having thus overtaken me, I am constrained as an honorable man to offer an honorable man the means to avoid possible—unpleasantness—accruing to one in my employ."

Cheever chewed it over and finally had to shake his head. "Looks me like you're gonna need an extra gun, if these circumstances of yours're liable to turn ugly. Told your cousin Shan I'd keep an eye on you—part of the deal, see?" He thought some more, oblivious to the speculation in Pat Rin's eyes, and finally summed it up. "Might bc he knew you were prone to circumstances, huh? Might he thought you'd be better off with some help this time out."

"It might be, Pilot," Pat Rin said gently. "Who am I to say?" He stared at the screen again for some minutes, then extended a languid hand and cleared it before looking back at the bigger man.

"You must understand," he said, "that there may be danger,

or there may be none. At the present we will merely extend our itinerary and give over any plans of a return to Liad."

Cheever frowned. "For how long?"

Pat Rin adjusted the ear-stone a final time and stood with sensuous grace. He bowed ironically and smiled. "Why, Pilot, only until circumstances resolve themselves. Do wake me when we land." And he strolled off toward his cabin.

VANDAR

WINTERFAIR

The key was the green light.

When the green light was lit, the broadcast was going out from the stage. When both red and green were on, it was going out from the microphone on the tables at the back of the hall. The yellow light meant that the hall was on standby.

Miri studied the competition rules while Val Con kibbitzed with the radio techs. He left the board with reluctance after a technician pointedly asked him not to touch, and climbed the steps onto the stage.

"No go?" Miri asked.

He moved his shoulders. "There is not much to be done from here at any rate—a relay board only. To subvert the system, I would need to be in the main shack." He grinned at her. "And we have already agreed that hijacking the station is not efficient."

"Probably just as well," she said. "Looks like that zhena up there—in the gray—decides what goes on the air." She shook her head. "Rules say they're gonna have each group play twice—two three-song sets. They'll do random drawings for play slots each time. That gives us a couple chances to catch the green light—you think Hakan'll be okay?"

Val Con sat on a bench and patted the spot beside him. "Hakan will be fine, Mini. He sees that you have done only proper things—the zhena has indicated what is required, and it shall be done. If he is not comfortable with our chances of winning he has not told me."

"What's the Loop say?"

He raised a brow. "Nothing. Lack of information."

"I don't mean about winning, damn it, I mean—"

"Miri, Miri . . . Both questions have the same answer. We cannot predict how the judging will go because there are different judges. We cannot predict who will be broadcast because we do not know what criteria the zhena in gray applies to her decisions."

"And if they put us on the air we don't know if anyone upstairs is still listening!"

"Exactly."

Miri grinned. "If it's Edger you can bet who'll be right down."

Val Con smiled and squeezed her hand. "I suspect even he would not be so hasty. Besides, Zhena Brigsbee would only say to Zhena Trelu, 'I told you there was something strange about those two . . .'"

MIRI was sweating, but so were Val Con and Hakan. The first two songs had gone over well, and they had weathered the minor problem of having to use another song for their opening number—the one they had planned to play turned out to be the closing number of the preceding group.

So far they had followed Miri's direction to play for themselves rather than to fit custom. Val Con's piano solo had certainly scored some points in the first number, and Miri and Hakan's switched roles in the second—he singing the female side and she the male—had drawn attention again. Though whether the attention was good or bad was more than Miri could tell. Worse, the green light had yet to come on.

Hakan moved against the wave of applause to his microphone, grinning fit to split his face.

"Now," he said, then paused to catch his breath. "Now, the Snow Wind Trio is pleased to bring you something a little different. We'll sing a song you all know well—first the way Zhena Robersun learned it when she was young, then the way Zamir Robersun heard it as he traveled on his brother's ship, and finally as I learned it as child, here in Gylles. Here, then, is 'Leaf Dance.'"

The audience was silent. On the board across the room, the green light came on, and Miri gulped; hearing the introduction roll off Val Con's piano, she closed her eyes and broke in on the beat, concentrating on the words she had set to the Benish music. The original was a simpleminded, happy hymn to autumn, admirably suited for rounds. Out of some perverse sense of obligation to Hakan, innocently assisting in the shattering of galactic law, Miri had tried to stay as close as possible to the spirit of the original.

In what seemed like no time at all her part was over and Val Con took up his, the liquid sound of the Liaden words transforming the sweet little melody into something exotic and sensuous. Miri slid her hand into her pocket, wrapped her fingers around the absolutely forbidden harmonica nestled there, and quickly brought it to her mouth.

To Hakan it looked like magic: Miri's cupped hands were somehow producing an eerie, unexpected sound, playing haunting counterpoint to Cory's part of the round.

And then it was his turn to take a step closer to the mike and give the audience the song they had known all their lives, Miri's harmonica a faint, warm buzz beneath the familiar words.

He finished his verse, caught the signal from Cory, and kept the music coming, while Miri played the harmonica solo to the world, reminding the audience that as leaves dance, they die. The thought hooked her, calling up memories of friends, dancing and dead, recalling her to times when the harmonica had made the sounds the unit had dared not: the laughter, the curses, the sobs.

Coming back to herself, she let the improvisation flutter to an end. First Hakan and then Val Con let their music fade and stop. Miri whipped the harmonica across her mouth one last time, and bowed.

She bowed to a silence so absolute the wind could be heard against the door flaps. Then, in the silence, people began to stand, and for a heartstopping moment she thought they were going to storm the stage. Not knowing what else to do, she bowed again. Then she felt Val Con's hand in hers, felt him bowing with her, while the sight of him inside her head was a marvel of brightness and warmth.

The cheering started then, and lasted a long time.

The judges had not been as impressed by the performance as the audience had. The Snow Wind Trio was tied for second at the end of the first round; and that second was a long way in points from the first-place group, which was—as Zhena Wrand had insisted—as traditional as possible.

On the other hand, popular sentiment was clear: The Snow Wind Trio was a success. There was still a chance that they could gain more points in the second round, after the dinner break. In the meantime, they had been besieged as they walked through the hall.

Hakan stood with a list of offers in hand, reading them off one by one to Kem, Miri, and Val Con. "This one is for Lax-aco's spring fest—three days at a club, one night in concert at the fest. This one is for a tour. I don't think it's so good—it's mostly one-night stands at smaller clubs. This one's an offer of a year contract, four nights on, three nights off . . ."

"Hakan?" Miri asked finally.

"Miri?"

"Why don't we wait until after the fair to count the pennies? The wind doesn't finish blowing yet."

"But some of these people say they need to know tonight! Zhena Ovlia, for example—"

"Ought to learn something about manners," Kem said, and Miri gave a crow of approving laughter.

"No, wait," Hakan tried again. "I mean she's trying to get things moving in a hurry and if we can say yes tonight—"

"If we can say yes tonight," Val Con said softly, "we can say yes tomorrow. After our second set we see: Do we get on the radio again? Do we get the award? Are we second or third? All these add up. Tomorrow is time enough to see what we have. Let us be patient."

"You be patient for everybody," Miri told him. "Me, I'm going to see when we play tonight."

In a moment they were all on their feet.

• • •

The luck of the draw made them spectators for most of the evening: They were scheduled last, right after the leading group.

"Cha'trez, have you considered a short walk?" Val Con asked after the second group played.

Miri blinked at him. "What for?"

He laughed gently. "For your tension. You are concerned?"

"Yes, dammit, I'm concerned. You'd be, too, if you had any nerves. I never sang in front of a group as big as the one this morning, and it looks like the evening show's gonna be a sellout. Feel like I'll probably freeze up and forget the words, or fall flat my face, or—"

Val Con took her hand, offering çomfort and assurance. "Miri, you will do fine. You always do well and more than well—and then belittle yourself, eh?"

He smiled at her and reached to touch her hair, oblivious to the shocked zhena sitting just behind. "You are very bright, cha'trez. I see you as you see me, remember? And this edge, this concern, is not bad to have. But further—"

"I feel like I'm ready to fight, and it's only people with guitars and words! Wish that damn idiot upstairs would *do* something, if he's still hanging around. And Hakan's so set on us going on tour and seeing the world, I feel like we gotta do it for him, so that he won't be disappointed." She took a deep breath, looked at him, and grinned. "Never pays to let a Merc think, you know? I'll be okay."

As he watched with his inner eye he saw a slight wavering of Miri's fires, a mistiness, and then she was brighter than ever, the melody of her absolutely true.

"We're playing for joy," she said slowly, shifting so that her shoulder touched his companionably. "Just like I said to Hakan."

"We are playing for joy," he agreed. "It is the best of all things to play for."

INTERDICTED WORLD
1-2796-893-44

It was a marvel the place did not take fire. The fairground was a maze of unsound wooden buildings, wooden walkways, wooden trade booths, and scattered mountains of chopped wood. And everywhere there was open flame—braziers, torches, cooking pits—tended by a half-witted barbarian or two, some clearly the worse for a jar or more of the atrocious local spirits.

More disturbing than the dangerous mix of fire and wood was the crowd itself. That this group of locals was as backward and ignorant as those in the south was expected; that the signs of disease and early aging were on many of them was not unexpected. Yet sig'Alda found the presence of so many infirmities distressing, so that he constantly reminded himself that his immunizations were current and that no disease known to modern medicine was capable of infecting him.

Out of the crowd bumbled a group of the local young, shouting and shrieking. One lost control of its balance and crashed heavily into sig'Alda, wrapping its arms around his legs in a clumsy attempt to save itself.

sig'Alda clenched himself into stillness and waited with what patience he could muster for the thing to sort itself out and be on its way. Instead, the cub tipped its face up, a vacuous smile on its fat face in loathsome parody of a proper and well-behaved Liaden child.

sig'Alda frowned. "Leave," he said curtly, and the round face puckered as it struggled with the meaning of the word.

"Laman?" An adult swooped out of the crowd and plucked the cub free, smiling to show a mouthful of crooked teeth. "I'm sorry, zamir, but you know what the young ones are!"

"Yes, certainly," sig'Alda said with scant courtesy, and

moved on, counting wooden auditoriums until he came to the
fourth on the left.

The music came up softly: "The Ballad of the RosaRing."
They had schooled Hakan for an hour in his pronunciation of
"Fly on by," the sum of his singing part. Val Con had a couple backup and fill-in lines, but primarily it was Miri's song
to sing.

The audience, respectful, may have been expecting another set of rounds: what they got was the ballad, in Terran,
of a pair of lovers separated forever when an experimental
virus got loose on the RosaRing.

The translation they had given Hakan for the audience
had the Ring a resource-rich island cursed with a strain of
infectious madness—which to Miri's mind was as close as
made no difference. The Ring virus had been deadly, the
world it circled rich, and three rescue teams had been shot
down by automatics before the fatcats had finally seen the
stupid waste of it and quarantined the sector. The lover had
been on the last rescue team. For Hakan—for the Winterfair—he escaped.

Miri sang the last "Fly on by," bowed low to hide her
tears—which annoyed her—and lifted her head to the thun-
dering crowd.

"Forget the words, Miri?" Val Con murmured at her side,
and she laughed, breathlessly.

The crowd kept them at the front of the stage a moment
more, then Miri unshipped her harmonica, ripped off a
quick zipping sound with it, and the trio launched into the
high-spirited Benish standard, "The Wind's Going My
Way." The harmonica added a zest to the song Miri liked,
and she dropped back to make room for the maneuver they
had practiced.

Hakan dove for the piano, and passing Val Con the guitar,
then Val Con was at the front lights, picking the tune rapidly
with the harmonica's support. Some in the crowd laughed;
there was even a sprinkling of premature applause, and, over
on the side, the green light glowed steady.

They increased the speed of the song again, and once

more, Miri watching for Val Con's signal. It came and they stopped, all together, bowing on the same instant.

The crowd stood, cheering and applauding and stamping their feet as the emcee stood uncertainly on the stage side, prepared to step up; but she stepped down instead as the cheering took up again.

"This never happens," Hakan whispered.

"No?" Miri said. She moved to the mike.

"Thank you! Thank you all!" she called, and the crowd grew quieter. "We are almost out of music now—" There was laughter as she paused to catch her breath. "But we know one more. Would you like to hear it?"

The audience roared assent, and Hakan stood transfixed.

"Zhena—" he began, but Cory was already back at the piano, and Miri was saying, "On the beat," with the hand-twitch that was the signal for "The Windmill Whirl." Hakan caught up his guitar and began to play.

DUTIFUL PASSAGE

"Be certain," Priscilla said for the third time, because that was the ritual—and because she distrusted his mood, all emotion bright and hard-edged and deliberate.

Shan folded his shirt neatly onto a chair and looked up at her, amusement flickering through eyes and pattern. "Come now, Priscilla, am I as faint-hearted as that?"

"You did say," she reminded him, "that it was madness for both captain and first mate to risk themselves when the Clan was in danger." She slid her trousers off and straightened, stern and lovely in her nakedness. "There *is* risk. One or both of us could die, if the Goddess frowns." She leaned forward, holding him with eyes alone. "Be *certain*, Shan."

"Well, I did say so," he agreed, sitting down to pull off his boots. "But that was before we had assassins at Trealla Fantrol, and the Clan spread to the Prime Points, and the

Passage taking on weapons. All very well and good for Val Con to send a message telling us to stay out of trouble while he and his lady vacation. We're *in* trouble, damn him for a puppy!"

He unfastened his belt and sighed. "We need him, Priscilla. There's a reason why the Delm is chosen from yos'Phelium, and if the Ring falls into yos'Galan's keeping, we serve only as First Speaker-in-Trust, surrendering it with a sigh of relief the first moment duty allows."

He finished undressing, folded his trousers atop his shirt, and stood straight. "And now?"

"Now." She came across the room in a smooth glide and wrapped her arms around him, her breasts pushing into his chest as she kissed him deeply and thoroughly. When she was certain of his arousal, she stepped back, motioning to the bed. "Lie down."

Wordless for once, he obeyed, his eyes not moving from her face.

Priscilla nodded. "There is sometimes a danger, when you are soul-walking, of forgetting the pleasures and the pains of the body. Remember them, and cherish them all, so that when you come home, joy will ease your way back in."

She sat on the edge of the bed and touched his cheek very lightly, allowing him an instant to read all the tenderness and love she held for him, allowing herself the same instant to embrace the singing brightness of his regard for her. Firmly, then, she closed it off and composed herself to teach.

"You will enter trance," she instructed. "You will do this with all inner doors open and unguarded, with nothing at all left behind your Wall. You will remain in trance, awaiting my summons. It will be my responsibility to carry us both to your brother. It will be your responsibilities to keep your essence centered and balanced, and to be sure that you have left a connecting line between your soul and your body." She paused, considering him. "Can you do these things, Shan?"

"Yes."

"Be sure," she said, though nowhere in all the Teachings was a fourth asking of that question required. "Because, if you lose your lifeline or can't maintain your balance, I'm not strong enough to keep us both alive."

"I understand," he said. "I'm to stay in one piece and keep the way home clear. No matter what."

"No matter what," she agreed. "Even if something goes wrong. If I seem to fail, or you reach out and cannot find me—come back to your body!" She read his objection and repeated her order more gently. "Come back to your body, even if you think you're without me. Remember, my body is here, too. If I can, I will come back to it."

"And if you can't . . ." He closed his eyes, and she waited, listening to the hum of his thoughts, watching the interplay of needs and desires. At last he sighed and opened his eyes. "All right, Priscilla. May your Goddess have room in her heart to forgive me."

"She forgives everyone, my dear." She touched his bright hair. "Whenever you're ready."

Again he closed his eyes, and she watched him bring down his shields and his protections, extinguishing alarms—all with deft skill. He entered the trance quickly, his pattern thickening as he went into the second level, then thickening again, reinforcing itself and shining with the energy of his will. He achieved the final level, heartbeat slowing, breathing long and deep and leisurely, his pattern so solidly formed that it seemed to overlay and partly obscure his physical self.

Priscilla waited a bit longer, analyzing pattern and body. Only when she was satisfied that both were sound, that both trance and soul-shield were solid and unlikely to fail, did she lie down beside him and begin her own preparations.

INTERDICTED WORLD
1-2796-893-44

Tyl Von sig'Alda stood in the noisy, smelly hall, watching his prey on stage. He had seen the sketch in the primitive newssheet, of course, yet the actual sight of a Liaden gentleman with his face marred in such a way was nearly as unsettling as the noisome proximity of so many locals.

There was a small percent chance that yos'Phelium had seen him from the stage and, a smaller percent chance that the Terran bodyguard had, though the Loop noted the imprecision of attempting to calculate the reactions and alertness of a chronic user of Lethecronaxion. If yos'Phelium had seen him, completion of the mission could proceed rapidly. Events, however, would seem to wait upon a contretemp upon the stage.

The precise nature of the difficulty was not apparent. The Terran bitch was near incoherence—not unexpected in a drug-taking sycophant—and the local on stage also displayed attitudinal positions consistent with anger.

yos'Phelium had been standing quietly at the bodyguard's side. He now attempted to say something to the female local, which interrupted him with a brisk hand-wave and stepped to the front of the stage.

At the bulky microphone it spoke in a stilted, slurred version of the language sig'Alda had picked up through sleep-learning; he surmised that it was being formal in order to add legitimacy to the delivery of negative information.

"Our judges, zhena and zamir, families and friends, have asked you to do as they and disregard this performance of the Snow Wind Trio. In order to avoid disqualification the group will be required to play a set of the correct number of songs after the performance of the solo guitar semifinals because they overplayed in time and number—"

All around him the crowd roared disappointment and disapproval; the stands themselves shook. The female's announcements were overwhelmed for some moments— sig'Alda's Loop went into action, informing him that the likelihood of an actual riot was small.

sig'Alda brought his attention back to yos'Phelium, who had begun packing instruments in a businesslike fashion. The Terran was speaking urgently to the local male, all some distance from the female announcer at the microphone.

Carefully sig'Alda began to move against the crowd. yos'Phelium would have to descend the side steps from the stage. With fair fortune, sig'Alda would intercept him there, and they could depart this place and return to the calm dignity of Liad.

It appeared, however, that his thoughts of waylaying them at the stairs were echoed by dozens of locals. The slender walkway was crammed with jostling, shouting barbarians, making a smooth rendezvous with his compatriot impossible.

sig'Alda sat on a bench near the aisle, awaiting his moment, counting through an exercise designed to give patience in frustrating situations. That accomplished, he pondered variables.

He had not known that yos'Phelium was such an accomplished musician—his record had spoken of an *inclination* for the omnichora—yet the sounds of that last piece, though obviously of local origin, had been refined by the agent's contributions into something with merit. And the agent himself—sig'Alda made use of the Loop's recall mode to watch again the last moments of the performance—the agent himself had been unfettered and full of energy. The music had been played with passion by all.

The Loop came up suddenly, without bidding, even as sig'Alda found himself reciting the formula half out loud: "Dispassion, calculation, control, success—"

The probability was .82 that yos'Phelium's actions were inconsistent with those of an Agent on Duty. sig'Alda con-

sidered further. Lost without a ship on a barbarian world one
might easily give up hope, attempt to throw oneself fully into
a new and successful life . . . He shivered, half from the cold
that had crept into the hall when the audience had begun to
sift out the doors, and half from the thought of attempting to
live at all long, depending solely on passion.

Consideration, of course, would have to be given to the
possibility that the facial scar—and the Juntavas report of the
incident had come from a drunken underling, after all—was
the least portion of a grievous and partially disabling head injury. Mere proper Liaden medical attention might be all that
would be required to return the agent properly to the fold.

Finally the trio was permitted to move, but so ringed with
admiring locals that sig'Alda found his best tactic was to
simply attach himself to the tail end of the throng and follow
where it led. Eventually opportunity would arise.

As if the thought was the trigger, there was an unexpected
event. The bodyguard was separating herself from the group!
If he might intercept her, perhaps remove her from the equation, options would be clearer. He hesitated for a moment and
saw the crowd close in again around yos'Phelium and the
local musician.

With the Loop's approval, sig'Alda moved.

VANDAR

WINTERFAIR

"Another set?" Miri asked rhetorically as they
walked down the midway. "Is she nuts, or what?"

Val Con grinned and pushed the hair out of his eyes. "At
least we have an hour or two to prepare—and to rest."

"Yeah, well, I don't know about you, but I'm strung so
high, I wouldn't sleep if you whacked me over the head with
a brick."

"Performance exhilaration," he murmured. "It means you sang with all your joy."

"I guess." She stopped, staring at the entrance to the hall, while the wind thrummed against the canvas stretched high above them. "Tell you what, boss. I'm going for a walk first; try to get this exhilaration thing buttoned up. Tell Hakan I'll be back in ten minutes, okay?"

"Okay," he said, squeezing her hand gently. He turned to go in and, vaguely uneasy, turned back in time to see her disappear into the tall crowd, heading toward the perimeter.

The Terran female had stopped, attention apparently engaged by the low-tech transmitting station and the landtrain that housed it. Tyl Von sig'Alda paused some distance back, closer than he liked to a smoky brazier, watching and considering.

The Loop counseled a direct approach and indicated a possibility as high as .99 that the Terran was currently drug-free. Certainly the performance he had just seen it deliver, though rude and barbaric, was inconsistent with an individual operating with Clouded faculties. sig'Alda stepped forward.

As he came to her side, she turned, eyes going wide. He bowed, not low, but enough to flatter and confuse.

"Good day," he said, speaking most gently in Terran. "You are Miri Robertson, are you not?"

Eyes and face had gone wary; stance suggested puzzlement and indecision. sig'Alda smiled, delighted to find her so very easy to read.

"Yeah," she said, her voice firm and fine. "Who're you?"

"A friend of your employer's," he said smoothly. "It has been noted that you have guarded with excellence, in circumstances both trying and unusual. Now that your duty is completed, and your employer going home, he sends me with this gift, indicative of his esteem." Sliding the little packet with its blue dot out, he saw the Terran's eyes widen, heard her breath catch, and saw the pale skin pale further as he pressed the thing into her hand.

"Cloud?" The fine voice rasped a little on the word, and sig'Alda inclined his head gravely.

"We have made a careful study of your preferences," he said, seeing how her fingers closed tight around the plastic envelope. "And when it came time for the gift to be chosen, I offered my knowledge of your tastes, so that the gift would be certain to please. I hope that you will allow yourself to be pleased and to look upon the gift with favor."

"Sure." The voice had flattened, and she stared at him out of sparkling gray eyes, eager, no doubt, to sample what she held so fiercely. "Thanks a lot."

"It is my pleasure to serve," he told her, and bowed once again. He left her still staring with those brilliant eyes, the little packet completely hidden in the clench of her hand.

VANDAR

WINTERFAIR

The rehearsal hall was hot, and Val Con was sitting as far away from the corner fireplace as he could, restringing the mandolette and listening to Hakan chatter.

"We could," the younger man was saying, "just replay the set they disqualified—well, not the fourth song, but the first three. Except I hate to do that and take away the impact of that RosaRing ballad of Miri's." He shook his head in wonderment. "And she said she couldn't sing in front of a crowd! There wasn't a dry eye in the house, man—I'll bet you my share of the cash prize!"

"If we win the cash prize," Val Con murmured. "Perhaps we should do a new set, starting with the song that disqualified us."

"Something to that," Hakan said reflectively. Then he stood with a huge smile, opening his arms and hugging Kem, right there in front of everyone. Kem hugged back, steadfastly keeping her eyes away from the shocked faces, and Val

Con shook his head to himself, remarking what a bad influence he and Miri had been on Hakan and his lady.

He picked up the last string, tied it, and threaded it, carefully turning the knob and—

The string snapped in his icy, clumsy hands, sweat beaded his forehead and panic blossomed in his belly. Heart stuttering, he dropped the mandolette, tears starting to fill his eyes.

"Cory?"

Val Con looked up with a barely stifled gasp as Hakan bent to his shoulder. "Are you all right, Cory?"

He took a deep breath, reviewed the Rainbow, and managed a shaky smile at his friends. "Nerves. I think, Hakan. I'll go outside and—get some air."

Hakan frowned uncertainly. "I'll come with you, if you want. You don't look so good, man."

"Miri—Miri will be coming soon." He came almost clumsily to his feet, snatched up his jacket, and went raggedly down the crowded room. Hakan looked at Kem, then bent to pick up the mandolette.

He leaned against the rough wooden wall and filled his lungs with knife-cold air. The violence of the panic had ebbed, leaving a clammy residue of despair in its wake. Val Con focused his attention inward, seeking the source of his feelings—and found it nearly at once.

It was emanating from the song that was Miri.

The terror this time was his own. Coldly he stepped away from it and turned his attention to determining her direction. The song tugged him north, and he went at a rapid walk, barely aware of the people he pushed past and sidestepped.

He turned the corner into a cross-street at a pace approaching a run, passing the infrequent fairgoers and the row of empty craft booths without seeing any of it, all attention fixed inward, where despair had solidified into something drear and nameless, and her song fragmented toward discord.

The man came out of nowhere, wrenching his attention outward with a touch on his sleeve and a murmured bit of the High Tongue.

"Good evening, galandaria. Where to, in such a haste?"

Val Con checked and danced back. The other checked, as well, and Val Con found himself looking at a slight man in a pilot's leather jacket, black-haired and black-eyed, face beardless and golden and curiously lacking in mobility.

"The commander sends greetings, Agent yos'Phelium." His voice was cultured and smooth, devoid of warmth.

Val Con raised a brow. "It must naturally gratify one to hear it," he murmured, "though I protest my unworthiness of such regard." He shifted slightly, testing the other man's reactions.

The man shifted in response, checking the foreshadowed charge, radiating self-confidence and control. "You mistake the matter," he said, "if you believe the commander allows even the least of us to fall from sight, uncounted and un-searched-for." He offered an arm imperiously. "Let us depart, Agent. The commander requires your report."

"My report . . ." Val Con frowned, counting the steps bearing down upon them, then spun and dodged away, putting a group of six fairgoers between them. Whirling back toward the top of the street, he found the nameless agent before him, poised for the throw. Val Con slammed to a halt, an empty craft booth to his left, the agent ready to leap in any direction he picked to run.

"So," the other said, pointing to the empty booth. "We will continue our discussion in there."

"No." Miri, where was Miri? He touched that portion of his being that reflected her—and pulled away, half-shuddering with her dread.

The inflexible face before him was shadowed by some unreadable emotion. "Will you die for so inconsequential a thing?"

Slowly, watching the man tightly, Val Con stepped back, muscles loose and half foolish, as in the *L'apeleka* stance named Awaiting. Cautiously, making no move that might be read as a threat, he opened the door, stepped into the booth, and retreated, though not nearly as far as the farther wall.

The agent came after him, sure-footed and assured as a tiger, and shut the door behind him.

"I will repeat my message," he said. "Agent Val Con yos'Phelium is ordered to Headquarters by the commander's own word, that he may be debriefed, recalibrated, and if necessary, retrained."

Val Con bowed, briefly and with irony. "As much as it grieves me to say so, I find that the commander's words leave me strangely unmoved. Pray carry my kindest regards with you when you go."

"So," the agent said again. His eyes closed, and the next breath he took was noticeably deeper than the one before; but Val Con was already moving to take advantage of that unexpected lapse. The agent opened his eyes, ducked, parried with a fist that came nowhere near connecting, whirled out of immediate danger, and cried out, fully in the mode of Command, "Val Con yos'Phelium clare try qwit—"

A string of no-words, meaningless in the necessity of battle: Val Con stumbled, twisted, and came barely erect, body half-sketching a *L'apeleka* phrase.

"Who secures Liad?" the agent demanded, and Val Con heard his own voice answer.

"The people of Liad."

"Who secures the people of Liad?" the agent persisted. The answer was not the one he would make: It came unbidden and uncontrolled. Even as he heard the words, he tried to shake them away, to form them into something else.

"The Department of the Interior secures the people of Liad," his voice said, while he hated the lie and his body continued, slowly, to move, developing more fully the phrase it had fallen into.

"Who secures the Department of the Interior?"

It was as if there were fog suddenly in the booth, or a shimmering veil between him and the agent. Through it, Val Con read the other's rising confidence and ground his teeth to keep his traitor voice silent.

"Who secures," the agent repeated, "the Department of the Interior?"

It was useless to fight. He grappled with his thoughts, trying to remember just what it was he must not allow, and heard himself murmur, through a mile of fog, "The commander secures the Department of the Interior."

His body continued of its own momentum; he paid it as

little heed as the lessening distance between himself and the man who asked these tiresome, tiring questions.

"Who secures the commander?" his interrogator demanded.

"The agents," Val Con's voice told him. "The agents secure the commander."

The man before him smiled. "With what do the agents secure the commander?"

"With actions, and with blood."

"When the commander calls you to duty," the man demanded, the High Tongue knelling like a death-bell, "what do you say?"

Val Con's body twisted silently in the dance; he came to a point of fulcrum and smiled peacefully upon his questioner. *"Carpe diem."*

The words were like bright sun, burning away the fog. In the instant of answering, he recognized the *L'apeleka* dance named "Accepting the Lance;" recalled that the one giving ground before him was an enemy; recalled that there had been another answer to the last question, an answer that had made no sense. Miri had given him the proper answer—the true answer—and he had danced it into place in Hakan's barn . . .

"Val Con yos'Phelium," the agent cried. "try clare qwit—"

The cycle went faster that time: Again he was shackled; compelled to reply, mind slowly clouding while his body relentlessly repeated the pattern of "Accepting the Lance."

When the commander calls you to duty," the agent snarled, "what do you say?"

"Carpe diem!" Val Con cried; and the dance described acceptance while the agent's hand flicked toward his pocket and Val Con loosened the throwing blade.

The knife struck the enemy high in the chest, close to the throat, and bounced away with a hollow *thunk* as the man brought his gun around.

Val Con dove and rolled in the narrow confines of the booth; he jackknifed and kicked the other's legs out from under him. The man used his fall to advantage, coming up on his knees, gun steady. As Val Con braced himself to leap, the

Loop calculated the angle that would permit the greatest chance of nonfatal injury.

"Val Con?" The voice was in his very ear, instantly recognized, dearly loved, and absolutely impossible. Before him, the agent held his fire.

"Surrender and accompany me of your own will," he said. In his ear Shan's voice was worried, insistent: "Val Con!"

He lunged.

The agent fell badly, gun spinning out of his hand, head striking solidly into the thick wooden wall. The man was moving again, instantly, throwing himself over the weapon—but Val Con was already out the door and running.

Beyond the depot, half a mile closer to Gylles, Miri shuddered, stopped, and stiffened, head up, questing inside herself: Val Con's pattern was—*wrong*.

Even as she watched, the colors dimmed, and several major interlockings shuddered as if under insupportable strain. Directional sense wavered, failed for an instant—then the whole structure was back as it should be: bright and strong and sane.

She relaxed, then stiffened as the cycle began once more; watching the colors dim, she spun back, terror for him overcoming dread for herself and loathing of the plastic envelope in her pocket.

"Dammit, Val Con!"

He slammed around the side of a food hall, glued his back to the wooden support, and whispered, "Shan?"

"Where the devil are you?" demanded the voice in his ear—in his head—bringing with it a static crackle of concern/annoyance/determination/love.

"The Winterfair," he whispered, craning to catch sight of the enemy among the thronging midway. "Where are you?"

"The *Passage*. Give your coords, approximate local fix—"

"No!" Val Con cried. He shrank back, biting his lip. "Shan, you must not come here! There's appalling danger—"

"Plan B!" Shan's thought-voice overrode him. "Speak to

me of danger, do!" Frustration, full anger, and not a little fear
were added to the static pummeling him, and Val Con pushed
hard against the wall, closing his eyes in an agony of emotion.

"Don't . . ." he whispered, though the snow wind tore the
word from his lips. "Brother—beloved—I cannot go mad
just today."

Abruptly the punishment ceased and was replaced before
his knees began to buckle with a steadfast bone-warming
glow. Val Con drew a hard breath against his brother's love
and began to murmur again to the wind. "There is a man with
a gun who will have me dead, and my lifemate is not with
me. I've no time to argue points of melant'i with you! Stay
clear—stay safe . . ."

"We need you." There was a wealth of emotion attending
that, mercifully damped to shadow.

"The gunman has a ship," Val Con murmured. "Must have
a ship! If the luck is willing, it is ours."

Warmth faded to coldness; the inner ear perceived an
echoing vastness . . .

"Shan!"

Warmth solidified. "Here. Running close to the time—uses
too much energy. Assume the ship—what then?"

"I'll take Miri to her people. Meet us—" In the midway
crowd he glimpsed a familiar leather jacket on a man much
shorter than average. The man checked, turned his head to
the left, then to the right, and came confidently toward the
corner of the food hall.

"Go!" Val Con cried to his brother, and—*pushed*—with
his mind. Vastness roared, emptily; then Val Con was slipping silently down the wall, toward the dim back of the
building.

Shan rolled and snapped to his feet, hand outstretched toward that last horrific vision: a man stalking purposefully toward him/Val Con, the outline of the gun clearly visible
beneath his coat.

"He was right there, Priscilla! I saw him! Gods—" He
spun back toward the bed, confounded by his familiar room

aboard the *Passage*—and then hurled himself forward, horror filling him completely.

Priscilla was not breathing.

What by all the gods could have made the man bolt like that?

Miri leaned against a rack of skis, breathing hard and trying to track him. His pattern was steady at the moment and seemed rooted in one spot, a real relief after the crazy zigzagging and dodging he had been doing for the past ten minutes. She squared her shoulders and set out again, keeping her pace down to jog now that she was back among other pedestrians. All the hell clear across the fair. If that just wasn't like his wrong-headedness! Why hadn't he run *toward* her, if he was running from trouble? No sense to have—

She swallowed hard, remembering the envelope of Cloud in her pocket; remembering the Liaden who had given it to her. Gut feeling said that Val Con was running from the Liaden—except that didn't make sense at all. Nothing about the whole setup made sense, but it suddenly looked like a good idea to get to Val Con and face whatever was after him, back to back. After that—she squashed the thought. Ain't any "after that," Robertson, she told herself harshly. Get used to it.

Grief threatened to strangle her; instead, she put her attention back onto his pattern—and slammed to a halt, a cry caught in the knot of grief in her throat.

Someone pushed into her, cursing; she moved until she came up against a wall and put her hands against it, fingers digging into the wood, eyes staring straight ahead, seeing only within.

His pattern flickered, danced, expanded, distorted, all seen through a shroud of swirling flame and color. The flames drew in upon themselves briefly, then expanded and remained constant for a moment. The pattern seemed as if it were going to fade altogether—*did* fade . . . There was a touch, like a cold kiss upon her cheek . . .

And Val Con was gone.

"No . . ." It was a whimper, short nails scoring hardened wood. "No!" she cried again in a burst of anguish as she

slammed her head against the wall and thrust her whole self
into the void where his pattern had been a heartbeat before;
she went through that space and out, so it seemed, to a place
of flailing wind and burning ice-falls and a woman's voice
crying out despairingly, as Miri reeled and went to her knees
on the frozen ground.

Swallowing against nausea, steeled for silence and empti-
ness, she probed the place. And swallowed suddenly against
joy.

He was back: whole, scintillant, sane. Alive.

"Alive," Miri whispered, she climbed to her feet, rubbing
her forehead where she had hit it against the wall.

Shakily she got her bearings and, walking steadily, she set
out to find him.

DUTIFUL PASSAGE

"Priscilla!"

Empty. A void where her mindsong should be—and the
failing glow of the autonomic system.

Healer training took over, forcing the horror he felt out of
consciousness, forcing his attention to the details that made
up life. No breath; no heartbeat; autonomics fading to nothing even as he scanned . . . He needed a medic! But there was
no time to call: Priscilla's body would be dead before Vilt
could hope to get there from sickbay.

Terror lashed him, but was shunted aside as he lay his hand
on her cooling breast; he grabbed and molded that terror in a
way he had never been taught—and released it in a bolt of
mind-searing energy.

He went to his knees with the shock of it; feeling the heart
flutter beneath his hand, he began the sequence: press, release, press, release. The body caught the rhythm, lost it,
caught weakly—and steadied. Breath began raggedly; the autonomic system glowed to full capacity. Shan withdrew his

assistance, watching breathlessly as the body lived on without it.

He dragged himself to his feet, casting with Healer's senses for the thread that had anchored Priscilla to her body.

There was nothing—no strand, no echo of emotion. Priscilla was gone, as if she had never been.

Horror rose again, and he welcomed it, using the energy to cast his Seeking wider, touching over the patterns of all who remained within the *Passage,* searching for a hint, for a memory, for a chord that was Priscilla.

Lina's pattern held him longest, and then Gordy's—but Priscilla had not fled to her friend or to her foster son, and Shan sought further, opening himself as he had never done, reading as he knew he could not . . .

There! An echo, a glow of recall, a familiar, warm touch of comfort.

Following the hint, Shan encountered a scattering of human patterns, the random buzz that was the pattern of lower animals, the near-cogent hum of the norbears—the Pet Library, Priscilla's first refuge aboard the *Passage,* nearly eight Standards earlier. He narrowed his scan, searching minutely, and found her at last, hugged tight within the devoted, comforting pattern of Master Frodo, king of the norbears.

Recklessly Shan expended energy and found himself for a disorienting heartbeat not nearer the norbear and his beloved, but back in his body, slumped over Priscilla's, head pillowed on a breast that gently rose and fell, as if in sleep.

"No!" He wrenched himself away, and fled back toward the Pet Library, homing in on Master Frodo's pattern.

He extended a tendril of affection toward the tiny empath and received the usual happy greeting; but the creature's joy was somewhat mixed with puzzlement, so that he fed out, too, a line of comfort to the norbear before seeking Priscilla herself.

She was wrapped tightly behind an intense shield, reinforced at several points by the norbear's natural defenses.

Shan came as close as he dared, trying to recall exactly how he had bespoken Val Con, then once again expended energy and thought of calling her name. *Priscilla!*

The surface of her shield shimmered, a wisp of pattern escaping; then more slipped out, displaying recognition, quickly followed by dismay, fear, and love. He returned love, comfort, and security; he tried again to bespeak her, to urge her to leave Master Frodo's protections for his own, but she gave no sign that she heard.

Gently, infinitely patient, he kept sending love, comfort, and security, paying out a Healer's line of rescue, and finally he felt her first tenuous grip on the line strengthen and grow certain.

He ignored the strain and payed the line out, feeling her shed defenses, hesitate, and stand away from Master Frodo's shield, exposing the kernel of her being to the void.

Shan *reached* in some indefinable way, encircled his beloved, and shook them both loose of Master Frodo's influence.

He reentered his body with a suddenness that was agony, and Priscilla seemed to join him there for a moment before she fled, pouring across the physical link of their bodies until, with a shocking break, she left his awareness.

Vilt had come and gone, after administering vitamin shots and a very sound scolding for whatever it was that they had done to make each of them shed so much weight, so quickly. While he was scolding Shan, Priscilla had called Lina and asked her to go to Master Frodo with an extra ration of corn; then she had ordered two complete dinners to be delivered immediately to the captain's office.

The dinner itself was gone and Priscilla was sitting next to Shan on the couch, head resting on his shoulder as she thought about what he had told her. Finally she sighed and stirred, sitting up to look into his silver eyes.

"Shan?"

"Yes, Priscilla?"

"Why didn't you go to the Wizard's College in Solcintra?"

Surprise flickered. "Because I'm not a dramliza, Priscilla; I'm a Healer."

"Yes, but you see," she said, very gently, "Healers can't do the things you've been telling me *you've* done—that I know you've done, as I sit here in body before you! And no wizard that I know of—or witch, either—can speak directly, mind to mind."

He frowned. "Nonsense. You yourself left a dream with Val Con's lady—and she replied!"

"Yes, of course. But neither of us spoke *directly* to the other. Think how much easier it would have been, if that was a common sort of ability. Anthora might have spoken to Val Con months ago, relaying Nova's order to come home!"

He shifted uncomfortably, then finally grinned. "Well, what can my excuse be, except that neither Val Con nor I knew the thing was impossible, and so we had a very nice chat!" The grin faded. "More—he was receiving me as another Healer might: asked me to damp the emotional output. And I saw through his eyes!"

He straightened and grabbed her hand, his own eyes near-hypnotic in their intensity. "I saw a man with a gun come out of the crowd; saw him turn toward Val Con . . ." He slumped back. "Then we were cut loose."

"Where is he?" she asked, after the silence went beyond a dozen heartbeats.

Shan laughed sharply. "Refused to tell me! Stay away and stay safe, he said! No time to play melant'i games with me— by which I assume he means he speaks to me not as my brother, but as my future Delm! Hah! There's a change of song, Priscilla! And finally, just before he pushes us away and all but loses me my lifemate, he tells me to meet him. The man with the gun also has a spaceship, you see, so that all Val Con need do is murder him to be free to leave the planet at his leisure and go to Miri's people. Wherever that may be."

"Miri," Priscilla said. "It was Miri who cut us loose." She sighed and added, as the Goddess demanded truth to be told, "My fault."

"Your fault?" Shan blinked. "Miri shoves us out into the void, and it's your fault? Priscilla . . ."

"My fault," she repeated. "My pride. I was so sure I could keep you safe! And when you turned your attention to Val Con—you used energy at such a rate, I was frightened for you, for the link with the *Passage*. I gave you as much as I could, but it wasn't enough. You faded, and I nearly lost you, and I reached out, tapped the lifemate bridge between Val Con and Miri—there's so much energy there!" She paused, gripping his hand, the gem in his ring biting comfortably into her palm, and she gave thanks to the Goddess, who had tested her fully and allowed her to remain yet a time in the active universe.

"Miri felt the interference in the bridge," she told Shan. "I must have obscured her vision of Val Con—she must have thought him in great danger . . . dead. Think of the shock, when you are used to being in harmony with someone, when that person goes behind a wall and shuts you out . . ." She shook her head. "She's not trained—didn't know how to see me; didn't know how to seek. All she could do was thrust out with all the power of her will and try to reestablish her link with her lifemate."

"Casting us loose in the process," Shan finished, and sighed, "Formidable." He looked into her eyes. "But what you tell me indicates that you're not at fault—nor is Val Con, nor is Miri. The person who bears blame—for terrifying you; for all but killing you—is Shan yos'Galan, for his greed and the selfishness of his necessities."

"No—"

"Yes!" He touched her face and ran his fingers into her hair. "Priscilla, you must not allow me to endanger you! You see what I am—a man so lost to anything but his own desires that he may slay his lifemate!"

"Shan!" She drew herself up, hearing the resonance in her own voice. "That is untrue."

He started, stared at her face—Goddess alone knew what he saw there—then pushed forward, his arms going around her, his cheek against hers.

She held him, and he held her, for an unmeasured time; then she asked the question he must have been asking himself, over and over, since his conversation with his brother.

"Would Val Con kill a man for his ship?"

Shan stirred, sighing like a weary child. "yos'Pheliums have a peculiar passion for ships, Priscilla; family history is full of chancy deeds done for the sake of the things. Val Con?" He sat up and shook his head. "My brother tells a story of the time he had captured an Yxtrang—to talk with him, so he informed me, and have an open and equal exchange of views. He says that when they had finished their chat, he let the creature go, because there was no sense in killing him, though that argument has never stopped Yxtrang from killing as many non-Yxtrang as they chose."

He sighed again. "How do I know what he'll do, Priscilla? Would *you* let an Yxtrang go?"

VANDAR

WINTERFAIR

The agent came forward, confidence in every stride; Val Con slid toward the back of the food hall, slipped around the corner, and ran, nearly knocking over a young couple lost in each other against the back wall.

Back on the midway, he became one more of a knot of fair-goers traveling in the general direction of the Winter Train. An agent *might* attempt a kill under such conditions; the Loop indicted that this particular agent had an overriding need for more discreet manners.

His thoughts ran in layers: one relieved by the stabilization of Miri's song; another, an amalgam of the Scout and the agent, concerned with weighing the likelihood of an attack, with being sure he left as little trail as possible, and with watching for signs of pursuit.

Another layer of thought wrestled with the puzzle of the agent's ship: was it on-world or in orbit? Was the agent alone, or did another wait with the vessel? How to find it? How to obtain the ship keys? It was unlikely that the man on his trail would voluntarily answer those questions, though coercion might be brought to bear. Val Con nearly sighed. It was possible to kill an agent, though difficult. But it was immeasurably more difficult to capture one.

"Plan B," Shan had said. What could have gone wrong? Was the Department openly attacking Korval? The Juntavas . . . He closed off that particular layer of thought. It merely distracted and brought unresolved emotions to the fore, when he needed all of his energy to preserve his life and that of his lifemate—and to gain that ship!

The crowd changed direction; he exchanged it for another, checking his song of her to make certain that Miri was still in the vicinity of the train.

The agent was good and knew that he was good; he was perhaps just a shade overconfident. The general speed with which he moved argued enhanced reactions—stimulants—which meant he would tire more quickly, over an extended period of time. Neither factor was significant in the short run. That he wore body armor indicated that he had studied Val Con as Val Con had studied his own targets in the past. Had he studied enough to know of the other blade—the blade Edger had given him? The possession of a weapon that could slip through body armor as easily as through water significantly altered the situation in Val Con's favor—and was negated by the burning necessity to keep the man alive long enough to learn about the ship.

The group he was traveling with turned off. He continued toward Miri at a somewhat quicker pace, the skin prickling at the back of his neck, while the Loop gave .99 surety that the agent was following behind.

sig'Alda identified the tread of the shoe, lost it, found it, and lost it again, which reminded him that he was chasing no mundane Terran politico but a trained agent.

An agent could not depend on luck. Already, though, he had been lucky in the extreme, for had the knife struck a bare two fingers higher, his body would even now be cooling in the dark shed. The speed! The anticipation! One moment to be beyond even the control of his own thoughts—and the next to conceive and execute that attack!

His chest hurt from the knife's strike; no doubt he was bruised. That such excellence should be lost to the Department! sig'Alda sighed in irritation. Regret of that had been the source of the second introduction of luck into his mission: that he should have had his target within sight and failed to neutralize him; that he should, instead, have offered the choice, already refused . . . Had yos'Phelium been carrying a gun, or even another knife, that mistake would have been fatal, too.

His quarry was ahead, sighted for a half second.

Ah, but it would not do to catch him too soon, would it? In the open light, with a crowd around?

sig'Alda slowed, allowing the other a more respectable lead. The Loop gave yos'Phelium a slight edge, if they fought hand to hand immediately. Barely considering the necessity and never doubting the wisdom of it, he took his third dose of accelerant.

Why was yos'Phelium running that way? Why not back toward the area containing the draft animals and vehicles, to escape to the larger countryside? Why—but wait. He had found the Terran in this general direction—at the base of the hill, by the transmitter; and he had originally found yos'Phelium rushing in that same direction. Now, given options, the man broke again for—

The transmitter. sig'Alda smiled. It fit one of the models perfectly. The songs had been a signal, deliberately timed, meant to be received by one who knew when and where to listen. The commander's words came back to him, saying that only Clan Korval might mount a military threat to the Department. Suppose the *Dutiful Passage,* large as a battleship, stood off-planet even now?

The Loop produced percentages that he did not like. That the songs had been deliberate signals—.97. That they had been prearranged and intended for a particular listener—.93. That they had reached their goal? No percentage.

Suppose they had not? Or that they *had,* and that his own advent had required a change in plans, which they were already radioing into space?

The Loop supported the hypothesis.

He ran, heedless of complaints, neglecting to follow Val Con yos'Phelium, now that he knew where he must be going. sig'Alda would be waiting at the transmitter when the traitor arrived.

• • •

Miri marked Val Con's progress. He was heading for the train on the far side of the depot, or for her, maybe—it was a little early to tell about details. He was not running a race anymore, which was good, and his pattern had steadied down after going through all those loopy changes.

As she trudged through the snow she wondered what *her* pattern looked like just then. Must be shot all to hell, what with the shock of that Liaden . . .

She squelched the thought, the packet of Cloud riding like a fifty-pound weight in her pocket.

Val Con had been running away from something, but she had seen nothing in his pattern that made her think he had killed anybody. That meant the skypilot was still at large, either walking toward her with Val Con, or maybe coming after him. Which meant— Ah, hell, Robertson, who you trying to kid? she demanded of herself. You don't know what it means. She saw the train, steam pouring from the boilers that fed the generators, and heard the occasional hiss of valves above the constant rumble of the huge belts.

What an arrangement they were. Some kind of cloth and rubber getup, looping between the big power takeoff reel, the generator, and the flywheel. Between them all, they fed the electric power from the generator to an enormous set of old-fashioned wet-chemical batteries on the railcar in front. The radio station drew its power from the storage batteries, which made sense: If the belt broke or the steam went down they would still have power enough to broadcast until the monster could be restarted.

Miri shook her head. Who would have thought that something so primitive could be so complicated?

One of the cars way in the back of the train was a studio, duplicating the setup in the music hall. There was no longer any need to invade that, since they had attracted the attention of someone with a ship. All according to plan.

She sniffed. *Carpe diem,* eh, Robertson? Now what?

Up the hill, limned by the reflected glow of the main fair lights, Miri saw someone going quickly toward the train.

She frowned and checked her pattern of Val Con. Then she faded carefully between the heavy couplings between two of the cars, watching the skypilot approach and taking a rapid inventory of her person, looking for something more potent than the skinny stick-knife and a handful of true-silver coins.

VANDAR

WINTERFAIR

"Cory!"

Val Con continued hurriedly forward, ignoring the call.

"Cory!" The voice insisted, and out of the corner of his eye he saw a man moving clumsily to head him off. The man was tightly wrapped against the evening chill, and Val Con frowned, then caught the details of nose and chin: Hakan's father.

He waved and turned his steps slightly, as if to pass on by.

"Wait!" Zamir Meltz called, disastrously skidding on a patch of ice. He waved his arms, tottered, and muttered "Thank you," as Val Con caught his arm and held him upright.

"There you are, sir . . ." Val Con helped the older man to safer ground and stepped back, only to find his arm caught in a surprisingly strong grip.

"At least give me a chance to thank you—and to apologize."

Val Con sighed and forced himself to stay within the man's grasp. "I do not—"

Zamir Meltz smiled thinly. "I wish to thank you for your friendship and your partnership with Hakan. I've never seen him with so much energy, so many ideas! And I wish to apologize because the judges have done a stupid thing. They put rules before music—before art! I helped elect those judges, and I see I made bad choices." He bowed his head.

Val Con shifted, seeking Miri in his head. "Zamir, it is a difficult thing that happened. Miri is—distressed. She feels that she led the band wrongly when she called for that last song. That she played the mood of the crowd perfectly—that the performance itself was correct—is something you and I and Hakan know." He shifted again and, with relief, felt his arm loosed. "I am going now to Miri, to try to show her the difference between judges and art."

The elder Meltz smiled. "You have a good zhena there, young man—bold and full of life. You tell her I know she'll be sensible, and that I respect her art and herself, whether she plays to satisfy their rules or not!" He shook his head. "Next fair, there will be musicians instead of politicians as judges, as the breeze blows the leaves!" He nodded to Val Con and strode off, his spare shoulders square with purpose.

Val Con checked his sense of Miri once more, hearing a welcome change in her song as it smoothed back toward cohesiveness and became more and more the Miri he had come to treasure.

The melody went abruptly sharp in an echo of the extreme concentration that she had displayed during the Bassilan invasion. He took a quick fix on her location and quickened his pace to a jog, though his heart argued for more speed yet.

Carefully Val Con hurried, half searching behind for the agent, half searching ahead for his lifemate.

Equations flowed and altered as sig'Alda ran; certainties became questions. Assuming that the Terran had been near the transmitter—had been *stationed* near the transmitter—as part of a deliberate and prearranged plan, the chance that she had taken the drug was markedly less; though, of course, for an addict, such possibility was never entirely eliminated.

The Loop offered figures that were marginally in favor of her having used the Cloud, noting that she had had none prior to the performance. Cloud was potent; its lure to one sensitized was irresistible.

The light was uncertain, mostly derived from the glow of the fair behind him and a few lanterns and electric lights set about the train. The red-haired Terran was not where he had left her, and the multitude of tracks about made any attempt to discover her direction hopeless.

He glanced behind. There was no sign yet of yos'Phelium.

sig'Alda sought further and found his quarry still within the limits of the fair light, speaking, it seemed, with a local.

The conversation ended abruptly, with the local walking back into the depths of the fair and yos'Phelium all but running, in sig'Alda's very direction.

sig'Alda smiled, admiring the clearness with which he could see that backlit runner. At this distance, it was still a chancy shot with a handgun, depending more on the luck that had saved him twice so far than any amount of skill he might bring to bear. But there was no hurry. yos'Phelium was coming to the transmitter. It remained only for Tyl Von sig'Alda to find an appropriate place to wait until his target ran within range.

VANDAR

WINTERFAIR

Miri crouched behind the flatbed, watching the Liaden watch, fuming and trying to think.

Val Con had not killed the guy, though she was sure some of the craziness in his pattern had had to do with a conflict between them. Ergo, she thought, half grinning in self-derision. Ergo, Robertson, this monkey's more valuable alive then he is dead. Figure out why.

The answer was so simple, so pure, that it took her breath away. Spaceship. Damn and hell and blaze it all to cinders! She fingered the coins in her pocket, pulled out the stickknife and flipped it—open . . . shut—and sighed. The way she saw it, the patrol broke down into two separate options.

One: Keep an eye on the Liaden until Val Con arrived and gave her some kind of clue to what was going down. And two: If it looked like the target was moving out, stall him—without killing him.

Always draw the challenging watch, doncha, Robertson? she asked herself sardonically, remembering that Skel had always accused her of deliberately taking the storm shift, as if a body knew when trouble would break.

The Liaden she was watching moved, reaching into his fancy leather jacket and pulling out a gun. Miri craned around the corner of her protection, trying to sight along his line of vision, and nearly yelled.

Val Con was moving toward the train, backlit from the main fair—a target even a mediocre marksman could hardly miss. She checked his pattern and found it alive on several levels, encompassing that twist she associated with consciousness of danger. But he was running, all the same. And in another few moments he would be within range of the Liaden's gun.

All bets're off, Robertson, she told herself. She slid forward, knife out.

Her melody changed again. It was denser, more brilliant, and intensely alert, as if she had suddenly slipped into a role where intuition, reflex, and intent were inexpressibly more important than thought.

As if she were—hunting.

He broke into a run, flat out and danger be damned, as the Loop leapt to full life, elucidating .85 that she was stalking the agent; .35 that she would survive the first encounter by more than a minute; .20 that she would survive at all.

Miri, Miri, Miri! He flung his will out, trying to speak to her as Shan had spoken to him. *Miri, DON'T!*

There was no sign that she heard; her song reached a plateau, drew in upon itself, and formed into a lance.

Heart wailing, mind cold and certain, Val Con pulled on deep-buried reserves, feeling *L'apeleka* and override programs and desperation fueling the fresh burst of speed. Hunch prodded him into evasive action, and the next second he saw the flash; he heard one pellet snarl by his ear as another ripped the sleeve of his jacket.

The Middle River blade was loose in its special arm sheath, ready to slide into his hand in an instant. Before him—still so far away!—he saw the agent turn, gun rising; he saw Miri coming in, low and fast and mean, knife gleam-

ing in her hand; saw the agent take the force of her charge on
his gun arm; saw the downward slice and—

Saw the gun fly away.

The agent snapped into offensive, missed his setup as Miri
dodged and ducked and slashed low, trying to cut his legs out
from under him, and recovered enough to slap the knife
away, arcing silver into the shadows.

Miri twisted and landed on her feet, countering the next attack—blindingly fast—with a move he had taught her. The
agent was surprised to meet that familiar counter: he slowed
minutely, slipped in the snow, and twisted as if to regain his
balance, throat exposed and defenseless.

Val Con drew one last burst of speed from somewhere, not
daring to scream and risk destroying her concentration, hoping against all knowledge that the agent's misstep had been
real.

Miri lunged forward and took the bait.

The agent steadied, accepted her weight and momentum,
bent, spun, and completed the kill with the sureness of a man
thoroughly trained.

Miri went up and over his back, arching high into the air—
a thin, red-haired doll in a blue hooded jacket—and smashed
down onto the hard-packed snow.

She lay utterly still.

Val Con heard himself scream even as the blade came into
his hand, saw the agent bend over to make certain of his
work, then saw him start back, choking and gasping. Ship be
damned and kin be damned and Liad and universe and life:
the crystal blade caught and held the light as it came to ready,
and Val Con jumped forward to close with the murderer of
his wife.

The cannonball hit him just below the knees, pitching him
into the snow while a banshee voice howled in his ear, "Stay
away from him! It's Cloud—poison!"

He rolled and came to his feet; one glance showed him the
agent snatching something that gleamed black metal out of
the snow; saw Miri completing her own roll and diving toward him again, knocking him sideways.

Heard the cough of the pellet gun and felt Miri's body go
stiff, and then slack, against him.

•   •   •

He was alive. No second shot had been made, either to be certain of the first kill or to set up the next. Val Con shifted Miri's weight, sighted through the splash of her hair across her face. The agent was standing perhaps three feet away, gun held ready, an expression of most unagentlike vacancy on his face.

Val Con brought his attention to his lifemate, discovering a feeble pulse in the thin wrist under his finger, and a patch of sticky wetness that seeped through, coat and shirt, to his skin, that could only be blood. *Her* blood.

Gently, reverently, he slipped from beneath her and came with slow fluidity to his feet and faced the agent, Middle River blade held in plain view, ready for the kill.

Gun steady, the agent looked at him out of wide, soft eyes, but he seemed inattentive. Val Con hesitated, then walked forward, extended a hand, and plucked the gun away. The man blinked but offered no resistance.

"I was to have shot someone," he said, the High Tongue registering wondering confusion. "I cannot properly recall . . . I was to have shot—*some*one . . ."

"And so you have!" Val Con snapped, his own voice taking on the cadence of authority. "Give me your kit!"

Dreamily the agent reached around his belt, unclipped something from beneath his jacket, and held it out.

Val Con snatched it out of his hand and spun back to the small huddled shape on the snow.

The wound was just above the right breast. His hands shook as he sealed the entry and exit holes and sprayed the dressings with antiseptic. Gods, gods—so close. And what he had to give her was rough first aid, though better than the rough-and-ready assistance a local medic might offer. For surety, for complete and quick healing, it was imperative to get her to an autodoc.

"Is she hurt badly?" the agent inquired from just behind his shoulder.

Val Con spun on one knee. "Badly enough," he managed with some semblance of sanity. He considered the agent's soft eyes, dreamy face, and careless stance. Cloud, Miri had said. Memory provided the relevant bit from the Lectures.

". . . *Lethecronaxion, street names: Cloud, Lethe, Now:* memory inhibitor; effects lasting from one to twelve hours; physical addiction, as well as psychological need of user to shield painful associations, make Lethecronaxion among the most deadly of the unregulated drugs."

Val Con sighed. "What is your name?"

The agent looked startled; covered it with a bow of introduction. "Tyl Von sig'Alda," he said most properly. "Clan Rugare."

"So." Val Con stared deep into the pupil-drowned eyes and saw nothing but guileless confusion. "Where is your ship?"

Confusion intensified. "My—ship, sir? I—Rugare is not a . . . I have no ship—of my own. I am a pilot-for-hire, if you have a ship but do not care to pilot yourself—"

Val Con cut him off, the High Tongue shaping the words into dismissal. "I see." Miri *had* to have assistance, and an autodoc was so far superior to a local hospital . . .

Gylles itself did not have a hospital, the nearest being in the next town, thirty miles southeast. Too far, mind and heart clamored, while his finger tracked the thready, ragged pulse. He looked again at the agent, trying to recall if there had been a way—*any* way—known to his instructors to bring an individual out of a Cloud-trance.

After a moment, he gave up. If the instructors of agents had the key to unlock a mind shrouded in Cloud, they had not shared it with Agent-in-Training Val Con yos'Phelium. There was, however, something else . . .

Slowly he came to his feet, careful to keep his body between Tyl Von sig'Alda, Clan Rugare, pilot-for-hire and Agent of Change, and Miri Robertson, lifemate, partner, lover, and friend. The dark, clouded eyes followed him, distant puzzlement plain on a face peculiarly vulnerable.

"Do you know me?" Val Con demanded.

The other signaled negation, half bowing. "Sir, I regret . . ."

"I am Val Con yos'Phelium." He watched for the flicker of recognition, hoping that the stimulants the man had taken were of the more powerful variety, and that the dose was sufficient to speed the Cloud through his system.

Nothing showed in face or eyes, then slowly something dawned. "Clan Korval?" he asked hesitantly.

"Exactly Clan Korval," Val Con snapped. "And this lady you have shot—in your passion to shoot *some*one—is my lifemate! How came you to do something so ill, man? And now you tell me you have no ship, when I know you must have, and are denying me the use of the 'doc out of murderous spite! Do you want my lifemate to *die?* Do you want the weight of my Balance to come down upon your head?" He leaned close and fancied he saw a glimmer of some returning sense deep in the dark, dark eyes. "Have you heard the tales of Korval's past Balances? They are true—every one!"

"Yes." The agent's voice held a note of actual ridicule. "Terrifying—the Balance dealt Plemia!"

Val Con smiled. "My brother is a merciful man," he said softly. "Do you think to find me so?"

The agent leapt forward and to the side, muscles coherent and alert. Val Con twisted and got a grip on him—then lost it as the man dropped, feinted, and came up with a palm-gun. Val Con froze, watching the eyes, which were changing yet again.

The gun was steady, the face firm and full of purpose. Val Con saw the finger tighten on the trigger—and he dove, tackling the man as Miri had tackled him.

The gun discharged into the air; the agent twisted, trying to lever himself to the top; Val Con countered, grabbed the wrist of the other's gun hand, and slammed it against the hard snow until the fingers opened and the tiny weapon spun away.

Again the agent tried to twist free, to gain the advantage. But Val Con willed himself a boulder—a dead weight to pin a struggling, hasty man—got his hands around the other's slender throat, and exerted pressure.

The agent froze.

Val Con kept the pressure constant, neither increasing nor decreasing, and let the silence grow for a moment while he felt the frenzied beating of the pulse beneath his fingers. Gods, how many stimulants had the man taken? Or had the Department merely issued their most potent because one of the commander's arcane calculations had rendered acceptable the odds that Tyl Von sig'Alda would achieve mission success before the accelerants wore out his heart? "Where is the ship?" he demanded.

The man beneath his hands was silent.

Val Con dared to raise himself and look into the other's face. The black eyes glittered with an inward-looking intensity bordering on madness; the face was flushed, the muscles painfully tight. Val Con felt hope flicker. This was a state he knew well: a deep MemStim frenzy. Carefully he took his hands away from the other's throat and sat next to him in the snow.

"Agent Tyl Von sig'Alda," he said, reaching into his memory for the commander's nightmare voice and speaking the High Tongue in the dialect of Ultimate Authority. "You will report as questioned. You will speak to answer questions. You will be silent when ordered. Is that understood?"

"Understood." The ravenous eyes looked upon him without recognition; sweat dewed his upper lip and forehead, and the pulse in his throat beat fast and ever harder.

Val Con willed himself into patience, making himself consider the proper questions and the proper order of asking.

"Timeframe," he said. "Directly before tracking the target to the Winterfair. You landed and secreted your vessel, correct?"

"Correct."

"Exact location, local longitude and latitude."

sig'Alda read the numbers unhesitatingly out of a mind that could not forget them.

Val Con touched his tongue to his lips. "What measures were taken for concealment?"

"Ship's ambient field." The voice sounded a trifle breathless, as the heartbeat continued to accelerate.

"Detail other protections and solutions."

There were three, detailed entirely, while the voice grew faint and breath came in gasps.

Val Con looked at the man's face, locked as it was in his frenzy, then recalled it, in sharp counterpoint, clouded and confused. Tyl Von sig'Alda, Clan Rugare . . .

"Describe, briefly, makeup and known antidotes of accelerants ingested within the last one to three hours, as well as the drugs forced upon you by Miri Robertson."

"Lethecronaxion—no known antidote. MemStim—no known antidote. Accelerant—name unknown; antidote unknown; runs system in approximately three hours."

"Loop reading!" Val Con snapped.

"Chance of Mission Success: Point oh one. Chance of Personal Survival: Point oh three . . . falling— Point oh two, oh one! Chance of Mission Success: Zero!" Horror in the gasping voice. "Chance of Personal Survival—"

"No!" Val Con slapped the mad face before him, trying to pull him out of the trance. "Tyl Von, it lies!"

"Chance of Personal Survival . . ." The pulse was beyond repair, beyond belief that any heart could beat so and not rip itself to bits.

"Tyl Von sig'Alda, Clan Rugare!"

The man's body spasmed, his back arching as every muscle in his body locked, then slumped back in a bonelessness that had nothing to do with life, pulse and heartbeat gone forever.

After a time, Val Con reached out and closed the staring black eyes, then quickly and efficiently removed everything from the man's pockets, belt, and person. The leather pilot's jacket he left, despite the fact that it was not of Vandar and should not be found there.

"I will tell your Clan," he said, very softly.

He found the palm-gun and Miri's stickknife, slid them away with the other gun, went to Miri, and knelt at her side, laying his fingers against her throat.

She stirred, eyes flickering. "Skel?" she muttered. "Dammit, Skel . . ." Val Con waited, hovering over her, but the moment subsided before she came to true wakefulness.

Carefully, then, weary in bones and soul, he picked her up and began the long trudge back to the Winterfair, leaving Tyl Von sig'Alda alone and unburied on the hard, dark snow.

VANDAR

WINTERFAIR

The walking was all there was; that and the slender body in his arms. He listened to her breathing, agonized that it was so shallow but joyous that it continued at all. Twice more she stirred and spoke to Skel, directing him once to put her down and go on alone: "s'an *order*, damn you . . ."

He spoke to her then, hardly heeding what he said, and it seemed that the sound of his voice calmed her. But for most of it, he walked, fighting the snow and a sort of leeching exhaustion, as if his strength were running out a drain rather than being efficiently expended.

It took, in fact, several heartbeats for him to recognize the lanky shape and concerned face before him. He frowned, studying the blondish hair, the bristly mustache, and the myopic blue eyes. "Hakan."

"Cory," the other said carefully. He gestured. "What happened, man?"

"I—" Val Con sighed. "Miri is hurt."

"Alive?"

"Alive," he agreed, feeling the sluggish beat of her heart and hearing the rasp of her breath.

"Right. You stay here and I'll get the fair med—"

"No!"

Hakan froze then frowned. "Cory—"

"She has had—aid. The fair doctor will not do more. I— Hakan, will you take us? It is wrong to ask . . ."

Understanding dawned in the nearsighted eyes. "Hospital's in Vale, Cory. Sure she can take the ride?"

"She can take the ride," Val Con said, "to the place we need to go."

"Right," Hakan said again. He glanced around, jerking his

head at an alleyway between two wooden pavilions. "Short-cut to the parking lot."

"All right," Val Con said, and started walking once more.

Hakan did not speak again until they were clear of the buildings and had started across the field that had that morning been the site of the log-pulls.

"I can carry her, you know," he said, hesitantly. "Give you a rest."

Val Con blinked. Hakan to carry her? Nonkin, when there was her own lifemate to aid her? With an effort, he perceived the kindness of it and the concern for both that had prompted it, and noted his growing weakness. It was imperative that he conserve his strength for the tasks ahead, or Miri's lifemate would fail her at the last.

He smiled up at his friend and nodded. "Thank you."

"No problem." Hakan took his burden gently and set off across the field in a consciously smooth stride.

Val Con followed, fumbling among his store of *L'apeleka* dances. "The Spirit Demands" presented itself and he danced two steps as he walked, his mind encompassing the whole. His heartbeat increased, though not nearly to the level that Tyl Von sig'Alda's had; his breathing deepened; his body began to work with more accustomed efficiency, drawing on stored vitamins and other reserves.

"Thank you, brother," he whispered to the memory of Edger, and stretched his legs to catch up with Hakan.

"Turn right," he said sometime later. Miri was on the seat between them, her head on his knee, a scruffy lap rug tucked around her.

Hakan blinked. "Hospital's in Vale, Cory," he said with a sort of nervous patience. "That's left."

"We go right." Val Con reached into the High Tongue for the proper cadence of authority. Hakan frowned, his mouth straightening stubbornly—and, slowly, turned right.

"Thank you," Val Con said softly, but Hakan only drove on, silent.

Three times they passed spur roads going left, toward Vale and the hospital. Three times Hakan made as if to turn in that direction, and three times Val Con had his way.

The next time, he thought, seeing the determination in Hakan's face, in the set of his hands on the controls. He'll take the next road left, no matter what I say. He sighed to himself. Maddened with grief, I suppose, and don't know what I'm about.

"Skel?" Miri asked and shifted fretfully.

Val Con stroked her wild hair and touched her too-pale cheek. "Skel is not here, cha'trez. Rest now."

But she would not be soothed so easily; she moved her head on his knee and tried to toss the rug off. "Skel!" she insisted. "Damn weather. Damn weatherman. Take readings five times a day and what's the good? Weather ain't got a pattern down here, Brunner. World's comin' apart—the *land's* movin', Brunner—like walking on wax. Lost a squad this morning. The hill they were camped on just—fell down . . ." Her agitation was growing; Hakan glanced over and then back at the road as he touched the accelerator, his face tight with resolve.

Val Con captured the questing hand and held it tightly, one part of him trying to think how to calm her while another coldly and continually counted distance and direction. They must not overshoot the ship.

"Gonna have to ditch the machine, Brunner, you hear me? Unit's pinned—what's left. Told Liz I'd kill the gun—give 'em a chance to get out . . . What does 'galandaria' mean, anyway?"

"It means," Val Con said softly, stroking her cheek, willing her to be calm, "compatriot—countryman. Miri—it's Val Con, cha'trez—you must rest . . ."

She stilled abruptly. "Val Con?"

Had she come out of her memories then, back to the present? "Yes."

"Don't leave me, Val Con."

"No," he said, touching her lips lightly. "I won't leave you, Miri."

She sighed then, like a child assured that a dream-monster

was well and truly slain, and slipped back into unconsciousness.

"Stop here," Val Con said, and sighed at Hakan's glare of stubborn denial.

"There's nothing here," the musician said flatly. "Just rocks and snow. Miri's *sick,* Cory—she needs a hospital, not a walk in the weather." He turned his eyes back to the road. "There's a turnoff about a half-mile up the road, get us to Vale in a little less than an hour."

"Hakan, stop the car."

The glare this time was less hard-edged, and the car actually did slow a bit.

"Miri is sick," Val Con said softly. "She needs the best medical care it is possible for her to have." He extended a hand. "Am I so mad with grief that I will murder my zhena?"

Hakan looked at him long and hard, then turned away and looked out at the crisp, starry night and the wild tumble of snow-covered rock. "Here?" he asked uncertainly.

"Actually," Val Con said, "approximately a quarter-mile back." He held his breath as the car slowed, stopped, and began to back up.

"Thank you, Hakan," he said softly. But the other only shook his head.

The ship itself was easy to find—merely a matter of following the line of half-filled footsteps back to their source. Val Con held up a hand as the turret beam lit. "Stay here a moment, Hakan," he said, and went on alone, clutching the multi-use key he had taken from Tyl Von sig'Alda's pockets.

The turret rotated, its beam seeking: Val Con twisted the thing in his hand, brought it to his mouth, and blew two sharp notes. After a pause, he added two more.

The turret stopped its rotation. Val Con pulled the portable beacon from his pocket, flashed a series of long-and-shorts at the beam, and sighed with relief when it simply went out.

"All right, Hakan," he called, and went to the ship's belly. He twisted the multikey, used it on the obvious hatch lock, then bent to find the hidden latch and disarm it.

The hatch slid open, silent in the silent night. The interior lights came up, touching the silver snow with gold.

Hakan stood holding Miri in his arms, mouth open. "An— airplane?" he asked doubtfully.

"Aircraft," Val Con corrected softly, and held out his arms. "I will take Miri, Hakan. Thank you for your aid."

"What?" The stubbornness was fully back in Hakan's face. "You have me drive you to an *aircraft* in the middle of nowhere, with Miri hurt and raving, and I'm supposed to just *leave* you here?" He shook his head. "No."

Val Con considered. Balance, after all, was owed. He bowed, very low. "As you wish. Come with me. Quickly."

The 'doc was behind a partition directly opposite the entrance to the control room. Val Con punched the emergency access, and the clear hatch cycled open. He had Hakan lay Miri on the pallet and then forgot him as he stripped off her coat and the bloodstained shirt, pulled off her boots, and peeled the skirt down. He scanned the board, relieved to find that the Department had thought enough of Tyl Von sig'Alda to supply his ship with a top-of-the-line autodoc, then cycled the hatch closed and watched the lights flicker as the 'doc cataloged Miri's injuries, taking blood samples, X rays, and brain scan. A chime sounded, and a line of characters appeared in the screen directly above the observation window.

GUNSHOT WOUND, HIGH RIGHT CHEST. NO FOREIGN BODIES NOTED WITHIN CHEST CAVITY. COMPLICATIONS: BLOOD LOSS, SHOCK, EXPOSURE. TRACES PSYCHOSTIMU-LATIVE DRUG DETECTED. PROJECTED REPAIR TIME: TWO HOURS FORTY-FIVE MINUTES.

The observation window opaqued. Val Con shuddered, knees sagging. It was going to be all right.

"Cory?" Hakan's voice was not doing well. Val Con straightened and turned to look at his friend.

Hakan's face was unnaturally pale, and he seemed to be trembling.

"Yes."

"Where's Miri?"

Val Con pointed. "In the—healing unit. This—" He

touched the readout. "This says that she will be—repaired—in three hours." He smiled slightly. "She will still need to rest and regain her strength, but she will be out of danger."

Hakan frowned. "That machine is fixing Miri, right now?"

"Yes."

The musician nodded, glancing around, then squared his shoulders. "I've seen planes before, Cory—and this isn't a plane."

"No," Val Con said softly. "It's not."

"What is it, then?"

Val Con sighed. "An aircraft, say, Hakan—and now forget that you have seen it."

Hakan stared at him, and Val Con sighed again, moving out of the 'doc cubicle and crossing to the menuboard. "Would you like a cup of tea?"

"Tea?" Hakan shook his head, perhaps to clear it, and then sighed in his turn. "All right, Cory. Tea would be fine."

Val Con requested two—sweet for his guest, plain for himself—then took the cups out of the dispenser and handed one to Hakan. He sipped, astonished at how good the spicy Liaden tea was; then he saw his friend still staring about wild-eyed, and waved him toward the co-pilot's chair.

"Sit down, Hakan, and rest."

Hakan did, gingerly, and sipped his tea with caution. "Where did this come from?" he demanded.

Val Con looked at him levelly. "Out of the kitchen. You saw it."

"I saw you punch a couple buttons on that wall there, and then you handed me this!" The musician closed his eyes and seemed to be concentrating on taking deep breaths. Val Con wandered over to the pilot's station and sat down.

After a time, Hakan opened his eyes and looked at him, very calmly. "Where are you from, Cory?"

Val Con sighed. "Away."

"Not," Hakan insisted, "Porlint."

"No," Val Con agreed. "Not Porlint."

"Where, then?"

"No," Val Con said. "Hakan, I cannot tell you that. Ask me again, and I will lie to you—and I would rather not lie to my friend, to Miri's friend. I should not have brought you here.

For anything less than Miri's life, I would not have brought you here." He smiled ruefully. "I have played a sorry joke on you, my friend—you have seen something that you cannot have seen. Not only that, but if you describe this ship—the kitchen, the medical machine—no one will believe you."

"Why not?"

Val Con moved his shoulders. "Can you go to a wall in any house in Gylles, push a few buttons, and get tea, hot and brewed to perfection? When you are hurt or ill, do you go to the doctor and have him slide you into a machine for an hour or two, until you feel better?"

Hakan shook his head.

"So, these things do not exist, do they? Cannot exist, I think Zhena Trelu would say."

Hakan closed his eyes.

Val Con sipped tea, cautiously allowing his body to relax; he ran the Rainbow very quickly and looked up to find Hakan's eyes on him.

"How long has this been here?"

"No more than a day," Val Con said softly. "And it will be gone before the start of another."

Sorrow shaded the mustached face. "You're leaving?"

"We don't belong here any more than this craft does, Hakan. It is an accident that we are here—a happy accident, as it turns out. We found friends and music—and anything that gains us so much is to be thanked."

Silence grew as they both drank their tea. Val Con shifted slightly, drawing the other man's attention back to him. "You should go, Hakan."

"Now? But, I mean, Miri—" He trailed off in confusion.

Val Con considered. "It is not safe to stop the healing once it is started, and Miri might not wake naturally for some hours after the machine releases her. She cannot say good-bye to you, Hakan, though I know she would wish to. I . . ." He shrugged. "Come back to this spot tomorrow," he said slowly, "and take away what is here." More regulations shattered by whim, he thought ruefully, reaching to touch the other's arm. "Be very careful, my friend."

Tears shone in the blue eyes as Hakan stood. "Kem's never

going to forgive me for letting you two get away like this. She—we—love you both."

"And we love you." On some impulse he did not fully understand, Val Con extended a hand and touched one stubbled cheek very lightly, as if they were kin. "I see you, Hakan Meltz." He stood back. "Live in joy, you and Kem—and may all of your children love the music."

"Yeah . . ." Hakan followed Val Con to the hatch and stood looking out at the night.

"Can you find your way, Hakan? Should I walk with you back to the car?"

"I'll be all right," he said, pulling up his hood. "Just follow the footsteps out, like we did on the way in." He hesitated. "Good night, Cory."

"Good night, Hakan."

Val Con watched until he could no longer see Hakan's outline against the stars and snow, then he sealed the hatch and went back into the ship. The 'doc's timer showed one and a quarter hours still to go on Miri's treatment. Val Con set the ship's clock to wake him in an hour, then reclined in the pilot's chair and went to sleep.

VANDAR

KOSMORN GORE

ADDITIONAL TIME REQUIRED TO COMPLETE REPAIRS: TWENTY-FIVE MINUTES.

Val Con touched the query button, frowning as the reason for the additional time took shape on the screen.

BLOOD FILTERING AND RECALIBRATION OF NUTRIENT LEVELS REQUIRED DUE TO STRONG ADVERSE REACTION TO INGESTION OF PSYCHOSTIMULATIVE DRUG.

"Psychostimulative drug?" he repeated. Then, face clearing, "Ah." The Cloud-and-MemStim mix she had flung into Tyl Von's face; she must have inadvertently swallowed some of it herself. He shook his head, keying in a request for the doc to send the makeup of the drug to auxiliary screen three. How had Miri come to have such a thing? he wondered, and shook his head again. He would have to wait for her explanation.

He bent and picked up her clothes and shoved them into the cleaning unit along with his own, adjusting the setting to "superclean" and "repair." The 'fresher also had a "superclean" setting. Val Con chose it and stepped under the deluge.

The observation port had cleared, allowing a view of a slight, pale body, a swirl of red hair, and a pair of languorous gray eyes. The new scar was a smooth patch of pink above her small breast. Val Con smiled and touched the release.

"Good morning, Miri."

"Hi." Her voice was husky, and she moved her head on the flat pillow in a half-shake. "Think I don't know how to fall?"

He sighed. "I know that kill so well . . ."

"Yeah. Me, too." She grinned, a trifle lopsidedly. "Don't teach your grandma to suck eggs, spacer."

"I would not dare."

She snorted. "Guess not, grandma you got. Feisty old toot, was she?"

"No more than the rest of us," he said softly, touching her face. "Are you hungry, Miri?"

"Could do with a snack." For the first time her eyes left his face and looked at the room beyond his shoulder. "Mind telling me where we are?"

"The agent's ship."

She frowned. "Just us?"

"Just us." He looked away, picking up a lock of copper hair and running it through his fingers, studying the process with intensity. "The agent—died. The Loop lied to him—as it did to me, on Edger's ship, you recall?" He looked back into her eyes.

"Yeah."

He sighed and shook his head. "He had taken stimulants and the—other drugs. The Loop added adrenaline in a massive dose, into a system already overloaded . . ."

"He had a heart attack," Miri said very quietly.

Val Con nodded. "Tyl Von sig'Alda," he murmured. "Clan Rugare."

She frowned. "You knew him?"

"No. He told me his name." He shook himself out of the memory. "What will you have to eat?"

"Whatever it is, I ain't eating it here," she said with an abrupt return of energy. "What kind of shape my clothes in?"

"The valet was adequate to the task," he told her. "A moment."

He returned almost immediately with her clothes, but she had already squirmed upright and sat with her legs dangling over the edge of the pallet. He shook his head and handed her the shirt, gritting his teeth against his need to help, trusting that she would ask his aid if it was required.

She finished up the buttons, sighed, and looked at the skirt. "Dump that thing over my head, willya?" He did, and she fastened it, then grabbed his arms and slid to her feet. "You didn't get hit, did you, boss?"

"No," he said softly. Then he began more urgently, "Miri, you must never—"

She held up a hand. "Don't say it, okay? Heard you screaming like death, coming up that hill. Ready to jump on him and hack him to pieces, was it?" She sighed and leaned against him, her arms going around his waist with unexpected strength. "Couple certifiables."

After a moment, she stood away from him. "Don't suppose there's any coffee."

"This is a Liaden ship," Val Con said, "so it is doubtful. We might check, however." He offered his arm.

She took it without hesitation, and together they went out into the main room.

There was no coffee, but the tea he ordered for her was nearly as good: dark and spicy and rich. She sipped her second cup half reclined in the copilot's chair, watching Val Con clean up the remains of their meal and wishing her brain would stop asking "Now what?"

He's gonna ask you about the Cloud, Robertson, she told herself. Whether that Tyl Von guy was lying to you or not. He's gonna ask. What're you gonna tell him?

Val Con came back to sit in the pilot's seat, carrying another cup of tea. He settled in and sipped, then lifted his eyes to her face.

Gods, she thought. Gods, please . . .

"Miri?" he said softly, and she swallowed a deep breath along with some more tea and met his eyes, level.

"Yo."

"Who is Skel?"

She shook her head in surprise. "Skel ain't nobody, boss. He died on Klamath." She took another breath. "Where'd you hear about Skel?"

"You were talking to him rather constantly at one point," Val Con said gently. "Ordering him to put you down and go on."

Miri closed her eyes and leaned her head against the rest. "Way it was supposed to go," she said tonelessly. "Liz's orders. Everybody for themselves, she said." Her voice took on a harsher cadence, as if words and tone were burned into memory forever. "If your partner falls and don't get up, run. If *I* fall—run. If you get hit and fall and it ain't fatal—get up, damn you, and *run!*"

"Miri . . ."

She opened her eyes, mouth tight with old pain. "'Nother unit—had us pinned with a heat-seek. Wasn't many of us by that time—twenty-five, twenty-six. Needed somebody to kill the gun, see? And I told Liz I'd do it." The eyes closed again, and she took a shuddering breath. "Made sense—I was smallest, fastest. Best choice. Liz saw it; said okay. Skel—he waited, after the gun blew. I took a hit on the way back, then the—the land moved—was movin' a lot, by then. Rocks fell—busted both my legs. Skel carried me. Got me to Liz before he got hit himself. Then *she* carried me, like she'd ordered us not to."

She sighed, her eyes opening to stare up at the ceiling.

"Liz, Scandal, Mac, Win, me. Five. Klamath killed everybody else. Wasn't for the weatherman, we'd been dead, too."

She touched the chair's control and brought herself upright. "Never got a chance to thank him—Brunner, his name was. Ichliad Brunner. Don't know his Clan. Faked a report or something—never got the right of it—made the station send in shuttles—pulled off maybe five hundred, all told, before everything went to hell. Heard he got in trouble, later . . ."

"Miri . . ." He was standing over her, one hand half extended, pain and sorrow in his face. Her heart twisted in her chest, and she clenched her jaw against the wrenching need for him.

"You better hear the rest of it."

"Later." He touched her jaw, his fingers stroking the tight muscles.

"Now," she said, pulling her head back. His hand dropped to his side, wariness joining the other troubles in his face. Miri sighed. "Ain't much more."

"All right," he said softly, his eyes on hers. "Tell me the rest of it."

"Finished up in the hospital, got my legs back in shape. Wasn't sleeping so good—nightmares. Got to thinking about how everybody I knew was dead and how I *should've* been dead. Got to drinking too much kynak, but that just made the memories clearer, see? Tried a couple other things, trying to shake the memories—all the dead faces. Finally got hold of some Cloud. The memories went away. I could sleep and think and I wasn't so—sad—anymore." She sighed. "But the Cloud would wear off, and the memories would hurt worse than ever, 'cause you just put 'em on hold for a little while, you don't turn 'em off completely."

She broke his gaze and looked into the empty teacup, then looked back into his eyes. "I took a lot of Cloud."

There was silence. Val Con stood, apparently willing to hear even more. Miri sighed and forced herself to finish.

"Liz got me in a rehab program—took a long time, but I kicked it. Most people, with Cloud, they never made it back out." She gave a harsh bark of laughter. "My luck."

"Ah," he said.

"What in *hell* does that mean?" Tears, sudden and appalling, ran down her cheeks and dripped off her chin. She lifted a hand and scrubbed at them as Val Con came over and perched on the edge of the chair, facing her.

"It means," he said softly, "that, if I had been on Klamath, seen a world shake apart and my unit—my friends, my lovers, my family—die, I might wish to forget, also."

She shook her head. "That Tyl Von brought me a pack of Cloud, when I went out to calm down. Said it was from you, for doing my job so good."

"Must I say that he lied?" Val Con asked. He sighed. "The packet that he gave you was a mixture, Miri—half Cloud, half MemStim—a drug that is given agents when they report. It stimulates complete recall."

Her eyes widened. "No wonder he had a heart attack. From forgetting everything to remembering everything? It'd pull his brain apart!" She stopped. "Hell."

Val Con nodded. When several minutes had passed and she said no more, he touched her hand. "Have I now heard everything that I must hear this evening, Miri? For I think you should sleep so you may continue healing."

She stared at him. It's all right, Robertson, she told herself. It's really all right.

Peace, as shocking and unexpected as her tears, flooded in, and she leaned forward to hug him and put her cheek against his. "I think I ought to go to sleep and continue healing, too, now that you mention it. But if you want me to sleep anywhere but here, you're gonna have to carry me."

"That," Val Con said, "can be arranged."

VANDAR

KOSMORN GORE

Sunlight glittered off the snow-covered rocks, bringing tears to Kem's eyes as she followed Hakan. If the whole thing were not so wild—but, there. Miri hurt, and Hakan and Cory bringing her out here, and Cory putting her in a doctor machine . . . and cups of tea coming out of a wall and panels of lights in an aircraft that was like no aircraft possible.

Kem shook her head and squinted ahead, looking for the aircraft. Something as big as Hakan had described should certainly be visible in the bright sunshine.

Ahead of her, Hakan stopped, staring at an oblong depression in the snow. She came to his side and slid her hand into his.

"It's gone," he said, and looked at her, desolation in his eyes. "They're gone, Kemmy."

She looked at him helplessly, then looked back at the depression, squinted against the glare, and pointed. "What's that, Hakan?"

It turned out to be a flat wooden box, with a fitted, sliding top. When they slid the top back, a strong, spicy aroma was released, somewhat reminiscent of tea. Inside was a sheet of paper and a pouch.

"Dear Hakan and Kem," the note began, in Miri's slanting, rounded letters.

> *"We're sorry we have to leave before you can see us again. Please believe that I am much better and that I'm not going to die, probably for a long, long time, so pity Cory. In the box is also the money we got from the king for being heroes. There is different money in the place we're going to, so you use this. Please. Hakan, I'm sorry we couldn't finish the last set. You're a good musician and a good friend. Remember to always play for joy. Kem, I owe you so much! I'm sorry we put you and Hakan to such trouble. Thank you both for all your help. Tell Zhena Trelu we won't bother her anymore. We love you. Miri."*

There were several blank lines, then in a sharp, backhand script: *"Be well and be joyful, both of you. We'll miss you and think of you often, with love. May the music never stop for either of you. Cory."*

That was all. Kem blinked back tears and looked up from the letter to see Hakan pacing around the oblong indentation, peering carefully off in all directions. She went to him. "What is it?"

He pointed at the unmarked snow all around. "No running start," he said. "He lifted that *aircraft* of his straight up!"

She looked at his face, around at the snow, up at the sky, and back at his face, worriedly. "Is that possible, Hakan?"

He started to say something but instead shut his mouth and looked at her for a long, long time. Then he reached out and hugged her to him, pushing his face into her hair.

"No," he whispered. "No, it isn't."

ABOUT THE AUTHORS

Sharon Lee and Steve Miller live in the rolling hills of Central Maine. Born and raised in Baltimore, Maryland, in the early '50s, they met several times before taking the hint and formalizing the team, in 1979. They moved to Maine with cats, books, and music following the completion of *Carpe Diem*, their third novel.

Their short fiction, written both jointly and singly, has appeared or will appear in *Absolute Magnitude*, *Catfantastic*, *Such a Pretty Face*, *Dreams of Decadence*, *Fantasy Book*, and several former incarnations of *Amazing*. Meisha Merlin Publishing has or will be publishing four books set in the Liaden Universe: *Plan B*, *Partners in Necessity*, *Pilots Choice*, and *I Dare*.

Both Sharon and Steve have seen their nonfiction work and reviews published in a variety of newspapers and magazines. Steve is the founding curator of the University of Maryland's Kuhn Library Science Fiction Research Collection.

Sharon's interests include music, pine cone collecting, and seashores. Steve also enjoys music, plays chess, and collects cat whiskers. Both spend way too much time playing on the internet, and even have a website at:

www.korval.com